PRAISE FOR AMITY GREEN

"Amity Green proves that there's still room for invention in urban fantasy. Leave it to a Texas Gargoyle in London to teach us what it means to be human."

— D.J. BUTLER, AUTHOR OF WITCHY EYE

"Amity Green's novels will hold you spellbound from the first page to the last. Wise and witty, Amity proves that she is a talent to watch!"

— DAVID FARLAND, NEW YORK TIMES BESTSELLING AUTHOR

PHANTOM LIMB ITCH

BOOK 2 OF THE FATE AND FIRE SERIES

AMITY GREEN

Petrichor Press

Cover art and design: Consuelo Parra

www.facebook.com/C.PBookCoverdesigns

Model: Saphiriacat.deviantart

Photographer: Martin Erker

ISBN 978-1-949906-00-4

Edited by Mia Kleve

❀ Created with Vellum

For Ronin. Thank you for making the wait worth every second.
#levelup

INTRODUCTION

A small piece of Fate was mine. I hacked it off when her guard was down, feeling it twitch and wriggle in my bloodied claws, brutally taken just like parts of me. Fate can't complain. Comeuppance is a bitch. She took from me, so I took from her.

Weeks ago, the world as I knew it—as everyone knew it—became a whole different planet. Other things live here, too. And I am one of them; no longer human. Ancient souls breathed right alongside me. Gargoyles, ethereal water beings, creatures thought only to live in dreams, nightmares, and Fairy tales, fought to hold their ground.

So much was gone, sent away in vaporous wisps like dew in the hot, southern sun. I mourned youthful simplicity and mortality like the loss of my right hand. That emptiness—the line of demarcation where I ended and my new life began—created phantom-limb-itch, a memory from being whole and owned by no one but me. Being a hybrid, half gargoyle and half Celtic goddess, topped teen angst, any day.

So much remained. Something in my soul needed out, was scratching and clawing at the pit deep in my chest, the place that swells with love and pride and aches like shattered bone when my heart hurts.

I begged for Change to find me, sinking deeper, hitting my knees on an altar in denial and grief. Fate and Change owned me equally, but I wouldn't stay down long. I would dance a circle, burning them both to the ground in a flame-kissed night when the thing in my soul was freed. And damn anyone—winged or not—who might stand in my way.

1

W hether it was morbid fascination or my own desire to understand the changes of my body, I had to watch the transformation from human to gargoyle with my own two eyes to get a better understanding of what I'd become. What happened to my shoulder blades when I had wings? Did my tail sprout like a new leg? Where did my breasts retreat to? Would scales replace my skin, no matter what, at sundown?

A true friend is precisely what I needed to stand by and witness me whittle flesh from my forearm, and Bree was that girl. My squeamish friend handled it well. Neither of us were biology majors by a long shot, but we agreed, both of us wanting to get a better understanding of the transformation. The question: Did my flesh have to be attached to my body to experience the change? Would it get scales if the skin was removed? I was concerned, and Bree got that about me. Maybe she was just as curious. Perhaps she was blatant in her musings, like me. We could do that—be morbid together. Whatever the case, she had my blessing when I carved out a hunk of skin the size of a twenty pence piece and she slapped a palmful of gauze over the pool of blood that filled the hole. I winced but barely flinched. I couldn't be all that proud of holding still. It wasn't my doing. We'd cinched my arm to the ironing board with one of Bree's long, braided leather belts. I set my dirk down and took a breath to chill out.

"Tee minus two minutes and counting," she said, with her spare hand tapping the screen of her iPhone. "How ya doing?" Voice calm, she caressed and patted my strapped down hand.

I did everything I could to avoid fidgeting. "You could so be a nurse." I grinned and chewed my cheek, looking from her to the ceiling, to the walls, keeping myself occupied.

"Ha ha," she deadpanned. "So really, you okay?"

"I'm okay," I lied. After all the wounds I'd suffered, some of which would have been fatal to a human, a self-inflicted-by-proxy biopsy had me rattled worse than facing down another gargoyle bent on murder. "This'll heal up when I Garg Out."

Bree tipped the tea saucer that was her make-shift Petri dish, examining my flayed-off skin in the light. The good news was the flesh just lay there like a good little severed hunk rather than doing something freaky like sprout wings of its own. She looked back to her phone while keeping pressure on the wound so I didn't lose a lot of blood. It was her idea to run the test so close to sundown so I didn't bleed a lot. I could only hope to develop her forethought. I'd save myself a lot of pain and grief. And blood.

"Crap," I moaned and rubbed my forehead with my free hand. True to form, I hadn't thought it out thoroughly. Not only would Bree witness what happened to the specimen in the dish, she'd see me transform right next to her.

"What's crap?" She looked worried, tucking a strand of spiral-curled hair behind an ear.

I loosened the belt and stood. We were downstairs in the living-quarters part of the building that housed The Bochord, the bookstore where we worked. We'd planned it that way because of the sink and proximity to the first aid kit Peter kept in the cabinet.

There wasn't even a closet in the room. I'd be in plain view. She released my arm and stood, too.

"What's wrong, Tessa?" Lacking a better place to put it, Bree fastened her belt around the waist of her Big Bird pajamas. I wore my old cream-colored camisole and lavender skirt, stained and tattered from months of being my go-to outfit for the transformation. Once my favorite, the lace hung free in places on the top's hem and the shape of the skirt was distorted and stretched with worn out elastic barely doing the job of holding it to my hips.

"Promise me something?"

She nodded, agreeing blindly to my request. "Of course."

"I haven't even watched in the mirror when I change yet and you're right here with me. I haven't been able to bring myself to see it take over my face. I mean, it's the most personal thing I lose when I change—"

"I won't look."

I sighed. "Thank you." The backs of my arms began to tingle. "Here we go." I turned toward the wall, entirely self-conscious of becoming a monstrosity in plain view of my best friend. I took note of the smallest detail, doing my best to commit each feeling to memory, to log every single sensation.

The overhead light in the room built to a new level of brightness, losing the slight yellow tint I'd paid no attention to before. The color of the tiled floor sparked with glinting bits of mica mixed in the sandstone. Bree's heart thumped in a tale-tell rhythm with her excitement, speeding up nearly as fast as my own. A clock *tick-tocked* in the kitchen, and there was a cat happily rummaging through the garbage bin outside, smacking his little kitty lips.

I held my hands at eye level as the ceiling grew a little nearer. I'd be darned, but I did actually get a little taller, although I was still a runt of a gargoyle next to Peter's sister, Petra, when she Garged Out. My guts roiled like a loose egg flipping in a frying pan or the first, tensing part of a menstrual cramp, but went away painlessly. The tips of my shoulder blades burned like Icy Hot meeting a cold wind, becoming heavy at my back, but balancing at the sides as hard, leathery wings unfurled with a tugging sensation that was rooted in my spine. Each vertebra seemed to pop just beneath the skin, my tailbone burned as my spiky tail slithered down my leg and wrapped around my left ankle. Cool air swirled at my feet in little gusts, disturbed by the slow beat of my wings. The sensitive fork of my tongue slid along smooth molars and pointed canines. Pinpricks ran down my extremities. Scales formed inside pores, little blade edges sticking straight out before coming together, weaving into plated silver and charcoal grey hide that was thick on the tops of my hands and arms and thin on the sensitive backsides. Talons sprang from each blackened cuticle, forming points that curled in at the tips. My scales gleamed in the light.

I smiled. It all happened inside of a couple moments with no pain. I was a little hot and pretty hungry.

"Well, shoot," Bree muttered.

I turned to see what she was doing.

"This just laid here." She shook the saucer, watching the skin closely. She put it close to her lips and blew on it. "Nothing."

I snorted. "You're hilarious."

"That settles it then," she said with an affirmative nod.

"Yeah," I agreed.

She discarded the sample dish onto the folding table. "The mojo's inside of you, chick."

I grinned. "Thanks for indulging me."

"Anything for you, Tessa. I love you."

Inner battles aside, if Peter got one inch further onto my last nerve, we'd throw down, gargoyle style.

He always had something to say. *Stay off the radar, yes?*—when

I'd go out for a moonlit flight. *Keep to the shadows, yes?*—when I went out for a run before work. I wanted to scream "Yes!" before he even opened his mouth most times.

Dealing with my new gargoyle form at night, and as a human with what I'd call a strong allergy to sunlight during the day was hard enough without Peter riding my case. And not to mention what I'd found out a few short weeks ago: A deity resided somewhere inside me, sharing my body and soul.

I was a gargoyle with strong goddess tendencies.

Bree didn't get it. At least, I was pretty sure she didn't understand how ingrained it had become. There were more than a few times when I couldn't tell if a particular thought was the goddess's or my own.

"It's like everything I knew, or thought I knew, about myself isn't really me. I mean, is it me who likes catsup, or the goddess?"

"Of course you're you," said Bree. "You've always loved too much catsup on everything, and that was way before all this stuff happened."

"That was just an example. Here's another. What if it wasn't me who liked Kai so much last summer. Yeah, he was hot and fun, but he'd also been an ancient killer and a monster. What if it was her who liked him and wanted that short relationship, and not me?"

"Tessa, we've all had guys we wish we'd never talked to or whatever. Just admit he was a mistake. You don't need to reason it out or blame it on an alter ego."

"I don't know. Looking back, I think if it was just me I would have told Kai to cram it long before we finally broke it off. I used to feel like the goddess showed up only once in a while and I wrote it off as another freak fever, like I've had since I was a kid. Now I don't know if every thought, memory, or idea I get is mine or hers. Our minds and existences are getting more and more seamless, with big blocks in between where I don't even sense her."

Bree had given me the pitiful smile version of a pat on the head.

Bandia Na Teasa, or Goddess of Fire, slumbered most times, unless I got agitated. When she awoke inside me, I became a super-fast and lethal killer. However, her aid was nothing I could count on. During the last four months, I'd been kidnapped, beaten nearly to death—*twice*—almost drowned, and been tortured by having two of my fingers snapped as I watched. The goddess hadn't done much to earn my trust. Although, she'd saved my infant life when my parents were killed in a car accident. I would have bled out on the asphalt that night if she'd not come along and jumped in here with me. The price for my rescue was sharing my existence with hers. Sometimes my will flipped a 180 like Kai's Aston Martin on hot asphalt. I was getting better and better at calling up my super-speed when I needed it.

Kai was a rotten Ancient I used to have a crush on but had to kill in order to save the whole of humanity. They could thank me later, but my heart had learned to be wary. Kai wasn't what he pretended to be, just wanting to be close to me because he already knew about *Bandia na Teasa,* even though I didn't yet. That still stung. So I stole his book, too. It was mine in the beginning, but he'd taken it and hidden it for a few centuries.

I opened that magical tome weeks ago. Then it truly became *my* book, and was something I craved, the closest thing to addiction I'd ever known. I holed up in my room at least once a day petting the stained, leather cover, cradling the thing like a baby. I cooed questions to the blank pages, hoping to see answers form before my eyes in brilliant, silver ink, scrawled in painfully slow script. Did it only make me feel like it was mine because I was the one it currently graced with its usage? Could I call what I got from the book "usage" at all? Maybe I wasn't that special. The tome had given me nothing in over a month but still I tried. I got the vibe it was pissed off. Could a book be vengeful? If it could call me by name and answer a few questions, I was placing no boundaries on other things it could be capable of. Bottom line, the tome wasn't telling me how I could become human again, adding to my frustration.

What Peter didn't realize—or at least I don't think he did—was that if I didn't do things like take a run or a quick, liberating flight, I'd lose it. I ran hot and cold, crushing on Peter and then avoiding him. I needed to expel energy. Craved fresh air. Yearned for sweet independence and freedom. He was like a ball and chain, keeping me tethered to the bookstore. As much as I loved manning the register at the bookstore, it was a prison. I dreamed of leaving and never coming back. I wanted out.

But then I'd wake up. Leaving the bookstore wouldn't fix a thing. The problem wasn't *where* I was, but *what* I was. That was the doozy. Part of me wanted to crawl out of my own, scaled skin, renounce the bars keeping me caged, and reclaim the fleeting chance at freedom I'd owned as a teenager in the US. Though, I wouldn't be going back to Austin. There wasn't a thing left there for me anyway. No one claimed me as family.

Two people comprised my list of friends. Bree proved herself as my bestie and made extended plans to stay in the UK, a decision that meant everything to me. Mr. Douglas was so much more than I thought. Turns out he's a quirky mage from Scotland, daylighting for nearly two years as my British Lit professor. I'd been crushed at the thought of never seeing him again. Not a problem now that I knew he'd been with me all along. So the two people on the planet I might have missed from home resided close. The blessing was not lost on me. I counted it every day on ticking fingers, and every night on clicking claws.

Icy, late summer rain pelted my wings, beading and sloughing away like drops on a sixty-mile-an-hour windshield. So much weighed on my mind that I had to get out for a while. The temperature dropped the higher I flew but the cold didn't bite at me. My breath clouded behind me in streaming puffs of frosty air. Chill was a sensation of memory when I was in gargoyle form.

Pent up energy was my battery; dark attitude my heater core. Water became a thick, vaporous layer of clouds that I busted into like a bull through a quiet rose garden. In the starry darkness above, I found a glistening fall of midnight snowflakes, beauty and serenity that stilled me to a glide.

Growing up in the American South, snow was a rarity. If flurries really did fall like the weatherman said—most times they made a liar of the poor guy—they melted on the ground, leaving no opportunity to touch them. In the sky above London, I did something I'd always wanted; I caught big, melty snowflakes on my tongue. I must have been quite the sight, winged, fanged, forked tongue, darting around the sky like a deranged, pug-nosed fairy. But it was awesome. No one told me to stop. No one saw me.

Chasing snowflakes wore me out eventually, so I drifted back toward the city, tiny streetlamps coming into view through the dense fog that dampened everything from the wet sidewalks to the echoless alleyways. The mixture of darkness, silence, and musty, wet air made Cecil Court miserable. I alit gently on the bookstore's rooftop, just like Peter showed me, coming to a quick crouch on the ledge. Water dripped from a downspout, spattering on cobbles below. Ice would form, freezing the little fall before dawn, just like my mood. I snorted a quick blast of short-lived steam that was taken away by drizzle.

"How was it?" Peter said, just behind me.

I didn't get up, or even turn to face him. "Soggy," I hissed. Articulating an S remained a challenge with sharp teeth and a split tongue.

He squatted beside me, his huge wings folding carefully behind us. They popped loudly against his back. I gritted my teeth with irritation.

"Where did you go?"

"Don't worry, Peter. I didn't do anything to draw attention to our little enclave." I rose and stalked toward the stairs inside, shaking water from my wings, umbrella style.

Peter stood when I did, towering above me.

That chapped me, too. If I was going to be a gargoyle, why did I have to be a little one? Peter was a dark giant next to me. Powerful and intimidating.

"Not so fast," he said.

"Give it up Peter. I'd outrun you and you know it. I'm going to bed." I tossed the words over my shoulder, not bothering to look at him.

"Get something to eat, Tessa. You look like you haven't eaten in a bloody month."

I wasn't in the mood for a lecture or food. I just wanted to lock myself inside my room and consult my book to see if the sources-that-be felt charitable enough to tell me how to get my life back. Just weeks ago, when I'd recovered the book during a brutal fight among gargoyles in Scotland, words formed on the first page when it told me it belonged with me. Sooner or later I'd have answers. I hoped.

PETER DIDN'T FOLLOW ME. Dawn chased my gargoyle-self into hiding, leaving me to dress in twice-worn jeans and a wrinkled Misfits T-shirt after another sleepless night. I hadn't worn mascara in weeks and my hair practically braided itself every morning. My book sat open on my crossed legs, unresponding. Although I'd been told otherwise, I was sure the answer was somewhere within the thick pages. The danged thing just wouldn't give it to me. I was through being a gargoyle. Flying was nice, but I wanted to be me again, so I wasn't willing to give up trying to pick the answer from an obstinate book.

I'd struggled my entire young life feeling unsubstantial, easily brushed aside. Being ignored reached a boiling point for me. I snapped the book shut, threw it to the floor, and kicked it under my bed. "Screw you, then!" I yelled. A vision of flames encapsulating the thick book as I bopped around it in merry, leaping circles tottered through my exhausted mind. I let out a high-pitched, psychotic giggle into the stillness of my room and smacked my forehead.

Before, when the book wouldn't respond to me, it was because I asked the wrong type of questions. Try as I might, I couldn't think of anything more important than finding a way to become human again. I requested information from the book daily, sometimes twice. Tears of frustration added stains to thick patina on the blotchy, leather cover.

My life as a human lacked a lot of the things normal teens had. I'd grown up orphaned. But coming to London had cracked my shell, setting me in motion. I'd just begun to really live and stretch out. I wanted to teach British Literature at the University of Texas. I wanted to meet someone wonderful and know love, have a family for the first time ever. All those things were now gone. I would never feel sunshine on my face, never again spend a day walking Lakeline Mall with Bree shopping for sundresses. I was suffocating.

Heat erupted in my chest as I came to my feet. I kicked completely through a bedpost, sending the whole frame smacking onto the carpet and shards of wood spraying my room. The sound erupted, loud enough to carry into the store downstairs. That didn't bother me nearly as much as the fact that all I could think of was my book getting smashed. My priorities were completely jacked.

Sure enough, pounding footsteps came from the hallway toward my door. "Tessa? You all right?" Peter called.

"Go away, Peter." Seeing him in his rather excellent human form wasn't on my To Do list for the day.

He tried the door. "Let me in. Now."

I sighed, stalking to the door. He'd just come through like a bulldozer if I didn't. I let it swing wide, displaying my retreating hind end. I turned around and glared at him.

My jaw went a little slack. He'd cut his hair into a wispy, collar-length style. I nearly screamed but snapped my mouth closed. He didn't have to ask me if I agreed with his decision to get rid of the length.

Peter eyed the busted up, listing bed, then his beautiful, sterling gaze flashed to me.

I crossed my arms on my chest. "I'll fix it."

"Fix?" He waved a large hand at the damage. "Really, it's beyond that!"

"I'll get a new one." If he was going to start preaching to me about the cost of bedframes, I'd freak. I made more than enough working at the bookstore to replace the stupid bed.

"What's up your ass lately?"

"That's just it, Peter. Mind your own freaking business."

"You'd be dead in a day if I did that." His tone didn't match mine. His words were soft-spoken, soothing. Making sense.

I hated that about him. He flipped a switch between compassion, stoicism, and rage like Mr. Rogers, Jekyll, and Hyde.

"Try me."

"You don't mean that." He smiled cockily, leaning in the door.

"Get out." I jabbed a finger into the hallway.

He strode inside my room, stopping close and peering down at me. "You don't mean that, either." Hot breath fanned my cheeks. His stare held a warning.

The floodgates released my temper. I hit him, and immediately hated myself for it. Not just a slap either. Hard, with a lightning quick hand. Before it registered, I landed my other fist. His head snapped to the side. I bounced on the balls of my feet, ready to let fly with another.

Peter surprised me. Rather than hitting me back, which I really wanted him to do, he grinned, catching me totally off guard. I stared at his face, wonder on my own, when he tackled me, pinning my arms above my head. I growled, thrashing beneath him.

He responded by letting his weight crush me to stillness. "That, little girl, is not advisable if you want to continue breathing. You may be fast, Tessa, but you're also naïve." His gaze searched mine for understanding. "If you decide to hit me again, I'll return the favor." Blood formed a fat drop from a split in his upper lip, the same one I'd loved to feel against mine over a month back.

I cringed inside. I didn't want to hurt Peter. My bottom lip quivered. I didn't dare speak or I'd start bawling like a baby. Instead, I looked away. *Coward.*

Peter lifted me so my feet were dangling in the air and held me against the wall. Air huffed from my lungs with the impact and my head smacked against the plaster.

"Ow, dammit!" My ears rang. We stared, eye to eye, an inch apart. "I meant it." My words fell flat, a staccato trail of whispered syllables because I couldn't draw a full breath. It wasn't what I really wanted to say. I'd never stop being a smartass. And just below the thin façade of tough-guy-Tessa, the words *I'm sorry* played in my mind, begging to be spoken out loud. I didn't know what stopped me from saying them, but I hated it.

"Clean up, get dressed, and be downstairs for work in ten minutes or I'll come back up here and we'll continue this rather than wait for your next tantrum."

I glared.

He shook me against the wall. "Understand?" Straight, white teeth gritted the word.

"Yes!"

Peter lowered me slowly, eyes locked on mine as I slid against the cold wall to the floor. He released my balled-up shirt and left without another word. I stalked to the mirror to wipe away the teary evidence of my frustration.

Something had to change. I had so many things on my mind. Sadly, I knew I wouldn't be able to find a psychologist who'd buy into any of my worries.

Weeks had passed without me killing anyone. Death rattles rang in my ears. Faces of those I'd "dispatched" reflected back at me each morning in the mirror when I changed, my gargoyle retreating for the day and sending me back to my slight, human form. I was dishwater-blonde, sort of short, and slightly pretty in a nerdy type of way. Having a few kills under my belt sure did change my self-perception. A year before I never would have seen myself capable of such thing as tearing out someone's throat.

Days ago I'd banished my guilt, considering what I'd done to Kai more of an extermination than murder. He'd been around for centuries before I led him to a watery death-by-Tyrens. I considered such a long life a damned good run for him. Blood stained my hands, even if I hadn't pulled the figurative trigger. Kai wasn't human when I killed him. He wasn't the charming Scot I'd begun to fall for; he was a monster capable of torture, bent on murder to get his means. Back then, I was just an orphan with an abnormally high body temperature, my dreams the only part of me capable of seeing anything outside of St. Vincent's Home for Girls or study abroad programs.

Were we entirely that different, Kai and me? We both killed, our perspective on right and wrong peppering our motives, deciding who lived and died. Those of his henchmen I'd murdered were simply collateral. Kai had used his mind and power over others to kill, never getting his hands dirty. I used my claws and took lots of showers. We each murdered, no matter how we justified the act or lied to ourselves so we could sleep at night.

I'm Tessa. I'm 19. I kill people if they threaten to do the same to those I love and that's okay because I say so.

He'd been a beautiful man with long blond hair and glinting brown eyes that danced with humor and wit. It was just a look, an act to bait my trust. We'd barely made it to first base before things got sticky. Now, months later, I was crushing on Peter for entirely different reasons, but both of them were gorgeous men in their own ways.

The romance Kai had introduced me to changed me nearly as much as the mysterious, dark side of the UK. Great Britain was a place I'd yearned to wander since I began to read. But sticking with learning the art of the historical literary masters wasn't in my cards, apparently. I'd begun to fall for Kai, found myself lost among volumes of beloved old books in The Bochord (we'd renamed our jointly-owned bookstore), and lived through my humanity being exchanged for that of a living gargoyle.

I looked at my hands. Had I been standing in full sunlight, my skin would be transparent, showing sinew, muscle, bone, cartilage, and what little fat remained here and there on my body. Even standing clear of direct sunlight, I was a monster beneath the façade of human skin, certainly lethal, but a bit of a hero by my way of thinking. When I found out what Kai was up to, I did everything short of sacrificing my life to save those he tortured and held captive. I would be indebted to Peter, Petra, Clan Logan, and the watery world of the Tyrens as long as I drew breath. We were the good guys, gargoyles that retained our humanity and fought the evil side of my new brethren, the henchmen, who left their lives in the light behind and never looked back. Unless they were hungry.

Kai and his henchmen had claimed lands in Scotland and all but demolished the rightful clan's once regal castle beside Loch Ore, while imprisoning Clan Logan. The clan was now free, and, aside from the absence of one brother, Teigan, the group of Scots reclaimed their lives and planned to rebuild their home. I'd promised to find Teigen and held my vow close. Kai was gone, plans were hatched, and construction was underway. They were free because of me, in part. There was a little good in the things I'd done, but there was so much blood, so much bad. I saw it in everything.

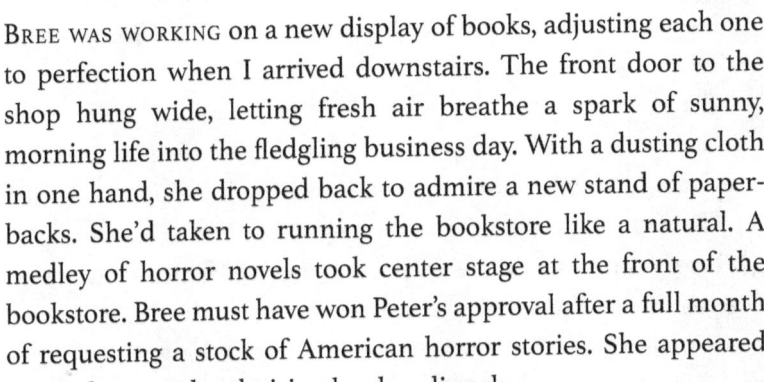

BREE WAS WORKING on a new display of books, adjusting each one to perfection when I arrived downstairs. The front door to the shop hung wide, letting fresh air breathe a spark of sunny, morning life into the fledgling business day. With a dusting cloth in one hand, she dropped back to admire a new stand of paperbacks. She'd taken to running the bookstore like a natural. A medley of horror novels took center stage at the front of the bookstore. Bree must have won Peter's approval after a full month of requesting a stock of American horror stories. She appeared pleased as punch, admiring her handiwork.

I couldn't help but smile. The scene was infectious. "Nice."

Bree grinned when she saw me on the stairs. "Good morning, sunshine." She turned back to the display. "These came in yesterday."

I skirted the sunlight, waiting for Bree to come along with me to the register. She gave one last look at her work and met me, smiling as we walked.

Bree was happy. She'd become fast friends with Crispin Logan, despite their differences. Bree was an American college student who'd grown up with support and love of a wealthy family. Crispin was an 11th century Scot who'd been transformed into a gargoyle. Over the centuries he'd barely survived numerous battles, at first. I'd seen him in action, and my life was safe in his skilled hands, or claws, as the case might be. I lived and breathed as a testament to that skill. The comparison between the two of them was polar, but Bree and Crispin took to each other like salt and pepper; different spices in a rack of blended flavor.

A couple walked inside the store and Bree grinned at me, turning on her heel to meet them with a warm smile.

Peter leaned against the counter, arms crossed over his chest.

The damage to his lip was small, thank goodness. If a person wasn't looking for the little cut, they'd likely miss it altogether.

I sucked it up and took a spot next to him. "Sorry about earlier."

"I know."

"I am truly, really sorry, Peter. I would never want to hurt you like that." I looked at him dead on. "I mean it."

"Don't make it a habit. You're angry, but you're also going to get hurt. A man can only hold back so much." He turned to watch Bree as she led the patrons to the new rack of books.

"Something has to change, Peter. I've got a lot bothering me, and I have to do something to feel like I'm doing some good somewhere. I think I need to go back to Kelty and keep looking for the cell where Teigan's hidden." He continued to watch the front while listening intently, so I continued, "I mean, I'm all bunched up. They're rebuilding the castle out there. Maybe I could help."

Peter snorted, smiling at me. "Fine way to refer to it, 'bunched up.'" He shook his head.

Crispin emerged from the back room toting a tea pot and a big fist of mugs. "Morning," he said, setting the steaming decanter on a hotplate beside the register. He pulled two packets of sweetener from a pocket, gesturing toward Bree. "Maybe if she tries the tea with some sugar, she'll like it more."

"Good luck with that." I grinned. They were quite the team.

Crispin left us to go talk with Bree and her patrons.

"I'll drive you," Peter said. "These two can handle things for a bit. The store will be fine."

"It's okay, Peter. I can drive myself."

"Absolutely not."

"I can handle it." The Aston Martin we'd taken from Scotland was quite the beast, but I'd watched Peter closely as he drove. Driving a car was something new. I'd never had the opportunity to get a driver's license back in the States. An Aston would be an awesome car to learn with, in my opinion.

"You'll wreck. Driving in London is never pleasant, and it won't do for a first run."

"See? This is what I'm talking about." I kicked at the wood floor, scattering imaginary dust bunnies. "I have zero independence."

"I hardly think getting yourself killed on the M is a good option to seek liberty, Tessa. Get a grip." He refilled his cup from the fresh pot of Earl Grey. "And I've got the keys."

"Well, la dee da."

Peter shot me a crusty look.

I really couldn't expect to make it by myself in one day, anyway. Kelty was over a half a day's drive from London and I didn't know my way there that well. With my luck something would happen and I'd get trapped in the open at nightfall. That scenario broke loose a whole world of crazy possibilities. I shouldn't risk Garging Out on the road. I could barely stay airborne for three hours as a gargoyle before I wore out and had to land. My choices were to drive with Peter, or not go.

"Fine. We leave at sunrise tomorrow." Maybe we could talk more on the way. Although I'd apologized, I still felt horrible about losing my temper.

He leaned close to my ear. "Three cases of periodicals await your attention in the back, Tessa. Need I clarify, once more, you have a job to do?"

THREE CASES of magazines turned into a day of stocking and dusting. I worked hard and fast, and was exhausted by mid-afternoon. I waved to Peter, pointing upstairs. A good night's sleep hadn't happened for me in weeks and a catnap sounded perfect. The store would be locked up for the night soon, anyway.

Peter acknowledged, so I went to my room, stripped down to shorts and a T-shirt, and climbed into bed. Two concrete blocks from the back alley were my method of fixing my broken bed frame. Not fancy, but it would work until I picked out a new one. The damned book hadn't been so much as scratched. Thinking again about the way it wouldn't answer me got my goat.

Never before have I fallen into a dream so quickly. It was more like being pulled through my surroundings by something I couldn't see, which held fast to my hand. My mind seldom quieted, instead building anxiety like a stockpile of slugs, slithering, clinging to the edges of my consciousness. Even in my sleep I sought escape, gasping, trying to claw my way loose but stuck in the dream. I wanted to wake up, and my brain was the only thing fighting to do it. Each breath was labored and panicked.

Something immensely heavy held me firmly against the mattress. My mind was awake, but my eyes refused to open on command. Not one part of my body responded to urges to get off the bed. The weight intensified. Finally, I managed to jerk my eyes open, clearing the blur of sleep from view.

I was crushed into the mattress cover as if I was vacuum sealed by the sheet. Terror overtook my entire being, but I didn't shiver. I wasn't sure I was even breathing because the sheet was so tight against my throat.

Something moved at the foot of the bed. I squawked, trying to kick my feet. A bubble of icy air pushed toward my face, but I was unable to move my arms. It kept coming, coating my body like cold paint. My ankles felt cuffed, as if thick fingers held them in a vice-like grip. I began to cry through sealed lips.

The bubble continued to creep up my body, clawing, grasping hands visible under the fabric. Tears ran from the corners of my eyes as I considered what might happen when the thing covered me completely. Gooseflesh rose on my thighs as the icy figure slid upward, filling the curves of my body, leaving no intimate part of me untouched.

The bubble grew into a monstrosity sitting on my chest, between me and the clinging sheet. The cover was pushed upward as the thing sprouted above me. Shoulders formed, like a kid in a homemade ghost costume. The selvedge of the material began to lift from my chest and the smell of decay gushed from the gap between. I dreaded what I would see underneath as the sheet fell back.

Long, twisted strands of filthy black hair fell over my chest and throat. A bowed head hung on a thin neck just below my face. Boney shoulder blades protruded like abbreviated wings. Labored, wheezing breath racked the body so hard my spine tingled.

The head rolled back, revealing gleaming, black eyes in recessed sockets. Two seeping holes divided the face where nose cartilage should have been. A wet maw parted, revealing serrated teeth, too numerous for the size of the mouth. It crouched back inside the sheet, coiling to strike, snarling like a feral beast ready to fight for its life.

I inhaled deeply and screamed with every bit of strength in my soul. The shriek resonated, pitching through my room with a shrillness that carried my helplessness.

"Bree!" My voice resounded like it came from a loudspeaker.

The thing shot from under the sheet, straight at my face. The room was oily, changing from grey to black-on-black. I slammed my eyes shut. Death was everywhere; in my mouth like rotten milk, pushing into my nose as if a rat, dead and bloated burst in my face. Decay leaked through my skin, creeping inward in a cold rush, carrying hate and disdain straight to my heart. I swung my arms, thrashing.

My ears popped and my skull bounced off the mattress from the force of the thing striking me. My face stung on one side. I'd been hit, hard enough to start my ears ringing in two different pitches. My arms went lax. I waited to feel those serrated teeth rip into me, sure I was finished for good. My legs twitched, and blood ran inside my mouth. The thing hissed.

I looked it in the face. It smiled, the grin spreading so wide, crows' feet forming so deeply, it appeared the temples might crack open.

"So sad," it said, black tongue smacking too hard against jagged teeth. "*Bandia na Teasa* leaves you now and where to go?"

I gagged, dodging a dribble of dark foam that dripped from its chin.

"You will know nothing more, little girl." It barked a delighted laugh, spraying me with muck.

"No!" I screamed, raising my knees. It might eat me, but it wouldn't be while I lived. The beast rocked forward, straight into my oncoming elbow. It thumped down to the floor, but only after raking my leg with its fingernails. I sat up, blinking to see where it had gone. I couldn't let it get away. The thing was hatred in physical form. Something like that held a grudge and would return.

The thing screamed from the foot of the bed and I came to my feet, intent on grabbing ahold of it and bludgeoning it to death, with a shoe if that's all I could grab. Balance was a trick after being struck in the head so hard. I fell forward, reaching, but coming up short as the thing flattened itself out like a weasel and skittered beneath my bed, where the book was. For an instant I worried it might tear the book apart. The room fell still but I didn't chance that it was gone. I crawled to the door, grabbed the handle, and pulled myself up with a slippery hand.

I stumbled into the bright hallway, squinting. Peter's room wasn't far, so I ran for it. Three steps into my flight my toe caught on the opposite heel and I fell forward. My temple smacked against the doorjamb hard enough to make everything go black.

~

DREAM A LITTLE DREAM.

The words replayed like a recorded female voice. I startled so hard when I woke up, my stomach muscles locked up. My head split with pain. I twisted against sheets, searching for the evil thing that had attacked me, balling the fabric up and flinging it to the floor.

The room was lit with soft, pale light. The sheet lay crumpled on the carpet like the monster abandoned its cloak. Back at the Home for Girls, I grew up thinking monsters only came out at night. What the heck could a bunch of nuns know? They were way off. The thing was in the room somewhere, waiting to jump me again. I could smell the rot.

"Monsters only come out at night," I whispered.

Warm arms circled me. "It's okay. I'm here." Peter rocked me slowly.

I searched his steel-grey irises. *Peter. Thank God.* "Where is it?" I yelled in choppy syllables, scanning the floor.

He held fast when I tried to get up. "Calm down, Tessa. You've hit your head really hard. You'll start bleeding again if you keep thrashing." He ran a finger along a sticky bandage clinging to my forehead above my left eye, sealing the adhesive back down.

Monsters only come out at night . . . monsters only come out at night. . . .

I lacked energy to do anything other than wrap my hands in the fabric of his shirt, inhale the familiar scent of capable, strong man, and cry like an infant. All I wanted was sleep.

"Tessa? Try to stay awake."

His voice wasn't enough to keep my eyes from closing.

2

I clung to Peter and he held me against his chest. He didn't talk or answer my ramblings. Darkness blacked out the corners and depths in the room. The thing was there, in shadow where I couldn't see it, waiting for him to let go. I kept my eyes shut and buried my sweat-soaked face against his shoulder. My forehead screamed with pain.

Peter read my mind, hitting a lamp switch, ousting night. If the sun had set by that time, I didn't know it. Dusk called forth gargoyles, but the close contact between Peter and me bound us to our human forms. I prayed to something unknown that he wouldn't need to abandon me for any reason.

Time didn't tick by like normal. My mind replayed images that tormented me. I cried, Peter rocked me. I trembled, he tightened his grip as if he could squeeze the shakes out of me. I slept, awakening to relive the horror, brought back to my senses just long enough to fall back into fitful sleep.

I cycled.

Peter remained.

If I awoke alone, he was there in an instant. Light blended with darkness outside his window and I locked my eyes shut against them both. I buried myself against him, his reassuring voice bringing me back before I slid away again, soothing, gradually replacing terror. Warmth began to swell in my chest. The goddess stirred while I slept, ousting my nightmares.

Consciousness ebbed. Heat expanded into parts of me I didn't remember being fevered before. Lucidity left me, but it was okay. The goddess awakened and wouldn't leave me alone again. She led me to focus on things that normally escaped my attention. The scent of man greeted me in that place just beyond awakening, doing new things to my senses. My hands wandered hard flesh. Warmth. Muscle. The raw, satisfying sound of fabric shredding in my hands. Bared flesh against my own, foreign but feeding a craving deep inside me.

He caught my hands.

"No, Tessa. You're not thinking straight." Big, beautiful hands held mine still and he pulled away, creating a barrier between us.

Noble.

Light faded and I relaxed, allowing myself to drift off. Sleep felt positively great, but it only happened for what couldn't have been longer than five minutes. I was recharged and ready to get up and get back to life, but then I'd be tired again. Each time I closed my eyes and woke up all I wanted to do was put my hands on him. Semiconsciously pleading for his touch, I offered my own in exchange. I was blind to everything but the two of us, begging for something I didn't fully understand. Each time I fought the urge to pull back, something told me to keep going. So I did.

"Bloody hell, Tessa. You're burning up." His accent poured over his words like warm honey.

I laughed. "God, I love to hear you speak," I said.

He groaned against my touch, pulling my hands from him. His grip tightened on my arms, flattening my shoulders against the mattress.

The gap between us chilled me. Cold air scorched my

burning flesh like ice on a sunburn. I trembled, grasping fistfuls of dampened sheets. My hair clung to my wet, glistening skin.

Peter blew lungsful of cool breath from above me. "You don't really want this."

I nodded like a kid wanting ice cream. "Yes, I do. And so do you."

"We'll talk when you are more lucid." He pushed clear of my hands and I was furious, but I knew I needed to get a grip on the bravado *Teasa* brought out in me. She knew how to awaken my appetites, apparently. All too soon, I was aware of what I'd been doing to him and I covered my face with both hands.

Peter tucked strands of sweat-dampened hair behind my ear. "You're going to be fine. Drink this." He held a tumbler of water to my lips.

A tentative sip became a long pull. Cold seared my throat and stomach, moisture filling cracks like rain on desert ground.

He took the glass away. "Not too much," he warned. "You'll be sick."

I coughed, nauseated and groggy, feeling a familiar heartbeat against my cheek.

Peter set the water aside. "Thank you."

"For what?" I croaked.

"Drinking without breaking the glass or cursing me out this time." He laughed.

I pushed away from him, damp skin pulling away and chilling. "Gross. You're all sweaty."

"You're like lying beside a thermal mass."

Daylight pushed against lowered blinds at his window. I blinked hard, focusing, trying hard to shake the grogginess.

Peter rested against the headboard in a pair of his workout sweats. Strands of hair clung to his neck. Angry, crimson scratches ran the length of his biceps. Similar marks raked across his chest next to a neat set of teeth marks.

"Holy hell!" I sat up quickly, searching his torn skin. Each individual drop of blood and color drained from my face. "No . . . no! What did I do?" I tucked the sheet around my naked form, placing my arms over my breasts, my face in my hands. "Dammit!" I fumbled, looking for words. An apology was necessary, but *"I'm sorry"* didn't seem like it would cut it. Had I done all that damage? What was I apologizing for? Had we just—

"Hey," he said, softly.

"Oh, my God! I'm . . . so sorry."

"Best battle wounds ever," he laughed.

Not funny. I didn't recall the whole thing. I remembered touching him, pulling at his clothes. I didn't feel any different, like I thought I would after the first time if we had actually done *it*. A sick feeling grew in my stomach. I'd blacked out and the part I couldn't remember seemed to be the most important part. I looked down at everything I *wasn't* wearing, spellbound.

"Ah, God." My face went back into my hands.

Peter sighed. I didn't move, not knowing if I would cry or punch something first. He got out of bed and pulled a T-shirt over his head. "Wait here. You haven't eaten in days. I'll go find you something." He smoothed his hair back from his face. At the door, he turned to me. "I mean it. Stay here. In my bed—"

"—yes." It figured he could just flip a switch and be back to business.

He frowned slightly, shaking his head, then left.

I waited just a moment to make sure he wasn't going to come right back in, then sat up despite a spinning head. I peered over the side of the bed. My T-shirt and sleep shorts were piled on the floor.

There was no way in hell I would wait around in his bed, naked, no matter what we'd just done. Or not done. It was hard enough to digest that I probably just had sex for the first time and didn't remember a measly thing about it. Or had I?

I put on my wrinkled sleep gear and slipped into the hallway, moving close to the wall. Dizziness swarmed in my skull like hornets and my stomach lurched. I paced softly to my room.

Afternoon sun fell toward the horizon outside my window. Disgruntled, dying rays shone against my skin, revealing bared muscle, sinew, and bone. I held up a hand. Sunshine gleamed between skinless, grey fingers. Dropping my arm, I leaned on the window to feel the warmth, despite my appearance. My hair fell forward, smelling of sweat and *him*. My hands curled as foggy, distant memories courted my mind, just out of reach and growing more distant. *Peter's voice, his scent, his heat.* I shook off the feeling quickly before my imagination got the best of me.

Something dark moved in the alley below my window. I leaned close to the warm glass. Two people split off at the sidewalk, each taking separate directions away from the store. They were just far enough away I couldn't see anything but hoods and black jackets. Their movements were quick and determined. There was no friendly wave goodbye or meandering in the direction of cars.

Peter called from the hallway. "Tessa?"

I hurried to let him in.

"I'd like to point out, you said you'd stay put." He didn't look shocked.

"Meaning. . . ?" If he thought I was going to just lay there in his bed and wait for him to come back, he didn't know me at all. Surely he knew better.

Peter sighed and shook his head. "Really, Tessa, you've given me some bloody lame excuses before, but playing stupid takes the damned cake. There's food ready downstairs." He gave a disappointed look and closed the door, leaving me no opportunity to answer. He didn't let on that anything new had developed between us. I knew I could be that smooth about it, too, if I used the same forced stoicism. I practiced that state of mind and went for a much-needed shower.

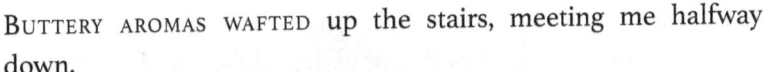

B<small>UTTERY</small> <small>AROMAS</small> <small>WAFTED</small> up the stairs, meeting me halfway down.

"We need to beef up security around the store," I announced.

I'd decided to ignore my inner turmoil at not being able to remember my sexual encounter with Peter by concentrating on fixing something else. Cowardly? Yes. Productive? Yes, again. The shower renewed my outlook. I was rested but famished.

Peter sat at the tea bar next to a delectable looking spread of fried fish and chips with a little bucket of minty mashed peas at the side. I accepted the plate he handed me, claimed a seat, and began helping myself.

"Security? The old wards are in place." He'd showered, too, and his hair was still long enough to tuck behind his ears. The short cut made the shade appear darker, showing off his eyes and tawny skin. He was the only person I'd ever known with hair that grew as fast as mine. His would likely be back down past his shoulders in a couple months. I wasn't complaining. Not many guys could pull off the look, but the dark hair, silver eyes ringed with black around the irises, and a short outgrowth of a beard was a good look on Peter.

I pulled my gaze away before the feelings of guilt and dread came back.

"It was just a dream, Tessa." Peter pushed a bottle of water down the bar toward me. "You went on and on about monsters while you slept."

"A dream?" Seldom remembered, my dreams generally didn't hang around long. Gargoyles healed during transformation. Although no wounds remained, I hadn't dreamed the attack in my room. That was a certainty. I'd been wide awake, trapped, fully realizing something crawled from under the bed sheet to snarl and lunge at me.

Hunger outweighed the urge to relive the experience. I tore

into a crispy cod filet, relishing the flavor of salty, greasy manna from the ocean.

"Yes..." Peter drawled.

I just shook my head and kept eating. He was way off. I didn't suffer from nightmares, and that wasn't why I wanted to talk about security. I'd tell him about the men in the alley after we ate. I doubted extra security would keep out a monster like the one in my bedroom.

Peter's fork clicked against his plate. We locked gazes for a moment. I washed a mouthful down with a big gulp of water so I could talk without being gross.

"I'm not talking about a dream. There were two men in the alley today. I didn't get a good look at them, but they acted sort of suspicious. They were dressed in dark clothes and in a hurry."

"I'll look into getting cameras angled on your side of the building, if that will help." He looked into his tea mug.

"That would make me feel a lot better."

He still wasn't looking at me. I think a bruised ego was new territory for Bigger Than Shit Peter. Getting to know him had revealed a man who was used to getting a certain type of attention from girls. No, not girls, *women*. My ability to hold character, to continue to talk business was throwing him off. I wouldn't be joining a harem any time soon. I was grateful for his help, his healing me. The rescue, and even the tenderness and his ability to offer it without making me ask for it. But I wouldn't allow myself to fall for him. At least not completely, no matter what had happened between us. There was too much grey area between Peter and me. Knowing where he stood with me was the only solid part of our arrangement since I never knew where I stood with him.

"Thank you for helping me." I watched him carefully, hoping he'd look up and see the sincerity I felt. He didn't, so I waited another beat before giving in to hunger again.

"You healed up well. How are you feeling?"

"Better. This," I lifted a grease-soaked filet in a messy wrapper, "is awesome. Thanks." I beamed around a mouthful of fish.

"That's good. Anything you want to talk about?" He popped a French fry into his mouth with casual ease.

I froze. That was the mother of all loaded questions, considering. For some reason I swallowed the half-chewed food and choked. He handed me my water bottle.

I got control quickly, a little angry. "What's with the inquisition?" He was acting like I'd done something wrong, like peed the bed or something. *His bed.*

He nodded, turning to his plate. "Good to hear you're fine with it all. A couple day's sleep can be quite satisfying."

My appetite died the more sarcastic he got. I wiped my fingers and pushed the plate away as his words hit home. "What do you mean 'day's'? I know I slept in, but I see no reason to exaggerate."

He looked at his plate. "You should thank Crispin and Bree. They watched the store for you."

"Both of them? Crap. I didn't realize I was out the whole day." I fingered the spot on my forehead, the new flesh there sealed and good as new.

A frown pulled at the corners of his mouth. "You did more than oversleep. It's been nearly four days."

"No way." I tightened the lid back on my water bottle in a restless habit. "Where is Bree?"

"Crispin took her to the Victoria and Albert. They wanted to get out for a while. They'll be back before sundown, of course."

"Of course." I felt horrible. They'd worked through their days off to cover me.

They'd be back soon. Crispin wouldn't risk changing into a gargoyle when he was escorting Bree. "I'll look for them a little later."

I was a real shit. I'd let everyone down and Peter wouldn't even look at me. Maybe I should have reassured him what happened between us was great, in some way tell him he'd rocked my world. I would have been lying. I woke up in his bed. I remembered coming to a couple times, touching him in ways I was embarrassed to think about.

"Sounds good," he said. "I'm closing the store for the next two days. We all need a break."

I nodded, looking down. "I'm sorry, Peter." I couldn't tell if he was trying to make me feel guilty on purpose or if he was genuinely upset. It wasn't like him to let his feelings show. He was all façade; an act that he had down to the point of callous nonchalance most times. Anger seldom broke through, and I doubted sadness had a chance.

"For what now?" he shot back.

My mouth worked but I didn't know what to say. "For . . . everything." I felt like an idiot.

He snorted, then slowly nodded, looking over at me. He searched my eyes, my face, body language, every means of silent communication he could to get something from me, but I honestly didn't know what to say. I panicked a little, the last of my will to keep up the "just business" attitude sloughing away. I had nothing on Peter. He could switch gears like a pro, letting a glimpse of his heart show at the perfect moment to throw me off.

"Let's go lock up." Peter folded his wrapper and dumped his plate in the rubbish bin, the awkward conversation tossed out with it.

I followed suit and washed my hands, thinking about a nice, long run to sort through my thoughts. They always helped to keep me grounded before. He joined me at the sink with his hands under the faucet.

"Sounds good," I agreed.

3

But it wasn't good. I'd hurt Peter, and not remembering what happened between us two after I awoke in his bed, horrified me. I didn't sleep much as a gargoyle anyway, but I was tormented by what I'd done. The old Tessa would never hurt someone she cared about. The new Tessa stomped around like the world owed her a favor, throwing over-heated hissy fits and hitting people.

The next morning, I splashed cold water on my face and searched my gaze in the mirror for some semblance of who I used to be. I'd lost weight but toned my body into something that looked more mechanical than feminine and curvy, like before. My face was thin and pale from lack of my beloved southern sunshine. Something moved just behind my gaze, like I was still in there someplace hopelessly locked away, calling out unheard, pounding on thick glass as my world happened around me.

I forced a smile into the reflection. Someone else grinned back, taunting me. The smile dropped away. My right fist shattered the glass, leaving behind a spider web of fragmented images of the bitch snarling back at me. Chest heaving and

knuckles bloodied, I strode past the busted-up bed in my room to
get dressed in running gear, grabbed a few bills from my under-
wear drawer and left the Bochord with my heart in my throat.

A purely volatile feeling owned me as if I was a bomb waiting
to go off. I ran, craving sunlight and the empty air offered by freedom, taking to the streets like I was whole. I sweated beneath the
hood of my sweatshirt, weaving between people. My feet touched
the ground like every other human on the sidewalk that morning.

I cried a little, feet pounding away, eventually slowing to a
fast walk.

A silver haired man walked beside me, compelling me to slow
to his pace when I saw he tapped a white cane before him. He
said, "You know, I live just up there. I'll be home soon." He kept
up a steady pace, smiling a toothless grin below sightless,
grey eyes.

He couldn't look at my tears and I didn't have to worry,
although it was cloudy out, that he would see my skinless face if I
got in the sun. To him, I was just me. I'd sound like my old self,
full of zest for life, like I'd been just months ago, pre-gargoyle.

My feet struck concrete at the same pace as his. Finally, I
offered, "I live back there." *Lie.* I lived nowhere. "I just need to
run. You know?"

"I know." He laughed. "Believe me."

That was nice to hear. He didn't know the things I'd done. To
him, I was just a sweet person out for some air, like him. We
continued in comfortable silence for a while, through drizzle
that broke with momentary shards of reluctant sunshine. I
buried my head at the back of my hood, creating a cowl over the
transparent skin of my face so I didn't scare the people we
passed.

"So many people out today, looking around," he said.

I've always admired the tenacity of the blind. The man used
his other senses to gauge his surrounding, listening closely,
hearing the others passing us by as we walked. I gave up my

silence to answer, hoping he'd stop talking. "Yeah, despite the rain."

"Nice day for a walk," he said, between taps of his cane. "But a young girl like you has reasons to be out looking around on a day like today. In the rain." He smiled.

The guy was flawlessly perceptive. I was out blowing off steam with a run-turned-walk, craving understanding and companionship, and I found it in a stranger I felt safe with, and searching the damp streets of London for *me*. I said nothing. I'd likely offer up another lie, anyway.

"Soul searching the walks of London, then," he baited.

"Mm hm."

"Start with where you live. Back there"—he motioned behind us—"just the advice of an old, blind man."

"Thank you."

"Of course."

"Have a good day," I called when I broke into a run at the next corner.

I didn't wait for a response, stretching my legs, fighting impulses to pour on speed that might draw attention. I ran a really long time, and the neighborhoods, businesses, even the trees changed. I slowed, gawking around.

Far more birds sang than I'd heard anywhere in the UK. I crossed the street to get beneath the amazing canopy of dense greenery. An old, gilt street sign was draped with yellow blossoms.

"Petrichor Lane." Someone had chosen the most awesome and fitting of names for the most gorgeous, ivy dripping, dewy street I'd been to in England. Trees grew tall and extra leafy, boughs touching above the lane to form a canopy over the deeply shaded street. Gas lamps shone low and yellow with long tendrils of ivy spiraling their posts. Big, bird-sized insects chased around tree trunks and pillows of blossoms so quickly I couldn't focus on them.

I'd entered a square court. There were no cars and only a few faceless people walked around. The shop windows were neatly adorned with heavy planter boxes of greenery and flowers that overflowed, hanging to the mossy cobbles. The air was sweet with fragrant nectar and rich from rain-damp earth. Flute music flowed from the distance, echoing, bringing the image of a piper with a wooden reed instrument held to his lips, fingers working away. I was utterly charmed.

My stomach rumbled. The concept of time and the fact that I needed to get back to the bookstore was lost on me as I ran earlier. It had to be well past noon and I hadn't eaten a thing. Returning to check in with Peter would do no good if I hadn't worked out any of the issues causing my inner turmoil. I needed time to think and this was the perfect place to recharge.

A plate of hot food was my goal. I selected a doorway with a big, dewy looking pendant light hanging down in front and ducked inside, plopping into a booth midway in, while my eyes adjusted to the lack of lighting. The place smelled delicious, making me crave a thick, American-style cheeseburger.

A sign above the bar announced *Jonnie's* in a welcoming scrawl. It seemed quite popular among dressy looking professionals at lunch time. I was the only one wearing sweats and a hoodie. It was a high probability I was also the only one that smelled like a locker room at Gold's Gym. I shrugged mentally. It was getting easier and easier to quit giving a damn.

Voices blended, mixing with the din of low, unrecognizable music. Only one empty table remained in the whole pub. People picked up drinks from the bar and plates from a window cut into the wall just beyond the drink station.

Not one server worked the area so I left my seat to cut around sipping, ritzy looking groups to get to the bar. I expected scathing looks down long noses, but the opposite happened. I got a couple polite nods as I brushed by, and one lady gave a warm smile when I passed. By the time I stood at the bar waiting to order something, I didn't know what to expect. I'd had the pleasure of many polite servers, but a few had been downright pissy with me the moment I let my accent slip, indicating my nationality. A guy stood behind the bar with his back to me.

"Be right there," he tossed over his shoulder. He shuffled tickets at a register, tucking a pen behind an ear hidden by rings of thick, brown hair.

"Okay." I was in no rush, and I didn't want him to be grumpy. I could be patient.

"Almost done," he replied. "Honest."

That made me smile. I looked at a sandwich menu lying on the bar.

"Just one moment. . . ."

His words poured from a smile. I couldn't help but look up into the bar mirror to see what he looked like.

Gleaming brown eyes watched me. He held up a finger, grinning. A cell phone was tucked against his cheek. I couldn't see it before because his entire head was obscured by all that spiraling hair that hung to his collar. White teeth shone through a neatly trimmed goatee.

"It's okay," I mouthed at his reflection.

The menu offered a surprising diversity of sandwiches and salads. I chose one of the beefier looking ones and a fluffy bowl of greens while I waited.

"Sorry 'bout that." The bartender slid his cell phone into the hip pocket of his jeans while stepping into place in front of me. "Welcome to Jonnie's."

"Are you Jonnie?" He looked like a Jonnie.

He laughed, holding a hand over the bar, "I'm Adam."

I took it and we shook. "Tessa." I smiled. His grip was firm and gentle at the same time, rather than one of those weak, noncommittal handshakes. I was relieved his demeanor didn't flip when he heard my American accent.

Adam reached for a pad and pulled his pen from the mass of

curls. "I was on the phone with my dealer in Belgium. Sorry to be occupied when you're ready to order. Didn't mean to make you wait."

"You're fine. I just now made up my mind anyway. A turkey and Swiss on marble rye with that salad," I gestured to a beautiful pile of veggies with a fat pickle beside it.

"Be right back." He wrote on his pad while he left to place my ticket on a ledge beside a narrow window in the wall at the end of the bar. A hand snatched the paper as Adam spun back around.

People accumulated behind me, waiting to place orders.

"Dealer?" I couldn't help it. Dealer was just one of those words. You could really get to know someone quickly knowing they had a dealer of any sort.

"Antiques." Adam pulled a glass from a rack, scooping two cubes inside. "I know," he shook his head, "I'm a junkie. I found an old Hoosier in Belgium. Beautiful baking cabinet. It will look magnificent in my kitchen." He grinned.

"Antiques?" Not in a year would I expect the guy to say he collected antiques. There was a day not long ago when the thought of checking out collector's shops in Cecil Court was my dream. I snorted. "That's awesome. I love old things. Especially books."

"Always nice to meet a fellow junkie, Tessa." He smiled. "Now what can I get you to drink?"

He caught me off guard. "I have no idea." I searched but there wasn't a drink section on the menu I held.

"I have one you'll love. I'll bring it out in a second. Best go grab your seat before you lose it."

"Thanks." I headed back to the booth, grateful it was still unoccupied. Stretching my legs under the table felt good. I took off my hoodie and smoothed my hair back into a tail, salivating over the wonderful aromas coming from the kitchen. I really needed to start eating more, or at least more often to keep up with my appetite as a gargoyle.

Adam placed a tall, fizzy, amber drink in front of me with another charming smile. "Strongbow. It's quite popular here and one of my favorites. You'll have to tell me what you think." He slid a carbon copy down beside it. I was number 133 for the kitchen.

I wrapped my hand around the glass, which was cold, thank goodness. I'd learned the British were stingy with their ice. Warm soda wasn't as good.

"Thanks, Adam. I'll give a full report."

He sped back to the bar, leaving me watching his retreat. His jeans were extra wide at the leg, and it seemed he limped somewhat, perhaps even on both feet. The backs of his knees seemed to pop against the denim when he took a step. Maybe he wore leg braces? Whatever the case, it didn't slow him down. He moved pretty fast, nimbly picking a path through people.

I sipped the strong drink. The flavor was a lot like apple cider. The real stuff, with a quality that went beyond just juice. The experience was new and it took me two swallows to decide it was quite to my liking.

By the time my number was called from the kitchen, my glass was nearly empty. I walked to the window, ticket in hand, smiling a little too wide at anyone that made eye contact. I gathered my food like a ravenous honey badger and went back to my booth to find my glass refilled.

"You looked thirsty," Adam tossed over his shoulder as he went back to his station.

"Is this beer or what?" The legal drinking age in England was 18. With my youthful qualities dissolving like sugar in black coffee, I certainly looked my age, and old enough to drink so it wouldn't have surprised me if Adam the Bartender and Lover of Antiquities had just offered up an alcoholic drink without much thought. The thought that Adam had chosen an apple flavored drink for me made me snort back an ironic giggle.

"One of the best ciders," he called.

"Great, thanks," I answered, unenthusiastically. *Crap.*

The lack of enthusiasm didn't stop me from enjoying the extra pint. The sandwich and salad were extra good, too.

4

Jonnie's was a riot. I finally warmed up. My belly was full. I loved the new kind of apple cider Adam recommended.

I gave up my booth to stand at the bar, dancing in place with a diverse row of people, who'd loosened up considerably from when I first arrived. I took my hair tie out and let my hair fall, swinging in a long mass of humidity inspired waves. Everyone at the bar had one thing in common: we loved music. That inclination was all we needed. Two darkly clothed Grumpy Gus types loomed over the bar on the far end, hulking atop stools. They watched my antics with the other "lighter" characters, drinking from brown beer bottles, obviously green about my ability to blend.

I was back. Tessa Marie Conley stood in my shoes, smiling and meeting new people. She'd been gone far too long. Whimsy rocked me to the beat. Carefree drove me forth. Abandon told me everything would be okay.

Adam told me I'd had enough to drink.

"Whatever do you mean, dahling?" I slurred, in what was far from my best British. I grinned.

"You can't weigh much, even soaking wet. Our ciders and ales are stronger than what you're used to in the US." He winked and took my empty glass. "You're having a good time and I'd hate to see that go south."

I'd never had alcohol before so I'd be taking his word for it, which wasn't a problem. He knew more about the stuff than I did. *All hail Adam the Wise.* I sniggered.

Adam shot me a curious look.

The crowd had thinned to only a handful of us perky fun-lovers. The sulkers were long gone, creating an emptiness at the far end. They had perfectly seasoned my fun. Knowing I was having a better time than someone else was a nice turn. Now that they were gone, the scene was bland, falling tasteless against my cottony palate.

I shrugged, the perma-grin loosening its grip on my face. A familiar sensation tingled along my arms and cheeks. I knew I should be alarmed but couldn't pinpoint why. Everything was going to be all right.

"We should get together and talk about this duplicity inside you," Adam continued with his curious expression. He handed me a small, black envelope over the bar. I took it and put it in my pocket without much thought. "I've got a feeling you're a very interesting girl."

"What?" I drawled. *Duplicity?* Did he sense something was different about me? There was no way he could have any idea I was a gargoyle. Or that I harbored a goddess inside me. That was *triplicity.* Tah dah, a new Tessa-ism. *Not funny.* My smile melted like soggy corn flakes in warm milk. My stomach flipped from a mixture of alcohol and realizing I was in trouble, and about to make a big, scaly, Garged Out scene.

"What?" Adam asked.

"Nothing. I should probably be heading back."

"Will I see you again, beautiful?"

"Of course. . . ." *Not.* It was ironic how one, nebulous word can sober a person. "How much do I owe for everything?"

He tapped a few rhythms on an antique cash register and gave me a curled ticket while I tapped a foot, looking around for a nonexistent window to see just how screwed I was.

I paid hurriedly and left him a tip that was probably too generous, but I didn't want to spend any more time at the bar. I'd let myself forget who—and what—I was. Gargoyles didn't hang out at bars drinking to the point they forgot themselves. Not responsible ones, at least.

"Thanks," I said. I pulled my hair back into a ponytail and flipped up my hood out of habit.

He nodded. "See you around."

He probably wouldn't. Being outside the walls of the bookstore at nightfall was a monumental screw-up. Despite wanting to kick my own ass, I needed to hole-up in private.

The next two seconds were a slow blur. Goosebumps rose. I panicked, gasping, feeling the waistband of my running pants grow tight over my hip bones. Choosing the lesser of ways to scare the hell out of people, I opted for "fast" rather than "monster" and spun, closing the distance to the exit, picking up speed. My scaly right hand jerked open the thick door to Jonnie's. Freezing drizzle greeted me in the gloaming outside. Water danced on the deserted street as sleet struck puddles and bounced off leaves, miniature meteors pelting a dark ocean. The gas lights struggled, casting gloomy halos, ringing in the hard rain. A carriage alley offered seclusion from the sidewalk as cloth began to shred at my back and my hood popped off the top of my head. My running shoes burst like over-boiled hot dogs on the next two impacts and were kicked free as my flight came to a skidding halt before I slammed into a dingy wall of wet bricks.

My breath came in rapid, steamy snorts through my nose as I realized I'd done it, I'd made the change without notice from humans. Picking the shreds of my favorite running attire from around my waist where it hung like a hula skirt, I watched the mouth of the boxed-in alley as litter soaked up melting sleet in pockets of dark liquid I didn't care to identify. Several heaps of garbage hulked against walls. I'd sped past them in my oblivious race to solitude.

Backing into a corner, I crouched and wrapped my wings around my knees, making sure I could see through a gap to keep an eye on the opening of my cave, like a bat that preferred not to hang.

I was secure, for the time being, although I had a huge problem. Waiting out the night in the alley wasn't a good option because the moment the sun came out I'd be a naked girl lost in London huddled in a dark alley. I'd be stuck worse than I was in darkness as a gargoyle. I'd have to fly out. The good news was that the dizziness from drinking cider for a few hours inside Jonnie's faded the moment I hit the sidewalk. Retracing the route of my run earlier that day would be easier from above. With the cover of the storm, I just might pull off getting back to Cecil Court without being seen.

I was an ass. Peter would be good and pissed by then. The whole day got out of hand. All I wanted to do was go for a nice run to try to clear my mind and come up with a plan that would lead to some clarity. As usual, it all backfired like a beat up, old pick-up truck in a hot hay field. Remorse was a bitch. I needed to get back to the bookstore and apologize to Peter and Bree for running out without leaving so much as a note. Then I'd keep it simple, do my job and concentrate on the fact that a handful of people in London cared about me. I'd be good.

Face to the sky, I closed my eyes and let frosty drizzle patter away at me.

The sound of soaked cardboard sliding on concrete tore through the alley. Two piles of "garbage" stood, wings unfurling and tails lashing with the anticipation of an alley cat that cornered a mouse. The shorter of the two started in my direction while the larger one stayed back, making a point to block the exit.

"You're not in the US anymore, Toto," the big gargoyle taunted.

That was lame. But it did the trick to create fear of larger things. Even the one that drew nearer had to be two feet over my head. It laughed at the other's attempt at humor. *Obviously British.*

I came off the wall a bit.

"Don't do it," the giant back at the mouth of the alleyway warned.

I looked up at the clear path to freedom, back down at the approaching gargoyle and launched into the darkness as if I knew where I was going. Any place was better than having my back in a corner.

They were fast. I could only pray to tap the speed of the goddess, but I didn't feel the least bit hot. I pumped my wings as hard as I could but the meager speed I built up did nothing to outrun the beasts chasing me.

"Come on, you bitch!" I shouted. My voice shook, echoing the frantic feeling in my chest. No heat. No speed. No goddess. The air stilled, allowing only the sound of my wings. I knew it for what it was, the calm before the ass-beating.

One of them hit me from the right, laughing like a demon. I kicked and clawed but he grabbed onto me, twisting his legs around my waist and hanging like dead weight.

My wings and shoulders burned with the strain of remaining airborne with the burden. I balled up a fist and pummeled his head as he snarled and tried to impale my hand by moving his horns in the way.

He slammed his wings closed like a shut umbrella against his back and sunk his teeth deep in the flesh just above my collarbone.

I screamed as burning pain tore through my whole arm.

I cried out and pushed at his shoulders in a weakened attempt to free myself as we began to fall. Relentless, knowing he had the best of me, the bastard chuckled around the mouthful of muscle he held onto with his jagged teeth.

A gothic church spire came into view below just as the other gargoyle glided up beside us. "Keep a good hold, Tal." He grinned at me.

They were waiting for me to give up, to tire out and quit beating my wings so Tal could flip us in the air and carry me off to my death. The two had to be henchmen, Kai's boys from Scotland. Maybe they would murder me and dine on my cooling flesh like they'd done to a college student one night when I walked in on them around their blood-slicked, macabre banquet table. They'd kill me and move on to the next, making meals of victims forever, like they'd probably been doing for centuries. I'd helped "end" Kai and now they were back, free of his rule, but ready for vengeance.

The spire neared. The smaller of the two gargoyles continued to escort us, gliding beside me as I strained to stay in the air. All three of us knew I wouldn't make it much farther carrying Tal's weight. Only two of our trio expected me to keep trying to fly into hopeless oblivion.

I pulled my wings together and plummeted straight at the church and onto the sharp point, feeling it jab through Tal and dig past the plated armor of my abdomen and into my belly. The metal burned, but the pain wasn't what I expected. Disoriented and in shock, I thought I might live.

We hung, skewered above the rooftop of the church, adding winged death to the gothic appearance of the architecture. Tal's jaw released me along with his legs, and his body went limp, wings flailing out to his sides like a crow hung spread-winged on a fence post as a warning to others. Tal wouldn't be biting anyone again. Ever.

Panic set in at the thought that I might simply let go, my body falling limp with his as I was snuffed from the world. I couldn't give up after all I'd been through. I had to warn Peter and Bree

—*Bree!* If I died there, atop the church steeple, right next to someone—something—so evil I couldn't warn them about Tal's friend who still flew around, free to kill.

Using the spike atop one wing and the arm that didn't ache from Tal's bite, I rolled to the side, shoved a knee between us, and freed myself from the tip of the spire, sending Tal's body lower onto the spike with a sickening squeal as metal grated on bone. A scream was torn from my mouth before I knew it was coming. Blood sluiced over the scales of my chest, arm, abdomen, and legs. I couldn't tell if it was mine or Tal's. A hole about the diameter of a Texas grapefruit gaped where my navel should have been, and a wet chill ran down my neck and shoulder. My hoodie hung by the waistband around my middle like a torn skirt. Looking up, I wobbled in the air as I kicked off Tal like a springboard.

Confusion set in at the same time I took flight. I didn't have a lot of pain. Either I wasn't hurt that badly, or I was mortally wounded and in shock. Whatever the case, I was far from out of the woods.

Tal's friend loomed ahead, pulling a U-turn in the air and coming fast, straight at me. He'd hit me like a missile. That would be my end.

I flew straight up, hoping to gain enough altitude to get lost in the heavy, wet veil of clouds and fog. I began to cry, knowing I would likely die. I wouldn't see Peter to apologize and tell him he was the greatest guy I knew. Bree would go back to the States, grieve, and be heartbroken. The goddess, well, she could go straight to hell for not helping me when I needed it most.

The telltale *huff* of enormous wings pounded the air behind me. I didn't look, just kept flying up, higher and higher to get to the fog. I was almost there but my shoulder throbbed where the muscle was torn from Tal's teeth and my back muscles grew more fatigued with each pump of my wings. I ignored it the best I could and concentrated on getting away. Gravity tugged at me and I was so frustrated and scared, I screamed over and over as I flew, wondering what was taking Tal's friend so long to get me.

A grunting *"Hu-uhck,"* sounded at the same time something hit the unnamed gargoyle like an owl hitting a pigeon. The silhouette of two winged forms tumbled against a backdrop of light grey clouds beneath me as they grappled, growing closer. A dark ribbon of thick, liquid splattered them, making one of them look up, the whites of his eyes the only thing discernible in his face. Either they were flying up to me or I was drifting down toward them.

"Aw, dammit, Tessa" he said, "you're bleeding."

"Peter?" He'd found me somehow. I started crying harder as they passed me, going up. "Don't leave me." My confusion deepened. I didn't see where either of the two bled from. I doubted somebody my size could have been the one shedding so much blood. I tumbled, trying to keep Peter in my line of sight but I was losing him.

One of the other gargoyle's wings flopped, out of control on the air current.

"Tessa!" Peter called. Gravity had me. The other two gargoyles passed me easily as I spiraled. At least my wings didn't burn or cramp anymore.

Peter let go of the other gargoyle and lunged for me, catching me just before I hit a patch of grass that appeared out of nowhere. "Don't leave me, Peter. I'm so sorry," I whispered. He set me down gently and turned away despite my pleas. I tried to get up but failed to find both feet.

Tal's friend landed in an ungraceful, contorted mess in a rose garden next to a gilded church fence but managed to stand right before being tackled by Peter. Dry leaves and mulch exploded where they went down, grunting and punching each other. Few blossoms adorned the plants at such a late time of the season, and they'd been cut back some by a careful gardener. Thick stems punctured the membranes of the other gargoyle's wings but they kept brawling.

Darkness began to give way to a comforting, sleepy haze. Footsteps approached and one of my arms was pulled vertical. When I turned my head to see who might be finishing me off, Adam clamped a hand over my mouth.

"Quiet, understand?" he whispered.

I nodded. He looked ferociously determined. Wasn't he scared of me? Maybe he knew gargoyles existed and he was going to keep me as part of a collection. I could see him with his phone pressed to an ear. Probably wheeling and dealing with his "dealer" in Belgium. I'd end up in a tank like Daryl Hannah in *Splash*. There was no way I could fight him off. My arms felt like logs and I knew I couldn't stand, let alone run or fly.

I stole a hopeful glance at Peter. He was occupied, still thrashing around with the other gargoyle. Adam wasted no time, just bent and pulled me up like a sack of potatoes over his shoulder, tucking my wings in with one arm. He was pretty strong for a guy who only stood a few inches taller than me. He took off at a run around the stone wall of the church, bounced up a series of steps like we'd hit washboards on a dirt road, and pulled open a thick, heavy door with groaning hinges. The pain in my abdomen came and went. Blood ran down my neck and into my ears. I felt the urge to cough, which was beat out by the will to draw breath, but only barely.

Adam sprinted past a row of pews that seemed to go on forever in the darkened church. The image of Jesus in his crown of thorns hanging on a huge cross passed by. A steel basin of water rested against one wall, just below the crucifix. Another door swung open and he hunched, dropping me onto a little bench against a wall. My right wing clattered across a grate-covered window like a playing card stuck in bicycle spokes. I wheezed. I was dying. Jesus peered at me through a hole in the window. I huffed an ironic snort realizing Adam had just deposited me in a confessional; and not the side where I was made to go as a child to declare any wrongdoing or wrong thinking. I closed my eyes.

"Hey," Adam said, tilting my chin up, "you're a damn mess." Adam surveyed my tattered hoodie where it hung around my waist, tried to pull it free but gave up when the thick waistband wouldn't rip. He took off his shirt, quickly tearing a long shred from the back. I closed my eyes again. It was easy to give in to the urge.

"Ah, Gods. Tessa!" His hand popped against the side of my face.

"Ow," I groaned. "What the hell?" The words came out in a gurgled whisper. I peered at him through squinted eyes . . . and blinked. Just behind the peak of his forehead, on the right side, a little brown horn nestled in all that curly hair. I shook my head, sure I was losing it.

"Stick with me, here." He ran out of the tiny cubicle in his fast, limping gait. Things clanked and rattled against wood and his footsteps were so frantic they sounded more like hooves stamping pavement. The door flew open and he crouched in front of me, holding a tin cup of water to my lips. It rapped against my fangs. Blood dripped onto the toe of one of his black boots.

I was hardly thirsty, and the water tasted like metal and blood, and was a little thick and oily. I turned my head. Sucking in air was much more important. Adam stood, grabbed the back of my head, tipped my face back and dumped the stuff in my mouth while he plugged my nose. I swallowed as fast as I could as the chilled liquid spread down my throat.

He put the end of the shirt in his mouth and ripped another strip free. As he crouched down I saw a long, ropey looking scar ran from the hollow of his throat past the button of his jeans. It wasn't quite a straight line. The cut had meandered off, slightly to the left of his belly button and continued toward his hip. I'd never seen so much chest hair. Even his arms were coated in thick hair along the tops, which got thicker toward his forearms. He pulled me off the wall so my head hit his shoulder as his arms worked around my midsection.

I cried out briefly when he pulled the fabric tight and held it in one place with a hand. The second strip was cinched around my stomach so tight it felt like it cut through my scales. The pain burned for a millisecond and then simply faded into icy cold.

"Holy water isn't gonna help. I'm dying," I grated.

"I'm trying to change your mind," he said. Carefully, he leaned me back. One wing hung under my butt and my tail stuck upward behind me, the tip listing over my shoulder.

"That can't feel good." He pulled my tail down and untangled it from my wing as he straightened me up. "The water is more than just holy. Give it a chance." He looked hopeful.

My mind drifted. I'd tried to rescue a sparrow that'd been hit by a car when I was little. I'd pushed through the wrought iron fence of the orphanage and picked it up out of the road. One wing was badly busted up and the bird just stared at me, didn't try to fly or run. It didn't squawk or try to peck at me as I put its wing back where it belonged, tucked its legs beneath it and set it gently inside one of the nuns' flower boxes. It regarded me as if watching clouds move in the sky. Moments later it closed its eyes and didn't open them again.

I got that. I was Adam's sparrow. He'd just tucked me neatly away inside a box. I didn't want to die, but I understood why it was happening. I was never really meant to be, past the age of two. All the extra years were just bonus time until Fate caught me. I'd taken out one, final killer. At least I got to meet Bree and Peter. Tears ran when I let my eyes close. My head lolled. It was so heavy I had no idea how I'd been holding it up.

"That's right, rest. Go to sleep."

"Tessa!" Peter's voice was a thousand miles away.

"Shit," Adam swore viciously.

The wooden door screamed free as the hinges were snapped. The bench beneath me shuddered. Adam snarled as wind blasted us from beating wings. *I sure hope it's the good guys.* It was all happening too late.

"Get the hell away from her and you'll continue to breath," Peter growled.

My eyes closed a final, blessed time.

A HEARTBEAT SURGED against my ear. My eyes were stuck shut so I squinted to break the matting around them and was finally able to see after several blinks. Peter cradled me with one powerful arm under my knees and the other under my shoulders, holding us apart. He was so beautiful and majestic when he flew. Try as I might to keep watching him, I couldn't keep my eyes open any longer.

"We need to talk, once I get you bandaged up."

"Mm hm," I agreed. *I'm telling you just how the cow ate the cabbage, Mister.*

"Can you hear me?" Peter's voice sounded a little panicked.

Drama queen. Leave it to him to get all worked up over nothing....

5

"You'll take a while to sleep this one off."

Somehow my mind acknowledged Peter talking to me. He let me slough off his shoulder, slapping me flat on the mattress. Semi-consciousness was my friend. I just drifted along, refusing to think about how badly I was hurt. I checked out as often as I could, a little aware I almost died, but mostly dreaming.

The goddess watched him from my eyes like Rapunzel in a tower, pent up and pissed off.

❧

I SEETHED, *remembering times long ago. A past I'd buried was resurrected to create a new threat. Even a goddess will err occasionally; however, my mistake was nothing small. No tidbit of reactionary afterthought would fix the subsequent mess. I could rest on laurels. My heart had been in the right place, a trait my father attributed to my love of humans.*

But humans sickened me with their lack of respect for life. I'd grown restless. Father's flame would dawn to the Earth shortly, although even Lugh's light wouldn't be enough to thwart an attack from the beasts that readied their weapons.

Six brutish males lumbered from a crudely made float, stalking one slumbering family on the outskirts of an encampment.

Just that morning, I'd lounged in the trees above their hut, watching the antics of twin baby girls as they learned of the beauty surrounding them, aided by the gentle hand of their mother. The children chased and played in thickets. I played, too, the young eyes of innocence seeing only the beauty I was given at birth, which matched that of a human without the pocks from disease. I hid from the adults of the tribe. Adult humans saw me as a beast—a punishment dealt by my father for my involvement in the natural turn of mortal life despite his wishes. Although he was the God of Light, Lugh's patience at my rebellion gave out. It broke his heart to make his daughter appear as a creature of darkness.

The attackers came after the family while Lugh slept. Those from the dark side of human nature would snuff fledgling life to sate their hunger. I wept, then grew angry. I wasn't to meddle. But I would not allow my beloved, toddling girls a mortal death of such pain. Resigned to again break my father's law, I dropped between the invading men, intervening, disrupting the flow of human life.

Lugh would be angry.

Innocents would be saved. I would deal with my father's wrath later.

One brute laughed, thinking me a fallen bird of night. All six watched me, a small, wounded animal in the midst of giants. They circled me, only one of the beasts wary and confused by my fanged smile—the hunters unwittingly becoming the hunted.

Heat burst from my center as a halo of white light illuminated the forest, cascading free as fingers of lightning splintered, impaling each beast. Silence pounced, and darkness reclaimed the surroundings. I lost the guise of injury as the men stirred. I spread my wings. Cautious eyes scanned my appearance. They prayed to their gods. I shook my head, smiling.

One of them leaned forward, vomiting, not bothering to clear the fluid from matted and clumped facial hair. Another yelped as bone expanded, base, human makings, unmade. I searched their faces as they warped, soft flesh taken by the plaited weavings like my own. Panicked cowardice compelled one to attempt to impale himself on a blade, which was entertaining, but temporary. He would not die by his own hand. None of them could. Their wings expanded in dark hues. Excrement formed, gathering dirt and debris to fresh, serpentine skin.

I left them, circling above as they stumbled into their new existence. Never again would they stalk among humans at night, hidden by a kindred appearance with those they preyed upon. They were marked, winged beasts in the absence of Lugh's illumination, mortal transformation gruesomely apparent if they strode into his light.

Just like me.

Wood planking beat against rocks as waves tossed their crude vessel. Six gargoyles, my creations, mounted their boat and pointed the bow into the tide, a mock, carved head of a beast driving forth, pointing into the impending dawn. A neat row of stone place-markers held space for their mortal souls, standing statuesque on the deck, beyond where the would-be murderers rowed, pained and burning, screaming as my darlings would have.

I flew back to my perch in the trees above the human camp, eagerly awaiting sunrise and loathing it in the same instant. Soon, children would wander from their shelter to frolic and grow, to learn and sing. I smiled, waiting for them to awaken.

Dawn broke.

"Teasa!" Father thundered.

Undoubtedly, Lugh witnessed the departing beasts on their boat. I would be punished.

~

"TESSA!" Bree gripped my shoulders. "Wake up. You're crying."

"Hey," I whispered. I held up a hand to see peachy flesh. It was daytime and I was in bed. "Crap!" I sat up, remembering. Pain tore through my gut and bile surged to the back of my throat. I doubled over, clutching the sheet against my abdomen. A smudge of crimson grew to a soaking pool.

"Peter, she's awake," Bree called. "And she's bleeding . . . again." Bree removed my hands from the wound, bunched a towel and placed it against the site where blood soaked through the sheet.

"Lay flat, Tess, please," she asked, pushing gently on one shoulder. Worried tears edged her lashes, making my heart break. She was hurt because I made a stupid choice.

I tried to lay back but when I straightened too much, it felt like something tore inside. I held my breath and tried again, gritting my teeth hard and looking at my bedroom ceiling to concentrate on anything but the pain, but I couldn't do it. I grabbed Bree's hand.

Ever perceptive, Bree piled pillows behind me and helped me sink back. The tearing sensation was gone, replaced by the constant burn of damaged organs. She replaced the towel and applied pressure as if she'd done it before. She probably had, judging from the piled up, blood-streaked terry cloths in a bin next to my bed. Torn shreds of my hoodie lay on the floor near the door. I remembered it flapping around as I flew.

Trying not to yelp at the compression, I closed my eyes, concentrating on anything else.

Teasa's "flashback" stuck to my freshly wakened mind, oozing into cracks and filling my consciousness with past awareness. She'd—I'd— created the gargoyles I knew as the six original henchmen. Two of them had tried to take me down when I wandered off the day before. We'd ousted them from their haven in Scotland, and now they were all about payback, on two counts.

If they knew who I was, really, deep inside, they would hold me responsible for their lost humanity. Teasa had changed them into gargoyles as punishment for raiding and plundering, centuries ago. More recently I'd helped free Castle Logan. Osgar and the other "good gargoyles" had lived there, trapped by Kai. That gave his ousted henchmen, the original six and the uncounted others he'd created more recently, two really good reasons to be seriously angry with me. They'd tracked me—us— back to London.

"You should have stayed here." Bree pulled the towel away, checking for seepage.

I nodded.

"Peter trashed the balcony reading room."

"I'm sorry, Bree." It sounded artificial, like I dodged her point. I'd have rather dealt with Peter separately.

"Don't apologize. Just get your head on straight. You were never all flighty like this before." Her voice broke but she took a breath and continued. "You were always careful. Thoughtful of others." She tossed the towel into the can with the others and stood. "Why won't you talk to me about any of this? I know you're going through a lot. You have been since you left Austin, but you also used to tell me everything."

I inhaled to speak but phlegm caught in my throat. A cough racked my entire body despite an attempt to hold my breath. I put my hands over my face to cover my agony.

She sat on the bed placing a fresh towel over the new bunch of blood caused by my coughing fit.

When I felt like I could bear to move, I lowered my hands. "There's no way anyone will ever understand what this is like."

"Well you could at least try. I'm not an idiot."

Ouch. "I didn't mean it like that."

"Peter and Petra are gargoyles, and so is Crispin," she retorted.

"I'm not just talking about the gargoyle part. You're right, if it was just one thing, one freaking element of what I have to deal with, I could handle it better." Exasperation hung in my words. Having such a heavy conversation when pain tainted everything I said and heard wasn't easy.

Bree rose from the bed and went to my window. Her arms crossed over her chest as she stared at the alley below. I wondered if she thought about how Kai had once forced her to stand down there, tape over her mouth and hands bound, as leverage to get me to follow him to Scotland. She'd been kidnapped and terrified, because of me. I didn't like the theme that emerged, with the people I cared about getting hurt due to the situations I kept getting myself into. Whether my choices created the trouble or others intervened, I was done watching the people I loved be hurt.

"Maybe the rest is BS," she tossed over her shoulder.

"It's not. Too many things make it real, Bree."

She whirled from the window. "See, this is what I mean. What the hell are you even talking about?"

Bree seldom cussed. My temper surged to meet hers. "Teasa, the goddess? Remember? Unexplained high fevers all my life? Superfast speed? She's in my dreams lately. She was the first-ever living gargoyle."

"Really, Tessa? You believe that crap? You nearly died last night. You're still bleeding. If there really was some goddess in there with you, do you honestly believe you would look like this?" She waved a hand, gesturing too wildly, tears in her voice.

"Yes, I do believe it. I've felt her. She's done incredible things, including giving me the strength to save your life when that guy attacked you in Scotland. That speed, the whole kill, was Teasa."

"Where was she last night when those two gargoyles attacked you?"

Good question. "I don't know! I haven't got all this figured out yet. And this is why I don't talk about it."

"So how do you even know she's real? Did you ever stop and think maybe you're the one who killed that guy?" She barked the question at me.

"It was her!"

"Prove it."

"The book—"

"Again, totally unreliable," she interjected. "That book tells you nothing. You can't count on it, either."

She'd cut me off. I bit my bottom lip, shaking my head, pissed. She was oh, so lucky I loved her. "Sure, these things don't help me when I need them. I was thrown to the freaking wolves. Do you understand now?"

She didn't move, her arms crossed tight over her chest, jaw locked. I'd seen her look like that before, but never at me.

I continued, shaking my head. "I told you. I can't explain it. It's not because you're incapable of understanding. It's because I'm incapable of conveying what this is like."

"You were tossed to the wolves because of your refusal to keep yourself safe," Peter said, leaning in the doorway.

I huffed my disagreement with his statement, turning away to look out the window. They both had excellent points. One on one I might have been able to interject, but with Bree, and then Peter, bringing up good arguments, I was stymied. Everything that fell out of my mouth sounded like excuses.

"Be as huffy as you like, you know I'm right. Had you listened, you wouldn't have run into Kai's men."

"How was I supposed to know they were watching for me?" I yelled. I clutched my stomach, wincing.

"They're mad as hell, Tessa. They've been run out of what they consider to be their home. Of course you're a target. We all are."

"You knew they were in London?"

Peter said nothing, just held my gaze.

"You did. You knew." I thought about chucking something at him, but the only thing within reach was a pillow. Twisting to grab one and throwing something that soft wouldn't yield the pain I wanted to inflict on him so I just smacked the mattress. That hurt, too.

"Nice. Throw a tantrum like the brat you are."

"You're one to talk," I shot back. "How's the upstairs library looking?"

Peter gave Bree a look that clearly said, *Thanks for telling her.*

Bree shrugged. "Most times when a guy has a fit, he does it for attention. So why keep it a secret?"

Peter sighed. "Bree, would you leave us, please? Tessa and I need to speak."

"Sure." She paced past me to the door, then turned. "Even if I'm frustrated, I love you, Tessa. I'll always be here for you." She glanced at Peter and left.

"Before you even get started, Crispin's downstairs in the back room. They'll find one another." He sat on my bed, calmer now. "So don't get onto me about keeping an eye on her. She's fine with Crispin here."

"Why didn't I heal when I changed back to human?" I pulled the crimson-splotched sheet back to reveal a blood-soaked bandage taped across my abdomen. I wore a tank top that was rolled up away from the wound, and a pair of pajama pants. "Thanks for dressing me."

"That was Bree. She was quite distraught when I brought you in. You were in rough shape."

I sighed and looked down again.

"We can't make this a habit, Tessa." He started pulling the tape away from my skin.

I wouldn't get a "You're welcome" from him so I changed the subject. "So why am I still injured?"

"Well, that one," he pointed to my neck, where the gargoyle sunk his teeth the night before, "is healed. But this was far worse. You nearly died on the way back to the bookstore."

"Adam tried to bandage me up."

Peter looked away, shaking his head.

"He's the bartender at Jonnie's." *Who just happened to be out running around waiting for me to fall from the sky . . .*

Peter paced toward my window and leaned a shoulder against

the wall, peering out. "You know, Tessa, just because you're given aid doesn't mean it was going to be all better."

"He helped me, Peter!"

"Oh, he helped you, sure enough." He crossed his arms.

"What is your problem? You were busy—"

"Saving your ass again," he snarled.

"I said I'm sorry."

"That doesn't even begin to cover it. You have no idea what could have happened."

"Yes, I do," I said, gesturing to the bloody mess down my front. "I know I made a mistake by getting lost in the first place —" It had gone downhill from there, in a big stream of screw-ups all night long. "I'd be dead if it wasn't for you and Adam."

"Really, you're giving that *thing* credit for your rescue?"

"He carried me into the church and used his shirt to bind this . . . hole in my stomach," I said weakly, remembering the terrible scar on Adam's chest. There was more about him, something even more substantial that I knew I wanted to remember. "I passed out from loss of blood!"

"We don't do that!" He spun away from the window. "You would have stayed awake, despite losing blood. You would have felt yourself dying and stayed aware the whole damned time. I've been there, many times."

"I know what I felt, Peter. I *was* dying." I would have yelled if I had the energy to do it. Speaking like a mouse frustrated me but it was all I had.

"Yes, you were dying. And I agree, you might have if Adam wouldn't have stopped the bleeding. But if I hadn't seen him carry you off, you'd wish he would have left you for dead."

"Why does everyone always have to be out to get me? He helped me!" My voice rose to a squawk and I regretted it as I scrunched up against the pain.

"He drugged you."

"That's completely ridiculous."

"Why are you defending him? You just met him. He could be any damned thing out there."

"You sound paranoid. He was just a guy, just a bartender." I didn't want to admit I'd put my trust in someone so easily. Peter was right. Adam could have put anything in the drinks he gave me. "Ohhh," I moaned.

"What?"

"Holy water."

He just shook his head.

"He gave me a cup of something at the church. I thought it was water at first, but it was like, thick or something. Like swallowing cooking oil."

"Don't you wonder what his plans were?"

"No. I mean, this is coming back to me slowly. I don't remember it all clearly." I picked a strand of my hair loose from the medical tape.

"I'll fill you in. Adam," he pointed out the window, "isn't human. His intentions, although seemingly innocent, were definitely not in your best interest."

I sighed. "Don't tell me. He was going to eat me." *Bitchy.* "Why is it always a conspiracy with you?"

He laughed. That pissed me off.

"It amazes me how easily you forget what you look like as a human." His grin remained, but at least he wasn't laughing at me anymore. "They have far more uses for human *women*," he drawled, the word "women" spoken carefully.

"I was roofied?" I cried. I was nearly date-raped, without the date. "I'm a gargoyle! He can't do that," I stated.

"Don't worry, Tessa. If I hadn't pulled you out of that bloody confessional, he would have saved you for daylight."

"Dammit!" I slapped the bed. Fresh blood spread across the gauze, quickly soaking through with bright crimson that overflowed to my hips.

"Stop this," Peter said as he sat next to me. "You can beat yourself up after you've healed."

With a sure movement, he peeled off the entire bandage, slowly, watching between the site of the wound and my face to measure my pain. I didn't let on, despite the fact it stung like a mother. Peter dropped the soppy mass of gauze and tape into the bin.

I couldn't help it, I looked. "Holy hell." The entire flat of my stomach, from just below my breasts leading to the waistband of my pajamas was mottled black, purple, and blue. A hole gaped just above my navel, which listed below, displaced and twisted. The center of the wound jostled as I sobbed. Things moved inside as I inhaled and exhaled, and as other organs did their regularly scheduled duties to digest the sandwich and salad I'd eaten at Jonnie's.

"It's looking a lot better," Peter said, surveying the hole with a furrowed brow.

"Better?" It was hard not to sound completely incredulous. Haven't you ever heard of stitches? My stomach is just . . . open!"

"Calm down. Stitches would cause more pain and aggravation than they're worth. You're healing quickly."

"Why is it taking so long? I've been nearly pounded to death and I healed up fine, in one day."

"The book healed you that time. This time, all that's come to your aid is the transformation, which heals us quickly in most cases." He paused to tuck a stray tangle of hair behind my ear. "You almost bled to death," he reminded.

A hiccup rocketed through my torso like it was on fire. I doubled over grasping at where it hurt, then sat back with two handfuls of fresh blood. The hole had filled up once more. Peter snatched two big pads of gauze and covered the wound, both of us cursing my hiccupping, nervous tick with clenched teeth.

"Be still and look at the ceiling."

"We have to get out of here." I diverted my gaze above, the stinging growing at the site of my wound.

"As far as I know, the gargoyles haven't found the bookstore. You can look now. Just be calm." He tore a piece of medical tape with his teeth and one hand. "We were planning a trip before you ran off, as I recall," he said, still working on me.

"Okay. I made a huge mistake, Peter. I'm sorry." Tears ran alongside my mouth. "I hurt Bree and scared her to death. I'm an ass. I got you all worried . . . again—"

"—Still," he retorted.

"And I almost got myself killed—"

"—Again."

"And I'm so, so sorry." I wiped at my face without thinking, drawing back streaked, pink fingers. "I really am. One of the reasons I went out for a run in the first place is because I was angry at myself for hitting you." I accepted the handful of wadded gauze pads he offered. "I'm all messed up. I can't even remember our first time and it's killing me," I said, around a sob.

Peter quit doctoring me to stare at me wide-eyed. "Our first time where?" he asked, with choppy, disjointed words.

"You know, together."

"What exactly do you think went on?" He went back to bandaging.

I gritted my teeth, trying to hold still when I wanted to squirm away from his touch. "We had—"

"We absolutely did not have sex," he exhaled in a gust.

I let my head fall back and looked at the ceiling. "Thank you, Little Baby Jesus."

"Thanks a lot." Peter went from being relieved, like me, to cranky in a beat.

"I didn't mean it like that."

"Mayhap you should engage some forethought before you speak, since you apologize so much after opening that trap of yours."

I gaped briefly. "That was mean."

"Just a thought."

"I just felt like I'd been cheated by not remembering the first time we ever . . ." I put my hands over my face. There was no way I was going to tell him that I wanted to remember each second of intimacy with him, hear each sound he made. Touch each part of him again. The entirety of what we'd done remained a mystery. I wanted to know each detail.

"You've still never. You're safe and intact."

The sound of medical tape screaming off the roll offered a change of subject. I lowered my hands, and from the look on Peter's face he was just as happy about that as me.

"My stomach's kinda numb." I watched him apply a new bandage without feeling him touch me.

He held up a syringe with a thin needle. "I shot you up."

"Thanks." I let my head fall against the pillow. "Still want to take that trip to Kelty? I mean, after I'm healed up?"

"I think that would be best."

"So do I."

He set the medical supplies on my nightstand and retrieved a bottle of water from my mini fridge. When he handed it to me I got a better look at him. Darkness circled his eyes. More than a five o'clock shadow grew, making his silver eyes pop so bright they glowed. His shirt hung untucked and unbuttoned to mid-chest and several dark spots of dried and smeared blood stood out on his jeans. He reached into a pocket, withdrew something small, and placed it in my other hand.

A small, baby-blue pill with a line across the top rested in the crease of my palm.

"Goodnight," he said.

"Thank you for helping me live."

"Of course."

I swallowed the pill with about half the bottle of water,

hoping it would stay down. I knew better than to ask for food with a wound to my guts. "Stay with me until this kicks in?"

He said nothing, but bent and slid an arm under my knees, the other cradling just beneath my shoulders, effortlessly lifting me to the side of the bed to make room. I didn't want him to let go, but I wasn't telling him that. He released me, lifted the side of a blue pad that was apparently there to catch dripping blood, and settled in beside me with the pad between us.

Remembering the feeling of resting my head on his chest was the happiest place I'd ever been. I longed for that closeness, hearing his heart surge. Wondering what he thought about holding me. If he felt the same way I did.

Peter must have heard my thoughts because he slid against the headboard, wrapped one arm around my shoulders and grabbed both my hands so I could lever myself closer to him.

"On two," he said.

I nodded.

We counted together and when he pulled me closer I bit back a yelp as the tearing sensation dug into my belly button. Although it hurt like hell, I needed the contact with him. I quieted as quickly as I could, trying to calm my amped-up breathing so I could just listen to the rhythm in his chest and try to sync my existence with his. The room twisted with midmorning sun. I balled a fistful of his shirt, inhaling his scent like I lived on it.

"You'll feel better after you wake up. Your body is working hard, healing at a fast rate, from the inside out."

"I'm dizzy."

"You're blonde. You're supposed to be."

"You're a funny guy."

"You're a pain in my ass."

I smiled.

6

Waking up in fresh clothes that someone else put there was climbing the list of things that put me in a horrible mood. Although it was done with love, the gesture was an indicator that I was a burden, whether they thought so or not. My tank and pajama bottoms were folded neatly on the bedside, where Peter had been. Heavy scents of antiseptic and household cleaners swirled together, forced through the air by a little fan in my window. The container of bloody towels and gauze had been emptied into a now-tied rubbish bag, and the ripped up hoodie I'd worn when I Garged Out downtown was piled next to it, ready to be tossed out. I squinted, remembering the black envelope Adam had given me.

Perky sunshine slanted through the gaps in the blinds. A small amount of gel—a side effect of Garging Out—had dried on my sheets, telling me I'd barely moved a muscle as I slept, neatly curled on my side. I'd been positioned that way by Peter, no doubt, so my wings didn't hang up on my bedding when they sprouted at nightfall.

Thoughtful.

Really, it was. The pill he gave had knocked me out hard. Usually, if I'd been sleeping when the sun went down, the tingling feeling I get in my arms and legs woke me so I could get out of bed and didn't trash it and save my clothes from being destroyed.

Medical tape caught the skin of my belly as I rolled onto my back. Pulling the sheet lower I began to loosen the bandage. Only a couple small dots of dried, black blood soaked through. That was a good sign. Under the gauze, fresh, smooth skin had knitted into place over my abdominal muscles, nearly covering the entire wound. Dark bruising had faded to run a gamut of pastel colors, like Easter exploded under my skin, and it appeared my belly button survived, after all. Vain as it was, I wanted to keep my navel.

The true test to measure my healing was sitting up, which was pain free, although I felt like a complete cyborg, using someone else's muscles to move. Abdominal tissue was tied to the subtlest of movement, the pain made even breathing a substantial price for bad choices. Fear of what was worse than death was the most lethal, eye-opener of the lot. I had managed to dodge more than death. Two days of my life were wasted while I healed, and I would do my damnedest to hold on to whatever Fate decided remained.

I leaned over, letting my hands and knees touch down on the carpet. I pulled the tattered material of what was left of my hoodie toward me and retrieved the black envelope from the zipper pocket. It was wadded and torn up a little, but still in one piece. I ripped it open and removed a folded card.

"You're Invited!" I read aloud, smirking. Adam had handed me the envelope before I Garged Out. It was hard to tell if he thought I was just a naïve human, American girl in London for the first time, or if he'd known something was up with me and been intrigued. "Please be my personal guest, for a Thursday

evening of music and exquisite cuisine at The Church in Petrichor Park. Cocktail hour at 10. Music to begin at 11." A map
detailed the location of the immense church just two blocks away
from Jonnie's, on a corner up a street. I'd run a fair distance from
Cecil Court to an area of Northeast London I was completely
unfamiliar with, which wasn't saying much. The church, which I
decided right then and there shouldn't be named like it was a
special musical venue the way Adam had done, was on the corner
of Courtene and Braene, according to the little map. I'd never
heard of those streets. Jonnie's was on Braene and Petrichor Lane.
I hadn't paid too much attention on the way over there. Rain had
started about halfway through my run and it had been one of
London's dreary and dark days later on. The blind man walked
with me for a little over a mile, I guessed, but I'd likely run
around five miles before I met him. I dropped the card onto my
bed. There was a display with maps for tourists downstairs in the
bookstore that would surely have better detail.

I reached between my mattress and box spring to retrieve my
dagger. The blade chimed when I slid it from the leather scabbard, anxious to get back into my hand. I sheathed the jeweled
dirk and put the invitation away with it. I'd keep the date with
Adam, that was for sure.

A question burned in my thoughts, pounding at me to let it
out. Why, if people like Peter and the Logans knew about Adam
and what he was up to at the church, didn't someone ice the
bastard at the earliest convenience? Was there some rule between
species that I wasn't aware of? An ancient pact or something?
Although the reasoning bothered me, I wasn't a part of a prior
plan to avoid stopping a predator.

A test drive of my mended body proved to be shaky and weak,
and I walked hunched over, afraid to straighten all the way.
Healing took a toll. I braced against a wall in the shower, my arms
trembling above my head just long enough to wash my hair.

Handrails were the reason I made it downstairs to the back room. Nothing sounded better than a southern-style breakfast taco, but I'd settle for anything hot that would fill the crater where my empty stomach seemed to be rubbing a blister on my backbone.

The kitchen was deserted. I selected a bag of leftover scones and a tub of clotted cream, chucked the entire bag of thick, biscuit-like bread into the nuker with a heavy thump, and filled a mug of tea from a pot on the hotplate. Bringing my bounty of scavenged food to the bar, I dug in.

Two bites into the meal, Crispin peeked around the corner, a broad smile tugging at his dimples. He pulled the chain of a pocket watch loose from his jeans and cracked it open. "You always have been an early riser."

"I think starvation woke me up," I said around a bite of scone. "Sorry I've been out for so long."

"Apology accepted, but quite unnecessary." He winked, which was adorable. I loved how well-spoken Crispin was. His brogue was all proper-like.

"Seems we share the ability to survive a death-blow to the gut, you and I." He pulled up a stool and dropped a rag magazine on the bar.

"Glad you're back. I hear you're off to Kelty tomorrow."

"Well, I don't know when for sure, but if Peter says so, I'm game." That would be perfect since it was Thursday, a great day for "music and exquisite cuisine." I grinned.

"It's tomorrow," Bree confirmed as she entered. "I'm packed." Clad in a creamy, thigh-length, hooded sweater, brown leggings and boots, Bree looked well-rested and excited about the trip.

"Are you coming, too?" I asked Crispin.

"Yes, he is." Bree answered for him when she saw him stuff half a scone into his mouth. She stooped to give me a quick hug, holding piles of long, spiral curls and waves back with one hand, trapping her hair against a shoulder. She wore Victoria's Secret Incredible, one of our favorite scents back home, to add the perfect fragrance to her cute outfit and expertly applied makeup.

I looked down at my faded sweats, Chuck Taylors, and Dropkick Murphys T-shirt. I hoped my shampoo smelled good because I hadn't even bothered to apply deodorant. My hair hung in a frizzy, damp fall nearly to my waist. I slathered another scone with clotted cream and crammed too much in my mouth, grinning at Crispin. We chewed like cows on cud, barely holding our huge smiles closed.

"How are you feeling?" she asked.

I nodded and smiled a lumpy, affirmative grin as I chewed. I chased the mouthful down with a few sips of tea to break it up. "Tons better. The wound's healed over, but I'm still bruised. I'll survive."

"Peter wasn't too hard on you, was he?" She filled a glass of juice and eyed my scones.

"He was great, actually."

"He's a good one." Crispin added cream to another scone. I was grateful there was a huge lot of them.

Bree and I shot Crispin equally quizzical looks. We never knew when he might chime in.

"Known him all his life," he concluded. He gathered his remaining breakfast and pulled the strap to a messenger bag over his shoulder and strode to the door. Before he stepped out he turned. "I'll watch the bookstore, Tessa. Today is for rest and recovery. Miss Morgan," he said with a beaming smile, "take a day off. You have been invaluable, helping me to keep the shop running for the last weeks . . . which reminds me . . ." He came back to the tea bar and set his things down, fishing in his bag. Withdrawing a small bundle of envelopes, he flipped through them, handing one over to each of us. "Peter asked me to hand these out."

"Thank you," I said, accepting mine. It was payday at the Bochord. I hadn't worked much, so the fact I got an envelope at all surprised me. Bree had worked tons of hours to cover my absences. I'd always been paid well at the bookstore so I was certain Bree had made quite a bit of cash in the last few weeks.

"Thanks," she said, returning his grin.

Crispin left us as we peered inside at our earnings. It was a good thing I'd been rat-holing my paychecks because, just as expected, I didn't earn a lot.

"Mani-pedi?" Bree asked.

"I wish. I can't risk scaring some poor nail tech if we get caught in the sun."

"Well, I've been thinking about the things you can't do because of your new allergy to the sun," she said, making air quotes around the word "allergy." "I went a couple weeks ago to this place in Piccadilly. They were great. I talked to a lady named Rose. She is willing to make a house call."

"No way." I couldn't imagine one of the ritzy salons in the Circus taking that kind of time out of their day.

"Well, it's not cheap, but here's the funny part," she pulled out a stool and sat. "I told her you're agoraphobic."

"I'm not scared of leaving here." I laughed.

"I know that, but it's not really a complete lie. The beauty of the story is, turns out, her sister has agoraphobia. Rose understands completely. Your situation is similar in some ways."

"That's true. I guess the thought of terrifying someone else keeps me out of sight during the day." I'd nearly scared the bejeebies out of too many humans for my own comfort. Going to a salon didn't sound like much fun if I had to wear a hood the whole time.

"Good. I'm glad you feel that way because they'll be here at ten."

"They?"

"You're getting your hair done, too."

"Nice. I haven't had a haircut since I left Austin." I picked up the ends of my hair and surveyed the multiple split ends. "This is just what I need."

THREE LADIES, including Rose, herself, showed up at ten, and transformed the backroom into a makeshift salon for the day. They parked a long van in the alley and carted in their supplies, including full-length mirrors, footbaths, and an electric towel heater. A slightly older lady, Rose was a petite blonde with a genuine smile set in a face gently touched by laugh lines. Although she looked stuffy and like the goody-two-shoes type, she was sweet and had a dynamite sense of humor. The other two girls were pleasant and chatty. It became obvious Rose loved what she did and was thrilled with the opportunity to come to the aid of another who suffered from a fear of leaving the house, like her sister. I didn't talk about that much, but Rose was so kind at heart and determined to help me, I resolved to tip her extremely well to help deal with my guilt at letting her believe I was afflicted with agoraphobia.

Peter and Crispin walked through from the back-alley door while Bree and I reclined in portable, wheeled, spa chairs, getting our pedicures. Peter shook his head all the way through the room as he went toward the storefront, but Crispin popped his work shirt off over his head and dropped into the adjustable salon chair where Rose swept up from trimming my hair. He removed the strap he used to tie back his long, straight hair and let it cascade like dark corn silk over thick shoulders, down to his waist. He beamed at Rose with boyish charm, the "boyish" part only evident in his dimples, the "charm" dominant because he was absolutely beautiful.

"Sign me up, lass."

The women stopped working, staring like nuns at a Chippendale's show.

Bree bristled.

I laughed.

Crispin winked. "C'mon then, I don't get to the city much."

Rose draped his shoulders, pumped up the chair, and trimmed Crispin's hair with a wide grin pasted on her face, chatting away. I couldn't help but smile and watch.

7

I wasn't a child, so I don't know why I felt like I was sneaking out when I left the bookstore. It was nonsense. I'd rested the entire day and eaten well. Perhaps an impromptu outing at night wasn't the most intelligent choice, but if Peter knew "things" like Adam were around, preying on women, and he wasn't going to do anything about it, I was. Peter's motives were a mystery. I used to think he was just like me, trapped by a crazy bookstore owner who changed us both into gargoyles.

So not the case. Peter had stakes in things I didn't understand. It seemed my big motive was survival, closely seconded by finding Teigan, thirdly, stopping Adam. Peter wanted something else. I'd handle Adam. Then I'd find Teigan.

Even if it wasn't night time it would have been dark out because of the storm. There was the normal freezing drizzle, but far more lightning than I'd seen since I left Austin. Thunder was killer loud, being up high and closer to it. I flew in the direction I had run the day before, looking for the church and the spire where I'd killed Tal. The maps I'd found in the bookstore didn't show the neighborhood where I'd found Jonnie's. I was winging it, literally.

Darkness and cloud cover forced me to drop lower so I could see the city below. I had to rely on intermittent pops of lightning and fought the feeling I was flying in a big circle over London. Many fears kept me alert; the biggest was being hit out of nowhere by one of Kai's gargoyles so I held a keen ear.

Finally, after frustration nearly beat me to tears and I had to land twice just to rest, I nearly ran into the tall spire. I swooped low, careful not to beat my wings and draw attention, and glided into the darkest side yard of the church, silent amidst the loud music that poured from the building.

Bass vibrated the cobblestones, drowning out any other sounds. It was past eleven if the band had started right on time. Adam would have to forgive me a lot of things after the night was through, the least of which would be missing his cocktail hour at ten.

The din of voices and shuffling footsteps indicated the place was full of people. I crept toward the building and tried to look through a window, but it was stained glass all the way to the top. I thought of flying upward to see if I could look inside one of the lighter colors, but with my luck lightning would show my silhouette and set off a panic. I wanted to get at Adam but didn't want to cause people to trample one another to get out. It was hard telling how many others had received the same black invitation. I would be forced to wait out the party. Most bands played for two or three hours, I figured. I skirted to the corner and pumped my wings softly, hunching atop the roof and likely looking quite natural considering the architecture.

The thought of girls inside being drugged and kidnapped made it hard to sit still. Would I be guilty of letting that happen, in a passive way, if I waited the party out before I did something? What if I could save just one girl by acting sooner? I looked around, having no idea how I would get to Adam while he was inside. There had to be a way to crash the party without scaring people.

The soft coat of mist turned to big raindrops that fell at a slant on a puffing breeze. I waddled around on the roof, looking for a way in; an attic access, a cellar or basement door on the ground below. I found stairs leading under the main floor, but more interesting was the beautiful little breaker box for the electricity. After a quick glide to the ground and a brief wrestling match with the box's metal door, I kicked over every switch on the panel, listening with satisfied glee when first, there was shocked silence followed by a collective "Awwwwww" within, once the amps lost juice. I shut the door and ducked into the wet, brick stairway to the basement, peeking over the edge of the wall.

A flashlight beam popped along the ground from the front door and a squatty troll of a guy walked out and opened the breaker box, shaking off water like he was afraid he might melt. He began flipping switches and soon the inside lights came on. A few disgruntled party-goers left but most remained inside, hooting when the band began to strum up again. The troll waited in the doorway with the door open, which showed all the pews had been scooted toward the back and the band, a dark trio of men, had set up on the stage with the crucifix behind them. They scampered to adjust equipment, strumming lightly.

Both guys and girls were in attendance, sipping drinks and sitting in the pews. Some had little plates of what must have been Adam's idea of exquisite edibles. Others completely made out as if they were in private, and certainly not in a church, apparently not too put off by the temporary outage.

Adam came to the door to meet the short guy with the flash-light. I scrunched down with my heart suddenly beating a zillion miles an hour.

"Every single switch had kicked," the troll reported.

"No kidding?" Adam said. I held completely still, like wet paper against the bricks. The beam swept the side of the build-ing, the sidewalk and trees. They remained in the door, despite the storm.

The rain settled into more typical drizzle while I waited, taking slow breaths to calm down. They'd stopped talking so I guessed it was Adam who stood in the doorway for a very long time holding the flashlight. Finally, the light stopped scanning, but the door was left open so the loud music and pulsing, foggy light continued to spill out onto the front cobbles and gardens, which was quite the effect since it was a church yard. I had no choice if I wanted to avoid being seen, so I slunk down to the blackened door leading under the building.

An ornate, weathered knob wobbled when I touched it. Carefully, I gripped it and gave a turn and, sure enough, the frickin' thing broke off in my claws.

Dammit!

I started heating up from frustration but kept focus and momentum to get inside. The door was thick, solid against my shoulder. I put an ear to it, testing for noises on the other side, but all I could hear was the music from upstairs. I set the busted handle down, took a breath and shoved a palm against the broken nub that protruded. On the second thrust the mechanism popped inward and I shot my claws forward to grab it before it hit the wall inside. I was left holding a metal rod with a handle stuck to the inside of the doorway.

My tail twitched with agitation. I waited a beat, dropped the handle, and shouldered through the door to try to make all the noise at the same time, hoping to minimize the disturbance. On the second try it gave way. The whole right side of my body tingled from slamming it against the wood.

The excitement got me a little amped up. I stood in the doorway, gleefully looking around, hoping Adam came down to investigate. I'd pop his curly head off his shoulders and be home before anyone knew I was gone. The broken door handle rattled and rolled in a semicircle on a thinly carpeted floor. I grabbed it and threaded the rod back through, then pulled it closed holding the broken part. When I let go, the handle dropped on the other side, but I got it to stay in the hole. If anyone looked at the door closely they'd surely see it was broken, but at least the door stayed shut. I turned, needing to get my bearings quickly.

The ceiling was low, but I was an abbreviation of every other gargoyle I'd met, so I could walk upright. My sight adjusted quickly, with darkened splashes of color and variances of grey to black, much more vibrant than I got when human. I paced around the open basement. The walls were the same cold brick as outside and the way my claws ticked on the floor told me it was made of concrete with cheap carpet stretched over. The air was thick with an overpowering scent of mildew mixed with chemicals probably used to try to kill whatever mold or fungus was growing down there. I tripped over a pile of something ropey and barely caught myself without falling, my wings splaying. The black horn on top of my right wing grated against the wood ceiling like steel on a dry sponge. Chunks of dust-coated wood poured from above in a musty spray.

A slinky, sequined shirt of some kind was hung up on the side of my scaly leg. I pulled it loose and ignored the feeling of rough skin catching on satin. Bling jeans, faux, gaudy jewelry, and other items of lady's garb twirled together in a heap like overcooked spaghetti. I kicked loose of the mess, eyeing other little piles of discarded clothing. Jewelry, shiny peep-toe heels like the ones I used to love, and a petite cocktail purse formed another pile. My heart lurched when I realized how many outfits were down there and how many girls had been taken. Adam was responsible for many killings. I was incensed. The freak had to be put down before he got ahold of more innocent girls. Just because they were out partying or whatever didn't make them his to pick off as he chose. I'd give him about ten minutes after the place cleared out and then Adam and I were having a Come-to-Jesus, gargoyle-style. I wasn't thrilled about the wait.

That's when a junction of thick, white, important-looking wires caught my eye.

I moved swiftly to the wall where they hung, wrapped my claws around the mass where they gathered below a grey electrical box, and yanked them free. I grinned, tail lashing to and fro like a happy, ornery church cat.

The band didn't even try to start playing again. They banged around above, packing up. Maybe it had happened just like I hoped, and they thought the circuits couldn't handle the usage for their equipment. Whatever the case, I'd succeeded and just needed to wait for Adam to be alone.

I hunched with my wings comfortably meeting my heels in a stance I'd once hated but now found natural. I touched the straps around my calf, where I'd tied my dirk, for reassurance. Maybe I wouldn't need it; my talons had proven deadly enough. I tucked my pointy chin and smiled. There was no such thing as too many weapons. A chilly feeling of excitement knotted my guts and my claws curled in anticipation of getting them wrapped around Adam's throat. The plan was working. I was a success!

Feet pounded upstairs until the sounds became a trickle as the partiers bottlenecked out the front door of the church, clomping down the front steps and talking too loudly outside. I watched the basement door until silence announced they'd all left. I didn't know Adam well, although he didn't seem stupid and he likely knew I was there messing with the power to his domain. Finally, light footsteps sounded outside the door I'd busted up and the handle fell from where I'd propped it. Metal met thinly covered concrete, ringing like a doorbell.

"Daddy's home," he called in a low voice. He held his arms out to the sides looking around the room. Only the whites of his eyes gleamed in his dark face. He knew I was watching, but he didn't have a clue how much I raged at the thought of what he'd intended to do to me.

I came out of my gargoyle stance and hit him like a missile, sending us both flailing through the random clothing. Finally, my super speed had returned, just like I'd seen in my mind's eye. The goddess must have preferred lending her ability while I was angry rather than when I was fleeing for my life. I let go of him and rolled to my feet, wings fluttering so hard I nearly floated into a rough-cut wooden support beam.

Adam rolled quickly upright, grinned and walked backward with his eyes locked on me. He shut the door and slid a deadbolt into the jamb. An odd popping of his knees was in front when he walked backward and I found it impossible not to watch.

"You and I need to talk," I said, returning the smile.

"About?" He stopped a few feet before me.

"About drugging me." I inhaled slowly, trying to calm down. "And here I thought you were trying to save me. Just a nice guy doing the right thing."

"I did save you." He winked and pulled his shirt over his head, letting it fall to the floor. The scar on his chest stood out deep purple amid swirls of thick, dark hair in the dim light.

"Put your damned shirt back on."

Adam continued to smile.

"If Peter hadn't found me, I never would have been heard from again," I said, doing my best to ignore how he kicked off one boot. When the sole hit the floor, I could only stare. Rather than a sock-clad foot, a bare, black, cloven hoof touched down. I looked at his face. He smiled wider and kicked off the other boot by prying it off his heel with the hoof. His hands went to his belt.

"Stop it!" I yelled.

He didn't. He came toward me taking his belt off and I was so bewildered with his feet that I actually took a series of steps backward. His jeans hit the floor and he stepped out of them without stopping his advance.

I didn't remember it this way, but Adam was taller than me, and a lot stockier. His chest was thick and arms hugely muscled. He shook his head, curls falling away to show two stubby horns. A rough pattern of ridges sprouted across his forehead.

I couldn't help it, I kept staring. His abdomen was rigid with an eight-pack and knotty obliques, nearly devoid of body hair. A very long, semi-hard, uncircumcised penis hung heavily against one bulging thigh. I blinked, not because of the huge dick but because his legs were on backward, like the hind quarters of a goat.

"So, let's talk," he said. "In just a couple, very short hours the sun will rise." He threw back his head, laughing the way he had at the bar. His teeth had become jagged, like too many were crammed in his mouth and they fought for the right to tear into something before the others.

"You're not human," I whispered.

He nah-nahhed back at me. "Let's not throw stones. Neither are you. Yet."

"A satyr," I thought, out loud. I didn't know why it mattered. He had to be stopped, no matter what sort of cloven-hoofed freak he appeared to be.

"A faun," he snapped. "There's a huge difference. A satyr would have killed you already. I'm far more *man*, than beast." He circled, taking in my wings, plated skin, and talons. "This thing that happens to you when the sun sets," he said, *tsking* and shaking his head, "is a bloody pity. You're beautiful, otherwise. As you can tell, I'm rather excited about daybreak." He reached forward, letting strands of my charcoal hair fall through his fingers. "Amazing how your hair changes, too."

He wouldn't get away with touching me. I smacked him as hard as I could with a balled-up claw, right in the temple, and ran from the wall, leaving him growling and grasping his head. While he was dazed I came around to stand in the center of the room. He whirled with me and I only had time to hit him once more before he launched himself forward on those strong legs and took me to the floor.

We thrashed and snarled at each other, his face losing the remaining humanity and becoming a twisted monstrosity. My limbs were dark and skinny in contrast to his. Scales snagged and ripped into his skin. Even the human parts of him were foreign. His flesh was softer than mine, easily torn, and it didn't bother me to rake any part of him that came close enough. He mistakenly thought I'd be thrown off by his lack of clothing.

I wasn't wearing anything either.

Adam should have looked at me as an enemy, a combatant. Something that was capable of killing him. Instead, he toyed with me, making a game of wrestling with me. I raked his side with my left claw, drawing a lot of blood. That brought him out of his playful mode. But I used the hard plates on the tops of my forearms and thighs as if I wore gauntlets so his blows glanced away. He managed to sink razor-sharp teeth through my scales and into my neck. I panicked and shoved three talons from my left hand into the soft flesh under his chin. He released like a dog under fire from a garden hose, tucking his chin and grasping at his throat.

I wrapped my legs around his waist and tore four new crimson lines down his chest to match his other scar. He shrieked, tried to stand, and got tangled in my legs. I bit into his forearm and he blasted my cheek with his other fist. My jaw relaxed with tingling numbness and he pulled free. Dazed, I tucked my head under an arm while my senses tumbled. I did my best to shake it off, but stars danced around everything I saw.

Just before he got both hooves under him, I tightened my grip on his shoulder and got him in another leg lock. He was upright in a second and I held fast, wrapping my wings around both of us so tightly I could smell his skin and blood. Panic left me and was replaced with the odd sense that I was doing what came natural, sort of like a beast with its prey. I locked down tight around each part of him with every muscle and extremity I could. Even my tail twisted around his leg, constricting so it clung to his skin with barbed scales. He beat at the walls of my wings with his elbows, but I tightened around him like a snake swallowing a rabbit.

"You bitch," he growled in our cocoon.

"That's offensive," I said, with a laugh. I hung onto him like dead weight. He took blind steps forward, then sideways, and we bounced against a wall then toppled to the floor. He thrashed, and I let him wear himself down, tucking my face away from flailing fists and elbows, biting down hard where I could and tearing his flesh open when he hit me. It was strangely disturbing, but his flesh tasted a lot like chocolate chip cookies.

Adam got the picture and quieted, but it took a long time. Our sweat created a weird aroma inside the shell I'd made. Between that and the taste of his blood, my stomach roiled.

He was still, but I could feel his pulse as strong as his breathing. I didn't want to bite him any more after my reaction to the taste of him. I needed to reach for my dirk and end it. His eyes were closed and his weight was heavy on my chest and abdomen. I waited for as long as I could handle it, afraid I'd throw up. His breathing calmed after a while. Slowly, I relaxed the grip of one hand and reached for my calf . . . which made a damned gap in my wings and showed me how long I'd waited for him.

Lavender, predawn light shone against the top of a small window that was just above ground level outside, but near the ceiling in the basement. The light fragmented into a blend of colored rays through a slender, horizontal stained-glass window I hadn't seen when it was dark. I held my breath, still trying to reach my dagger without releasing him fully.

My scales tingled. I hiccupped. Adam opened his eyes. I gave up holding onto him and reached for my blade, feeling my fingers close around the hilt as my bare back hit the cold floor beneath us when my wings retreated and disappeared.

Shit. Not good.

The first light of day popped silver over the horizon, and the colors from the little window brightened immensely, shining in on us where we were crammed against the wall. My scales softened to peachy skin and talons receded back to cuticles as sure as clockwork. I shoved at him, wrestling to get out from underneath his weight.

Adam grinned, locking his arms around my shoulders and slamming down on top of me, deepening the saddle of my hips around him. As he did, my dirk slid free and fell softly onto the floor, hopefully within reach. I locked eyes with him, feeling around the carpet with my fingers, trying to find my dagger.

"Good morning, sunshine." He looked down at me beneath him, letting his eyes roam over my breasts. I hit him hard across the face, snapping his head to the side, my other hand flailing blindly for the dirk. He returned the favor and hit me so hard my ears rang, and I went limp for a second. He dipped his face, nuzzling and kissing my left breast, his dark hair shrouding my face as he pulled my nipple into his mouth. I elbowed his cheekbone hard with my free arm, frantic and desperate to get him off me.

The point of my blade poked my finger. I slid my hand as low on the cool metal as I could, finger-walking it into my grip. Adam's breath came hard against my chest as he switched to my other breast, raking his roughened forehead beneath my chin. He throbbed on my thigh and I jerked out of reflex, my legs constricting. He picked up his head and looked at me with squinting, yellow, animal eyes. One of his hands moved to my hip and the other reached between us so he could grip himself. I pushed back against the floor with my feet, trying to scoot away but his grip was vice-like, much different since I'd become smaller and so much weaker than before. He regarded me quietly, both of us still. My insides all cringed. I would die before I allowed him to take the next step.

I had to look scared on the outside because I was terrified and turning to Jell-O on the inside. Just as he arranged himself to do the deed, I leaned forward, locked both hands around the dirk's handle and drove the blade through his left kidney, pulled it back while he was shocked, brought it around front and shoved it forward, intent on his heart, shrieking like a banshee the entire time.

Adam screamed, grabbed my wrist, and stopped the dagger's momentum as he curled into a fetal position. The blade barely punctured his skin. I kicked from beneath him, crawling on all fours a few feet then got to my feet. He got up and took two really slow steps in my direction. Shock coated his features and the color drained from his face when he saw how much blood ran from the hole in his side. His eyes shot to mine.

I wiped the blade across my thigh, smearing his blood across my skin, warning him as he watched my movements.

"You have one working kidney and from the looks of it, you're not nearly as excited to see me as you were last night."

"Not to worry." He snarled and lunged at me in a quick, fluid motion in one last attempt to take me down. I spun, sticking him in the side just under his arm, clear to the lung. The hilt jammed against bone, the dagger buried as far as it would go. I yanked the blade free and jumped back. He went down, a bloody mess from both wounds. He began to wheeze.

I walked toward him looking down at his pale face. He coughed a spray of blood.

"I liked you, Adam. But that was yesterday when I didn't know you." There was no guilt for taking his life. I was sad that he was hurting, but it was a sadness I'd associated more with a spider I'd accidentally crushed, or a possum, dead on the roadside.

He closed his eyes.

My chest heaved as I stood in multihued sunshine, naked. A not-so-mythical creature lay dying at my feet. Toto and Kansas had nothing on me. I had so much to learn. How long had beings such as Adam been around, hidden in little enclaves? What else could be out there, aware of me while I flailed around, unknowing, dumb luck keeping me alive?

Peter had known about Adam, and knowing him, he probably

hoped I'd be scared into staying at the bookstore. He wasn't the only one I'd surprised lately.

I held up my bloody hands. Who the hell could do something like what I'd done and consider herself unaffected? I began to shake.

The security of the bookstore was all I wanted, and hopefully I'd get there before people worried about me again or realized I was gone. I wiped the dirk clean on the fur of Adam's leg and found my scabbard discarded on the floor. I tied it back around my calf and slid my blade into the leather sheath. I snatched a pair of the bejeweled jeans from the floor, disturbed at how well they fit. Trying not to think of the unfortunate girl who'd last worn them, I picked through the shirts and selected a long-sleeved, black sweater. They'd have to work for the run home. It was likely only about 6:30 or 7 in the morning and I hoped my sprint home, on bare feet wearing bar chick clothing would be undisturbed.

Without a last look at the dead faun, I left the church like an urchin who'd just stolen an apple from a street vendor, taking to the shadows in order to get home.

Two long hours later I let myself in the alley door of my sanctuary, exhausted, with bloody feet, and soaked because, of course, it started raining ten minutes after I left the church. It was 7:45 AM and Peter was already up. As I passed his bedroom door, his weights clinked, music played, and I heard his voice, like he was talking on the phone. I hoped he hadn't noticed my absence. I'd handled my business, which wasn't any of his.

I showered and climbed into bed but couldn't rest. Sleep was something I'd never needed much of. Even back at Saint Vincent de Paul's Home for Girls in Austin, a few hours a night would suffice. As a gargoyle I needed even less.

Being alone in my room still freaked me out since I was attacked by the thing under my sheet. I dozed but woke up moments after I fell asleep. My mind wouldn't quiet so I got up. I ate, listened to music on my iHome, wrote in my journal, and got more and more bunched up about leaving for Scotland as I managed to put Adam, my most recent kill, out of my thoughts.

Osgar and Iain Logan had just begun the rebuild on Castle Logan when Peter, Bree, and I left, weeks ago. I was curious to see what they'd accomplished in a month. Their home, before it was nearly leveled by Kai and his band of gargoyle henchmen 1,100 or so years ago, had been immense, according to Osgar. They'd talked about leveling the manor Kai had built in the center of the ruins, just to add insult to injury, but really, I didn't know where they'd all live if they did that.

Each member of Clan Logan had a room inside that manor. Petra, Peter's twin sister, had one there too. Kai's manor sprawled inside jagged rock walls that once stood at full height in 900 AD. The ruins ran for miles along the shore of Loch Ore, towering from the top of the brae, a deep forest flanking the stout curtain wall to the west, the east bordered by the sparkling waters of the loch.

Inside what was once the castle bailey, a circle of standing stones remained from centuries before. Clan Logan was as ancient as lore itself in Scotland, and they were happy as hell to regain freedom from the darkness. I couldn't blame them if they wanted to level the manor house Kai had built. Maybe, if it was me instead of them, I'd burn the whole thing to the ground, roasting marshmallows and singing Kumbaya while it disintegrated into embers in the night.

Kai had used my book to overpower Clan Logan. Gooseflesh rose on my forearms at the thought. I tossed the clothes I was taking onto the bed and squatted down, peering underneath the bed rail at the ginormous tome. Considering it mine might be a stretch, but it was Teasa's, apparently. If she was happy climbing inside my body with me and laying low, I didn't see the harm in sharing her book. Although, I didn't understand either the goddess or the book with any clarity.

Sitting back against my bed, I withdrew the volume from beneath where I slept each night. My sheet hung down, catching on the ornate plating decorating the corner, the form of the cast metal showing through the cotton like a face pressing through skin, or like a monster hiding just underneath.

I dropped the book on the carpet and skittered away on my heels and the tips of my fingers. Could the book have sent the monster to haunt me that night? Surely it wouldn't have done that. We'd bonded when it allowed me to open it in Scotland. Hadn't we?

Shortly thereafter, the book had refused to answer my questions or help me. It saved my life that day in the courtyard after a gargoyle, one of Kai's henchmen, Hamish, beat me within short reach of my demise. That was the first time I'd opened the cover, and I was healed that moment. Words formed on the pages, calling me by the goddess's name—*Bandia na Teasa*. After that I'd cradled the worn leather cover to my chest like it was the last infant in a dying populace. Weeks later, there in my room at the store in Cecil Court, I kicked it under my bed out of frustration.

Then I'd been attacked.

The timeline held true, as did the theme of my life lately, where I did stupid shit that caused me and those close to me grief and a whole lot of pain in the outcome. I'd also nearly been raped and ultimately killed because I was headstrong. I wrapped my arms around my chest, beginning to rock back and forth.

I could have been raped. I didn't know why that seemed to be way worse than the dying part that would have followed, but it was. The whole ordeal played through my mind again as if I was reliving each part. Adam's hands on me after I'd turned back to human form. His mouth tasting my skin. The look on his face when he was sure he would get what he wanted.

I shot to my feet, wiping away tears, shaking and nauseated. I needed to get far away from what had happened. What I'd nearly let happen. Why would I put myself in such a risky position? Who was I lately?

The clock on my iHome said 9:41 AM. The last time I went looking for answers I'd let myself into the records department back at the orphanage, looking for information about my family. That decision ended in monumental heartbreak when I found I'd been denied the knowledge that I had a brother.

Mentally slugging myself, I crawled over to the book and cracked open the cover, listening to the familiar sound of the ancient leather binding creak and smelling the wonderful scents of a time in ancient days.

The pages were, of course, blank as a new sketchbook. "Hello?" Feet flat on the carpet, knees spread, arms reaching to the floor, I smoothed a few thick pieces of bound parchment. "Please tell me how to find Teigan."

He'd been the member of Clan Logan trapped in a prison cell when we'd taken down Kai. Selfless was an understatement when describing his actions. Teigan spent his last free night guarding me from harm, although I'd mistaken him for one of Kai's henchmen. I'd been cold and mean to him. He'd been pulled into an unseen prison to spend a full cycle of the moon, something Kai did to keep Clan Logan in his power. To my knowledge, Teigan remained imprisoned in a cell, hidden from plain sight, somewhere near the castle in Kelty, Scotland.

I would free him if it was with the last breath of air I ever took. I owed him that.

The book remained silent, forming no silver words. I didn't know how many beings inhabited the pages, but I'd been told it was two: the life essence of a Roman scribe, and a Pict warrior. Whatever the whoever, someone had answered me before.

"Look, I don't know if you can see everything that goes on or what, but Teigan is a good guy and he deserves to be found and reunited with his family. All I'm asking is that you point me in the right direction and I'll do what I can to set him free from Kai's cell."

A bright ray of blue electricity zapped my hand, rocking me back onto my butt.

"Dammit!" My fingers burned like they'd been frostbitten. "Okay, just give me something. I don't want to be afraid of you all the time." I should have just kept packing. "Hello? Anybody? Make me human again?" I deadpanned, and sat back on the floor, my time wasted. My stomach rumbled. "Get me a Big Mac?"

Getting to my feet, I got out my backpack and began organizing the things I wanted to take to Kelty. Gotye serenaded me from my iHome while I sorted and folded, one of my favorite songs from a while back, "Somebody That I Used to Know," played while I worked, leaving me to draw ironic conclusions between the lyrics and how I used to know myself a whole lot better.

A hissing noise continued after the song ended, sounding like steam released from a pressurized valve, in a series of hot, little bursts. I held my breath, listening, afraid I would be revisited by the demon that terrorized me before. A surreal sensation pricked the back of my mind while I considered what I would do if the beast under my sheet came at me again. One thing was certain, I wasn't in bed, lying prone. I was on the edge, had just killed someone, and was fully awake. The little son of a bitch would have a fight on his hands.

Silver glinted, catching my eye, as words etched onto pages of the book, which I left spread open on the floor. Figures danced into place. I squinted at poured titanium ink as the diagram crept into clarification, despite the speed of an invisible quill. The map of a hill fort sprawled into a miniature depiction of stately castle grounds, complete with broad elements like an outer bailey and gatehouse, down to the great hall and larger chambers. Finer lines formed, though so small a magnifier would be required to read the complexity. The drawing continued; etchings creating shadows, blocking detail from view. The hissing finally abated, leaving my body stiff from holding position to watch. I was left with too much detail crowded into a diagram so intensely small, the human eye couldn't read it.

On the page opposite, writing started. *"A toll shall be taken."*

I was cheated, given something I couldn't use, although I doubted it was intentional. Sentience required perception. Whatever haunted the pages of the book was no longer human or simply never had been. For all I knew the tome had just rendered the key to everything I'd asked it for, the good hiding in the details, rather than the devil. I would look at the message in a positive light and find a way to use it.

"Thank you," I said, gently closing the cover. For the first time in weeks, I didn't feel abandoned by the things causing calamity in my days. Still, those things saddled my existence. I craved understanding of the new elements. I put the "toll" part in the back of my mind and moved forward.

8

After we cleared the heavy traffic of London that morning, Peter pulled the Aston off the M. Bree and I were in the back seat and Crispin sat shotgun. Peter and I hadn't spoken since he applied a new bandage to my wound. He didn't mention that I had possibly been out all night. I went with it gratefully, unsure if I was just buying into the convention that he really didn't notice me being gone, or if he simply didn't want to talk about it yet. The silence between us went beyond awkward into a whole new level, bordering on tension. I wondered, if he knew I'd done something as risky as chase down a faun and terminated it, would he be angry that I put myself at risk? Or would he be proud that I'd handled it myself? A part of me wanted to tell him. To find out which. But I balked against the idea of seeking his approval. That's not who I wanted to be. The only approval I needed was my own.

He pulled the key from the ignition and dangled it above the console, peering at me in the rear view.

"Really? You're going to let me drive?"

"It's a good day to die," Crispin drawled. "I hope the back seat has a safety belt."

"You got this, Tess," Bree chirped.

"Get over here before I change my mind." Peter bit back a smile. He popped his hood over his head and reached for the door handle.

Once Crispin let me out of the back, I jerked up my hood and trotted around the front of the car like the next contestant on *The Price is Right.* I grinned but Peter had already lost his smile, replacing any glimpse of good nature with stoicism bordering on a cloaked scowl.

"Are you worried?" I stopped in front of the awaiting driver's seat, eyeing the plush cockpit.

"Absolutely."

"Thanks for the confidence," I tossed at him, while he paced to the passenger side.

The first thing I did was adjust the seat. At a not-so-lengthy 5'4", my feet dangled against the floor, well short of the pedals. I tilted mirrors, buckled my seatbelt, and adjusted the volume on the stereo. By the time I started the engine, the cockpit cradled my form like it was molded to fit only me.

"When you put it in gear, don't give it fuel. Let it idle to motion." Peter nodded toward the highway as butterflies tapped against the walls of my stomach. "Now's a good time to get on the road," he said, peering over his right shoulder.

The gear selector clicked at D and the motor engaged, pulling us forward like a puck gliding over ice. I bit back a squeal, guiding the car between the lines on the asphalt as the Aston purred, crooning for the slightest urge from the throttle.

"Gently touch the gas pedal on the right," Peter instructed.

Determined to do well at my first driving lesson, I did just as he said. A little gas went a long way. We jetted forward with smooth transition as I learned the basics, hands glued at 10 and 2. The resonating hum of the engine and heavy scent of supple leather filled my senses, blending with each breath. Dimples burned my cheeks, but I kept smiling. Peter seemed more relaxed. We'd be in Kelty in no time at all, as good a time as I was having behind the wheel. I put everything but the drive out of my mind, listening to the world go by.

Bree and Crispin conversed softly in the back seat, only audible in mumbles and the occasional giggle from Bree. In the back, Crispin was able to let his hood down. Peter and I hid from sunlight that might blast us from the windshield, where the tinting was minimal. Our visors were down, but at the right angle, an oncoming motorist could be traumatized if all elements lined up perfectly. I wasn't complaining. I'd wear burlap and a bag over my head to drive the Aston Martin one mile.

"Nicely done," Peter said, just above a whisper.

I peered over at him. "Thank you, Peter."

"Get your bloody eyes back on the road."

"It's pretty hard to sound gruff with a smile. Just an observation."

9

"Can we please, please pull over?"

"No." Peter took no time to mull-over an answer.

We'd switched places miles ago, and just pulled into Kelty. My driving lesson went well, although we were on a highway, so there wasn't much excitement. We idled along Main Street, passing a sign on the right that announced the location of the Kelty Public Library. I recognized a resource when I saw one. Getting to the library could be totally simple, if he'd just let it happen. We had a healthy cloud cover. Just in case, I'd put up my hood, grab the book, and run inside. No big.

The book still held the map on the first two pages. I'd checked just before I tucked it beneath my backpack for the trip. Libraries held old records. I wasn't planning on letting an opportunity to research the area get away. Searching for Teigan was a priority. For that, I needed to get my bearings, and I was certain the answers were in the map. I just couldn't read the danged thing. The small-town library was a stretch, but I had to start somewhere.

"Who died and made you King of the Road?"

"We go to the castle, and from there, you go nowhere. You've done enough meddling with things you don't understand."

As if. I gazed out my window, fighting the urge to argue, a little embarrassed at being shut down in front of Bree and Crispin. He was sort of correct, but I still disagreed with leaving a kidnapping, rapey monster like Adam free to victimize people at will. I got that there had to be some big agreement put in place ages ago, one that afforded both sides privacy. But that was long before I arrived on the scene. Something small, I could turn my head. Not this.

Peter didn't offer to come with me to the library and I hadn't given him the opportunity to come with me to hunt Adam. I'd been right in my hunch to leave him behind. He'd have stopped me from going to protect the pact with Petrichor Park, if there was one. I prayed something substantial stopped him from doing the right thing about Adam. For all I knew there was some big deal about snooping around in Scotland, too. Once again, I was on my own. I'd risk my safety to find Teigan and Peter would never get that. Teigan had sacrificed his last days of freedom watching over me. I'd return the favor, alone.

Peter ran hot and cold. I understood keeping the peace to avoid bloodshed between all the beings hidden in the UK's twilight. What I didn't get was why not go out and do away with a scourge? I'd done it. Sure, it could've been a tidier job, but a murderer was put down. Peter could have done what I did and kept a secret. Instead he turned judgmental and condescending again. When he wanted to, he made me feel like the most important person in existence. The flip side was that he could withdraw and make me feel completely naïve, like a child, by tweaking the inflection of a single word. If circumstances suited him, he acted as if he had a stake in matters and could be amicable. When he treated me the way he did just then, I couldn't help but think he had ulterior motives, or a vendetta of his own. Being close to someone that polar was like trying to hug a porcupine in place of a teddy bear. We'd talk, but I'd have more class and confront him about letting Adam kill girls when we were alone.

What could he possibly lose by helping me look for Teigan? I knew Peter wanted to get to Castle Logan to see Petra, like a good brother would. I got that. He didn't offer to bring me back to Kelty later. He hadn't neglected to pose the opportunity. Peter was too careful for that. If he wanted to, he would have offered before I even asked. For some reason, he didn't want me to start my search. Asking him straight out would undoubtedly end in misery and embarrassing failure. I wouldn't give him the opportunity to respond in such a way again. I just hoped I could count on the other members of Clan Logan as a resource. He'd gone missing weeks ago. Surely they'd want to find their kin. Family should work that way. Not that I'd know anything about family, but if I had one, I'd die for them. Clan Logan was ancient, with centuries of war, tenacity, camaraderie, and love bonding them. Teigan had offered many times to take other clansmen's turn as Kai's prisoner in the hidden cell. That sacrifice meant love, plain and true. The fact that I'd been the reason they were separated, possibly forever, stung. I'd find a way to fix it, with or without Peter's help.

Maybe he thought it was a lost cause. The cell holding Teigan was said to be veiled somehow, by some magical conjuring Kai had created to keep the Clan under his control. If finding the prison had been easy they would have uncovered the location long ago. Each member had been locked up. Not one remembered getting taken there, or the return trip back home. The "lost cause" part Peter possibly considered would be that naïve, American me wouldn't have a wing or a prayer in the quest.

I beg to differ.

My tenacity, steel, and dumb luck had taken people off guard, including me. No one really knew what I was capable of, again, me included. I intended to use my standing as a wildcard to the fullest, to do right by the people who'd come to my aid when the straights were at their most dire. Maybe I'd surprise us all, again.

"Stop brooding, Tessa," Peter whispered.

"We'll talk soon." I didn't look at him when I answered.

My resolve grew as the forest sprang up taller and greener beside Black Road while we drove on. I was an underdog, but my growl might shatter some eardrums soon. I bit back a derisive snort, realizing I was getting ready to leave the assumed pecking order between Peter and me in a neatly-piled, hot mess.

"No way," Bree said. Our foreheads hit our windows at the same time as we looked out at the tops of tents through trees.

"It's a renaissance fair!" I squinted, watching two men walking up a dirt road toward the festival. "I love ren fairs. Can't we just stop for a couple minutes?"

"What the hell is that?" Crispin leaned over, peering out beside Bree.

"Only the sickest festival ever," Bree said. "People dress up and they have jousting and so many awesome clothes. And there are always fairies."

"That is not a renaissance anything, Tessa," Peter said.

I looked over at him as he drove, always the buzzkill. "Does it ever get old?"

"What?" he asked, a little irritated.

"Being such a frickin' stick in the mud."

Bree snorted.

"Those are just some freaks from that SCA thing. You know, modern day gamers playing in real life and all?" He talked like the people were the edge of humanity.

"Even better," I said.

"Can't we just stop for a little while? I'm cramped, and fresh air would be great. We're almost there now anyway." Bree looked over at Crispin, eyes huge. Her lips parted in the best smile I'd seen her pull off yet, and she actually batted her eyes.

I gave her a toothy grin. *Attagirl.* Bree didn't have to endure the same scathing I'd get from Peter if I'd done the same. Using my femininity for survival was a developing tool I would keep in a handy top drawer just in case, however. I just couldn't use it any ol' time the way she could.

She upped her game further and grabbed Crispin's hand.

"The trees are turning over there. Makes me miss autumn in the States." Bree didn't take her eyes from the window.

I was the reason she was in the UK. Thinking of her being homesick made me feel pretty guilty, but at the same time I couldn't deny the panic her words kicked up. They were the words of a person who was desperate for familiarity in a world she didn't belong in, even if she said them at an opportune time to get what we wanted.

I proceeded gently. "You could go home for a while, you know? I mean, you can still go. Your family would like that, and the holidays are coming up." I quit talking, realizing I was trying to talk her into doing the exact opposite of what I wanted, what I *needed* her to do, for me. There wasn't a single part of me that thought I could survive in this mad world without her.

"Mayhap seeing these idiots is a good idea after all," Peter said. He glanced in the rear view and hit the turn signal, edging the car to the side of the road. True to form, he didn't deal with sentimentality unless it was his own.

A collective sigh of relief blasted through the car. I reached between my feet to get some cash in case we saw something to eat. While I was looking down, something hit the Aston like a train, smashing me into the dash. I tucked my face in my arms on reflex, dazed, the concussion ringing in my ears and tingling down my spine. All the safety mechanisms in the car deployed, gasses hissing into the cushions, blasting into us from all directions.

Peter cursed viciously. I peeled myself free of the airbag and twisted to look in the back. My nose was numb, and the taste of blood coated my upper lip. Crispin and Bree peered out at a white van that was wedged against the back corner of the car. The image of a brightly frosted batch of cupcakes decorated the side of the delivery vehicle. People yelled outside, and cars accelerated as drivers hit their horns, like that would somehow help the situation.

"Screw you!" I yelled. Obscene gestures seemed appropriate, so I shoved two fingers around an airbag and against the glass for punctuation.

Bree slid back against the seat, rubbing her forehead.

Crispin and Peter made eye contact in the rear view. The men both popped their door latches, but Peter's front door was the only one that opened up. Crispin had to shoulder his loose, sending the sound of bending, scraping metal screaming through the car.

My jaw clamped shut at the grating.

Once outside in the din of passing traffic, a third man joined them. He kicked at the front of his van where it was jammed into the back of our car. Bree and I grabbed our stuff and got out, her curiously looking over the damage to the car, and my heart in my throat as I prayed my book wasn't damaged. I had some seriously screwed up priorities.

Cars and trucks revved by us, drowning my hope of hearing what the guys said. The bakery driver nodded, got back in his truck and started it. Peter waived Bree and me back. When we were at a safe distance from the roadside, he signaled the driver. He and Crispin rocked the Aston's bent fender and crushed bumper loose from the front of the van. The driver eased the van back. Metal groaned and popped, and so did our rear tire and axle.

"Dammit!" Crispin yelled.

I pursed my lips and Bree put a hand over her mouth. The car wasn't going to be drivable for a while. I contemplated just how screwed we were while checking the pace of the afternoon sun. We were still an hour from Logan Castle.

"Things just got a little hinky," I said.

Bree nodded. "At least it's off the road."

The only buildings or help around was the encampment of renaissance people. Even if we called the Logans, there wasn't enough daylight for them to get to us and then back to Logan castle before twilight.

Finally, the remaining backed-up traffic cleared from behind our wreck, leaving us in near silence. We all looked from the van and car to the sky and back again.

"Bloody hell," Peter muttered. He jerked the trunk open and had to hold it up while Crispin reached inside and began to set our bags beside the car. Crispin used both hands and began yanking on something for all his worth.

"Oh no," I said. A huge ball of dread gathered in my stomach. I ran over to them with Bree right behind me.

"Shit!" I hollered. My book was pinched hard between buckled metal and the wrinkled floor of the trunk. Crispin pulled again but a sharp edge was jabbed into the leather cover. Pages rose up against the disturbed line of torn binding.

"It's jammed tight," Crispin said. He backed away. "I'm doing more damage than good."

Peter scrubbed at his face.

I reached for my injured tome. It didn't budge. "Okay, so let's not panic," I shrilled. "We just wait a couple of hours until nightfall and any one of us will be strong enough in gargoyle form to pull it free. It's not a problem. It's all under control," I reasoned.

The bakery driver decided to take the opportunity to belt out onto the road and make his getaway.

"Hey asshole," I yelled.

Peter grabbed my elbow. "Just let him go. We don't need the complications. He's doing us a favor by getting the hell out of here."

"Speaking of which," Crispin added, "We need to get on the move." He donned his backpack and pulled the handle out of

Bree's hardback travel case as if we didn't have a huge issue with my book being trapped.

"Whoa, whoa," I interjected. "I'm not leaving it here."

"Tessa, we can't stay here on the road after dark and you know it. Cut the drama and get your bags." Peter didn't bother with eye contact, certainly expecting my protest.

"I'm not leaving it." I leaned against the door of the car.

"Tessa," Bree looked incredulous. "We have to get you three out of the clear. You know that."

"And what then? Some creep manages to get the book out of the car and finds a way to do something horrible? It's up to me to protect it."

"To protect others *from* it," Peter said.

"Exactly."

Crispin chimed in. "Nobody's going to get that book out of there before morning. And even if they did, the damned thing will not open up for them. Only upon a bloody miracle will it work for you."

"I'm not leaving it here." I locked my arms over my chest. "I'll find a place to wait it out and just keep watch until morning. You guys can go on ahead and come back with help at first light."

"Anyone hurt?" A lady in a big dress and apron called from beside a barricade marking the side of the camp of gamers. A group of three men started toward us, all dressed in tunics and knee-high boots. One held a contradictory looking cell phone against his ear.

"All's well but the car," Crispin called. "No injuries, but thank you for your concern." He waved them off.

"A tow's on the way," the guy with the phone said. He fingered the screen and slid it into the pocket of his pants.

"Crap," I blurted.

"Thank you," Bree called.

The group stopped, glanced at one another, likely perplexed at my outburst.

I waved and faked a smile, then bailed toward the back of the car, and tried one last time to free my book before the tow truck arrived. Bree was right beside me, holding the trunk open while I stepped up on the bumper, intending to climb inside and try kicking the metal back.

"Where is it?" she asked, peering inside the compartment.

"Right there, under that crack and bubble," I pointed, and stepped into the trunk.

"Hm." She looked from where I gestured and back to me.

I sat back on my heels. "You can't see it?"

Bree shook her head.

Peter came up beside us. "It's thrown up wards."

"Good to see the bloody thing still works, if only in the spirit of self-preservation," Crispin said. He held out a hand to help me out of the trunk.

I looked from the book to his face as a big truck came into view over his shoulder. Hope left me, and I deflated like a half-full balloon released before it could be tied. With a last glance at the buckled cover, I let Crispin help me out as the tow vehicle backed toward the bumper of the Aston Martin.

I doubted any of the paperwork in the glove compartment could possibly show any of us belonged behind the wheel of the car. The Aston was red hot, blatantly stolen, and considered the spoils of war by me and my little group of good gargoyles. The issue facing us was much bigger than deciding what to tell the tow driver.

Now that they'd found us in London, every one of Kai's henchmen living would be on the lookout for the car once night fell. We kept it out of sight for the most part and it would be hidden once again if we'd made it to Logan Castle.

The tow driver moved about like molasses in a cold jar. He smiled but was in need of a long bath, joked but had off humor, and disregarded my frown and Peter's snarls, going about his job with no hurry at all. Peter took the business card the driver offered and motioned toward the pile of bags.

We all grabbed our stuff and stood in silence as the motionless Aston Martin was dragged upward onto the slanted bed and then chained to its coffin. The driver hopped up beside it and tossed a cable over the trunk to keep the lid from bouncing en route to the tow yard.

I was dazed. Just like that, uncertainty replaced the awaiting safety of Castle Logan and the Clan. We were out in the open and would transform in less than half an hour, except for Bree, who had begun to beat a neat trail over little grass moguls toward the gamers' tents.

"Wait," Crispin called.

"For what?" she snapped. She tossed her hair to her back and released the handle of her travel bag so it stabbed upward. "Look," she paused and took a deep breath. "I know what happens at nightfall. We should get off the damned road and blend with these"—she waved toward the lady and men who still watched us—"guys. We need to come up with a safe plan and I refuse to stand in plain sight on the highway and risk being seen."

Sensing Bree's turmoil, the lady in the huge skirts smiled and waved her over with a flurry of little "come here" gestures. She had a very sweet, matronly face and I bet right then she could bake a mean cinnamon roll. I grabbed both my bags and passed Crispin and Peter up, falling into step behind my best friend.

Bree was right, crappy as she made it sound. She wasn't a gargoyle and would need protecting if something did happen.

I tried not to look when the tow truck drove off with my book, but a small voice screamed and cried for me, falling quiet as the top of the Aston dropped from sight. Bree and the lady chatted softly by the barricade, but the words didn't register. Peter approached.

"Discretion must be used around the humans, Tessa."

"I know that, Peter. And now isn't the best time for a lecture so tread lightly."

"Well, maybe you should act like you know what the bloody hell I'm talking about then," he snapped, in a harsh whisper.

"Okay, fine," I said, turning to face him. "Please enlighten me as to which part of my jacked-up life you'd like me to try to keep a secret from humans?" My lower lip tried to tremble, but I bit the inside to stop the traitor from belaying just how stressed out I was.

"Excuse us for just a moment, won't you?" Peter asked Bree and her new friend. Crispin stood beside Bree and nodded to Peter. Bree just stared at me, likely hearing the way I'd spat the word "human" a second before.

Peter grabbed my elbow and pulled me along toward the back of the row of tents and trees. We stopped, and I dropped my bags next to his.

"We've been trying to think of a way to broach the subject with you for a time now," he started.

I cringed inside. With a statement like that, the topic had to be a doozy. My plans to grill him over his inaction with Adam took a back seat.

"I know she's your best friend and all—"

"Wait, wait. Whoa," I interjected. "This is about Bree?"

He took a long breath and nodded. "She's human, Tessa, and it's not safe to have her here. For either one of you."

"It's Bree," I reasoned. "She's fine here. I mean, look how she handled this situation. She's smart, heading into this"—I motioned to the tents with a tilt of my head—"for cover. It's not like she doesn't know what's out there."

"You're not getting it." He stepped closer, which was always an indicator that he was about to talk down to me like I was stupid. I bristled.

"I get it just fine." I stepped back so he couldn't look straight down at me, thwarting his attempt to lord over me.

"Listen to yourself, won't you? We are here with this group of humans because your human is defenseless. If she was back in the US, where she belongs I might add, we would be in the bloody trees and halfway to the Logans by now!" The flutes stopped from inside the camp.

"She belongs with me!" I yelled back. He had it all wrong. "This is what family does. We look out for one another." I took a breath to try to calm down, which didn't work. Bree being in the UK was a subject Peter should have known better than to question.

"She's not your family and you know that," he snarled. "This schoolgirl sister thing you two have going was charming in the beginning, but now you're endangering the very person you want to protect merely by allowing her to stay. Are you so proud and selfish that you fail to see that?"

My bravado waved goodbye and the words I had prepped dissolved in my mouth. Was he right about that? I shook my head and looked down. The sun broke through the mist-filled clouds on the horizon of trees, making its first showing all day long. My hands turned skeletal and sinewy in the stray beams. Peter's face darkened, the tendons pulling tight as his jaw worked. We both popped our hoods up immediately, but the clouds fought back, gobbling the sun into their gullet of black anger to the west. We had a solid fifteen minutes before sundown. The little band started to play again and the smell of smoke from a new camp fire drifted over the tops of the tents with it.

"Here's the deal," I closed the space between us and glared all the way up at him, "she's here now and I will protect her with my last breath. If she decides to go home, I'll support her in that but there's no way in hell I'm telling her she's a liability to us."

"Hello, human here," Bree called from behind me.

I turned around to face her, guilty as hell and knowing full well Peter had baited me into saying what I did at the right moment. It hadn't been an accident that she'd shown up right then. He was just too good for that. Bree continued without missing a beat, neatly stepping around the elephant in the room like it hadn't just crapped on the carpet.

"They're cooking some sort of sausage and potato thing in here and want to know if you're hungry. I know you'll only be around for a couple more minutes, but I can bring you guys some when it's done."

Crispin was with her and he dropped the hood of his pullover while he approached. "They said we can use the back of their supply tent," he said, pointing toward the end of the row we stood beside. "You'll have to run interference for us during the night so we're not disturbed," he said to Bree.

She nodded. "Small price to pay for your protection." She didn't bother to look at me, although each of her words mimicked mine. "I'll go let Sinnie know you're in." Bree turned and left.

I spun and jabbed a finger at Peter. "You did this on purpose."

He didn't answer, just gazed at me.

I turned hoping to find Bree so I could smooth out the damage before I had to tuck myself into a tent and get scaly.

"Hold up," Crispin said. "We can get through right here." He pointed behind Peter and started that way. "We can't risk getting held up with introductions walking in. There are too many humans inside."

"So what, we have to go hang out in a tent all night?" I held my ground. Had everyone forgotten that my book was out in the world without me? Sure, the wards were up around it, but what if some magical-type just happened to work in the yard and saw through them?

"I have to go get my book." I looked at the horizon, where the dying sun streaked purple and pink through the storm. "I won't be staying."

"She's right," Peter said, to my surprise.

Crispin nodded. "I'll stay with Bree. We'll be in that one, there."

I followed his gesture to the large tent that was next to the last.

"There's a sort of sword battle getting ready to start at dusk. That should keep them all busy."

Peter scoffed. "Indeed."

"Aye. They use wooden weapons to keep it legal, but it seems the ones who are adept fighters are quite good and lethal with them. One of the men is quite bruised and banged up after the match earlier."

"That's awesome," I said, wishing I could learn more instead of Garging Out and chasing down a tow truck.

"If all goes well, we'll be back quickly," Peter said.

Crispin nodded and turned to go back into the camp. I envied him so much, wishing I had the opportunity to walk around the events with Bree, even if it was only for a little while. My skin began to tingle, scales waiting to erupt, laughing at my childish, human whims and wishes.

"Crispin?" I said, before he got too far away.

He stopped, waiting for me to speak.

"Tell Bree I love her, please? And that I'm sorry."

"She knows, lass. But I'll tell her anyway." He smiled and left, leaving Peter and me to the business of finding the wrecked car and retrieving my book.

Peter pulled the tow driver's card from his pocket. "Ready for this?"

"Born ready," I said. The enthusiasm I'd meant to pepper across my answer was a little limp.

"Come then, Tessa. You're the one always going out of your way to find adventure." He turned toward the thickest part of the tree line and I broke into step beside him without answering.

Hopefully, I could find a safe place to stash my clothes before we Garged Out.

～

MY ABILITY TO navigate while flying was lacking, at best. I didn't let on that it got my goat to have to follow Peter's lead. We'd waited well into the night to make a move and the moon was locked in clouds, so we soared over the streets of Kelty in near darkness, carefully avoiding lane lights. I knew we were close before we dropped lower, the smell of used oil and overheated electrical wires pulling us in. The boneyard of busted up cars was laid out in curving rows inside a concrete wall that twisted beyond sight. Piles of bumpers, fenders, and unidentifiable pieces and parts rose up here and there. The road butted up to a tall chain-link gate that had been peeled back from its posts on one side. A black car idled there with one door thrown open and the dome light lighting the ground. Peter and I glided in for a silent landing beside a truck and watched a huge lumberjack of a guy rattle the other part of the gate loose and toss it aside before getting back in the car and rolling through.

"So, this is shady as hell," I whispered. "Shouldn't there be an alarm or something?"

"I doubt this rubbish heap is that well-guarded," Peter said.

"Let's find the book and get out of here before we get in trouble for doing whatever that guy's got planned." I went to get up, but Peter grabbed my arm.

"Wait a moment." He motioned toward the black car as it rolled past. We crept along, hiding from sight, as the driver slowed, apparently looking from one wreck to the next.

"Ah, dammit. You don't think they're looking for it too, do you? We have to get to it first!"

"Relax. It's warded now."

I didn't trust that one bit. I'd seen others who'd found the book despite those wards. From the looks of things, it was too late, anyway. The car's engine idled down as the driver stopped and put it in Park. The door opened again, and the driver got out to hold the door for a petite figure who'd been in the back. The two walked through the headlights and stopped at a car with the trunk popped open. I leaned to have a better look, panicking when I recognized the Aston.

"Now's good," I said, and shot toward them, targeting the man who grew unbelievably larger as I got close. He put one meat hook of a hand on the trunk lid right as I hit him out of nowhere. A blast of breath exploded from his mouth as he tumbled to the side, into another torn up car. Not wasting time, I turned toward the last known location of my book and shoved inside the trunk looking for it.

The woman's short bob of black hair flew up in the wind when I burst past her. She growled, rather than blaring the terrified scream I was hoping for. I didn't stop to look at her, intent on getting my prize and being in the air long before the giant pulled himself free of the tangle of metal. I hoped Peter would hold them off for just a split second. I used the butt of my palm to beat at the torn fender inside the trunk, pulling on the book at the same time. The pinched metal loosened its grip as sounds of fists connecting began. The book popped free all at once and I had to use my wings to stay upright. I hugged the leather tome to my chest for a millisecond, apologizing for letting it out of my sight.

"Let's go!" As I launched my right wing smacked into the woman. She looked up at me with white-blue eyes. Her face was a stark contrast of porcelain skin and beautifully applied makeup framed by midnight black hair. She wasn't smiling until she saw my face. Recognition isn't exactly what I saw then, but she didn't seem the least bit shocked or scared.

Peter released the mountainous human who fell into a limp heap and took to the air. We didn't look back again.

WE FLEW in silence until I couldn't handle it anymore. There were things on my mind that I couldn't hold in. Apparently the same was true for Peter because he nodded and began to glide down. He hadn't made a peep when I jumped without him to rescue my book before the weirdos stole it, and I was certain he had two cents to share.

"We need to talk," I said, touching down. A slow drizzle had started so dirt and leaves clung to the scales on my legs and feet. I tried not to let my tail swish so the conversation didn't start off confrontational.

Peter sighed. "I'm relieved you want to talk about it this time." He crunched along beside me as we cut through the trees. "It's a good sign."

Confused, I looked at him, trying to understand what he could be referring to. I was still at a loss. "What the hell are you talking about?"

"I mean to discuss what you did back there. Flying off like that, you could have gotten us either killed or captured. Worse even," he answered, casually.

I stopped, looking up to the sky for the strength not to bite his head off. It didn't work. He watched me, jaw set.

"First off, I don't need your permission to go after what's mine," I punctuated number one by waving the book at him. "Secondly, you are so, very far off track with the meaning of this little talk."

"Don't shout," he growled.

I waved my free hand around the forest. "Sorry, buddy! All this nature's about to bear witness to you getting told to go screw yourself."

"Tessa, I am warning you, right now," he started.

"Shut it." He surprised me by doing so for just a second, so I continued. "You're not at all who I thought you were when we met. I thought you were the kind of guy who had a good heart and cared about people in general." I pointed a talon right at his chest-plate. "The guy you really are is bossy, borderline chauvinistic, and easily bought off of helping people. You're the kind of guy who lets a monster prey on innocent girls just to protect your own ass."

"You finished?" he drolled.

"That's it? You're not even going to try and explain?"

"Sounds like you're all set." He looked up and crouched, ready to leap into flight.

"Oh, hell no, you're not," I yelped, desperate to hear him try to save himself. Wanting him to somehow redeem my image of him. I jumped at him, stomping on his tail and wrapping him up in a bear hug to try to stop him from leaving. The book thumped to the wet turf.

The next thing I knew, the forest swept by as I was flung into the base of a tree. My spine might have snapped down the middle the way pain screamed from my neck to the back of my legs. The impact jarred all the leaves above me and water poured from above, splattering my head. All I could do was try to breath, but it wasn't working out.

"I don't owe you explanations. Understand? And you'll forgive me for thinking you would have other questions, yes?" Peter crouched in front of me. "Perhaps, like this," he said, preparing. "Gee, Peter," he said, fluffing imaginary hair back from his shoulders, "who is that crazy lady with the red lipstick who almost had my goddamn book back there?" he mocked, in his best American accent. "Hey Peter, did you mind letting that gargantuan pound on your head to keep me safe?"

I wheezed, not knowing which was worse, not being able to breath or being so mad I wanted to skin him to make thigh-high boots.

"What is it, beautiful?" Peter peered into my face with mock concern. "Can't back talk?" He slapped my cheek so hard my head snapped to the side. I inhaled with a gust, icy air turning to a blast of heat in my chest. My neck cracked when I straightened up. My fingers closed on a small stick, which I swung and stabbed into his ear canal on an urge. He fell back, bracing on a wing, both hands on the protruding end of the twig.

"Dammit, Tessa," he yelled. "You bitch!"

I was completely grossed out at the sight, but heavily disturbed at my ability to do something so vicious. Peter wouldn't die from anything I'd do to him. He wavered so I kicked him over and yanked the stick free.

"You're a dick. Don't ever forget that." I controlled the anger that accompanied the blast of heat, fearing if I let myself react I'd try to pummel him into jelly. Not that I'd accomplish that. Peter was tough and much stronger than me, even when goddess tendencies gave me a little bump of strength.

"I want respect from you from this point on. You might be killing the respect I had for you but I'm not here for you to lie to and toss around."

Peter got to his feet, snarling. His wings beat slowly, clumps of moist soil and leaves sloughing to the ground. Black blood ran down his neck, glistening against charcoal scales.

"You have no idea what you're in for. I've done everything I can to protect you from what's to come. You've made your bed, Tessa." He shot to the sky so fast his black wings were lost in darkness.

"I don't care! If you have something to say, say it! Don't just punish me and treat me like a snot-nosed kid!" There was no answer. "Do you hear me?" I yelled. Peter was gone. Not the slightest acknowledgement returned, even from the breeze.

I started for my book, moving a little slower than normal and flexing my wings. My legs ached and tingled, and so did my claws. Gingerly, I bent and grabbed the book, then started limping in the direction of the camp of stick-fighting, renaissance people.

I walked slowly at first, sort of nursing my wounds and all-around feeling sorry for myself. The more I walked, the more I thought. The more I thought, the more pissed off I became, until I reached some idiotic turning point where I was genuinely sorry for stabbing a piece of downed oak tree into Peter's head. Why did I have to lose my temper in the first place? Sensible people talked things out, sans violence. But the way he mocked me and refused to talk or to take me seriously was horrible of him. And where did he get off telling me what to do all the time? I wasn't his kid, his sister, his lackey . . . Just who the hell did he think he was? It took all of thirty-seven seconds for me to rage at him, ready to tear his arms off the next time he was close. I wouldn't be treated as someone's dog. If anything, it was Peter who should have been looking up to me. I was a goddess, once upon a time. That was freaking substantial, whether I spoke with an American accent or not! Like it or not, just like I'd learned, the people and gargoyles around me needed to start taking that into consideration before they made any more stupid decisions.

I kicked rocks and snarled to myself. The nerve! And to think I'd felt guilty when I saw him bleeding. What about the things he'd done to me? He'd actually touched me, thrown me into a tree, for crying out loud. By the time I was close enough to hear snapping campfires and tipsy flautists I was ready to search for Peter and smack him square in the snout.

"Hallo, you," a male voice growled. I stopped walking, ears pricked, listening for more noise in the brush. I sensed something old, a familiarity, which wasn't a good thing. All old things usually came from way back, the memories belonging to Teasa from her travels back in her day.

"Hello?" I saw nothing but picked up on a sense of aggression nearby. "Who's there? Show yourself." I picked up that I was being looked at like prey. There was anger on the air. Malice, mixed with a bit of glee at the thought of a game of cat and mouse.

"Why so damned bossy?"

I turned to my left and looked up in the trees a little, peering hard. "You've picked an awesome night to screw with me buddy,"

I stepped forward, cautiously, but doing my damnedest not to act fearful.

"What ya have there, lass? Bring us a prize?"

I looked up, following the voice. "That's none of your business."

His words turned to laughter as he landed in front of me. Wings expanded to block half my view as a big damned Ancient gargoyle stepped close. He grinned, eyes and horns gleaming. I backed in a circle as he came at me. He swung his wings wide, something I was sure he did just as a fear tactic, and then shook them into twin columns against his shoulders and back.

"We agree on one thing," the gargoyle said, waving huge claws around at the night. "Tonight is the perfect time. I wish to talk to ya, so don't be frightened." He was old-school Scottish with a brogue so thick I had to sift through it to find words that made sense.

I scoffed. "As if you frighten me." I might have been done for soon, but it wasn't like me to go down without talking a big game.

He drew entirely too close in two monstrous steps and arched his neck to peer down at me. "I smell it on ya. Fear has a scent akin to death. I like the smell of fear. It sticks in the air, sweetens it up. I'm willing to show you the difference."

I shook my head at him, absolutely hating being a short gargoyle chick, when inside I felt like I dwarfed the creep. Something clicked when I looked way up there at him. I didn't want to be there, with my life threatened, holding a book that I'd bonded with. I didn't want to be in the woods, or headed for a castle on a lake, or a freaking loch. I didn't want to be a gargoyle or a goddess. I wanted to be a teenager with a nice pad in the Hill Country, surfing the net to find the next great concert while I shopped for badass boots on Amazon. Worst of all, I didn't want to be a killer. A little sob snuck out.

The Ancient's grin widened. "Give us what you've got there, lass."

I smiled as a hot tear slid down my cheek. Everything was hot, my claws, the breath coming out of my snout, even my guts were burning up. I was going to erupt and there wasn't a damn thing around to stop me. And the fool tossing threats down at me was an idiot. The least I could do was enlighten him.

"Just leave," I said. "I'm going to kill you. You can't even see what I've got." The book was warded, making it invisible to most every other thing out there. I focused on the dim firelight in the distance and took a step in the other direction as he started laughing at my threat.

"Everyone knows," he said, putting a claw on my shoulder and stopping me dead as he laughed his ass off, "what you have. Give it to me and I'll make it painless."

"I can't. Even if I wanted to hand it over, it won't let me walk away." The thing's eyes grew a little wide and shocked, so I just kept talking about the things exhausting me. He really did expect me to fall apart and beg for my life, to cringe and cower. Every stinking thing on the planet had a purpose. He was about to be shown his.

"I'm tired of all this. The way you're familiar even though I don't actually remember seeing you. The fact that I have to take care of this damned book, like my sole purpose in life is to be its personal librarian who's willing to die for it!"

"This will go easy for you if you stop talking and hand it over." He didn't look too appreciative of all my jabber, but there was a new element, maybe caution, in his voice. He thought I'd lost my mind, had cracked up and become a rambling nut.

"I don't want it! If it was up to me, I might just give it to you. And it could be your problem then. It's not all it's cracked up to be. There are these crazy tolls to be paid, and I don't know what that even means, other than I'm going to lose an eye or something soon. It lies and ignores me. It only serves itself. Seriously, you and this"—I held the book out, as if he could see it—"thing, you deserve each other!" I twisted and whipped the book behind me, knowing full well I'd be the only one to see where it landed. As much as I'd love to rid myself of the wretched tome, it was my responsibility to make sure it didn't fall into the hands of those like this gargoyle and whoever he might be hunting it for.

"Why do you even care about the damned thing?" I blurted.

I was amped up. The pain from Peter slamming me into a tree seemed to meld with the heat and anger. Asking questions was probably a little pointless, but that one slipped out.

"I have my reasons, bitch." He regarded me like I was scum. Crazy scum.

"Don't tell me," I baited, laughing, "you want to be human again. You're tired of just eating them. You want to get back to your old self."

It looked at me like I'd finally sold the farm and lost my mind.

"Don't ya think maybe that's what I want, too? But look at me!" I gestured a little too wildly at myself, flapping my wings and whipping my tail. "Here I am, all Garged Out and getting ready to get my ass kicked again."

"Just give me the fucking book," he growled.

"Nope, it's not that easy. See, it's making me a little nuts. You're going to hear all about it."

A high-pitched, whining sound erupted from the direction of the camp. My ears twitched but I didn't take my eyes off my would-be assassin. Dread built to foreboding. The sound ate at my nerves. Something was very wrong over there. I tried to shake loose of his grip and failed.

"Let go!" I yelled. The whining gave way to a scream of alarm at the camp. I had to go check on my friends.

"There's more to the tale," he said, wrestling me close with a thick grip on both my arms. "This is about retribution. About taking an eye for an eye. You killed my brother."

"Adam's your brother?" The words fell out before I could catch them.

The Ancient stared for a brief second, then shook his head

and laughed at me again. "Not him. You'd be paying for that, too, if I'd not come across ya to get mine first."

"You've got me confused with somebody else. Now let go of me or I swear you're going to regret it!"

"Ah, it was you. On the steps above the Grotto. Callum was his name. Put in charge of watching over that little American twat for Kai. I helped put you down once. This time, I'll make sure it's done proper."

The lives I'd ended didn't count up to much, which was a matter of perspective, but there was one other than Adam. The creep had been attacking Bree when she escaped the Grotto. I'd lost it, knowing I had to save her after seeing her grabbed. It was the first time I could say the goddess inside me took over. I moved lightning fast and tore the creep's throat out before it registered I'd flown up the stairs. And it didn't stop there. I ended up caving his chest in and watching him expire with a smile on my face, all in front of Bree. That was the moment she found out I'd been turned into a gargoyle. I'd saved her life and destroyed her image of her best friend inside of about two seconds.

The Ancient gave me a hard shake. "Now that we understand one another, you can tell me where that damned book is and I'll make this quick and easy. If not, I'll take my sweet time watching you bleed."

I stared, realizing the beast was dead set on vengeance at the same time as stealing the book. Several crashes and screams came from the camp which was probably crawling with more escaped henchmen like the gargoyle holding me. My best friend was in danger again. I went for broke.

"The book's behind me, beside that thicket. Get it yourself." I yanked loose as he looked past me.

"If you lie to me, I will take that friend of yours and flay her alive. I'll feast on her while you watch."

I held my claws up to show him I had no intention of moving. I'd bought some time. The oaf bent, trying to keep an eye on me and feel around in the leaves and dirt. His wings stuck straight up and his tail cut a swath through the dirt behind him. The second his claws brushed the cover, his eyes lit up. The book must have dropped its wards right then because he certainly appeared to be seeing it. That made it free game for any number of players vying for the book, which would lead to catastrophe.

Holy hell, no. Fire ignited, and I shot into his side, oddly satisfied when his ribs cracked against my shoulder. Somehow, he kept ahold of the book while he wheezed and curled up. I kicked at the same batch of busted bones in machine-gun repetition until he finally cried out, hacking out a spray of blood. About three seconds had gone by since he'd first touched my book and he let go long enough to grab the end of my wing and ankle so I couldn't kick him again.

He knew what he was doing. I was completely off balance. Every time I tried to shift my weight he'd yank on my wing. It was all I could do to stay upright and keep the rest of me out of his reach. I tried to kick his hand off my leg, but he straightened on the ground and drove his horns through my calf muscle. That did the trick, and I fell down, grabbing at my skewered leg and cussing like a sailor. The horns ripped free and the night got a little darker as the huge Ancient rose to loom above me like death.

Looking at the latest minion Fate hurled at me was all too familiar and frustrating. I cringed in piles of damp leaves and black, loamy dirt waiting to see if I would die, thinking it was unfair, and wondering if I might actually, really be done. I hated it.

Following an urge from deep inside me, I grabbed a branch we'd knocked loose in our scuffle and squeezed it as hard as I could. The temperature in my palms rose and steam began to roll off the wet bark. A second later the smolder popped into a beautiful little flame. I was on my feet as the gargantuan backed off. The night was still too dark for my liking, so I turned in a circle, sending little sparks, one after another, into the surrounding brush until smoke and steam rose and gave way to flame. Orange and yellow reflected off the Ancient's scales. I smiled big with my fangs showing and looked for something else to light on fire.

He must have thought I was all-in because he charged me in a blur of beating wings and swinging fists. Two strikes connected hard with my face and left numb patches. The numbness would give way to pain the next instant so I braced, a little shocked that he had the balls. Recognizing my calm smile apparently meant a shit storm was on the way, he yelped a little when I used my amped up speed and caught the next punch he threw, twisting beneath his elbow and yanking his arm down across my shoulder with blurring speed. While he adjusted to the idea that his elbow was snapped, I spun around hard and jammed the flaming branch completely through his sternum, which looked sort of awesome because sparks flew and blood hissed on the embers inside the wood. Goddess tendencies traveled much faster than plain old gargoyle stuff. Thankfully, the beast took a knee as he gasped and clawed, trying to pull the wood from his chest. His face was level with mine. I snarled and started swinging. It took a mere matter of seconds to hack his blocky, sinewy neck apart. I was glad I got started in a hurry.

Ancient blood spilt on the leather book cover beside the twitching body. Rather than rescue the damned thing, I let it continue to pump across the pages and spine for half a second, mesmerized as the cover seemed to absorb the blood like an extra dry sponge. I grasped one of the dry corners and angled it so the rest would run off. I was completely creeped out. With my free claw, I grabbed the dead gargoyle's head by a horn and pitched it into a burning thicket. After setting the book on a dry spot, I heaved the body over a few times, rolling it into the leaves and brush so it would catch on fire, too. Once it ignited, I grabbed the bloody tome and took flight.

10

T he camp was a scene of chaos. Humans ran about the tents and wooden booths, hiding and yelling orders at each other. Random piles of unrecognizable things burned. I landed, and a man tried to run away from me but I caught him by an arm.

I spoke slowly and clear, knowing he'd be freaked out. "There's a pretty American girl here some place. She had long, light brown hair. Have you seen her?"

He didn't reply but a field of wet material grew around the front of his old-fashioned pants. His eyes scoured my face, taloned claws, and the horns on top of my wings, before coming to rest on the giant book I had in one arm. Yep, I was a living, breathing gargoyle toting a big book, but he'd have to get past it, pronto. I wished the book would simply keep up wards all the time.

"Hey! Can you hear me or what? What happened here?"

"Oh God!" he whimpered. "Oh God, please don't hurt me!"

Something cold ran through the membrane of my wing and jammed into the scales between my shoulder blades. "Ouch," I drawled, turning to see who the idiot was that tried to stab me.

A man dressed up in full meshed chain armor ripped an honest to goodness longsword free of my wing as I turned around. White eyes darted around inside his metal helmet and he drew back in a defensive looking maneuver.

"Hold on there," I said, putting my free claw up. "I'm not going to hurt anyone. I'm just looking for a human I left here."

The two men held very still.

"Okay that didn't come out right. I'm not a bad person or like a bad guy. I'm a good guy. I promise. And aren't you only supposed to have like, wood swords?"

"Tessa!" Peter called from above me. "I count five gargoyles over there. Crispin has Bree and they're headed out the back by the trees." He circled, pointing in the direction of the most recent crash and screams.

"Give me that," I said to the human knight wannabe.

"Like hell!" he yelled, and ran off, shadowing Peter on the ground. The other guy pulled a soggy cell phone from his pants pocket.

"Good luck with that," I said as I took off. Despite the wetness, he punched numbers and held it to his cheek.

The knight was fast for a human. He arrived on the other side of a row of tents as I touched down. Peter dove into the melee, taking on two gargoyles who were tearing the hell out of a tent. Sword hefted, the human yelled a battle cry and charged at one of the other gargoyles. Peter watched him, as shocked as I was, when he assaulted the stunned gargoyle with a barrage of sword strikes, dodging swiping claws and deflecting hits with a square shield.

I looked around to see if I was being watched and bent to stash my book beneath a pile of canvas. I kicked dirt beside it for good measure and was about to take off to join the fight when a gargoyle landed in front of me. Standing upright, it must have been over eight feet in height. Counting the twisting horns on his head, closer to nine. It held a brutal looking short sword with two hooked tines protruding from the hilt. It extended its wings once before folding them into twin arcs, the base of each tucked tightly against each thick calf. I knew right then something akin to Satan himself stood in front of me.

It looked from the piled-up canvas back to my face. My first inclination was to hand him the book and wish him a great night.

Another gargoyle shot into the giant from the sky and they wrestled and fought in the dirt. I watched, mesmerized.

"Get to the trees, Tessa," a voice called from above. The glare from all the fires made it hard to see right above me but I recognized the voice easily.

"Osgar?"

I didn't get an answer, but I was sure it was him. Following instructions came easily right then. I retrieved the book and ran to find Bree and Crispin, listening to fists connect and the human knight continuing to hack away.

Sure as more rain, Crispin guarded Bree in a grove of trees. They weren't visible at first and I'd been worried I wouldn't find them, but I caught the scent of Bree's body spray. They were crouched down low and well-hidden. Once I got close, Crispin flew toward the camp. I crouched beside Bree where she sat on a backpack. Neither of us spoke. Instead, we listened and watched smoke and sparks rise from the camp, praying for daybreak to arrive.

Gargoyles flew above the fires in silhouette and it was killing me not being able to tell who was who. The fighting seemed to go on forever and I didn't dare leave Bree. Humans ran, but some stayed, sticking close to the knight who refused to give me his sword. They were quick, small shadows on the ground, swinging swords and staves, concentrating on one gargoyle at a time. I prayed the ones that stayed had a good sense of who was good and who would eat them.

Finally, after listening to screams and other traumatic sounds of raw battle, the sky began to lighten to lavender. Hanging clouds were black pockets of drizzle just waiting to bust loose. A small exodus of gargoyles took to the sky leaving only the sound of fire crackling. One winged form held the arm and leg of a limp human as he took off and I wished deep down the unfortunate man was already dead. Hopefully, Peter, Crispin, and who I thought was Osgar, were able to save most of the humans.

Before I had time to worry, Bree pulled a T-shirt and a pair of pajama bottoms from her bag and handed them over without a word or a smile.

"Thank you." I took the clothes as pinpricks screamed down the backs of my arms and through the nape of my neck. My claws shrunk quickly, and I nearly dropped the shirt. Bree looked away for the duration of my transition back into the more familiar human form she was used to, and I had to wonder if she was disgusted, or just being polite. I hoped for the latter, although she'd been under a lot of pressure I got mixed vibes from her more times than a clear message.

"I hope they're okay," I whispered, after I'd dressed. My clothes and shoes were beside the road on the other side of the camp. As soon as we got the all-clear from one of our friends I'd go get them but for the time being, we stayed low and waited.

As morning broke, the full effect of the trashed and burned-out camp came into view. Humans milled, and Peter and Crispin walked beside Osgar, who pulled on a pair of loose pants he'd picked up somewhere. Peter pulled a shirt over his head, apparently having found a way to our bags.

"Thank God," Bree said. She straightened and pulled away from our hiding place. I ran and quickly pulled my book out of the dirt. Disgusting blotches of blackening blood held clumps of dried leaves and smears of grime. I didn't bother wiping it off before running back to the others.

"His name is Michael," Osgar said, as they approached. "I've talked to him before. I knew his father."

"They have one of them," Peter said.

"What, like the humans have a henchman?" I looked from face to face, needing to be filled in.

Peter nodded. "They dragged him off about an hour ago."

I didn't respond. Of the three, Peter was the last one I wanted to talk to. I turned to Osgar.

"What will they do with him?"

"Hopefully kill him slowly," he said. "Michael will make sure he disappears. He's a good man."

Crispin walked straight up to Bree and wrapped her up in a hug. She didn't say anything, just tucked herself inside his embrace. "I'm glad you're okay," she said.

"I need to go get my clothes from last night." I turned away and started to pick a path that appeared relatively stickerless.

"I'll get them. I have to go anyway." Peter didn't wait for me to respond, just passed me up. I didn't argue.

An old truck rumbled to a stop on the road and the driver's door creaked open. Iain Logan slid out and began stomping toward us.

"You could have told me you were leaving," he yelled. "I couldn't find you anywhere in the damned castle and woke up smelling smoke." He scowled at Osgar.

"The racket was enough to wake the dead, but not the likes of you," Osgar answered. "Don't be blaming me if you go deaf when you fall asleep like a babe on the teat."

"Okay," I said, waving a hand. "I'm going to go get my bag out of that tent."

"Hold up," Iain said. He and Osgar matched stride with me but I immediately slowed. Apparently I was the only tender footed person of us all. Each pebble or stick felt like a dagger wherever I stepped, and I imagined the weight of the book in my arms was making it worse. Osgar was shirtless and shoeless but he stomped ahead with no trouble. Iain stayed back with me.

"It's been a really long night," I said. "How did you know we were out here?"

"When I saw you didn't show up last night, and I couldn't find my boneheaded brother anywhere, I thought to follow the smoke and come check the road."

"So, we were close to making it?" I asked, skirting a pile of pokey looking rocks.

"Only a short flight. A longer drive on the ground and an hour's worth of walking."

"Well, I'm glad you're here. I don't want to walk the rest of the way." I gave him a grateful smile.

"We'll get your bags and be on the way home."

11

I found it crazy what one person considered home compared to the next. To my dismay, when I thought of the word "home" the orphanage came to mind. Peter likely thought of the bookstore in London. The Logans said home and meant their castle.

The crumbled remains had been cleared and freshly napped limestone replaced missing sections of the outer curtain wall, leaving everyone in the truck astonished, peering at the towering fortress. Bree and I rode in the cab with Iain and everyone else was in the truck bed. The stone gargoyle place-markers of Osgar and Iain stared a diagonal path from above, grimaces leveled at whoever arrived. When a gargoyle is created that person's soul is moved to a different place in time and a stone figure appears. My stone gargoyle remained above our bookstore opposite Peter's, holding the wooden sign. Both sets imposed a solid message, like watch dogs.

A square gatehouse stood inside the bailey, shooting to a height well above the new wall, sporting an arched window facing each direction from the loft. A thick, metallic antenna soared into the sky from the top of the tower. Some other buildings in town had a cross or another decoration for the top of a spire, but an antenna was more functional, for sure. I couldn't tell if it was a cellular phone tower or what, but it appeared Clan Logan had gone online and mobile.

The sliding wrought-iron gate remained, parting at a center point of the cobbles to allow us passage onto the grounds.

The manor house hadn't been demolished, to my surprise, especially after Clan Logan vowed to tear it down. The walls were intact, regally sprawling amidst the construction of a new castle. Care had been taken to preserve each tree, shrub, and garden just the way I remembered them. Late season blossoms weaved through lush ivy, stands of lavender, and sweetgrass. Even in the midst of an overhaul, serene, timeless, natural beauty prevailed. Fountains still rushed in place while birds danced in baths and ground squirrels teased in thickets. In a few weeks' time, much had been done to rebuild the safety features of the castle, including erecting a new inner curtain wall, complete with corner turrets. Even with modern equipment, the rebuild of Castle Logan would take months, if not years, to complete, but they had a decent start on it.

As it was late in the afternoon, heavy equipment—earth movers and cranes—had been idled down, buckets and blades laid to rest for the day. Iain eased the truck into a slot beside the garage, and we all bailed from it as if we'd not had fresh air for weeks. Gathering our things, we didn't talk much. I shouldered my backpack, cradled the heavy tome against my chest, and nearly tripped when memories whirled as I stepped in the exact spot I'd spilled the blood of another person, just weeks ago.

Reasoning in the fact that the man had been one of the henchmen, and that he'd likely help to cause my demise if I hadn't acted to protect myself, helped ease guilt, but not all of it. The scene replayed, him wheezing his last breath, air bubbling from deep gashes in his chest, heart pumping what remained of his life into the pea gravel at my feet.

"Tessa," Bree called. Voice gentle as her eyes, she waited for me at the start of the walk leading to the manor. She knew what happened before and, as pissed as she was about the last day, she understood where I'd just gone. Weeks ago she'd screamed as she ran across the grass between where we stood and the doorway to the manor, running for her life as death on wings barreled at her from the sky. Osgar had saved her. I wouldn't have made it before the henchman smashed into her. That guy was likely still hanging around somewhere close, and he was a cannibal. I couldn't bear to think of the dangers Bree, in her tender, human form, faced in the grips of such evil.

Peter stepped in front of me, breaking my stare. "Let's go inside, yes? The Clan's been waiting for us all afternoon."

I nodded but gave him a wary look, matching his stride. "This doesn't mean you're forgiven."

He ignored me, just like I thought he would.

The cobbled walkway leading to the grotto stairs was newly lined with solar lighting and berms of moonflowers awaiting twilight, buds at the ready to spread into bloom along the path in the darkness. Nectar hung sweet on the air, mixed with woodsy scents of oaks and pines from the surrounding forest.

I had an easier time walking around the grounds for once and was amazed at how a foreboding could pass with the execution of one man. Or one Ancient, as Kai was known. Although I hadn't been the one to actually kill Kai, I'd led him to his death. The Tyrens, mystic water-beings that dwelled in the cavernous grotto on the castle grounds, had been waiting for the opportunity to get close enough to Kai to literally squeeze the life from his body. I'd never forget the sound of flesh giving way to extreme pressure, or the feel of being splattered by the liquid shrapnel that followed.

Shaking off yet another flashback, I continued following Peter toward the manor, looking forward to seeing the place in a different light. Crispin and Bree had already disappeared through the front door.

Petra leaned against the jamb, arms crossed, obviously waiting for Peter to come inside. I knew better than to think she'd be waiting on me, too. We'd gotten off to a rocky beginning. Petra liked to push my buttons, and I'd retaliated by busting her lip. I'd tried to make it right with her, but she didn't like the possibility of her twin brother being involved with me. There wasn't much to worry about between Peter and me just then, though considering the last time Petra saw us, Peter and I seemed much closer. Peter stepped aside and gestured for me to take the front steps first.

"Hi," I offered, coming to the top of the steps. I figured I would try to be amicable. Maybe start things off on the right foot this time.

Petra acted as if she hadn't seen or heard me, diving into a bear hug with Peter the second he topped the stairs. I kept walking inside, not surprised, but a little hurt by her continuing attitude with me. I was ready to write off the twisted twins right then. They could have each other.

Osgar broke out with a huge grin when he saw me. He stood with Crispin, Bree, and Iain at the back of the windowed foyer, the four of them turning to acknowledge my entrance, which was a lot more to my liking.

I hadn't talked with Iain much, though I was under the impression he was another of Osgar's brothers. The way the Clan acted signified to me that it didn't matter if they were cousins, uncles, or brothers, they were family, and that needed no definition. I put my book on an end table and set down my bag, hurrying over, craving interaction of a friendlier nature than what greeted me back in the doorway. The sun's rays lacked the strength to extend much past the first set of windows, so no one was affected, leaving us all to appear just as human as Bree. I found comfort in the mock normalcy.

Iain held out a huge hand, which I shook with a grin. He had the same strong jaw and features as the other Scots in the room, although he kept his hair cut short. He wore a polo and khakis, a contrast to the traditional get-ups Osgar and Crispin wore. Crispin tromped through the house in a rather primitive-looking wrapped kilt. Osgar always wore soft, handmade boots from the most buttery looking leather. Usually he wore a kilt but sometimes he wore pants from an unidentified manufacturer. One thing all three men had in common was a tall, strong build. Although Bree was a few inches taller than me, she was just as dwarfed as I was standing next to them. I wondered if my grin matched hers in charmed awe. It certainly felt like it did.

"It's nice to finally meet you."

"The pleasure's mine." Iain dipped his head, bowing a little. I stared, briefly aware of Crispin sliding a protective arm over Bree's shoulders.

Osgar laughed, stepping toward me. Just when I expected him to extend a hand the way Iain had, he pulled me into a big hug.

"Glad to have you back, Tessa. You look well." The warmth of his words and actions was perfectly matched by the roll of his brogue. A hug from Osgar was like a warm blanket after being caught in a December rain. I didn't fidget, but tightened my arms around his back, digging my face into his chest. He responded with a chuckle, rocking me a little.

"I missed you," I told him.

"Same here, lass." He pulled back, grinning. His smile was kind. Big-brotherly. I could see the two of us growing to be closer and that did my heart a lot of good.

"Anyone hungry? We had dinner prepared, in case the road got to your appetites." Osgar released me, gesturing toward the massive, wooden double-doors to the great hall. I turned to get a look at Peter, who remained back by the entryway, watching me over the top of Petra's turned shoulder. Cutting ties with him was going to be tough when it was knee-jerk to see if he was okay with my plans, or at least coming along.

"I'm starving," Bree answered.

Peter gestured that he'd be along soon by nodding and holding up a finger, but Petra stood with her back to us, not bothering to acknowledge Osgar had said anything. I turned to retrieve the book from where I'd left it, following the others to the dining area.

The first of two ornate, wooden buffet cabinets held plates of warm, smoked fish, sliced bread, fried potatoes, and some sort of salad that looked like it had chunks of tomatoes and nuts in it. The second held silverware, plates, napkins, and drink pitchers with tumblers arranged neatly across the top. My stomach rumbled in approval of the wonderful aromas. I set my book on the table and filed into place behind Iain at the buffet and filled a plate.

By the time I took a seat, Peter was getting food while he talked with Osgar. He sat beside me, as we occupied one end of a thick, rustic table. Light poured from three chandeliers hanging from thick chains that disappeared into darkness above. Dishes clattered, forks scraped, and small-talk burst through pockets of silence.

"Wasn't Petra hungry?" I asked quietly, hoping my voice would get lost in the din and only Peter could hear. I hated the way I had to know how soon I'd find myself back under the bus when she was around.

"Apparently not," he said, matching my volume.

"So what was with the top secret convo? Is she okay?"

"She's all right. Just not in the mood to be around people tonight."

"Is it because I'm here?" It was a good question. Petra seemed pleased as punch to see Peter.

He didn't answer right away which gave me my answer.

"Really? You're kidding. That redefines juvenile." How hard could it have been to join in? She could have ignored me and talked with everyone else for all I cared rather than causing a scene with her absence.

"You two were in a fight at some point?" he said. His voice was gentle, and I could tell he worked hard to ensure I knew he wasn't being judgmental. That was good. His sister cornered that market the first time I saw her in human form. Oddly enough, I preferred Petra Garged Out. In person, she looked deceptively sweet.

"I thought you knew that. She said some hurtful stuff in the alley behind the bookstore the day Kai brought me back here for the first time. She wouldn't quit mouthing off and I warned her to leave me alone. She didn't. You saw her afterward. I mean, she rode up front with you with a split lip," I reasoned.

"She wouldn't tell me what happened."

"Ah," I drawled. "Well, now you know."

Peter didn't seem angry that I'd smacked his sister, which was good. After all, Petra had continued to pick at the fact that I was an orphan that day. I'd found out I had a brother once and that he was adopted without me. He'd recently been killed in Iraq. I'd only felt guilty about pounding her for a second and thinking about what she'd said still pissed me off. I shifted in my seat, picking at my food.

"I'm not mad, Tessa." Peter was looking at me, but I kept my eyes on my plate.

"Thanks." I smiled, but it felt weak. "Not that it matters what the hell you think."

He huffed and shook his head. "That said, it would be nice if you apologized."

"Are you freaking kidding me? Absolutely out of the question." Whisper-shouting drew a couple curious looks. I stared at Peter, feeling my lips draw into a tight line. Voice low, I continued calmly. "I know she's your sister and all, but if she's trying to play for sympathy, we're at a stalemate here. Unless you're buying in."

"I've an announcement," Osgar said, calling everyone's attention. I turned from the conversation with Peter, happy for a break in the tension.

"Our home has been recovered after centuries of loss. We have removed the old signage from the gates, as you noticed, I'm sure."

I nodded along with everyone else. A low-pitched "woot" rang from Crispin's side of the table. He grinned.

Osgar paced to the head of the room where a red cloth was draped over a partition. "I've had something created for my beloved clan." He grasped the edges of the heavy material and pulled it free.

I gasped softly. A beautifully carved slab of blond wood had been engraved with the name "LOGAN" in heavy lettering. A thick border of runes framed the outside. About three feet tall by at least five feet in length, the new property nameplate was huge, a gorgeous creation to mark the grounds as belonging to Clan Logan, once again.

Iain started a short round of applause as we stood.

Osgar smiled. "We'll announce the reclaiming of our home with a gala to be held Saturday evening beside the grotto pools."

I smiled. The more in attendance, the better. At least one person would have more information to help find Teigan.

On a purely childish, indulgent level, the prospect of plain old fun was inviting. Holding a party beside the hot springs was perfect. We could remain in human form during the event down in the grotto. Some mineral in the water and rock nulled the transformation during the night. I'd be able to wear a dress without the fear of wings and scales tearing it up. The event might require formal dress. I found myself happily munching away, looking forward to it.

When we were full of good food and caught up with the plans for the rebuild, I was exhausted and ready for some quiet. I struggled with guilt that Teigan wasn't around to see his family celebrate their freedom. No one had spoken his name, although I was sure they had to be thinking of him. Time droned on and I remained in the dining hall out of good manners. By the time everyone else was finished up, I was fighting yawns that I hoped didn't show. Bree looked just as spent as me after the sleepless night and all the excitement and fighting.

Peter didn't try to talk to me again. We rose and helped clear the dinner table and clean up the kitchen. When I went back to the dining room he'd disappeared.

I'd known the manor was larger than it seemed, but the next day Bree and I were given the nickel tour of the house and grounds by Iain and Crispin. It was easier to see the beauty of the place when I wasn't led in as a captive, and I was certain Bree felt the same way. The last time either of us had been up to the castle we'd nearly been killed. Bree was kidnapped by Kai and I'd been coerced into staying there so he wouldn't hurt her. She was the only "family" I felt I had at the time.

Things had changed. I considered Clan Logan my family, and they were. We were a kindred breed; no longer human. Bree remained my best friend, or sister, as we claimed, even though we weren't related by blood. I was an orphan and she was the only person on the planet I trusted. Even though I had a new family, my trust needed time to develop.

Crispin was easily my favorite of the clan. I'd known him and Osgar for the same amount of time. Osgar could be gruff, but still smiled easily. Crispin came back to London with us and our friendship grew deeper by the day. Iain was quieter than Crispin, who laughed and joked around a lot. Iain regarded situations with thoughtful silence, but when he did speak I listened with intent, trying to know him more.

Iain had one of those voices that was low and sweet. He could have done voiceover work or read steamy characters for audio books. His looks matched up. He was the only member of the clan who had hair above his shoulders and was smooth shaved.

He wore shirts that fit snugly over his chest, showing off just a little bit but not to the point he flaunted himself. The thing I liked best was his smile. It reminded me of Chris Hemsworth. He was impressively well mannered. I hadn't opened a door in his presence since we'd met, which took some getting used to. My face flushed a lot when we were together. I accepted each courtesy and thanked him, loving being in the presence of such a gentleman after being cooped up with Peter for so long. Peter had started off on a good roll, but as soon as I asserted myself and began doing my own thing he regarded me as something other than merely a mousy girl. And of course there was the discretion when he allowed Adam to exist and did nothing to stop his kidnapping, rape, and murdering. That was the difference. Peter knew me to be the potentially lethal gargoyle I'd become. Iain and I were so new together that he still treated me the way Peter used to, when we got along well. I didn't like the thought of Iain developing an opinion that made him view me differently. I wanted him to know the old Tessa, the girl who was so much like Bree. Sadly, the girl I used to be only made fleeting appearances. I felt her though, like the tales of people missing a limb. She was right there, just out of touch and fading, leaving behind a phantom itch.

I'd been right about the construction of the castle. The new manor house was being incorporated into the rebuild. Certain parts of the manor had been demolished and removed. Kai's study was gone, which made me happy. I'd been tortured in that room. The new foundation had been poured inside older, existing castle walls there and a solarium and a new library would be built in the newly cleared space, complete with a media center. A two-story east wing was revealed as we walked on, and that's where Crispin and Iain delivered our bags, so we didn't have to stay in the old room where we'd been locked up before. We'd stayed there the night before and we were both up before dawn because of remaining bad vibes. It could have been partially because we both fell asleep before nightfall, though. Four bedrooms made up the upstairs, each with their own full bathrooms. Bree's room was right next to mine. My room had a window with a clear view of the timber circle with the monoliths inside.

While we walked the grounds, we took our time watching squirrels and birds at the Roman-style fountains and flower gardens. Sunshine danced through clouds, glinting down on us at times. I didn't have a hood to pull up and my skin became transparent each time I was under a stray beam. I didn't look Bree in the eye when that happened, sure my appearance had to be disturbing for her.

Bree didn't let on if she was sickened when I became all seethrough and grey. For that I was grateful. She didn't look at Crispin when we stood in the sun, though. The tendons in his jaw worked against the darkened muscle there. I felt bad for him, his form bared that way in her presence. We didn't talk much, just walked and looked around until the clouds built again.

A neat swath had been mowed around the standing stones. Twists of ivy still crawled up the sides of the limestone, but the thickets and overgrowth had been cut back. A path was beaten into the grass from frequent walks to the site.

The driveway had new stone pavers rather than the gravel from before and the walkways all matched. The carriage house had four newly installed garage doors on the longest side. When we walked past, a soft mewling sound came from the back of the building.

"What was that?" Bree stopped, looking toward the garage.

"A cat had a litter back there last month," Iain said, gesturing to the rear of the building.

"Hoolet bait," Crispin said with a wicked grin. Bree slugged him in the arm and headed in the direction of the meowing kittens. I followed.

"Way to pour on the charm," Iain said as he passed Crispin.

"It was a joke." Crispin laughed. "Lighten up."

"I like owls," I said, trying to diffuse the tension a little.

A small hole had been dug beneath the concrete wall. Bree and I crouched, and she peered inside.

"Oh my," she said as she stuck her hand in the hole. Slowly, she withdrew her arm and brought out the cutest little ball of striped grey fluff I'd ever seen. She cradled the kitten and got to her feet. "There was just one in there."

"Mayhap the owl thing wasn't so far off," said Iain.

"I prefer to think he's an only child." I reached and stroked the tiny cat's fur. Crispin leaned forward.

"Hello, little one." The kitten sunk back into the crook of Bree's elbow and hissed, all fangs and venom.

"You're scaring her!" Bree twisted away.

"Her?" he asked.

"She's too pretty to be a boy."

I laughed. She was dead serious, which made the statement too damned funny.

We started back toward the manor, no one questioning whether the kitten had just become an instant house guest. I grinned inwardly. Seeing the kitten grabbing at strands of Bree's hair as she cooed to her about being safer from owls inside, made my morning. Crispin rolled his eyes, and I burst out laughing again. It was all very good for my soul.

When we walked in, Osgar was making lunch in the kitchen. Bree took off to her room with the cat. Iain popped a paper towel loose and used it to hand me a cucumber sandwich and took one for himself.

"The place looks great," I told Osgar. "You guys have been working hard."

"Thank you," he said. We sat at the breakfast counter. "The design is at a standstill until I find a better indication of the old layout." He bit into his sandwich, chewed, and moved the bite into the pocket of his cheek. "My memories are from childhood; a long time ago. I want it to be as close as we can get it, considering."

I flashed back to my book and the silvery map with the tiny detail. "Do you have some sort of magnifying glass? Like, a really strong one?"

"That's a random question," he said, smiling and chewing.

"Funny thing is I was asking my book some questions a couple days ago, and it drew the outer bailey of your castle. It kept going and the lines got so close together that I can't make them out now." I took another bite. There was no way I would tell them the map was revealed when I asked about Teigan's location. I didn't want to upset them by bringing up their missing clansman. The book showing me a map meant Teigan was hidden somewhere on the grounds. If Osgar had a good magnifying glass, I could search the map. He could check the old castle floor plan. We'd both be happy.

Osgar stopped eating. "What sort of questions were you asking that book of yours?" He wasn't smiling.

"Oh, just being curious about what you guys are doing up here," I said. *Lie.* I looked away, hating the way the statement just poured out of my mouth like dark water. I forced myself to take a bite of the sandwich.

"Well, let's see what you've got," said Iain.

"Okay. I'll go get it as soon as we're done."

Osgar gave me a curious look but nodded with a slight grin.

After a little hike up to the east wing to retrieve the book from under my bed, I toted it into the kitchen and spread the pages, laying it flat on the counter. Just like before, the outer lines of the curtain walls, corner towers, and bailey were clear. At such a small scale, the detail of the castle was just too tiny to see. Osgar held a round glass over the page, but sighed, moving the magnifier around.

"It's no good. It's a wee scale at best."

"Maybe there's something more powerful at the library? Like

one of those old microfiche things? They had one back at the Home when I was a kid. The nuns hung onto it because a couple of them needed it to read old archived stuff."

"Hold on," Iain said. He opened the pantry and rummaged through a bin. He returned to the counter with a flashlight. With the magnifier a few inches above the page, he shone the light through the glass. "There we are," he said, moving around over the page. "The light filters out the finer lines. At least this way one can see the more prominent detail." He handed the implements over to Osgar, who immediately took position over the page.

"Nice." After a moment he sighed and set the flashlight down. "I'll just make a few notes and figure the scale here. "This is fantastic, Tessa. Thank you."

"Sure," I said. "So, are all the rooms there? I mean, even old stuff in the basement and all?"

"It seems rather thorough. The labels aren't legible, although that might be because they aren't in Gaelic. If we get the chance to get a stronger magnifier, we'll be able to read it all."

"We could order one online," I offered. I needed to do some shopping anyway since I didn't have anything to wear to the gala. "That reminds me. This party you're throwing. Is it going to be fancy? How many people will be here?"

"It is formal," Iain said. "You'll need a gown." He was matter of fact.

"I'll have to get online for a dress too then, so I'll look for a magnifier."

Osgar nodded, closing the book. "This is the first time in centuries I've seen this book. Thank you for sharing this with us."

"Of course," I said, as he left. Hopefully the map would also show me the way to find Teigan. Then he would be extra happy. They all would, including me. I grabbed the book and was headed toward the door when Iain stopped me with a soft touch against the back of my arm. I turned.

"A gown. Not a dress." He winked.

"Noted." I nodded.

Dress shopping online wasn't nearly as fun as it would have been in person at Lakeline Mall in Austin. There was a killer shop there, and I never could remember the name, but they had the most fantastic gowns and cocktail dresses. I lied about having a date for prom one time just to feel okay about trying on one of their dresses. The sales lady was too kind, going out of her way to give me a bottle of water and hand selecting the perfect shoes for me to try on. She had a purely victimized look on her face when I left without buying anything. That was me, broke and guilty as charged.

Hours in front of a computer got dull quickly when I was surrounded by Scottish countryside, Highland foods and men who belonged on the covers of romance novels. Their unawareness of that last tidbit made the men of Logan Castle that much more appealing to a wide-eyed American girl. The Clan members were gargoyles and had been for centuries. There was something dangerously raw and downright animalistic about them. They treated Bree and me differently than any other man or teenage boy ever had. We didn't lift our own bags, open doors for ourselves, or pull out a chair at a dining table. They were old-school, treating us as the cherished, fairer sex, and the old-fashioned manners and courtesy compiled the most amazing charm. It was a lot to take in.

Crispin, I totally got. He was head over heels for Bree, and it was mutual. I knew he was one of the reasons she stayed in the UK.

If the opportunity arose to consider going back to the States —something I wasn't allowed to do—she simply called her parents and talked to them for long periods of time, catching up, and assuring them she was okay. She wanted to stay. They sometimes asked to talk with me, which was a huge treat. Her parents and brother were the only way I knew how a real family worked. I told myself they only wanted to talk to me to really check up on Bree, but hoped they cared. They doted on me by sending what they called "care packages" when they mailed stuff to the bookstore for Bree. We couldn't exactly tell them I'd been changed into a gargoyle, but we could tell them I simply didn't want to come back to the States. After all, what did I have to miss? Keeping everyone at an arm's length seemed to work out better in the long run. When Bree's parents got old and died it wouldn't be as hard on my heart. I would keep on living the ageless life of a nineteen-year-old gargoyle. The same thing would happen as Bree aged without me, but I didn't allow myself to think about watching her grow old.

She'd picked out a great dress hours ago and left to hang out with Crispin. My patience was drained. Bree looked great in anything. At my wit's end, I selected an elegant, black gown with some rhinestones in a size smaller than I'd worn pre-gargoyle, added it to the cart, tossed in a pair of overly strappy heels and called the excursion complete, with next-day shipping.

The front door shut below, and I scurried to my window just in time to see Iain walking around the side of the manor. The sun was shining bright and some fresh air sounded great. I decided to go on a little mission to get to know the clan better, and Iain was the one I'd spent the least time with. I tossed myself into running gear and chased him down just outside the busted-up bailey wall, where I'd never had the pleasure of exploring.

"Hey!" I called. He smiled, waiting for me to catch up. I trotted beside him and stopped, looking around. "What's up? It's gorgeous out here."

My jaw dropped before he had a chance to answer. A picturesque stone stable was tucked beside a proud grove of trees that stood out from the rest of the forest. Separate runs were attached to the side of the barn where feisty horses tossed their heads and nickered to Iain.

"You've got horses!"

"Do you ride?" He scooted over on the trail, making room for me.

"Heck, no. I've never touched a horse before. They're huge." We made it to the first pen and I looked up into the face of a black horse with shiny eyes. His neck was arched, and he stuck his head over the top rail of the pen, about a foot above me. He smelled salty.

"I thought you were from Texas," he accused.

"I'm from Austin, actually. It's just not the same."

"So no 'yeehaw' or 'yippie kai yay'?"

I laughed. "No. Austin's more about music, art, and college. It's the rest of Texas that has tumbleweeds and cowpokes."

"These horses are bred for hunting." He reached way up and scratched the horse's face hard with his fingers, on the flat part of his face between his eyes. The horse bobbed his head, enjoying the feel.

I stared. "He's gorgeous," I said.

"Give him some love then, lass. He won't know unless you show him."

I put my hand out so he could smell me, wondering if it was like a dog and I needed to show good intention. The horse actually snorted a big smell of my hand followed by two quick little breaths. I smiled, looking at his face. His pointed ears were forward, and he looked right at me with deep, kind eyes.

"Oh Iain, I'm in love with him." His muzzle was the softest thing ever. He bent his neck and stuck his nose right on top of my head, still smelling like a curious dog. I laughed hard, trying not to move.

"Horses have great senses about people. He's just getting to know you. He can tell a lot about a person just from his sense of smell." Iain rubbed at the horse's jaw then scratched behind an ear. "Would you like to learn to ride?"

"Really? I mean, yes. For sure." I eyed the top of the horse's shoulders warily. I'd be way up there, but it looked easy on TV.

"It will be an honor to show you, lass. We'll begin soon."

"Great." We grinned at each other. I allowed the horse one last smell and scrubbed his head, then stepped back. "Well, I'd better get back." I didn't want to wear out my welcome or appear desperate for his attention.

"I'll see you for supper, then?" he asked.

I nodded. "See you then."

THE NEXT DAY flew by and I fought nervousness until about noon when our package arrived and I saw that I'd done a good job selecting the size for my gown and shoes. I busied myself helping with decorations. The castle grounds were gorgeous when we were done, with candle lanterns and uplighting along the cobbled walks and gardens. Before I knew it, the time had come to head across the courtyard and down the stone stairway to the underground cavern.

I was amazed at how many people could fit inside the Grotto. We'd lined the stairs with twinkle lights that morning. I was a little crushed that I wouldn't be able to see the finished product all lit up against the moonflowers and hedges, but we'd leave them up to enjoy later. It was a small price to pay really, to be able to enjoy a night in human form, and in a black formal gown to boot. I was sequined and bejeweled, done-up and made-up, standing next to the horseshoe shaped bar with Bree.

"Cheers," she said. We tapped our champagne glasses together gently. I delighted in the delicate "ching" sound as we smiled at one another and took the first sips.

The stream sunk and boiled inside each pool, lit with blue, purple, and green bulbs. More soft ground lighting traced walkways and directed people to islands of hors d'oeuvres, carafes of water, and buckets of chilled champagne bottles.

"This is all very well done," I said.

"If we don't say so, ourselves." Bree tapped her flute against mine again.

The humidity was low inside the cavern because the place had been overhauled with new ventilation after the typhoon gutted the place when the Tyrens killed Kai. A couple new holes in the ceiling had been drilled and turned into vents with fans that hummed into the din of gushing water. To accommodate the gargoyle-types, full dressing rooms were built by the restroom and we'd taken advantage of them, slipping into our gowns and doing our hair and makeup in the Grotto. It had been doubly good because we were able to get into the sound room and upload playlists to the music system. The volume was low, but a mix of good music could be heard in little breaks in conversations. I peered at the mineral stream, wondering if we might be graced with the presence of one of the mystical water beings during the event. The water had been thick with Tyrens the last time I was in the Grotto.

Along the bar top, little satellite stations were set up on lazy Susans, containing neatly arranged embossed napkins and little plates of chocolates. We indulged, despite my guilt after remembering what happened the last time I drank anything with alcohol in it. It was sort of an accident in the first place, but I'd almost been killed. We were as safe as we'd get in current company so I relaxed some and enjoyed the bubbles, although the thought I was underage as an American niggled at the back of my conscience.

Bree would turn 21 in November. I was 19. By American standards I broke the law enjoying the champagne, but in the UK, I was old enough to take part in all the festivities with our British friends, all of which were completely dapper in tuxedos. No kilts. Osgar looked modern, which amazed me, and gave me a different perspective of the ancient Scot. He pulled it off with just as much comfort as he did loafing in his old boots and kilt.

Peter hadn't made it down yet, although it wasn't quite dark out. We had to be sure to clear the last of the steps into the Grotto to ensure the minerals could work their magic and render us human. He had about 45 minutes to arrive and change, or else he'd be Garged Out when he came down, and naked until he made it into the bathroom to change.

I grinned and snorted a quick laugh.

"What's so funny?" Bree asked. She placed her glass on the bar, smiling at me.

"Nothing really. I just imagined Peter arriving late."

"Oh." She wrinkled her nose.

"Like he'd come down and change in the doorway, wearing nothing." I sipped. "That would be fantastic."

"He's too careful for that. He'll be here. Don't worry."

"I'm not worried about it," I said. "Really, it doesn't matter if he shows up or not. I can have just as good a time."

"I'm glad to hear it."

"Really?"

"Don't take this the wrong way, but honestly, I've never really liked that guy."

I loved that about Bree. She was a Pisces and made me believe in the traits that clung to her sign. She had a sense about people sometimes. This was one of them.

"You're dead right about that one." I nodded. "He was good and deceptive for the first year, and he got more and more controlling. It was easy to let him boss me around when I first got here because I was scared and alone, and he was just all there was. He's good looking so I was crushing on him like crazy last year."

Bree gazed past me toward the door. "Too bad everything that looks that good can't be as awesome on the inside."

I turned to look. No one was there. I looked back at her with raised brows. "Not funny."

"He's fun to look at," she said with an ornery grin. "But you can do so much better."

"You're right. Look at us," I said, laughing, gesturing to she and I, in all our formal splendor. "We look like money."

"Yeah, we do," she agreed. Our glasses touched again and were nearly empty somehow.

"So, do you have a hard time understanding these guys? I was talking to Iain yesterday and he probably thinks I'm stupid or something. I have to wait and process for a second before I can answer sometimes."

"Yes." She tossed a mass of long curls behind her shoulder. "I suppose they think we're both slow."

I laughed again. No one would ever think Bree was slow on her most sluggish of days.

"It's yin and yang," Crispin said, approaching. He grabbed a champagne flute, sipped, and then waived it in an arc between Bree and me.

"But we both look fabulous," Bree added, with a wink. She wore a cream and white gown that contrasted again my black dress.

"Indeed," he said. "A couple of goddesses gracing our Grotto." He leaned against the bar, so relaxed in his tux that he looked sort of GQ. Bree stared.

"Really?" I said.

She smiled and looked at her glass, suddenly fascinated with the little bubbles.

"Well, it's about time." Crispin said.

I turned in time to see Peter step from the bathroom. He looked around, gazing right past me. Stepping to the left of the restroom doorway, he nodded at Crispin then stopped. Petra emerged from the ladies room in a brilliant, fire-red gown and took the arm he offered her. The two walked into the room together, Peter nodding and shaking hands, and Petra beaming and hugging people. I looked away, forcing myself to concentrate on the other guests. I took notice of the people I wanted to make it a point to meet before the night was through.

"How did they get in here?" I'd been watching, and they hadn't come through the front entrance like we had.

"Through the back." Crispin shrugged.

"There's a back?" Last year I'd been stuck in the Grotto, half dead, worried sick about never being found alive, and forced to walk up the stone steps at the main entrance with gosh only knew how many sprains, contusions, and possible broken bones that would never see a doctor. "You don't say."

"Sure do, lass. It's that way," he said, and gestured roughly to his left side. "Behind the stairs. We found it last week and cleared it out." He grinned and swilled his champagne. "Leads straight to where Kai's study used to be inside the manor. We installed full baths."

I nodded. Bree and I had dressed for the evening in the ladies room for no reason.

Clusters of people stood against the bar and walls, admiring the pools and talking. The groups varied in size from a couple men or women on up. The largest group was central in the room far from the pools. Conversation was probably easier there, away from the sound of the stream. I craned my neck to get a look at them, but so many had their backs to me and they were mostly men, so they were a big wall of black suit jackets. Short bursts of laughter erupted from their direction.

Bree followed my gaze. "Who is that?" she asked. We shared the love of meeting new people.

"No idea, but it seems like a good group to check out."

Peter grew closer. I had every intention of heading off before he made it to where we stood. I downed the last of the warm glass I held and stepped around Bree to help myself to my second. When we'd ordered our outfits I'd picked out really tall heels and so had Bree. I was still a shrimp, despite my efforts. Oddly enough, it was pretty easy to walk in them.

"Excuse me ladies," Crispin said. I followed his gaze to where Osgar stood by the little gate leading behind the bar, waving him over. Crispin gave Bree's arm a warm looking little caress as he left.

"Shall we?" I handed her a fresh drink.

"Thanks," she said, following me away from the bar. From the corner of my eye I watched Peter's head turn as we left. We skirted the group and I found a little space just big enough for us to fit. As we approached, the man next to us turned with a smile. The petite, redhead woman at his side didn't. Instead, she looked at my dress and up at my face, then out toward the crowded room.

Oh, screw you, girly.

"Meh," Bree intoned, quietly so only I could hear.

We beamed as we met the combined gaze of the others.

Opposite us stood a perfectly gorgeous woman. When she saw me she lit up. Familiarity accosted us both at the same time.

She'd been at the tow yard trying to steal my book. The bitch had nerve showing up at the Grotto. I was incensed that she was there, but at the same time something wasn't right with her recognizing me. I'd been in gargoyle form and a normal human would have no idea I was the same creature. She locked eyes with me and held my gaze, though, and I had no doubt we were on the same page.

She wasn't someone I would ever bump into on the street. Although she wore heels, she was still extra petite but curved perfectly. Her dress was more than a gown. The hem was high in the front and tapered to floor length in the back, hanging in a fall of the softest looking material that was deep emerald at the strapless corset bodice, fading in a rich palate of earth tones until it ended in lavender at her feet. Pearl drop diamonds hung from each earlobe and a larger, matching stone gleamed in the hollow of her throat, which was accented perfectly by her shoulder-length, glistening, black, Pantene-commercial hair.

Oh, barf, I thought. She was too perfect. I considered how making her bleed some would change her whole façade.

She was still looking at me. It was the first time someone shorter than me looked down their nose as they regarded me. Her eyes gleamed the same color as the top of her dress. Her whole appearance was simply regal.

I wondered if she had taken me in the same way I did her. I tried not to let the animosity ooze forth and sipped a little champagne. A fizzy little droplet splattered onto my chin. Somehow, I doubted she cared too much. There's no way someone so "put together" as she was would spend the time sizing me up. I tried to be cool, wiping at my chin with a quick brush of the backs of my fingers, hoping to look demure. Bree snorted softly beside me, apparently watching the whole event. I rolled my eyes at her, but she smiled beautifully at the woman, awaiting an introduction. I lost the audacity that carried me toward the group of strangers we stood amongst. A blonde girl with her hair jerked back in a bun so tight she was cat-eyed glanced at us, sucking in her cheeks so she looked extra pouty and pursed. I wanted to groan.

"Genevieve," Miss Perfect Book Thief stated.

Being ever polite, Bree spoke up. "I'm Bree, and this is my best friend, Tessa." I tried to match the smile Bree had pasted on her face but came up short.

"Hi," I said.

Genevieve looked from Bree to me then smiled, showing shining, pearl white teeth. "It's nice to meet you both. What brings you north?" she asked in a very Irish accent. I hid a bristle. Why did everyone have to be exotic? I felt dull and common standing close to her.

"Cody Allen," one of the men said. He stepped toward me and stuck out a hand. I looked into one of the most genuine faces I'd seen in months. He had a small, scraggly goatee and big eyes that were dark hazel. I took his hand, shaking it while his smile grew to infect my face. I didn't let go and neither did he. Soon the handshake turned into a little match of charm, both of us strangers to one another, but willing to do something a little silly to break up all the stuffy in the room.

"I'm Tessa," I gave his hand a final squeeze to end our little game. "It's great to meet you, Cody."

"Likewise."

"You're American," stated Bree.

"Guilty." He said it with a grin that admitted his guilt was intentional as he offered Bree his hand.

"What brings you to the UK?" If he told me he'd found true love I'd have to hide a facepalm.

"I graduated aeronautical engineering school at UT three summers ago and treated myself to a backpacking adventure."

"UT? Sweet," Bree said. "We're from Austin." She gestured between she and I.

"I went to UT for college, but I'm not from Austin. I'm a Colorado native."

"That explains the accent." I said, half teasing.

"Said the Texan."

I liked the guy. He was quick. It was confirmed; I was a fan of Cody the Coloradan.

"What a sweet reunion," Genevieve chirruped.

I smiled. Genevieve didn't look jealous, but I imagined she was the type.

"Must have been one heck of a backpacking trip. You're still here." I hated to point out the obvious, but he was standing next to a complete contradiction to his nature. Genevieve's perky "lording it over" demeanor had dropped out and was replaced by blatant jealousy that she was no longer able to hide.

"I didn't realize quite what I was searching for." Cody put his arm around the petite Genevieve. She seemed to calm some. "Fate works in strange ways. I was about to call it a trip and head home to start a new job at Boeing, then I met Gen and found true love."

I closed my eyes. Bree scooted closer and all but elbowed me. "I love stories like that," she said. I held my tongue.

Genevieve perked right up, grinning like she'd won a marathon. If she was one inch shorter, or Cody one taller, it wouldn't have worked out.

"How do you find yourselves here at the gala?" I already knew, but had to ask. She was here for the book.

"One never refuses an invitation from Clan Logan. You?"

"You must truly be a very old friend of theirs." I had to say it. I had two advantages over her. One was the book and the other was youth. "Bree and I are friends of the family, as well." I said, trying my best to sound obnoxiously polite.

"Clan Logan? Really?" she said.

"Very close friends," Osgar said, just over my shoulder. He and Crispin stood behind us. I wondered how long they'd been there, a little embarrassed at my antics. Genevieve made an odd "mmhh" sound, as if considering his answer deeply.

"Ladies, won't you come freshen your drinks? The entertainment will begin shortly," Crispin said.

"Nice to meet you," I told her. She was on my radar and would be there as long as it took to figure out why she wanted my book, and to make sure she never laid a perfectly polished finger on it. She just looked at me with a knowing, half-smile.

"Bye, Cody. It was great meeting you."

He smiled warmly and nodded.

Osgar put a gentle hand on my elbow and I stepped in front of him, heading back the way we'd come.

"What's up?" I whispered.

"You want to watch that bitch," he replied.

"Yeah. She tried to steal my book from the tow yard."

"There's more, trust me. Don't turn your back with her in arm's length of ya."

"Well, why the hell did you invite her?" I couldn't help but be astonished.

"To keep the peace," he replied. We were back at the bar and Crispin and Bree drew within earshot.

"The centuries have taught me that although they're not my favorite to share space with, it's best to keep them in the social circle, lest Gen get her knickers in a twist."

I outright laughed. The word "knickers" mixed wonderfully with champagne. And I'd recently learned a lesson in respecting prior "arrangements" in the UK. Genevieve probably respected the invitation for the same reason and showed up to keep the Logans in focus. I sipped lightly to slow the bubbles going to my head. I was feeling rather light-hearted, which was good, but I needed to keep my wits handy.

Musicians settled into heavy chairs on a stage at the back of the room, past where I'd once woken in a soggy, bleeding heap, to meet my first Tyren. The stream had eddied to form a pool there but the river bed had moved recently, likely an effect of the flooding that happened there. The area was clear and open, and a huge wooden dance floor ran the length of the new space at the far side of the bar and ended at the stage, where the band readied their instruments. An enormous pendant crystal chandelier hung on four chains anchored into the limestone ceiling.

A mousy looking girl worked to remove a cello from a wheeled case. The musicians wore tuxedos with tails, even the two female players. I'd never been to an event that was ritzy enough to offer such a band and I couldn't wait until they started. I wondered if people would dance, and caught myself looking around for Peter, but quickly got control and looked back toward the group around me. Petra's red dress caught my eye as she and Peter approached. To my delight, so did Iain. He flanked Peter as he approached, grinning when he saw me.

I couldn't help smiling back. He held out a hand in a flamboyant gesture and I walked toward him, straight past Peter, who assumed I was coming toward him. Petra actually grunted softly as I whooshed past Peter and took Iain's hand. He spun me around and I was thankful there wasn't much left in my glass. We bowed to one another, grinning like dorks.

"You look magical, lass. Simply beautiful." He kissed my hand.

"Look at you all dressed up," I said. "You look great. Very dapper." It was true. Iain was the definition of a beautiful man in a tuxedo. Almost a little *too* beautiful.

"We should dance," he said.

"I'm not a very good dancer," I admitted with a shy laugh. "And it's been forever, but indeed, sir, we should. I'd be delighted."

Peter, who was hardly out of earshot, huffed a little. Petty as it was, I was glad he'd heard us. The last time I'd danced, and the first for that matter, was with him back at the bookstore. On my nineteenth birthday. I was totally infatuated with Peter at that point. We danced the majority of the night and it had been so amazing we hadn't noticed when the music stopped.

"Let's start with a slow song?" I grinned, anticipating the feeling of being swept around the dance floor. I could handle being Cinderella for a night.

"Of course," he said.

I took my place beside Bree, and Iain joined the group. He picked a fresh, sweaty champagne flute from a tray, took my empty glass and handed me a fresh one.

"Thanks," I said, intending to drink under half of it.

Bree snorted at me, holding up her nearly empty glass. "Don't feel bad." She grinned.

Petra squeezed into the group right beside Iain. I wanted to dump my drink down the front of her dress. "See any interesting gents?" she asked Iain.

"A couple that could be my type," he said, grinning.

"Do tell." Petra's left brow quirked slightly.

"I'll give a full report." He smiled and sipped.

Bree nodded at me, giving me a loaded expression that said, *"It all makes sense now."* Conversations between us, typical best friend talk about guys and stuff included our wonderment at why Iain was single. He had to be in his mid-twenties. The fact he wasn't married with a couple kids was surprising. Iain was off the table if I was looking for a date.

Which I wasn't.

I grinned back at her. If I hadn't overheard the conversation between Iain and Petra, I never would have guessed he was gay. Except for the clothes and the perfect hair. And the way he looked at the other guys around us. Okay yeah, I decided, I could see it. For some odd reason, I felt ten times more comfortable around him then, knowing I'd been friend-zoned.

Peter stepped up beside Petra and I looked for a reason to leave as the group continued small talk.

Genevieve wasn't very far away from us. A man I hadn't

noticed before stood next to her. He must have just arrived because there's no way I would have missed him before. His skin, or maybe his entire body, sort of glowed. He had a silver-white outline like a cloud in front of the sun, but not quite that bright. I glanced at others around him and no one stared or even acted like they saw the iridescence outlining his body. I blinked, holding my eyes closed a little longer before checking him out again. It didn't work. The guy still glimmered a little around the edges, and the effect seemed to radiate toward the center of his chest. I wondered if I was seeing his aura. I'd watched a special on TV that talked about how certain people had that gift. His hair was white-blond but his eyes were so dark brown they could have been made of jet. I blushed some when he smiled at me after he caught me staring. The glow faded in and out as he moved. I made a mental note to track him throughout the night, so he couldn't leave before I got a chance to investigate who he was.

Genevieve traced his line of sight and grabbed his biceps, squeezing until he looked away and at her instead. I bit back a grin, oddly satisfied.

Our playlist faded, and the sound of strings tuning squealed into the room. People started migrating in the direction of the band. Bree and Crispin had joined up again, Petra and Peter strode ahead of me, and Osgar and Iain were nowhere I could see. I sighed and waited for my giggling best friend to pass and followed her, wishing I hadn't let Iain out of my sight.

Somehow the Grotto had filled with people. Through the countless and unfamiliar faces, a jeweled crown glinted atop a head of dark brown hair. The human who'd helped us fight off the henchmen at the SCA camp approached with a few other men following him. None of them wore a crown but they were dressed in the same period clothing, enhanced with velvet and finery. They walked right past me.

"You look damned different without wings, Osgar," he said.

Osgar turned and broke out with a smile. The two men shook

hands and started talking but I couldn't hear them. They continued toward the band area with the "King's" men at their heels. I was beginning to feel like part of the furniture. I took a huge, contrary glug of champagne.

"Tessa."

"Hm?" I said, turning in the direction of the voice. The white-blond-haired guy was there, sans overprotective, jealous, Irish book thief. A rude little burst of heat melted my insides at the thought of her.

"Cian," he said. When he smiled, childish dimples formed in each cheek. His eyes lit up, accenting their almond shape. I expected to see pointed, elven ears for a second.

"It's nice to meet you, Cian." We stood in semi-awkward silence for a moment, looking at each other. Cian was a little too perfect, from the way he was built to his flawless, softly bronzed skin. He was only slightly taller than me, which was a comfort in a world when it seemed everything male loomed above my head. He might have been about five ten. I decided that was a nice change.

"So, how do you know the Logans?" Small talk became rough and repetitive when I only had one thing in common with any given person I just met.

"I've known them for centuries and their ancestors for millennia."

I set the rest of my champagne on a nearby table without batting an eye. At least he was honest.

"You don't say. I just met them a few months ago."

"I know. I've been aware of you ever since you arrived back on your native soil."

"You and I need to talk, don't we?" The guy was a gold mine of information, although it was unnerving to hear him blatantly talk about, and actually know, sensitive things about me and my conflicted lineage.

"Indeed, we do."

Silence entailed, but it was a comfortable silence. He smelled incredible. Like nature, or a mix of something herby and spiced caught on a morning wind. A far-off memory hung just out of reach and that smell was a huge part of it. I thought of the conversations we could have. Was it really possible he knew me? The real me. The one who was melded inside, half goddess and half human. I'd have to test that.

"You have questions," he stated.

Damn right. I nodded.

Cian inclined his head to his left and I followed him through throngs of people until we were away from the noise and mix of voices and string instruments. We took a space close to a rocky corner, half-secluded by a long table with tall arrangements of flowers and ornamentally stacked champagne flutes.

Finally he said, "I can help with answers." He picked up my right hand, turned it over, and placed his lips against my palm. Heat erupted inside me, lava in my veins. Suddenly I was completely alert and aware of each beat of his heart and the rhythm of his breath.

I jerked my hand away. "Whoa, there. We just met." I took a half step away from him, creating a more comfortable buffer. Personal space was gold. Cian was undaunted. "Let's start with who you really are."

"Fair enough. We are from the same place in time, you and I."

I gave him a look. *You'll have to do better than that, buddy.* "I'm from Austin."

"Not that you, the real you," he said, matter-of-factly. I didn't know where that part of me was from other than way back, a seriously long time ago, when Vikings pilfered and pillaged.

"You talk like you're from around here though."

"I love it down here. Been visiting for eons."

"Down here?"

He nodded.

"On Earth?"

"Not quite. We are all of the Earth. This place and time are . . . a layer of that."

"That's an enormous thought." I wished I hadn't drunk a single sip of champagne. "You sound like you're from Ireland."

"Ah. Good ear. I'm from Tailtiu."

"And that's in Ireland?"

"These days it's referred to as Teltown, County Meath."

I didn't let up since he was answering my questions. "And who are you exactly?"

He smiled, beautifully. "I am your betrothed."

"Okay, nope." I shook my head and scooted back again. Sweat beaded on my shoulders and back. A drip careened down the front of my dress, between my breasts. I didn't get why I was suddenly so overheated. Nervous, sure. But I wasn't angry. I didn't really feel threatened, either.

Cian laughed, easing up on the weight of the conversation and adding some much-needed levity. "Relax. I was shocked at the news, myself."

"Nothing personal, but there's no way in hell. I don't know if I'm the type to get married. I'm just now learning who I really am, and it's been slow coming."

"Stop fighting it."

"I don't." He didn't answer, or even blink. "And you don't know what you're talking about, really."

"Lugh's your daddy."

I was a little stunned but recovered fast. "You overhear that somewhere?"

"I've known since my memory begins. Promise."

And just like that I didn't want to talk to him any longer. Admitting such things was the equivalent to baring myself to him on a deep level. I was completely convinced he knew exactly what we were talking about. I sighed and changed the subject. "Why were you with Genevieve?"

He laughed and looked toward the ceiling, shaking his head.

"We go way back. She doesn't like the idea of you being back and loathes the idea of me being with you."

"Really?"

"Really, really." He was stone-cold.

"Hm."

"I would have introduced myself to you sooner, but she intervened."

"What has she got against me? I know she's after something I have, but this personal stuff is crap. She doesn't even know me."

He pursed his lips.

I sighed. Being in a place where other people knew me better than I knew myself was tough, and pissing me off.

"Don't worry," he said. "You will gain remembrance." He touched my cheek, admiring my face. "And this being, this wonderful mortal before me will remain."

"I can't accept that without feeling that some part of me will like, disengage at some point. I've done horrible things—"

"No"—he shook his head—"you have not. You have done nothing you didn't have to do. You love deeply, and love like that should be protected. You're simply learning to become the warrior you were born to be." Gently, he pulled me closer. I recognized his request and respected that it wasn't a demand, allowing myself to move to him. Something deep inside me screamed a warning, then told me it was okay, then yelled at me to run. He placed his cheek against mine. His skin was hot, like mine. Warm breath caressed my neck. I closed my eyes and let myself feel *right* for the first time in my life.

"You are the daughter of Lugh, you are a battle goddess, and you are one whom we have all watched languish long enough."

He spoke my truth. Part of my soul rejoiced with relief and vindication. He placed his lips on mine and the only fear I had was his absence. The contact, the rush of my senses to his, was simply meant to be. Or was it? I had the urge to back away and run, never looking back. But we kissed like lost lovers, a reunion of stolen inamorata and sweet euphoria. I imagined being with him in the most intimate of ways my imagination allowed, hoping and pining for that time to come. Our bodies came into contact and the heat he threw off rivaled mine. I didn't need to ask why I caught glimpses of light around him.

I granted myself another moment of bliss, thinking about how Genevieve could sod off, and finally pulled back.

"You see, I'm not so bad." He laughed, and we stepped apart, gathering ourselves. "I want to take it slow, too. It must seem predatory, the way I'm here and looking for you. Please don't think bad things."

I was absolutely speechless, and my face was so hot I had to be bright red.

"Say something, please?" The vulnerability in his voice caught me off guard.

"Sorry. Of course. But when you toss around words like 'betrothed' it can be a little scary. I mean, a lot scary."

"Understandable. My apologies." He smiled. "I have something for you." He reached inside his jacket pocket and withdrew a carton, which was a little bigger than what a fancy writing pen would come in. "I wanted to give this to you when you first came back."

"Back?" I needed to catch up.

"It must seem odd, but for us, you've merely been missing. You must feel that you're new here, Tessa, but believe this: You've only come home."

Cian opened the carton to reveal a velvet box. I totally expected a bracelet to be inside. He opened the box and I was nearly blinded by the contents. Once my eyes adjusted I made out the shape of a long, skinny arrowhead that looked to be made of a glowing, hundred-watt light bulb. Cian turned the box so I could see the whole thing. The arrowhead had a handle. The light the thing threw off dimmed, like something died out now that it was in the open.

He took it out of the box. "This is a small part of your birthright."

"What is it?" I didn't mean to sound ungrateful, but I had to ask.

"Lugh's Light. A gift from your father."

Maybe it was the way he said it so softly and with such meaning, or maybe it was the word "father," whichever the case, I teared up. *Ah, jeez. Embarrassing.*

Cian turned it over and held the handle end out to me. I wrapped my hand around the hilt and he let go.

"It's a dagger made with you in mind, so it should fit your hand perfectly."

He was correct about the fit. Now that I could feel it and see it better I understood it was a small weapon, undoubtedly for protection, close up. It appeared to be made of crystal of some sort, but it wasn't nearly that heavy. Actually, it was oddly light for the size.

"The nature of the blade is to fight. Keep it close at all times."

"Thank you."

"I wish the credit could be mine, but it's not. This is a gift from Lugh and I merely delivered it to you."

"Tell him thank you for me."

"I cannot." He let his forehead touch mine.

"Oh. I'm not sure how this works." I turned the dagger over, adjusting to the feel.

"I can't go back now that you're home. You're here, and that is the important part."

Cian held out a piece of thick, soft looking material and I placed the blade on his hand. He wrapped it up and put it back in the box and tucked it inside his jacket again.

"Let's get you back before I insist on getting you out of that gown."

"Good idea." I cringed. "I mean getting back. Not the gown." *Shit!* "I mean yes, the gown should stay where it is." I needed air.

Everyone had probably noticed my absence. We started through the cavern and stopped at the horseshoe shaped bar.

"When you're ready, I'd like to walk you to your room."

"What? Why?" I laughed.

He winked at me and grinned. "I don't trust these fucking Scots."

13

"I don't trust her." I scrubbed my hands dry on a paper towel and toed the bin open.

Bree finished and looked up from the sink, meeting my gaze in the mirror. "Genevieve does seem like a conniver."

"Bitchy, too. Plus, she and some goon were digging through the tow yard looking for the book right when Peter and I showed up to get it. She knows who I am, even when I'm not Garged Out. Recognized me quick when we met her."

"Why don't you tell me these things?" She tossed her towel into the waiting bin. "I was standing there all trying to be polite while y'all guys were staring daggers. I was clueless."

"Sorry. When I got back to the camp there were henchmen everywhere and the tents were burning. Then the next day we were exhausted and there was the excitement of getting back up here and I just sort of forgot about it."

"Aren't you worried she might try to take it while she's here?"

"Not likely. She's on the Logans' radar. I'm certain she hasn't been out of their line of sight all night."

The door swung wide and Genevieve walked in. She glanced

at me and then stared Bree up and down with a smirk on her face.

"Can I help you with something?" Bree asked, with a too-sweet smile.

"Certainly. You can leave."

"Shall we step outside? I can show you how we take out the trash where I come from." Bree punctuated the offer with a wink.

Genevieve was stunned, and rightfully so. The perfect eyebrows were up. She wasn't used to the way we Texas girls rolled. I'd seen Bree offer to kick someone's ass before. No one suspected Bree of being full-on ready to pop someone in the lip. She was sweet, with compassion evident in her facial expressions, voice, and actions. She'd bloodied a mouthy drunk chick's nose at a UT football game once and then held her own in the resulting mini-brawl. Even sweethearts had their limits.

I understood why Genevieve was a little stymied. Hearing Bree suggested she'd like to throw down was a complete contrast to her physical appearance, especially all dolled up in an off-white evening gown and not a hair out of place. Bree didn't care about that when it came down to business. She'd swing. She'd break a nail and do a lot more than get her hands dirty. It wasn't the first time, but the current scene was by far my favorite, because audacity controlled the moment. I grinned hugely.

All too quickly, Genevieve recovered her wit. "How very uncivilized. You Americans love to act like Neanderthals, given any opportunity." Her words were clipped, bringing out her Irish accent even more.

"Mmff. We Americans, indeed." Bree shook her head with a pitiful expression on her face.

I'd have given anything to watch Bree pop her one, but I didn't trust Genevieve to fight fair. Something evil was up with her.

"And how about you? I suppose you were looking for your lost pot o' gold in that tow yard?" I gave her a once over, just for effect. "I mean, I'd hate to suspect someone as civilized as you of being a common sneak thief with below average skills."

Genevieve laughed. The crinkles around her eyes faded instantly when she stopped. "I suggest watching your tongue," she warned, looking at both of us. "I can always show you how I deal with people who stand in the way of what I want."

"Simmer down," I said. "We were both just leaving."

She grinned again, stopping me from walking out.

"Pretty low, just showing up snooping around." Of course she was. Why else would she hunt me down in the bathroom?

"Indeed, I am here to offer a trade. And congratulations for using your head for something besides a hat rack. Or a target."

I rolled my eyes. "No deal." Childish, for sure, but knee-jerk, too. I yanked the door open and Bree stepped out, letting the door swing behind her.

"I'm most certain you'll reconsider when you hear my terms," Genevieve said, sincerely.

"Whatever." I grabbed the door handle before it came to the jamb and went to follow Bree out, but Genevieve caught my attention again by waving a folded piece of paper in the air.

"I have something you want. Follow these instructions precisely or she dies."

I snatched it out of her grasp with a glare and kept going so she didn't see that she'd rattled me.

We walked back to where I'd found Bree talking with the Logans. I was ticked at myself for entertaining the thought of trading with Genevieve. Maybe on a deep level I just wanted to get rid of the cursed book and get on with life, weird as it was. The way the book had warned me about taking a toll inched back into my mind and I was worried. But I couldn't give it to Genevieve. Sure as rain and hot tea in the UK, Genevieve was evil at her blackened heart. God only knew what she'd use the book for.

I folded her note over again and flicked it to the floor. I was completely ashamed of looking for a way out, but at the same time I knew I was in over my head with the damned book. It was only a matter of time before one of the people or things wanting it finished me off and took it anyway. It was time to start playing a lot smarter.

Before we stopped, I tugged on Bree's elbow. She leaned close to hear me over the band. "There's someone I want you to meet. He's over here by the bar."

She nodded, and I led the way, relaxing when I saw Cian was still there. Cody Allen was there too, and they were deep in conversation.

"Hi," I said, stopping by Cody's stool. "You guys know each other?"

"Just met," Cody said, putting his glass on the counter and wiping his hands on a napkin.

Cian offered his hand to Bree, who took it. "Cian," he said.

"Hi." He gave her the most amazing smile. Just watching it ignited electricity down my spine.

"Delighted," he said, and actually kissed the top of her hand perfectly and gracefully, like a scene from a movie. Bree was charmed. It was hard not to be, which was good. I wouldn't have to work that hard explaining why I liked him so much. He released her hand and grinned at me.

"Hi," he quipped, giving me the short version after his intro with Bree. He drew me closer by a hand.

"Hey," I laughed and shook my head. He was hilarious.

"How's your night going?" Bree asked, looking at Cody.

"Great. I'm actually getting ready to cash it in. I've got an early day tomorrow."

"We just saw your girl in the ladies room." Bree smiled at him.

Cody sighed and smiled back. "You don't say." He stood. "I'd probably better go find her. Cian," he said, holding out a hand, "it's been an honor."

Cian grasped Cody's hand and the two shook, genuinely. "Likewise. Best of luck in your travels."

Cody left into the crowd to find his date and I wondered if I'd ever see him again as he went. I doubted it.

"He's a good guy," I said.

"Yes. Every once in a great age I meet a human I can tolerate. That is one of them." Cian held up his glass in a one-sided toast.

"That was the most bizarre, borderline offensive thing I've heard since I left the restroom," Bree said.

Cian looked from her to me, waiting to be filled in.

"Genevieve came into the bathroom exuding some charm, trying to be intimidating," I explained.

"Ah. She isn't happy that I introduced myself to you," he said, getting up from his stool. "She's not much to worry about. Merely a tired hag with a dodgy backstory." He pulled the little box from his jacket pocket and motioned toward the cocktail purse Bree had. "Would you hold onto this for your friend?"

Bree nodded and tucked the box into her clutch.

Cian turned to face me. "My assistance is required elsewhere for a short time. May I visit you when I return?" He turned my hand over and placed a soft kiss on the tender skin of my wrist.

Goosebumps screamed up my arm. "How very double-oh-seven," I joked. "I'd like that."

He smiled. "Until then."

When he let go of my hand, cold air replaced his touch, but the spot where his lips met my flesh burned like I'd touched it to a curling iron. I watched him go until he was lost in all the other black jackets.

"Where did he come from?" Bree tucked her clutch beneath an arm.

"It's a long story, but he's perfect." I grinned. "Can I ask you something without you thinking I've finally lost my marbles?"

"Of course. I mean, let's hope you can keep the two you have left clacking around up there." She nodded and smiled with a little bit of her tongue showing.

I ignored the jibe. "Does he have a thin grey line around him?" She was going to think I was nuts. I knew it.

"You mean like a belt?" she said, totally serious.

"No. It must have been the lighting. Maybe there was a light behind him or something."

"What's in the box?" she asked, fully expecting me to say something like "A diamond necklace," or another expensive gift.

"A dagger."

Her smile faded some. "Really? Another dagger? You need to meet a man who might give you a nice tennis bracelet or something."

"A girl can never have too many weapons." Someday, I'd be able to explain to her that the one in her purse was imbued with magical "light" from my father, who was the Sun God. I'd sound ridiculous trying to explain it right then.

"Well, now you've got one to strap to each leg, I guess," she said, with a laugh.

"What's a lad got to do to get a bite to eat in this dump?"

My blood chilled. A grungy unkempt lumbering brute of a guy stomped his way through couples and groups of people. He had to be a gargoyle. Even in human form, he was still a beast of a creature with a thick brow and constant scowl, although he tried to smile at the awed faces greeting him. Recognition built at the same time as dread.

"This one here looks good enough to eat," said the ogre who'd sidled up behind Bree. That confirmed my fears. I had a hunch they were old ones, henchmen gargoyles. Bree and I reached for each other and pulled away from him. They were the only two people at the event not dressed in a black tux or some other type of finery. Both of them were too familiar to me. Ages ago, when I was only Teasa, the goddess, I'd changed them into the first group of gargoyles ever, besides me. It was a punishment I still stood behind. The henchmen were cannibals, eating people when they'd been human. Even before I'd changed them, they raided villages in the Highlands, killing families and making use of the bodies in the most heinous ways thinkable.

The man behind Bree was a little smaller than the one causing the ruckus. His hair hung in a mat of locked-up, dusty red twists. Freckles marked every part of his face. For some odd reason, I imagined him as a young guy, like a teenager with a snowboard, or maybe a skateboard. He smiled and showed sickeningly brown teeth rooted in blackened gums.

"Aw God," Bree said. We backed away slowly. I didn't know what was right behind us, but I kept going, trying to guess how far we'd have to go before we made it to the exit by the bathrooms. It wasn't that far from where we talked earlier.

I took a quick stock of the guests, looking for any others. Some of the people still danced and most others remained undisturbed. Osgar and Iain cut through the people and headed our way. I hated the way I sought out Peter, but I found him, and he was on his way, too. Crispin practically sprinted toward us from behind the bar, apologizing to a couple for bumping them as he went by.

We made it to the wall next to the new exit.

"Come now, lassie, I donned my best for your party," said Brown Teeth. He pressed toward us, but oddly slow. Not far off, the other henchman swung an elbow and connected with a man's jaw, carefully pulling the poor guy's champagne flute from his grasp as he went down. The brute downed the dregs of the glass and tossed it to the floor.

"Where's the bloody drink in this hole?" he yelled, eyeing the closest group of guests. People grew quiet for a split second before the first screams sounded, echoing off rock and causing a ripple throughout the cavern.

Panic hung on the edge of busting loose.

"Please, remain calm." Osgar addressed everyone from atop a

stool by the bar. "As you can see, some rubbish has fallen from a bin."

Random, nervous laughter sounded from pockets of people. Petra, of all people, came forward to help the guy who'd been hit as Iain and Peter closed in on the henchman before he could hit anyone else. Brown Teeth and Crispin squared off, each waiting on the other to make a move.

"Psst." Someone hissed to my left.

Out of habit, I turned toward the sound, like a dope. A really big fist sailed out of nowhere straight at me. The last thing I heard was the *pop* when it made contact.

14

The scent of expensive leather always made me think of awesome cars. Bree and I went along with a group of students to an auto show once and that smell, the aroma of buttery, oiled leather, touched memory. I was surrounded by it, and moving, my head lolling to and fro and my neck screaming clear down to my shoulder blades. My tongue was fat and dry but still worked well enough to taste old blood. The side of my mouth was swollen, and a slab of flesh hung from the inside of my cheek where it had been torn by my teeth.

The more lucid I became, the more pain set in. Something else was keeping me fuzzy. On top of being smacked, I'd likely been drugged to keep me down. It occurred to me that going back to sleep wasn't okay and that I should be concerned as to whose car I was in, so I opened my eyes. A man in a pearl, pinstriped suit was seated beside me on a bench seat, back-lit against the window. Undoubtedly the owner of the fist that hit me, I instantly loathed him. There was just enough light outside so I'd have to wait to Garg Out and wrap him up into a bow tie.

We went over a bump in the road and I closed my eyes, mulling around the flap of my cheek. I used the motion lent by the rocking of the seat to turn my head a little to try and alleviate the pain in my shoulder blades. It didn't work. I opened my eyes to find the guy watching me. When he saw I was awake, he tapped on the driver's seat.

I sunk an elbow into the seat and began to sit up, stopping quickly when the pinch of pain that had been in my shoulder blades ripped along my spine. The idea my flesh was stuck to the seat crossed my mind and the jackass beside me found that delightful, smiling at my groan and grimace.

I wanted to tell him all the many ways he could get screwed, but even inhaling deeply hurt my back. Tentatively, I leaned toward the opposite window, carefully scooting my bottom under me so I was upright. The thick material of my evening gown didn't make it any easier.

The guy leaned forward and spoke to the driver in a guttural language I couldn't make sense of. The driver motioned with a tip of his head when he replied. My seatmate relaxed back again.

"Where are we?"

He ignored me, of course. We slowed down and began to rock over another series of bumps. I grabbed the door handle and yanked hard. It didn't open. I sighed and kept a straight face, not giving the man the satisfaction of seeing how much it frustrated me. The air inside the car took on a sweet, familiar scent, like flowers and rain.

We rolled to a stop, waiting for an iron gate to slide away. The driver proceeded to take us down a declining tunnel below a concrete building. Grey walls hugged the car and the sick sense I was being driven to the depths of hell boiled in my gut.

I started to count to myself so I had some gauge of how long we dropped. A neat beam of yellow light lined the ceiling as we went along. I made it to 54 as the car leveled out and we pulled into a bay beside a white car that Cruella De Vil certainly drove around stealing spotted puppies.

The door latch popped as the driver got out. The man riding

beside me nodded toward my door handle, so I obliged and opened it up. Intent on getting out quickly, I ignored the pain in my shoulders and stood, coming face to face with the business end of a stubby rifle.

"Whoa, Jesus," I snapped. As I stood fully, the guy on the other end of the gun followed me up, keeping the barrel leveled at my face. I found that profoundly sobering and suddenly my sliced-up cheek and shoulders didn't seem so daunting.

We were in a tight room, like a two-car garage with just enough space to move around. Gun Guy whipped his head to his left and I traced his motions to a wall where a glossy steel elevator door waited. I stepped toward the door, slowly, both to keep my balance on the heels and to make sure I didn't get shot. When we all stood in front of the elevator, one of the men hit the down button and the doors sprang open.

Cool air fanned from inside and as I put my back to the wall, the place along my back that seemed to be causing the pain chilled, like it was wet.

In about three seconds the door popped open again, displaying a beautifully lit sitting room full of ornately decorated, velvet and wood furniture.

I groaned. It appeared I'd unwillingly accepted Genevieve's invitation for brunch at her place.

I straightened my dress out and walked toward her. The elevator shut behind me, and to my astonishment, all three of the men stayed inside. Genevieve stared at me as she approached. The closer she got, the more pissed off she appeared.

"You look just like your father."

What the hell? Maybe she didn't know me, after all.

"Welcome," she turned to the side, gesturing behind her to the rest of the huge room.

"Where are we?" I asked, not really expecting an answer.

"Just north of Tara."

That was no help. The only Tara I'd ever heard of was in

Ireland and although she had an Irish accent, I suspected she was lying.

"I apologize we didn't have more time to become acquainted at the Logans'. They're barely cordial, even with Kai being gone."

"You knew Kai?"

"Mm hm," she said, with no other emotion.

I wanted to groan and smirk at the same time. That was a notch-on-a-bedpost response if I ever saw one. Depending on her fondness for Kai, and how much she knew about his "passing," I decided to stop talking. If she was lovestruck and held me responsible for his death, I was in some deep kimchi.

"So how far away do you live?"

"Well, it is Ireland." The look accompanying her words was the verbal equivalent of patting a dunce on the head.

She walked, and I matched her stride, waiting for her to do the talking she'd missed out on. My mind was chewing on the fact I wasn't even on the same land mass anymore.

"Please don't worry. After we talk things out, I'll have you delivered back to the Logans." I nodded my response, content to just listen as I looked around. Knowing I wouldn't be killed or worse made me feel slightly at ease, although I knew it wouldn't be that simple.

There must have been hundreds of thousands of dollars in just statuary and art hanging on the walls. The air was perfumed with the scent of a sweetly blossoming flower I couldn't identify. There wasn't a window in sight. The more we walked, the room grew in size and depth, giving it the feel of a museum.

Other things in the room seemed trivial when I saw the darkened, round aquarium running from the marble floor up into the ceiling. The cylinder was about ten feet in diameter. I mentally shrugged. If I was richer than Bill Gates I'd have a badass fish tank, too.

Genevieve picked up on my fascination. Her little heels

clicked on the stone floor as she walked to a small, gilt table to
retrieve a remote and turned on the aquarium light.

"Oh," I breathed, setting a hand against the lukewarm tank,
looking at the sole denizen. Long, white hair clouded around a
hollowed white face. Blackened eyes widened. Thin to the point
of jagged bones protruding from flaking skin over xylophone
ribs, she barely appeared female. One hand crept forth toward
mine, the Tyren's ashen fingers caressing the barrier between us.
No longer transparent and glowing silver, she had to be close to
death. My throat locked and my chin trembled. A pang of heat
unleashed in my chest. Thick tubing encircled her neck, full of
brownish goop with a big bubble here and there. I traced it to the
surface of the water then lost it.

Genevieve stepped beside me. The thing surged forward and
raged at the glass, swimming full on into the front of the tank,
smashing and beating against it. For the effort, the only sound
was sort of like a large pot of whole potatoes boiling.

"You kidnapped her?" Of course she had. Genevieve apparently practiced that often. I stepped away, hoping Genevieve
would, too, so the Tyren would settle down. She could hurt
herself with the assault on her cage. The tank light went out and
the tirade inside stilled.

"Her?" Genevieve snorted, placing the control back on the
table. "Personification of these things will get you hurt." She
turned away. I approached the glass, peering in through dark
water to the swirls of hair shrouding the Tyren.

"You're killing her." I sounded like a child when I said it, my
voice high, holding too much emotion. Sweat broke out on my
face and my hand fogged the glass. The Tyren's eyes were all I
could make out. She stayed at the back of container.

"She's dying. She's starved."

"Do you know what they eat?"

I gave an exasperated sigh, glaring at her. "Maybe you could
have figured that out before you did this to her."

"Mm." She nodded. "Well, it's not salt."

"You put salt in there?" I waved a hand furiously for a second before that spot between my shoulder blades reminded me I was hurt there.

"It's the only mineral I had. She could make due." Genevieve huffed, as if put out by the Tyren's inability to live off stagnating saltwater.

I grit my teeth. "What do you want?" I figured I might as well cut to it. She wanted the book.

"Well, now." Tossing her hair, Genevieve settled back in the stuffed throne with one of her dimpled smiles bordering on a smirk. "This will be easier than I thought."

"What's going to be easy?" I turned, eyeing her. Nothing from that point would be simple for Genevieve. I pushed an escaped strand of hair from my dampened face, tucking it behind an ear.

"Please, sit." She gestured to a matching, yet much smaller, Victorian chair. Deciding to humor her, I picked up a tasseled cushion and sat, my back screaming with pain when it brushed the back of the chair. I dropped the fancy pillow on the floor beside me and leaned forward. Genevieve smiled, knowingly. I tried to quit thinking of the caged Tyren and give her all my attention.

"You can have it—her," she inclined her chin toward the tank.

"What's the catch?"

Genevieve feigned shock. "It's simply a gesture," she waved toward the Tyren. "I bore of it anyway. I'd no idea you knew these things existed." She eyed me, that half-smile pasted into place, blood red against her pale face.

I stood, smoothing my gown. She'd just lied to me and I was wound far too tight to continue the façade. She continued to stare, likely another who'd misjudged me, selling me short. Earlier, when I'd met the woman, she made me feel typical and gauche. Even now, for our little play date, she was dressed in rich Victorian lace and a royal blue corset with spike-heeled leather boots and probably ten thousand worth in cameos and jewelry. I'd barely made it away from the Logans' with deodorant applied and my hair curled. The old feelings of being society's reject flowed over me as I took stock of her appearance compared to mine, while she tried to get a good read on the nobody in front of her.

I might look rough-hewn and denim clad, but my soul was good—I knew that, anyway. Genevieve turned out to be nothing but a spit-shined turd. In my experience, they still stank to high heaven.

"How much?" I crossed my arms, digging into my biceps with my fingers. It was all I could do not to unleash on her, the heat boiling just below the surface. "With transport. I have no idea how to get her safely back to the Clan's grotto." I inhaled through my nose and tried to tamp down the urge to pop her neat little head off her shoulders. I desperately wanted a window so I could gauge how long it would be until I could Garg Out and pull her arms off.

She stood too and walked to a bar to our left. I wanted to jump on her when she passed me but that wouldn't help the dying Tyren. Ice clinked into two glasses. "Tessa," she shook her head, back still to me. One graceful hand pulled a decanter of amber liquid close. The glasses splashed full, and Genevieve came back toward me.

I accepted the drink, sure I wouldn't like what was in the glass. She sipped and so did I. I kept a straight face despite the way the liquid seemed to try to bore a hole between my palate and nasal cavity. My gashed-up cheek burned like crazy for a split second, then went numb.

"Teasa," she said, drawing out the "s" sound into a long "z".

"What?" Surely I'd heard her wrong.

"Which do you prefer?" She sat, crossing her legs. She gestured at the seat she'd offered. I took the chair again, leaning forward with my elbows on my knees, staring at her. I shook my head and pursed my lips, swirling the ice in my glass.

"I am offering a barter for two things." She placed her feet on the floor, matching my posture. "Please take time and consider wisely."

I took a drink.

"The first item is silence. I will give you the Tyren and arrange to transport you both back to the Logans. If any of your"—she paused, looking for the perfect word—"enclave, pose the question of where you found it, you will not answer them. You will mention nothing of our meeting." Genevieve's features grew tight, her jaw set. "This is the way it has to be, lest every kilt-clad, wing-flapping Scot in the Highlands is over here in my business."

"And then some," I added. I figured, screw it, there were two people in the conversation, no matter her desire to dictate.

"Look here," she leaned closer. "You will stow your attempts at wit and listen to me with intent." She sat back and retrieved her remote control. After a couple clicks, the sound of a furnace kicking on puffed through the room, coming from the direction of the aquarium. Little bubbles formed at the base of the glass, some breaking free to boil to the top, past the Tyren who'd backed against the far curve of the tank. Slowly, she pulled into a ball and drifted toward the surface. The bubbles inside the tubing slid into motion, chugging toward where I lost sight of the tube.

"Turn it off!"

Genevieve tapped a button on the remote and hurled it at me. It hit my sternum and I grabbed it before it fell to the floor.

"Second thing," she said, balling up her fists, "you will bring me that goddamn book!"

And there it was. Confirmation. I wondered if there was one person or thing in all the UK that wasn't tormented by the thought of possessing the book. Part of me wanted to yell, "Deal!" and hand it over.

"You're weak, you know? The way you put stock into the meaningless things living down here. You buy into the plight of Clan Logan." She snorted. "You have the vision of a sheltered human." She downed the rest of her drink, in one sizable gulp, exhaling through her nose. Staring at me, she sat back again, relaxing on the plush chair, arms out at her sides, dangling the empty glass from her fingertips. She crossed her legs, one long fingernail *tinking* against the glass. "You don't even know what it's capable of, or how to use it."

I imagined smacking her in the nose and watching it swell. I owed her one.

"So, it's settled then. You get that," she said, gesturing with a tilt of her head to the languishing Tyren, "and I get the book and I promise no more of these, or any humans, find their way into one of my cages."

"That's not a trade. That's blackmail. You're holding leverage."

"You'd be doing your friends a service. And really, do you sleep well knowing the book is with you? Does it set you at ease knowing something so ancient and powerful, something potentially evil, has its hooks in you?"

"That's my reservation about giving it to you. Evil is one thing, but you're scrambled eggs." I'd been told not every person would be able to open the book. If I could tell Genevieve was missing a few blocks in her Jenga tower, it probably could, too. I'd deal with getting the Tyren to safety first and worry about the book later. It would buy me some time to get with the Logans and hopefully save the Tyren.

Genevieve slammed her glass down on the side table. Remarkably, it didn't shatter. "You, come with me."

I got up, tentatively, watching her, wishing I'd minded my words for the Tyren's sake. Genevieve and I both knew she could say what she wanted or else she'd torture the poor creature.

"Let me show you what your brand of wit has earned. This way please," she said, holding out a hand.

I followed her through her home, hating the way her heels *clicked* and how she didn't bother with words. We came through an ornate dining room, with too many chairs for people who couldn't possibly be comfortable eating in her presence, then entered a huge, galley kitchen with a walk-in cooler at the end. She stomped up to it and jerked the metal handle, swinging the door wide.

Cold air huffed out, along with the smell of fish and ripe produce.

"In you go," she clipped.

"Okay. I'm sorry I was rude. I'll agree to your terms. But if you go back on your deal and harm any more Tyrens, any of the Logans, or my friends, I'm coming back to get it and I will not be smiling."

"Noted. We agree then. Now get in the goddamn refrigerator." She grabbed my elbow and yanked me forward, amazingly strong for someone who appeared to value her manicure above physical strength.

I shook my head.

"Geo!" she screamed. "I want her in the cooler!" She raged.

A lout I hadn't seen on the way in hit me square in the back so hard my head snapped back and my spine popped. I went flailing into the cooler, barely staying on my feet. The door swung shut and latched heavily from the other side.

"I said I'd do it!" I yelled.

The light went out.

I went to the door and pounded hard. "Hello? You can have the book."

Nothing. The interior "button on a pike" safety opener slid in like it was going to unlock the door but didn't engage.

"Genevieve? Open up!"

A fan kicked on from the top of the rear wall. Gooseflesh emerged along my bare arms and the urge to pee hit me hard. My eyes adjusted quickly, using a faint glow from a digital screen beside the door. The square, red digits read 2.777 C. I was more grateful for the small amount of light than to know the air was slightly above freezing, although I would have traded it all to know what time it was. All I needed was nightfall. Genevieve would freak when I busted out and trashed her perfectly-placed, well-furnished abode on my way to rescue the Tyren and get out of Dodge. I just had to wait it out. The chill didn't bother me. I never stayed cold for long, anyway.

More bothersome was the niggling pain between my shoulder blades. The sensation had centralized there and was no longer a "sore muscle" type of thing. It still hurt but seemed superficial and it kind of itched. I pounded on the door again.

"Hello? Can we talk about this?" I didn't expect an answer and wasn't disappointed.

I paced a small circle, concentrating on keeping my thoughts from growing hysterical. The last thing I remembered before being hit was Crispin beside Bree, so she was likely safe. Genevieve's guys were apparently artists at their work. Interesting, too, was the fact that henchmen worked for her. I had no idea how long it took to make it to Genevieve's place from Logan Castle in Scotland, but it had obviously been a quick trip. It felt like it was early the next morning, but I hope it was later in the day.

I hadn't Garged Out since I put on the evening gown I still wore. The thing would have been shredded and there was no way the bodice would have survived the way my ribcage expanded when I grew into gargoyle form. As far as time went, my abductors must have kept me hidden someplace inside the grotto, using the minerals there to keep me in human form until morning so I didn't change. Then they simply put me in the car, or plane, or whatever, and moved me during the daytime. That explained why I felt drugged and fuzzy when I woke up.

Soon, my feet began to ache, pinched in places by the dressy shoes I'd picked out. I wasn't used to heels, especially strappy ones that were slightly too tight to begin with. Too many things irritated me. The itchy pain in my back, my feet being pinched, and the urge to urinate, all combined and made it hard to concentrate.

I felt along the tall, wire shelving, fingering boxes and looking for something large and round. A moment later, cold metal greeted my hands and I removed a large stockpot from eye level and set it on the floor with a heavy, sloshing clunk. When I removed the lid, a savory smell wafted out of the half full pot.

Hurriedly, I adjusted all the layers of fabric I wore and squatted over the pot to relieve my screaming bladder. The experience was a lot like using a portable toilet at a park event. When I was done, I simply replaced the lid and scooted the pot back against the shelving, hoping Genevieve was in the mood for soup.

I sat on the closed pot, unbuckling straps, and sliding my feet free of the shoes and onto the comfort of the inside of the bottom of my dress. My best guess was that I'd been locked up for around an hour. The fan continued to run so I took a quick glance at the temperature, which had dropped a bit, to -4.37 C.

Being an Austinite, I'd never experienced the outdoors when it was truly cold out. My internal temperature always ran high. The air inside the cooler was damp, so maybe that made it seem colder. At any rate, for the first time in my life, I was actually, really cold. I scrubbed at my arms and bounced my legs to warm them up. Moments later, I made the decision to tear the skirt off the dress and use it to cover my arms and torso, leaving the thinner, under-layer of the dress to cover my legs. My makeshift cloak brushed the sore spot on my back and I cringed. My nose was icy and it started to run. I snuffled and wiped snot on the dress. I needed the sun to go down. Any damned time.

I slid my shoes on and began walking again to get warm. Everything was off kilter. I had no help from the goddess, which really, came and went on her whim anyway. I counted steps and sang my ABCs. After that, I sang some Michael Jackson and waddled through what I could remember of the dance routine from *Thriller*. Time bled on. I got colder. My feet, legs, and fingers hurt. I moved increasingly slower.

The screen read -11.69.

Giving up on my sense of time, I tore into every box and container on the shelves looking for a misplaced knife or something to work the door latch with. The fan continued to run. My body ached but I continued to use my numb hands to fumble through boxes of fruit and plastic cases of meat. The cooler was about six by six feet with a tall ceiling, so trying to tear down a wall of shelving wouldn't work and would make it so I couldn't move.

-18 C, right on the button.

I found no wayward kitchen tools. I used my shoulder to batter the door, which stayed firm. I concentrated on everything in the world that made me angry, trying to incense the goddess for a nice, warm fever. I got nothing. She was unresponsive. Nightfall should have happened hours ago. My gargoyle was nowhere to be felt. I exhausted myself trashing the cooler.

The material from the dress didn't really help but I wrapped up as tightly as I could and tucked my feet under me, unwilling to look at the temperature again. Reading how much below freezing it was would give Genevieve some satisfaction, in my mind.

Life was a funny thing. My life came and went, built by others, taken away again, built back up and protected, then left for dead. There was no way anyone would know where to find me, or else they would have showed up by then. Cian was the one I held out hope for. Certainly a member of the Celtic pantheon could track me. Or maybe not. Maybe Genevieve lied. I could have been anywhere in the world. Maybe the building encasing her home was so far below the surface that I'd never be found. That was possible, especially considering Teigan was still missing and half of Scotland and London had turned the UK upside down searching for him. I'd failed Teigan, and myself, because I'd sworn to find him to repay him from saving me from my own stubbornness.

Without me around, Bree could go home to her family. She deserved that. Petra would be thrilled to have me out of the way so she could have all of Peter's attention. Not that I wanted to be around him anymore, now that I'd grown to know him the way I did. The nuns in Austin would find a new orphan to torment and beat over the head with their Bibles. I wished I would have done so many things differently. Damned those bad choices.

All that remained was to hold out faith that even if I drifted off to sleep, I'd awaken when I Garged Out. Tears solidified on my cheeks, numbing my skin. Letting the fan lull me to sleep was too easy.

SOMETHING BIT into the crook of my elbow. Elastic squeezed my bicep. Plastic popped against tubing. Drowsily, I fought to keep an eye open as plastic gloves removed a tourniquet from my arm and finished filling a vial of blood. A cotton ball was held in place by a random thumb.

I swatted at hands, but my arms only bent and moved from the elbows. Straps grated into my skin across my biceps. Antiseptic coated the air. My stomach knotted even though my mind said to relax.

A strand of hair was snipped loose from my nape and wound up on a black spindle. Vials of blood and the sample of my hair were dropped onto a silver tray on a stand. I concentrated on blinking because it made me feel as though I might be waking up, but sleep came back.

"Now tell me," the kind man said again, "where will you take the book?"

"Jonnie's. I will give it to Adam," I repeated, dutifully. I was a good girl. It's what he'd said, but that grew more and more confusing.

"Good girl," he confirmed. "Open up for me." I blinked hard, focusing on the green-eyed Brit with the partially obscured face. His mask puffed out slightly when he exhaled. I'd always had a problem with doctors. Maybe it was too much prodding at me when I was younger, and the nuns were trying to find a cause for my fevers. I'd just woken up with one of the bastards right in my face, stealing blood and God knew what other samples.

Fingers pressed down on my chin. I opened my mouth to feel a swab press against the inside of my cheek.

"One more. Hold on."

Things clinked on the tray. Fingers pressed against my teeth. I bit down.

"Mother—God," he grated. "Get over here and get her off me!"

My jaw locked down and I concentrated as hard as I could to focus. The silver haired doctor pried at my head with his other hand. I must have had his knuckle between my teeth because the harder I bit down, the more it reminded me of gristle in a piece of chicken. He hit me. I squinted and locked down with all I had, envisioning his finger chopping loose. Flesh popped free. Warmth coated my tongue and bottom lip. I held fast to shredded skin, busted bone, and ragged, powdery, plastic glove, as he continued to pound on my face. He screamed as his hand came free. I held on to his finger. The gurney toppled sideways and slammed onto a cold floor. I hit hard, growing foggy again.

Another guy scavenged the metal tray, too fast for me to get a look at his face. Both of them ran off with the doctor wailing and chuffing. A door slammed.

I let my head rest on my shoulder, feeling parts of my face puffing up from the beating. I'd be black and blue within the hour. I spit out the chewed finger, but it simply fell from my lips. Saliva built up in my mouth and I swallowed hard despite the amount of blood in my mouth. I didn't love reflexes right then. I had to swallow again when my stomach roiled at the thought. I concentrated on breathing to avoid vomiting.

The hazy feeling left in a hurry. I got the sense I'd just got a hit of caffeine, or maybe fruit sugar from an entire watermelon. A second later is was more like ten of those fruity, little bottled vitamin B shots all kicked in at once. Endorphins rejoiced. I sucked at every bit of moisture in my mouth as my body warmed from my throat outward. Maybe the guy was on something, and that affected me through the little bit of his blood I swallowed. I couldn't tell for sure, but it was possible that if I'd ingested just a little more, I could leap small buildings and stop bullets with my teeth. The cells in my body rejoiced like wilted plants in unexpected rain.

Where my mind went next made me sort of sick. As I lay there on my side, lost and head spinning, I thought about biting into that finger again. Maybe eating the whole thing like a chicken wing. The sweet, metallic tang still coated the roof of my mouth. I couldn't see where it had fallen, although it had to be right below the shoulder that held me off the floor. No one would know. I could do it.

I could eat one little bit more of the human doctor's finger. Just a nibble and I'd feel like a million bucks. I could bust out of the place without waiting to Garg Out.

The straps had loosened, so I simply slid one arm free and peeled thick Velcro from my ankles, arms, and waist so I could get myself up off the floor. It happened extremely fast, bordering on amped up speed.

The finger rolled off the shiny black fabric of my dress and dropped onto the floor, pale and fake-looking, with blood soaking into the cuticle. Maybe my brain didn't want to register that it was real. Looking at it then, I sort of wanted to puke. I scooted back, disgusted with myself and refusing to let the thoughts I'd had about eating some of the thing creep back into my mind. They had to have been produced by a drugged, starved, and weary brain. I had to get moving.

My shoes were gone, but I still wore the gown I'd torn down to cocktail length. Every part of my body throbbed back to life as I walked toward the door and turned the handle. It opened right up, and I peeked out into a white-lit corridor, which was so long I'd have to walk farther than I liked before I made it out. No one was around, so out I went.

The farther I walked, the less and less groggy I felt, but the giddy, electric energy from my tiny "drink o' human" wore off fast. As my legs and arms stopped hurting, the pain in my back twinged and throbbed, reminding me it was still there.

A sterile looking set of double doors were on my left, the twin vertical windows in each blacked out. A certain smell, like dirt mixed with fertilizer, earth, or soil from an old garden, hung around the hallway. Without any better idea to find the exit, I grasped one of the handles and pulled the door open a little so I could see in.

In my haste for a quick peek inside, I made out a few dark-ened tanks of what appeared to be water and some odd long boxes on steel tables. The tanks were arranged central in the room, like a pillar between the floor and ceiling. Considering what Genevieve liked to keep in tanks, I was incensed and horri-fied. More clear tubing came from each, leading to junctions. Machines hummed and monitors sent hues of blue and grey into the room, barely shedding enough light to make things clear. I stepped inside and let the door brush my bottom when it shut to make sure it was silent.

With the door closed, sound was amplified. Air filters bubbled softly, like walking into the fish section in a pet store. Monitors beeped subtly, in time to flashing numbers, each set eyelevel beside a tank. Wheeled stands rested beside each steel box on the metal slab workbench that ran the length of the room against the far wall. There were four "bays" there but only two of the long boxes—which looked more like coffins—had monitors flashing above them.

The smell was overpowering inside, permeating the room like I'd walked into a botanical greenhouse. It didn't stink, but it was certainly strong. A long air pocket inside the tubes running alongside one of the tanks bubbled loudly, emitting the sound of a straw at the end of a milk shake.

There was no other movement or sound at the tank. I tried the door with the heel of a foot to make sure it was still unlocked. It opened easily, but only very slightly. Once it was closed again, I started into the room toward the tank with the slurping tubes.

The same, mucky brown fluid I'd seen in Genevieve's Tyren tank earlier was being pulled from this tank, as well. I placed a hand against the glass. The water inside was cool. A soft current moved inside, swirling little bubbles around at the surface. There was a switch beside the monitor. I held my breath and flipped it up.

A male Tyren was secured to the back glass inside, upside down with his hands bound to the bottom of the tank. Emaciated and flaky looking, most of his body was atrophied and shriveled to the point it was hard to tell if he was male or just a white stick figure. Patches of long hair had fallen out and bare scalp shone through. The tubes were strapped to his body and actually pierced his skin. One each in his throat, chest, and a thigh. Seeing any creature tortured was horrific. The fact I could see the Tyren submerged in water meant there was a substance mixed in. I hoped it wasn't salt. Tyrens thrived in fresh water, from what I knew. The mineral water from the Grotto didn't have salt in it.

I crouched, looking at the bindings that held him flattened against the wall. They appeared to be large zippy ties. There was one around his neck, too. I peered harder at that one to see how tight it was. His eyes opened.

We made eye contact, my gaze feeling wild, imposing, and

tearful, his bleached eyes searching mine briefly with a small spark, then losing focus. I wanted to cry for him and tears welled.

I remembered the way the female Tyren raged inside the tank. This one couldn't do that, thanks to the straps. His mouth opened slightly then closed again, as did his eyes.

I sprinted around the pillar of four tanks, hitting the light switches. All held a single male Tyren in the same position. One of them must have been captured more recently than the other starved ones because he was muscular and strong, without flaking skin or lost hair. I stepped back, wondering how in the world I could manage to free starved, angry Tyrens who were in different stages of pre-death. I'd have to bring them to fresh water somehow, without letting them kill me. I shook my head, looking from one tormented face another, horrified and helpless to get them out.

I was shaken out of panic when one of the monitors sounded off against the wall, followed by the other one. A motor kicked on somewhere in the network of tubes and junctions where they came together to join a central, larger one. Bubbles began to march forward from each tank, each Tyren being siphoned of the fluid inside. Sucking sounds came from the top of each tank as I circled, watching in terrified fascination. One particularly huge bubble chugged through a tube and I followed it to the bench along the wall, where it joined a two-part manifold above the coffin-boxes. Each box sat atop a metal table attached to the bench.

I had to walk between the two tables to approach the moni-tors. I couldn't make out the info on the screens, but a caterpillar of letters and numbers ticked along, a system that someone had set up to track the intake from the tanks. I could guess that much.

Clear plastic sneeze guards, the kind I'd seen at a salad bar, covered each box. Dried drops of the brownish fluid, more like a fine spray in places, stuck to the inside of the plastic separating me from a waist high coffin filled with deep, blackened goo.

Sprayers were mounted at the head and foot, with two on each side. They pumped fluid into the boxes with a layer of clear water on top of darkened layers of sediment. A current pulled through the lower layer, pushing past eddies in the corners.

A pump kicked on by the wall, loud as hell, and I jumped away from the box I had been hovering over and smacked my butt against the side of the other. Out of reflex, I reached to catch the side in case it tipped. It didn't. My right hand smacked against the metal wall while my other hand and arm sank elbow deep into the tank.

Nothing will send you into a fetal position faster than having several invisible mouths suddenly nibbling at your skin. At least that's what my imagination told me was happening. Something in the tank touched my hand. It felt like little jaws and teeth scraping against my fingers and wrist. I yanked my hand out and spun in a tight circle, flinging goop in every direction. My heart surged into my throat. My hand was covered in a layer of oil-sheen-bronze material that swam up my skin as if my arm was a log under water. I yanked up the trashed and abbreviated hem of my gown and scrubbed it away. It took what had to be just short of forever. The stuff continued to nip at my skin the whole time. Finally, I got it all off. My left hand and arm were pink next to my right, exfoliated to the max. My skin tingled, shiny and healthy. I was amazed. Perhaps it wasn't trying to eat me. Rather, it might have been doing away with dead skin and old soap or lotion.

I was intrigued and grossed out. I leaned over the tub, watching the current wash clear water over the bumpy topography of the bottom layer. Dips and valleys made almost recognizable shapes. A large, central outcropping of piled sediment looked like wash boards from a country road. The liquid shifted around in the box, churning slightly opposite me. I instinctively leaned back. Slowly, a softened ridge came out of the watery top layer. It turned over slightly. The hair rose on the back of my neck and arms. One foot shifted behind me. The end of the ridge rotated then expanded into tendrils. Four long fingers and a thumb smacked palm first into the sneeze guard. I yelped and ran, putting my back against a Tyren tank.

The hand receded, leaving a smear on the plastic, and splashes of goop spilling out onto the metal bench and vinyl flooring.

I hit every light switch and was out the door seconds later, sick and shaken. I needed to pee, throw up, and cry, in no specific order.

Genevieve was cooking up humanish things, pulling the building blocks out of Tyrens. That told me the beings in the boxes were not likely to be gargoyles. The minerals in the Grotto, where the Tyrens lived, muted the transformation and rendered us into human form at night. The muck being pulled into the coffins had to be heavy with whatever it was. The tubing seemed to carry the fluid into a manifold of sorts where it may have been processed, maybe even run through some kind of sieve. The end result coagulated in the tubs, coming together into something creepily alive. The hand was human, no less.

Genevieve was kidnapping Tyrens and bleeding them. She probably drained them until death. Her purpose? Creating life. I'd bank the end result wasn't anyone I'd want to meet in a dark alley. And how the heck was she getting into the Grotto to get them? That wasn't a happy thought. Everyone who lived at the castle grounds in Scotland was a member of Clan Logan, except Peter and Petra.

Only one direction led away from the room I'd been in, so I opened the only door I came to, which led to a carpeted hallway with décor that matched the overblown, Victorian posh of Genevieve's living room.

Cody leaned against the wall. I could have cried happy tears.

He put a finger against his lips and waved me over. I was reserved and held back the urge to sprint at him. I got a sense there was something else that made him tick, rather than

Genevieve. Gratefully, I hurried toward him on dirty, sticky, sore feet.

"You okay?" He kept his voice low. "I've been looking all over this fucking place for you."

"I'm okay. A little sick, but fine, I guess," I whispered back.

"You sure?"

"No, I'm not. They're like, cooking up people in the next room. I just . . ." I took a deep breath. "And they took all kinds of samples from me, like blood and hair. And I just did something horrible." I stopped talking and took a big breath.

"No, you didn't," he said, rubbing my shoulders and looking straight into my eyes. "You're fine." His motions were quick and he looked worriedly toward the corridor.

"Have you ever just, like, done something and both scared and hated yourself afterward? Because that's what just happened. I need to get out of here. Did you hear me? She's making things with hands in there!"

He nodded. "I know. She's bringing someone back from the dead. Watch out for her. You have no idea."

Actually, I did have an idea now that pieces began to fall into place. I just didn't know how much I could say to him. I liked Cody. He was with Genevieve, but he didn't belong with her. I didn't want to hurt his feelings, but he could do a lot better than Miss Guano Crazy in the other room. "Genevieve. You're with her. I mean, do you know about all of this? There's a lot going on with her and it goes far beyond the stick up her butt and the psychosis. You need to get away from here."

"This is about your book, Tessa. It's a small price to pay for saving humanity from annihilation."

"You know about that?" My whisper shouted words came out too fast.

"I've been tracking that book for the last three years."

"You didn't come to the UK to go backpacking?"

"Not hardly."

I was impressed to the point of silence. "Who's in the box?"

"A guy. Someone she's known for her entire life. Kai, I think. I'm not familiar with him."

I was stunned. "Really? Why is every female over here hung up on that dick? He . . . he broke my fingers! I mean, I got back at him, killed him and all, but, he was absolutely freakin' nuts." I shook my head, digesting what I'd learned. Kai was being brought back to life using the dredges of Tyren essence or something. Of course, something beautiful and pure would have to die to enable him to live again. And why should he be able to? He was a monster. A murderer, a kidnapper, and all-around domineering freak.

"It's taken me this long to earn Gen's trust. It will all be over soon." Cody continued to try to calm me. It wasn't working.

"What are your plans for the book?" I liked the way everyone was itching to get ahold of the book and I hadn't made up my mind about giving it up. Just moments ago, I didn't even know if I'd make it off the gurney.

"I've got a buyer. But really, I'm fighting the urge to destroy it. I know about all of its power. What it does to everyone. What it did to you." He gestured toward the hall. "Just know, she trusts me with her whole heart."

"How can you be sure?" Her heart had to be a shriveled walnut of a thing. I would always have doubts about everyone. Cody was plainly noble and good-hearted, but plans failed all the damned time.

A door slammed from where I'd just fled. I jumped and fought the urge to bolt the other direction.

"Here," he said and thrust a small bit of folded paper in my hand. "It really is going to be okay. Head that way." He pointed across the room to a door. "It was empty a few moments ago. I'll hope to see you very soon. Just play it safe."

I crammed the note between my breasts as Cody vanished into the hallway and silently closed the door.

Gathering my wits by taking a breath and swallowing hard, I walked through the hall and to the first room I'd been in, to see Genevieve herself, tipping a glass and half-watching as the Tyren churned and bubbled in the tank, tortured.

She looked up at me, hit a button on the remote that audibly kicked off a control in the tank, and emptied her glass as the Tyren slunk to the back of the container like a spider running from a spray can of poison.

"What did those freaks do with all the samples they took?" That was a much better opener than "What the fuck do you think you're doing cooking up Kai in your back room?"

She didn't respond, just walked to a fancy, gilded bar and filled her glass from a crystal decanter.

"I swear, if you don't tell me, I'm going to beat it out of you." I stepped toward her, knowing I'd beat her to a pulp with my last breath. Hell, maybe I'd bite her, too. She might taste even better than her doctor goon.

"Be careful," she said, taking her seat. "Not one of us started off as a monster." She grabbed the remote and pointed it at the Tyren again.

I batted it out of her hand. As the plastic casing exploded on the floor, she blinked hard and took another drink.

"You're going to kill her," I pointed out.

Genevieve snorted an unladylike little laugh. "Can't," she admitted. "I've boiled that bitch for days on end. She won't die." She got up and walked toward the tank, deep in thought, trusting me far too much. She turned around just as I was going to jump her.

"It's what they call magic down here, the power that keep this thing moving. We get it at birth, those like you and I."

"We are nothing alike."

She laughed again. I grew tired of that.

"I've known you since the beginning of your time, Teasa. I was there when you were born to your whore of a mother."

"You're drunk," I accused. She was also delusional. And stupid. "Do you really think you should be insulting me right now?"

"Cheers," she said, with a little nod and a big grin. "I loved your father."

"I don't want to know this." It was odd how words could kill my moxie in a heartbeat.

"Oh, you're going to listen, and hear me well." She turned to face me, straight on. "You and I both feel injustice. We have that in common. Although, you are the source of mine." She swallowed hard, staring at me with a look of disgust. "You're not even supposed to exist."

"You don't know who I am. I'm not even from here."

Genevieve burst into laughter. "Oh, I know exactly who you are, Teasa, daughter of Lugh. You are the reason gargoyles exist."

She had me there. Although I didn't always get to act on it, that goddess was part of me. I was stuck in a weakened, human state right now, but she'd nailed it.

"I've thought about the day I would finally speak to you for centuries, thinking about all the ways I wanted to hurt you so you know how this feels. I'll start with some cold facts, and we'll go from there.

"I killed your mother."

I shook my head, trying to understand what the hell she was talking about. The only family I'd known was dead. My parents were killed in a car wreck and my brother was killed in Iraq.

"It is truth. And it's why I'm here," she said, waving her arms at the room around us. "She conceived you. I waited until you were born and they were attached to you to get back at your father. It's what he deserved for bedding a human. You got away, but poor mommy . . ." she bit her lip and shook her head, grinning maniacally. "I'm the reason you were on the run. I almost had you when Lugh found your mother's body."

"Toys in the attic." I shook my head. She was pathetic in a scary, psychotic way.

"All I had time for was one, fiery little car crash and you still managed to merge yourself with this human."

"You killed my human mother, the one who was also a mother to Robbie?"

"Both the human who bore your Earthen body and the one who bore you as a demigod, as well. They both died in fire," she said, much like a serial killer who considered herself an artist. "Boom."

I would never forget the sound of her voice when she said that last bit. The way her bright, red lips formed a perfect O before she broke into a proud smile. I don't know when I teared up, but I caught it before I made a mess of myself.

"And you did this to yourself out of choice," she said, gesturing to my human form. "What a slap in the face to your father, denying his resemblance. Denying your true identity as a demigod. I am in exile here, stripped of my identity and far from his grace. Lugh loves the craft of punishment. Even you, his once beloved daughter, sentenced to life as a gargoyle. It's fitting, really. A bastard deserves not the grace of the father."

No witty retort came to mind. I was in foreign territory. The best I could do was hold it together while she ranted.

"And to top it all off, I have to watch you plod around down here, denying your gods-given abilities when the likes of this," she said, gesturing toward the Tyren. "Even these things embrace their power."

I held my tongue about how I felt she was a freak for torturing the Tyren, remembering Cody's advice to play it safe. Mouthing off wouldn't help me to freedom.

"Geo!" she erupted. I jumped in my seat. "Load the tank and escort Miss Conley back to Logan Castle."

"That's it?" I asked. I'd been certain she'd off me, but of

course, she wanted the book, and I couldn't deliver it if I was dead.

"You know what to do," she said. "Adam seems interested to see you. Hand him the book like a nice human."

Holy shit. One of the rules in Zombieland was double-tap, making sure they were dead. I'd failed there, apparently. But he certainly had bled a lot.

"That book is the key to getting my life back. To regaining my status and leaving this place. I don't belong here. I want to go home, and your friends would be happier with me there. Make this trip easy on yourself and don't abuse my men, understand?" she asked.

I nodded.

"Good. Now get the bloody hell out of my house." She turned her back on me.

Geo arrived quickly with three other men who all started working on the aquarium. It was sectioned off and sealed using pieces of what looked like Plexiglas. The part the Tyren huddled in was laid flat on the back where casters were mounted at the top and bottom. The little wheels groaned with the weight. The men were careful, thank goodness, and the sloshing inside the tank was minimal. I followed them back to the small garage where a truck waited and stood by while they loaded up. A door was opened for me and I held down the back of my ruined dress as I got inside for the ride home.

"Thank you," I said. It was more out of good, Southern manners than anything, but I figured it couldn't hurt.

"Shut up, bitch," the man said.

Knowing right where I stood with the characters transporting me, I kept quiet, hoping the jostling from the trip back to the Grotto wasn't too much for the ailing Tyren.

Genevieve pulled a psychotic one-eighty as we left, waving and smiling as Cody appeared next to her. He grabbed her hand

and smiled, waving, too. I hoped he came to his senses and left before Genevieve got the opportunity to do something vile.

I rode along, quiet and polite, so I would arrive in Scotland in one piece but inside I seethed. Genevieve was going to die by my hand or claws. I would tear her apart. By my calculation, she'd ruined my life twice. I'd end hers for good.

Once the truck was headed up the ascent to the road we'd come in on, I tried to breathe deeply because my heart was racing so badly. Two thugs rode in front of the cab and I sat in the truck's backseat beside a goon with no neck. Frankly, I was scared and didn't know what to do. Pain pricked along my spine each time my back hit the seat. The tunnel drove me crazy, seeming much longer than it had before.

The passenger in front turned to the guy next to me and tossed a black sack to him. No-Neck pulled the bead low on the drawstring, opening the bag up wide.

"Hold still," he said, all business.

"What? Why?" I was genuinely confused and didn't get it until he came at me with the open sack. "Shit! No, wait. You don't have to. I won't look at anything," I said, grabbing at the material when he held it over my head. "I'll just look at the floor," I begged.

Everything was black in an instant and the drawstring closed around my neck. I began to think it would have been better to sleep through it, in some ways. Being awake and jumping at every sound and movement was the worst of terror, when I considered I was alone, lost, and in the company of three giant men, with no gargoyle happening, the goddess missing. After a moment I started to hyperventilate, my mind getting the best of me. No one helped. I came around without passing out and rode in silence. We continued to drive for what seemed like a day. Finally, we were on a winding, hilly road for a while. We slowed as my window rolled down. The bag was loosened and yanked off my head.

Once my eyes adjusted, the iron gates to Logan Castle came into view.

"Press the button and get us inside," the driver ordered.

I obliged, so grateful I nearly cried out once I heard Iain's voice on the com.

"What do you have for the castle?" he asked, apparently seeing the truck on video.

There was a pause and I didn't know what to say.

Shuffling sounded. "Tessa?" Iain said.

"Hi, Iain. We have a sick Tyren in here. Open up please?"

"Who are you with?" Pensive didn't mix well with his Iain's usual confidence.

"Genevieve's finest."

The gate drew open and the driver started through. Not five seconds passed before all the Logans, Peter, and Petra met us in the driveway. I bailed out as Osgar talked with the driver, which was just a series of warnings and threats from both sides. Crispin walked up to me and gave me a once-over.

"You hurt?"

"I'm okay. Just a sore back."

He turned me slightly to have a look. "Looks bruised and lumpy. I think you'll live. Feel that?"

"What? I mean my backbone stings like hell." He applied enough pressure to my back to push me away slightly, but the sensation wasn't isolated to my back. I couldn't tell where his hand was.

"It must be numb here," he said, tapping. Two quick taps resonated through to my sternum, but still no pain on the lump he was checking. "I'll have a better look in a wee bit. Certain it's nothing to fash yourself over."

"Sounds good." Really, it didn't. I was extra worried at that point. Something about part of my body losing feeling didn't inspire confidence. It hurt like crazy the day before and now had gone numb.

The others worked together to lower the Tyren and her refrigerator sized tank from a lift on the tailgate of the truck, onto a cart with handles on the sides. They began rolling her toward the back of the cavern, where the newly added access was located. She sloshed like grey meat and I wondered if she would ever shimmer with life again.

I gimped after them on bare feet. Instead of waiting in line, I went for the stairs and beat them to the water's edge. They wheeled the tank across the dance floor.

Most of them looked uncertain as to how to get her out of the tank and into the stream. I had an idea.

"Let's push the whole tank into the deep part here."

Crispin shrugged and helped Iain wheel the tank into the water while the others watched Genevieve's goons. I waded into the water and submerged, searching for another Tyren to help the injured female we were about to put back in the water. The image of bringing home a new goldfish came to mind, but it was much more involved.

I had a hunch she was pretty far gone. Genevieve had tried to kill her many times. I didn't know what was keeping her going. Even as she flowed out of the tank into the good, mineral-rich water, she still didn't have that silvery transparency Tyrens normally had. It was so bad, I could see all of her and she looked like a petite human with a sickly pallor. Her body was pale and sort of flaky looking, with dark splotches here and there. I did the only thing I could think of and held her up, as if she needed her face above the surface while I treaded water.

Something brushed my leg. I put my face in the water. Two male Tyrens were below the surface. I sunk and took her with me.

The males touched her tenderly as they moved away from me. I held my breath as long as I could before coming up for air. When I went back down, they were gone. That was very disappointing.

I emerged just in time to hear an argument between Genevieve's men and Osgar. They wanted to take the tank back to Genevieve but the Logans weren't having it.

"Get back in the lorry and get the hell off the grounds before I change my mind about allowing you to leave," Osgar said.

"*Psscht*," the driver hissed. "Genevieve doesn't need your charity."

They started toward the exit, the Logans escorting them out. Once the men were inside the truck, they sped off.

I was so grateful to be back with people who cared about me that I didn't know who to hug first.

15

A shower revived my senses and I could bet the Logans were happy I'd washed up, too. I lingered in the hottest water I could stand, letting the spray hit the sore spot on my back. It itched like crazy. My left arm was skinnier and I managed to get my hand between my shoulder blades to scratch at it. A hardened scab ran only about a half an inch long there. There were no stitches, or staples, but there was a knot higher up toward my neck that I could barely touch a fingertip to. Finding a lump beneath my skin was both gross and horrific, especially considering I suspected whatever material comprised the thing was keeping me from being a gargoyle. I weighed that thought, fully realizing what it might mean for my future. Bree and I might be able to go home, for instance. I let my cramping arm drop down, tingling and throbbing.

I might have been reading too much good into that finding. Something wasn't right with it. I didn't envision any saving grace. Instead, my imagination ran with my fear. Rotten things twisted there beneath my skin, poisoning me. Spreading like cancer and turning good parts of me black and dead. I knew intuition when I felt it.

One handheld mirror was a huge help when looking at my back in the bathroom mirror. I climbed onto the vanity so I could see better. An inch-long cylinder about as big around as a pen lay along my backbone, right between my shoulder blades. Black and green bruising surrounded the lump, with most of the black part starting at the top where a small cut had been made and closed up with three sutures of stiff black thread. My first inclination was to call Peter to help open it up. But then I'd have to endure a lecture about how I shouldn't have done something that led me to be captured, yada yada yada. And I wasn't thrilled at the idea of being close to him after what I'd learned about his principles. Yet he was the only one I considered asking. My level of comfort wasn't quite at the level of "shirtless" with anyone but Bree, who would have been traumatized. I opted to work it out myself.

I could only reach one of the stitches with the fingernail clippers. I hoped the thread was all attached, but it only loosened one side of the cut. It would have to do. The good news was that it didn't hurt much. The skin was numb. Probably from unskilled or uncaring hands who did the cutting in the first place. Each time I got my middle finger beneath the tube underneath my skin, I could get it to slide only a little way toward the incision. My arm would start cramping from the contortion of reaching between my shoulder blades. The hairbrush handle didn't work. Sweat ran down each of my temples from the exertion and some pain, plus frustration.

The last ditch idea I had was to use the vanity cabinet top. I spun around, flattened my back as best I could, and placed my shoulder blades just over the top of the cabinet. I squatted there, dropping down until the bottom of the thing made contact with the flat surface through my skin. That part I was guessing since the site was mostly lacking any sensation. I just let it stop me from dropping any lower. I hoped I had the base of it caught. Then I leaned back and pushed to trap the protrusion and then worked my way lower, keeping my back flat against the side of the vanity. The thing moved, and I felt it clear to my toes. I didn't want to have to endure more than I had to, or to try it all again.

I dropped back hard as a tearing sensation ripped up my spine and dropped me like a rock onto the tile. I bled like crazy, an enthusiastic little rivulet pouring down my back. It dripped onto the floor. My legs trembled as I clamored back to standing and grasped the mirror with a shaking, two-handed grip. On the vanity sat a blood streaked, metal cylinder, about the size of my pinky finger. I checked my back and it was still bleeding, but slower. It would be fine.

I grabbed a towel and pulled it around my back like I was drying off after a shower, then tied it between my breasts as tightly as possible to apply some pressure.

After a few moments of waiting around for my platelets to coagulate, I couldn't stand still any longer, so I took another quick shower and cleaned up the blood on the floor. Clean clothes were completely underrated. I dressed in an older shirt that I wouldn't mind getting a little gooey and ran downstairs to the kitchen with a towel around my neck.

"So, where's Bree?" I squeezed the ends of my dripping hair with the towel and grabbed an apple from the breakfast bar. The sun would set in just a few minutes and I wanted to check in with her before I Garged Out for the night. I expected to find her in the kitchen rather than in her room.

Crispin closed the book he was reading and set it down without a sound. "She's upstairs." He didn't smile, like usual.

I blew it off. "Cool. Thanks." I turned to run back upstairs but he reached and caught my elbow before I could go.

"We need to talk, lass," he said, gesturing to the stool beside his. I didn't care for his somber tone simply for the fact it held so much gravity that I could tell something was up. I just couldn't let myself succumb to more gloom and doom.

"Why? You're not pregnant are you?" I winked and crunched my apple.

No smile or reaction to the quip. Not even a blink or an eyeroll. Nada.

"Tough crowd." I swallowed and set the apple down. "Is she okay? Oh God. Is *she* pregnant?" My joke might have just landed both feet firmly in my mouth.

He shook his head. "No, definitely not. She isn't feeling the best, however." A small sheen of sweat broke out over his face.

I bounced off the stool and tore off toward the stairs, sprinting up them. Peter emerged from a sitting room as I blew past, but he didn't say anything, just looked down with a frown. Bree's bedroom was past mine on the left, and within a few seconds of running hallways with Crispin on my heels, yelling for me to stop and to please wait, I pounced on her door and pounded on it hard.

"Bree? Hey, it's me." I knocked again.

Crispin grabbed at my hand, but I dodged him and twisted the door handle, throwing the door open wide. "What is your problem tonight?"

He didn't answer. I walked inside to where Bree stood, already in pajamas, looking out the window at the waning sun. "Hey, you okay?"

"Yeah. I'm fine." She turned and lunged forward, embracing me in a hug before I could get a clear look at her. A strand of her hair fell across my hand. It was the first time I'd seen Bree's hair unwashed to the point of being oily. I picked it up while she hugged me, rolling the thickened hair between my fingers.

"You'd best head to your room. The sun's about to set." She leaned away with a poor attempt at a smile. The room was dim, but the dark circles under her eyes were a blatant contrast to her pale skin.

"You're not okay. What's going on here?" She didn't answer, and I glanced back to Crispin. He looked like he was about to speak but then shut up. Backing toward the door, he said, "I'm going to let you two talk." The door clicked shut and I turned back to Bree.

"You'd better go, too. Seriously. Any minute now you'll change, and I know you hate for people to see."

"I'll use your bathroom." I dropped onto the bed, sending the message that I wasn't going any damned place at all until she fessed up.

"Suit yourself." She whirled back toward the window. A second later, her frame shook from a sob she'd tried to suppress.

I didn't say anything, just waited for either my skin to tingle, announcing my change, or for her to start talking.

"Gloaming." She shook her head, speaking to herself, rather than giving me the explanation I demanded. "Out of all the new words I've learned here, I used to think that was the most distinctly beautiful."

"Bree, you know I love you. And you know you can talk to me about anything. I really need to know what happened." I tried not to come off like I was begging for her to talk to me but failed. I truly had to know. I had to help and make it right.

She only sighed and dipped her head, chin to chest.

The sun winked out and I headed for her attached bathroom, shutting the door as I shucked clothing. Wings jumped out of my shoulders and my tail hit the floor. I brought my wings in fast so I didn't smash anything up; the horns on top of them were a serious magnet for breakables. As certain as the sunset, there I was, forked tongue, scaly skin transforming, and muscles building in my thighs and shoulders. A gargoyle, plain as day. I'd known it all along but couldn't believe that someone could implant something beneath my skin to stop me from Garging Out. I grinned at my reflection as fangs cut my gums. I pulled the door open and walked out while the rest of my scales set.

The thought that I wasn't going to change hung at the back of my mind as I walked out, grinning. "I'm ba-ack," I said, still smiling. The room was a lot darker than I remembered. Silhouettes moved with sick noises.

Bree's head whipped back. In the next instant I was horrified when spiked wings burst through her pajama top and her bottoms split at the seams, refusing to accommodate her expanding thighs. Cloth shredded. She fell forward slightly, claws smacking the window sill. After a breath, she straightened. One muscular, scaled arm flew around to the wing on her opposite shoulder, where her claw jerked a piece of ruined, cotton shirt free and tossed it to the floor.

My heart broke while hers beat beneath a fresh, scaly chest plate.

"Oh no," I said.

She drew in a huge breath. "Let's just get this straight," she said, her speech a little slurred over fangs, but was understandable, nonetheless. "I no longer need you to protect me. Things can go back to the way they were in Austin, when I looked out for *you*. You will not blame yourself, and that's final." She turned around, finally showing me her features.

At some point I'd begun to cry and put my claws against my mouth. I did my best to stop the shock and dropped my arms. Her sky-blue eyes were still there but the rest of her skin had taken on a tan color that got darker at the palms of her hands and under her arms. Her tail lashed, and I stopped examining her, forcing myself to look at her face, to concentrate on seeing her soul looking back at me from inside. Shock faded quickly. Somehow, I'd known.

"Why didn't you change last night, Tessa? Everyone knows you didn't."

"I had this vial of stuff sewn into my back." Her tone was so abrupt and cold, I didn't say anything else.

She snorted. "Didn't you want to share that news?" She waved a claw full of talons between us.

"I wasn't sure about it until Garging Out just now. I'm sorry—"

"Don't!" she yelled.

I shook my head, remembering my emotional rollercoaster while I was trying to adjust to the change. Flares of temper were to be expected. "I was just going to say that was insensitive of me not to come and find you when I got back."

She looked down. The silence hung for too long.

"This wouldn't have happened to you if I wouldn't have stayed in that goddamned bookstore!" I exploded, needing to get it out. "No matter if you want me blaming myself or not, this happened to you because of me. I'm the one who got stuck in the UK. I'm the one who seems to be a beacon for screwed up shit to cling to." My wings fluttered slowly, and I did my best to furl them in, but my tail wouldn't stop lashing around like a beheaded snake. "I don't care if you want to hear it or not. This is my fault," I explained, my talons scraping against my chest plate as I gestured to myself. "I should have been watching that book closer so it couldn't be used to do this to you." I was trying to talk too fast. Spit flew from my forked tongue and I tripped up over half my words. I had a hunch about who would want to use the book to change her and he was about to have a broken nose.

"Oh, spare me!" Bree yelled. "I don't buy into the self-loathing crap, Tessa. I know it was you. I get it, I mean, I wouldn't want to live over here without you either. And you dropped so many hints! I'm actually a little glad this happened. I'll never have to walk into a conversation and hear how I need protection while you try to talk under your breath. Which, by the way, you completely suck at!"

"How could you actually think I changed you?" She couldn't be convinced of it. There was no way. Bree knew me better than that. I thought...

She took a long breath and started off in a calm tone, more like herself. "I've had time to think and I'm doing every-damned-thing I can to reason through this so I can still bear to look you in the eye."

"Bree!" I was stunned. How could Bree, my best friend, think I was capable of changing her into a gargoyle, of stealing her life?

"Get out of my room, Tessa!" She pulled her gaze away and ran to her bathroom, slapping her wings against either side of that jamb and slamming the door.

"So, do you remember when the book told you it would call a toll due, Tessa? There is nothing you could do to stop this." Peter stood in the doorway, large wings blocking out most of the light from the door. "And I know it wasn't you."

"Get the hell out, Peter!" I screamed. "That door was shut for a reason. Nobody in here needs your two cents or your arrogance."

He did the exact opposite of leaving and came toward me. "I'm here to take you downstairs, Tessa. We need to have a look at you."

"There isn't a thing wrong with me. We can talk later." I turned away from him, willing him to leave.

He didn't. He picked me up and simply carried me down the hall as I beat on him, biting and clawing. My wings scraped paint off the wall.

"Put me down!" I screamed. If I could have found some leverage I would have torn him up. My claws were numb when we landed beneath the banister in the front room. I continued to pound on him, aiming for his eyes since that was the only way I could see him flinch. Peter wasn't the only one who wanted to know why I didn't react to sunshine. The fact they didn't simply ask me what was up pissed me off.

I raged, screaming and kicking. My temperature spiked. Peter dropped me next to the stairs. My God, I hated him.

I exploded with heat that flew around me like a halo. A nearby armchair flew backward and smashed against the matching sofa, smoldering. Peter shaded his eyes but used his wings to steady himself. I bounded up to Peter and backhanded him as hard as I could, nearly falling down. He sprawled, catching himself. I twisted to hit him again, but Iain wrapped his thick claws around my arms and hauled me back a staggering step. A quick twinge of pain stung my neck but was gone as quickly as it came on. I needed to slow down before I hurt myself. I hadn't slept or eaten right in God only knows how long.

Peter shook his head, glaring at me.

I smiled. "I'm not as miserable as you think I am." I shook Iain's grip away easily, focusing on Peter. "I love being me. All of it. The powers, the killing. The saving. The loving . . . I just wish I wouldn't have let you slow me down."

"Whoa," Crispin said from the doorway. "Why is the furniture on fire?" He looked straight at me.

"What, one little fire and it's automatically me that did it?"

He blinked, looking bland.

"I'm going to ask you this one time," I said calmly. "Why did you do this," I gestured at both our gargoyle forms, "to Bree? She loves you anyway. You didn't have to."

"How could you think I would?" he yelled. I'd never seen him angry before. Fighting and killing, I'd seen. Pissed off, not so much.

"Well she thinks I did it!" Crispin shook his head, scowling. His wings beat softly in agitation. "And we both know it wasn't me," I said, fighting off a brief bout of dizziness.

Being accused never made anyone feel good and Crispin was not an exception. Worse, he was hurt. That was regretful, although he was the one who had something to gain if Bree became a gargoyle. She couldn't go back to the States that way.

"It wasn't him." Iain held up the thing I'd dug out of my back, using a little cloth to grip it.

"You went into my room?" Were they all a bunch of sneaks or what? They didn't trust me at all. That was plain.

"I just wanted you to know that I have it. No one could guess what you went through with Genevieve, or what condition you would be in upon your return. We are just covering ourselves."

"Going into my room was a dick move."

He didn't address that issue. "I know that neither of you did this to Bree. I remembered it like a dream."

Everyone stared at me. "You all knew? You let Bree think it was me?"

"She told no one of that notion to my knowing," said Crispin.

"I told them when it happened. Cris prepared her the best he could but he only had that one day. He hasn't left her side, unless by her request," said Iain.

The apology clawed its way from my heart to my throat but didn't come out. The dizziness was back in force. Why did it have to happen while I was gone?

Crispin stalked off, heading up the stairs. "That book of yours compelled him, Goddess," he said. No one had ever referred to me that way before, and it wasn't meant as a complement.

"I had no way of stopping it." I hadn't felt a bond with the damned thing since it saved me. I hated it, and every page between the covers knew that. It acted out and sent that juicy, rotted, hairy monster after me when I kicked it under my bed. The feeling was mutual. I wasn't the one to wield its magic, by any means. Maybe I was just too human for that.

"You saved us the trouble of removing this," Iain said, oblivious to the turmoil between Crispin and me. He carefully wiped blood from the tiny metal vial he'd retrieved. "I wish you'd have waited. We wouldn't have such a bloody mess and likely less pain." He used the cloth to shield himself from direct contact, grasping the end of the cylinder and holding it to the light with a huge but nimble claw. I couldn't see what was inside.

"I need that." I stared at it just long enough to lose balance and fall forward. Smoke was building up around us from the chair I'd lit up. Exhaustion took over. Peter stepped back and let me hit the tile, then stomped off toward the front doors with his tail twitching. I moved as quickly as I could, clamoring to my feet. Iain helped me reach the handrail to the stairs.

"Don't fash yourself over the burning furniture, Peter, I'll put it out." I couldn't tell if Iain was seriously offering to douse the upholstery, or if he was messing with Peter about being an ass.

Peter didn't let the door hit him, completely uncaring and pissed. I'd told him off good and true and had no intention of taking back a single word.

"I'm sorry, Iain. The flames are gone. I think it's dying on its own." I swayed, trying to focus on the blackened chair. Iain grabbed a fat vase off an end table and dumped it, flower stems, too, onto the spot that smoked the most.

"Atta boy," I commented.

"Let's get you upstairs so you can sleep this off." he said, a little too knowingly.

"I'm tired and pissed, and you violated my privacy," I retorted. "And you stabbed me in the neck with something."

"I hit you with a dart."

"What did you shoot me with? We have to work on your trust issues, pal." I held onto his scaly arm for dear life, feeling pretty buzzed.

"A wee bit of horse tranquilizer."

"Oh, my God," I moaned. "Too much, buddy."

"It won't last long. Gargoyles metabolize the drug faster."

My emotions ran wild, surging into sadness. "I'm so sorry," I said, slurring like a drunk. "I didn't mean to sound hateful before." I leaned too far and nearly fell again, but Iain held me up.

"I'm sure Peter will get over it."

"Not him. That dick deserves it. I meant Crispin. I shouldn't have said all that to him." I knew I half-mumbled the last part but felt he got the gist.

"Talk to him later, when you feel better and can speak clearly. Let's get you upstairs and you can see him in a while."

"Did you really think I'd keep things from you? I mean about the vial in my back?"

"I trust you. I do not trust Genevieve."

"Makes sense." I stepped slowly toward the stairs, quickly losing balance. He caught me, and I spun a little in his grip, heavy and off balance. We bounced into each other, chest to chest. I slammed my eyes shut. Iain was one of those great looking guys that always kept me aware of his sexuality, even when he was Garged Out. Just like when it had happened with Peter before, the second our bodies touched, our gargoyles retreated and bare, human skin met mine. He froze. I looked up at him as my vision swam in a circle.

"Hm," I mumbled, around a nervous laugh. I was careful to keep my eyes locked on his face. Iain checked the room to see if anyone else was looking at us, bare butts and all.

"You know about this?" he said.

"Yeah." I was secretly glad he hadn't moved. His skin was warm and cool at the same time. "It was just for a second."

Iain kissed my forehead and stepped back, keeping a hold on my hand. I started laughing when he did it. We both changed quickly, the force springing us backward. The eruption of my wings and tail nearly knocked me over. "Seemed like the thing to do," he said, with an ironic grin. He placed the wadded-up cloth and vial in one of my claws. "Hold on tight to that." He grabbed my elbow and we took the first step.

I squeezed my claw tight to ensure the little vial didn't fall out on the way to my room, glad I had it back and that Iain seemed to be trusting me again.

16

The book had to go. Whether I'd brought on Bree's change by my actions, or by giving the damned thing the right to take a toll, my decision was final. The book was far too powerful, much too sentient for me to ever keep it safe or to keep the world safe from it. It looked out for its number one, and so would I. The risk would be eliminated when I placed it in the most capable hands I knew of. The time was as good as it would ever get to create a little bit more safety for the people I loved.

The vial and cloth rested on the dresser, still wrapped tight, just like when Iain handed it to me. Carefully, to make sure the creepy thing didn't make contact with my skin, I tucked it beneath an arm and went out toward the stables and Iain's workshop. It was still early enough that dew soaked the grounds, darkening leaves and glistening low in the foggy morning. My flip-flop-clad feet were already wet, but since my shoes would take too long to dry out, I opted for thrifty convenience over elegance. Footwear was sparse in my closet. The other choice was a pair of strappy heels, which was a no-go.

If I'd thought it through correctly, Iain would be outside

feeding the horses and working, hopefully alone. As I stepped through the stable door, a few of the horses picked their heads up out of hay troughs to peer at me over the walls separating stalls, only to shove them right back in and keep munching. Iain had already fed them and wasn't in sight. I shut the door again and continued along to the smallish lean-to where he crafted swords and such.

The door was open, and he was seated at his workbench wearing blue plastic gloves and eye protection.

In spite of how odd that seemed, I stepped inside. "Hi, Iain. Do you have a minute to talk?"

"Tessa, hey," he said, standing up. "Certainly." He pushed the clear glasses up onto his head and began pulling at his gloves.

"You don't have to stop. I mean, I just have a question." I stopped myself. "I mean it's sort of a question. Or like a trade. Kind of, like a deal?" I squinted against embarrassment, hating the way I babbled sometimes. At least we both had clothes on this time.

"A deal?" he asked.

I opened my eyes just in time to see him eye the cloth in my grasp. "Yeah. An important one."

"Well, out with it then," he baited.

"Okay. Here goes. I need to borrow your work truck." I held my breath.

He didn't answer at first, just looked stymied. "The grain lorry? Why on Earth?"

"It's perfect, and safe, and inconspicuous . . . and, ah, God." The words had been so neatly aligned in my mind as I practiced on the way over. They'd come out all piled up and hectic. I sighed. "I just want to go to the library. Only for like, an hour."

He didn't answer right away, just considered quietly, watching me. "You can take the lorry. One hour. Don't make me come looking for you, and tell no one."

"So, that's it? I can take it?"

"Yes. And thank you for asking instead of acting as you have in the past when you want something. I appreciate that."

The bottom of the wrapped-up cloth came loose and I grabbed at it, trying to keep it clumped together. It was a lost cause. "I was going to make a deal with you for this," I said, still wadding the material. More came loose and I decided to check the ground to see if the vial had already fallen out.

"It's not in there."

I stopped shuffling material around and glanced at Iain.

"It never was. I took it."

"Wow." I didn't know what else to say. I'd never suspect Iain of something like that.

"You were faded and on the fight. I didn't think you'd notice for at least a day, but here you are the very next morning, of course." He looked down. "I'm sorry, Tessa, but you couldn't expect us to live this way for centuries and have you come along with an obvious cure for the change without us looking into it."

I nodded. He was absolutely right. And I looked like a cold bitch trying to use the vial as a tool for bartering. I tossed the empty cloth on his workbench and crossed my arms.

Iain spun on his stool and retrieved the vial, still intact, from behind a folded rag. "It doesn't work anymore, if it ever worked on contact. I tried it last night, with no results. I remained a gargoyle." He tried to hand it over, but I shook my head.

"Just hold onto it."

He nodded and set it on the bench.

"Did you happen to open it up and see what's in it?"

"That was the next step. Not as of yet."

"I'm sure it's the water from the Grotto." I nodded again, feeling sad and awkward. He picked a set of keys off a nail sticking out of the wall.

"Be careful. Best go early and be back before the noon hour."

I took them and nodded again. "Thank you." I turned to leave.

"Tessa, I'm sorry. Don't hate me."

"So am I. And I could never hate you, Iain. I'm just disappointed. But I am getting a feel for how the real world works thanks to all this." That may have been a little bitchy, but it was true. There were limits to what people would do for me. And vice versa.

I took my time heading back to my room. But once inside, I dug up the note Cody had given me.

∼

I DIDN'T KNOW which was worse, driving Iain's barge along the windy road to Kelty, parking said barge, or trying to act casual lugging the most awkward camouflage/oversized tote bag into the library. I let the truck hang a couple corners too wide, but it was easy to coast downhill to get to town. As luck would have it, there was a parking spot on the street, at the end of a line of spots. I backed in between the lines, like I owned the place. It was a little past eleven thirty when I made it across the stone courtyard and through the glass doors. Straight ahead was a check-in type desk with a lady standing behind it. She watched me from the moment I saw her.

Her lips parted in the most genuine smile I'd witnessed in months. Age-clouded blue eyes twinkled as I approached. She had a load of hardbacks, slender arms cradling them as she slung a waist-length silver blonde braid over a shoulder to her back. A name tag was pinned to her green clerk's vest, reading:

Kelty Branch Library

Anna

Just seeing her turned a switch in me. For some reason, I needed her to make sense in my life. *Please, just be normal.* Just one person to help me hang onto the world as I used to know it. Pre-gargoyle. Pre-goddess. Pre-dark magic.

Not that I'd have liked to go back to living with nuns in an orphanage, or even go back to Austin for that matter. I was in the

UK, the place I'd dreamed of since I'd first learned to read and surf the Internet. The museums, libraries, playhouses in London; my love of these things depended on my ability to skirt sunshine and get away from Peter. Those two working together made it hard to get out much. Looking at Anna gave me hope. She appeared simply pure and good. I just needed something to hang onto. Something that showed me there was still a measure of humanity around. I wondered what she would think if I let fly with the tears I fought back. I wanted to drop the damned book of curses and rush to her for a hug. Would I get a motherly embrace with a warm hand rubbing my back and a soft voice telling me "It's all going to be okay"? The way life had gone lately I was certain it was more likely to go the other way.

She looked at me like I was nuts, a girl on the edge.

I sucked it up, switched gears, and eyed the books she had.

"Hello," she said, in a welcoming voice. She set the stack on her desk. "What can I help you find?" She took her seat and pulled a mug close.

"Do you have any information on local history? Like, the clans and the, um, lore and stuff?"

Anna blinked.

"I'd also love to look through your Victorian literature section." I smiled, trying to look normal, thinking how I should have led with the request for the literature and then asked about the other.

"Perth land holdings and history are against the front wall, behind the travel section. There's a small collection in the Religion section, too." She picked up her cup and gestured straight out to her right. "Shakespeare's that way."

"Perfect. Thank you." Just for appearances, I headed to her right, when really I wanted to dive into the Religions.

"Have a library card with us?" She asked before I made it too far. I turned to see her glance out to the street, where I'd parked Iain's "lorry."

"No, ma'am." *Holy hell.*

"Well, you'll need some identification to get one." Her gaze rifled from my face to my thick book bag. If she knew the truck, she didn't let on.

I wasn't sure sharing my identity with anyone, even the seemingly innocent and kind librarian, was a stellar idea. "If it's okay, I'll just spend some time here, reading. All I have is my student identification from college."

She regarded me for a second before the smile returned. "That's fine."

I approached her, holding out my hand. "I'm Tessa."

"Anna. It's a pleasure to meet a fellow lover of literature and Perth, Tessa." She reached for a squatty honey pot with a wooden dowel for a dispenser. "Please let me know if you have trouble finding what you're looking for."

"I will." I smiled and went looking for Shakespeare.

It felt good to grab a book of plays to get cozy, whether I was just holding up appearances or not. I flipped it open but didn't read a word. What if I should have made a different choice about how to unload the book so Genevieve wouldn't get it? Maybe I should have just burned it instead of rehoming the piece of shit. It was much too late for that though.

Footsteps padded up the aisle and Cody smiled at me.

"Hey." I didn't have a smile to return.

"I just want you to know that I'm thankful. It's not all about the money."

"No?" I tried not to sound doubtful, but I was certain my handing over such an item to a treasure hunter would make said hunter very, very wealthy.

"Mm, nope." He just kept grinning.

"Well," I said, dragging my oversized bag from beside the chair. "I hope your buyer has a stroke of conscience and burns this thing." I zipped open the drawstring and pulled the leather tome free. The cover remained cool to the touch rather than warming to my hands instantly.

"That's the thing," Cody said, He whipped a pair of blue plastic gloves from his jacket pocket, then reached to relieve my burden. "This works with what it's given. It isn't always bad. As far as the buyer, I've been vetting this party for longer than I've been in the UK."

I nodded, looking into my lap. I was a little defeated, knowing down deep I wasn't the one to make the book the best it could be. I'd let it own me and to ruin part of me, to maim my best friend's heart, youth, and undying soul the same way I'd suffered. "I just keep thinking I should have destroyed it somehow, to get rid of it."

"You know it's indestructible, right?" A half smile tugged at the corner of his mouth. "Don't be so hard on yourself, Tessa. 'We know what we are but know not what we may be.'"

"Nice," I said, finally finding a smile at his quote.

"I'm a fan," he said, gesturing to the book of Shakespeare's plays resting in the chair with me.

"Maybe I need to revisit his wisdom."

"Do it." He slid his treasure into a foam sleeve and then a large bag of his own, shouldering the thing with a huge swing around his back. "I've got to get going. Crowds of belligerent British travelers are waiting for me at the airport."

"That bad?"

"Not really." He grinned. "I'm hopping a Cessna out of Perth." He winked. "Thanks again, Tessa."

"Thank you, too, Cody. Please be careful until you can unload it."

And just like that, the book was no longer my problem. Cody walked back down the hall, none-the-obvious about what he carried. I remembered the first time I'd touched that book, I'd been drawn to it, sat petting it for too long. Cody was a pro. He hadn't blinked, just slid it into his bag and let it hang off his shoulder while he said good-bye. He could have been carrying a bag of groceries and not let on differently. That helped relieve my tension. I had to trust that he knew what he was doing and how to handle himself with the sort that wanted the book. He just seemed so damned young. Like me.

I rose from the chair, feeling a thousand pounds lighter.

I'd done the right thing. The trick would be convincing the Logans.

I'd cross that bridge when I had to.

17

S pellbound. That was me as three dirty, shaggy men walked up on Iain's truck before I could get to it. Sunshine would have shown their insides. One of them looked around and then jerked the door open. Before they noticed me, I spun a one eighty and tried to look preoccupied with a statue in front of the library, hiding behind my hood. I fidgeted for a minute and then went back inside.

Anna slowly came to her feet and gawked with me. Through the paned windows, outside in the gloom, the men went about their expedition without once looking inside at us.

"Shit," I clipped.

Anna looked at me and back outside.

"This is going to sound a little crazy, but I need to know how to get out a different way."

Anna was so anxious that her words ran together even faster than a normal, native Scot dialect. After a moment and repeating half of what she said, she finally lost patience and jabbed a pointy finger behind us.

"Git yer arse on the back wall, far corner, and oot!"

"Thank you, Anna." I hated the way I had to leave so fast and hoped I could come back spend some more time with her. I was as scared as she looked, though. It was time to disappear.

I backed toward the farthest wall in the library while Anna turned the door's deadbolt with a defiant little click. She rounded her desk and picked up the receiver on an antique telephone with a freckled, blue-veined hand.

Outside at the truck, one of the men looked across the bed and through the windows at us.

I ran as fast as I could, right back at Anna. "You can't stay here. Come on. You're coming out, too."

"The library closes at twelve thirty on Wednesdays—"

"You locked the door! And it's not up for argument. Those are not nice men. They're going to try to get in here and when they do, you can't be here."

Anna considered, looking at me thoroughly.

"I'm sorry. They're here because of me." That was getting to be an all too familiar theme with people around me getting hurt. I was like a magnet for trouble and they paid the price. I couldn't let that happen to sweet, normal Anna.

She calmly set the phone on the desk, dialed the number nine three times, grabbed an old, leather purse from where it hung off the back of her chair, and led the way without another word. I hurried along, right on her heels, fighting the urge to shove her along ahead of me. She was a little on the light, frail side and her little trot was probably as fast the hitch in her get-along allowed. We finally made it to the back of the brick building and the door came into view. I ran past her and began unlatching the first of three different mechanical locks.

Glass shattered behind us. Anna looked like she might cry, then her expression changed to one that could peel paint. She didn't say a word, just locked her jaw and followed me out. We emerged onto a small patio with a short pad of fake grass and a few dried-up plant pots alongside a stand of metal lawn chairs.

I pulled her to a stop at a gap between the library and the

three-story beside it. "Okay. Just go out here through that gate and onto the road. Walk away."

Anna didn't nod, just looked from me, back to the library door, and then toward the narrow passage to the gate. I grabbed her and hugged her tight, releasing her quickly. "Be careful and stay gone."

She walked toward the gate without looking back.

I ran like hell in the opposite direction. My flip flops had about had it. Once I rounded the far side of the next building I slowed to a walk, headed down the next lane over. I crossed the street and waited for a red bus to go by. Once it passed, black smoke drifted upwards above the library. My stomach dropped.

A guy on a bike stopped ahead, looking up. I ran toward him.

"Can you call the fire department? I don't have a phone with me."

He nodded, digging in a fanny pack.

I walked to the roundabout on Cocklaw Street, where people had started to gather and point. Iain's truck was right where I left it, so I headed that way at a fast pace. Sirens erupted a few blocks away. I slid into the truck, started it up, and simply pulled away.

Gawking humans stared up in the sky and pointed as I rolled by, fighting the urge to floor it, and looking for Anna. She was nowhere to be seen. I turned the roundabout in awe of my ability to do something so stupid. The fire was my fault. I should have known better. I had no idea when I'd ever learn. Tears filled my field of vision, but I forged on toward the road out of Kelty. Once I was headed back to the Logan's, I was puttering along at a good pace.

I felt a little better the more I mulled it all over. True, they lit the library on fire. It was also quite probable that the fire department showed up fast. There was probably a sprinkler system inside since it was a government building. Anna was safe. I was safe. It could have been much worse. And the book was long gone. That thought made me pretty darned giddy. I smiled to myself. Mission accomplished!

"Shew," I said. Something died on the road at some point because the smell of decay overtook the truck like I'd driven through a cloud of zombie farts. I turned on the heater to clear out the air in the cab.

Over the sounds of the motor and the road, I thought I heard a little kid crying. I easily pushed the idea away, reasoning it out as a product of my guilt-soaked mind.

A sob erupted from the other side of the truck. There it was, huddled on the floorboard, squinting its black eyes and breaking into a shrieking wail when it saw me looking at it.

"Shit!" My eyes shot to the road just in time to avoid smashing into an oncoming car. The driver careened away, tires screeching, as he yelled and flipped out at me. I gripped the wheel, fighting the urge to cover my ears. The noise wouldn't stop. I gassed the truck to straighten out on the road, head reeling from the screaming. The peal wouldn't stop.

Three seconds seemed like an hour as I tried not to look down. The truck was in the correct lane, moving forward. I stole a glance.

The monster was back, black hair clinging to mucus and gunk on its face where the nose should have been. Its mouth hung wide, gaping too much, as it screamed at me and climbed onto the seat. I tried to let off the gas, but the road seemed to be a blur through the confusion. Pain erupted through my shoulder as the thing dove and latched on, sinking a mouthful of razor-like shark teeth into my flesh. I screamed and let go of the wheel, trying to stomp on the brake pedal, and slamming my foot down on the gas instead. I caught handfuls of greasy hair, trying to rip myself free. It swung its hands wildly, scratching into my face. One gripped my left wrist. We fell against the door as the truck swerved on the road. Tires squawked. I screamed as it choked up its grip, moving the bite into the soft flesh of my neck. My wrist popped, fingers going numb almost instantly.

We rocked to the opposite side of the truck cab as weightlessness carried us, then smashed against glass. I wasn't sure which window we'd hit but diamond bits of glass showered throughout the cab. Sounds of collision kept coming. God-awful scraping. More glass breaking. My screams. The sucking, growling noise the monster made as it tore into my flesh anew. The sounds were audible horror. It was enraged, mournful and crying, crazed and vengeful, yet elated by my screams.

I yanked out a fistful of hair, but then was out of control, like a rock in a tumbler. My senses screamed as colors swirled by, colliding with darkness. Blood filled my nose, mixing with upturned dirt and plant matter, and finally, gasoline. Another scent hung thick as the din subsided. It blended with pain and cold, hanging onto me, as I trembled, terrified.

Finally, everything stopped. The thing was still on me, but much quieter, almost as far away as the pain. Fear. It owned me. I didn't want to be eaten by a monster. I couldn't just die and know nothing more.

I was being punished. It was the book. The monster had appeared when I lost my cool with the book one time before. I calmed. I couldn't live with the book any longer. The book was likely thirty thousand feet above me, flying at seven hundred miles an hour, headed for who-knows-where. All that remained was the incarnation, the ugly awareness that it had been cast away. The monstrosity shouldn't be real. I wanted something deadly to ram through its heart. I wanted to cut off its head. Cut out its heart. Watch its twisted, pinched face melt in flame.

Fire. It was all I had. My body was broken. I couldn't let it win. Flame, beautiful, blue, orange, and red. Cold left me. I channeled all the energy I could muster, thinking of the palms of my hands and whatever matter rested in their reach. Fumes filled the bent cab. One of my eyes hung open a slit. I peered up toward the only light that seemed real, only to have it blocked out by the leathered face of the monster. It pushed its face into mine, turning its head like a dog's. I wondered it if was trying to discern whether I was dead. I didn't move, focusing on its face as it broke into a bloody-toothed grin.

You son of a bitch. How could it think I'd go out so easily? Evil incarnate was apparently very audacious. It pissed me off.

I let my eyes gaze blindly and unfocused. The rank smell of smoldering hair filled the cab. That cleared up what my hand was full of. I gritted my teeth the best I could, setting a jaw that wouldn't align anymore.

When the flame blossomed in my palm, I imagined that's what heaven felt like. Energy and air, fumes and wind all fought for a place in my grip. Another burst of fire erupted through the stench surrounding me and then the flash took us out.

The monster screamed.

I couldn't wait to see the bastard burst into flame. It tried to run but I wrapped my only working hand around a sinewy, rotted forearm and bore down to hang on. Beautiful fire ate at skin. It screamed as a tremor overtook its body.

It burned.

The cloth seat melted onto it, sticking and peeling off bits and hunks of flesh. Plastic melted and ran and more glass crashed in on us. The monster twitched, and soon I couldn't tell which part of the cab it had melted into. Things hissed as fire burned hungrily through the wreck.

I knew I wasn't going to die. The goddess wouldn't let that happen, but she'd damned well let me get charred and beat up. At some point, my thoughts would be hers and hers would be mine. I couldn't wait for the day it all made sense. Our minds would flow seamlessly together. I wouldn't lose any of my memories and neither would she. I worried about that, crunched up in that smoldering truck. Would gaining her knowledge and experience over millennia years melt my brain? I didn't think so. I had to face that as a gargoyle, anyway. My mind would absorb more time than a mortal. But the goddess had been alive much longer than any gargoyle I knew, and at some point that would be my existence. I supposed I'd start taking ginkgo biloba and give it my best.

I wondered if I'd ever be on par with Cian.

He'd breezed quickly into my life and left even faster. A girl had to wonder why. He showed up with all that blather about being betrothed, and then, *poof*, goners. I'd wondered what was up back then and still didn't get it. He was a god, and an old original Celtic deity, at that. We were obviously mismatched.

Maybe I'd see him again, and maybe not. Likely the latter.

God, I'm thirsty.

Everything burned down but me. Time slowed once the screaming stopped. I experimented with moving parts of my body which responded in a variety of ways that ranged from twitches to nothing at all. There was a ton of smoke and lots of wet things, clinging here and there. My eyes opened a little, impressing me.

Plastic does strange things when it's hot. Fire makes it pliant and it takes a long time to cool back down and set up in the form it melted into. Glass behaves the same way, which I totally expected since glass basically stays in liquid form at all times. That's why the old panes in Victorian architecture have distortions at the bottom. Even though glass was installed and meant as part of an exterior wall, a means to keep things out, it's still just liquid. A little bit of heat and it's a pool.

I thought the fire was out. Plastic melted off the steering wheel and flesh bubbled on my wrist where flame made contact, setting as I watched. My sense of smell left soon after the passenger side burst into flame, and the last scent I caught was hot, electric wiring. Metal creaked. Glass cracked. Being unafraid of the fire, not worried about dying, messed with me. I was more scared of pain from the wreck. The fire hadn't hurt me at all. I

passed out for a time, oddly sated by the thought that the book
was really, finally gone.

Voices grew loud outside, and I was more frightened than ever,
not of what would happen when first responders found me, but
of what the wrong people would do when no one was looking.

The wreckage creaked and rocked as they attempted to pull a
door open. An arm wrapped in yellow material came at me
through the window. A hand brushed my shoulder and I began
to cry.

"She's alive," a man said.

I tried to tell him I was okay but the sounds that came out of
my throat weren't words.

"Don't speak. We're going to get you out."

Scraping and knocking ensued. The man kept his arm thrust
through the busted window, barely moving his hand across my
arm to let me know he was there. Metal gave in a sudden jolt. My
back pulled tight, feeling like my hips broke apart with it.

I was tired.

There were a lot of voices around but the only one I concentrated on was the first man who'd spoken. He remained right
where he was. I wondered if the truck was back on its wheels. I let
my eyes close. Lots of things moved around me.

"Careful and slow," the man said.

I was lifted, then set back down. There were cold straps and a
plastic cup placed over my face. Someone held my hand.

I let myself sleep.

"Good fortune runs in yer blood."

A set of huge breasts rubbed against my shoulder and cheek

as a nurse reached across me. "Pulled from a smoldering wreck and not a burn on ya. A few knocks and bumps. Fortunate lass."

Machines beeped and hummed. Lots of what I focused on was plain white. The nurse's face came into view. She was a pretty lady with a red, round face and a boy's cut of brown hair. Green eyes peered deeply into mine.

"There ya are," she said, smiling. "I'm Nan."

"Hi," I tried. The H sounded without the I.

"Let's have some water." She turned her back.

A black and white clock ticked against the wall.

7:17. That had to be PM. If it was AM, Nan wouldn't be so friendly. I was relieved for about half a second, until I realized I was about to Garg Out with poor Nan in the room. Garging Out was a mixed bag of good and bad. I needed the change badly, to heal, and to get away. The time explained why I woke up. My skin tingled.

Nan was going to have to suck it up.

She approached me with a cup, holding a straw to my lips. I drank. It hurt like hell, making me wonder if water was leaking through cuts in my chest. I shuddered.

"Thank you," I rasped.

"You're very welcome, sweetheart."

A blood-pressure cuff tightened around my right arm. Nan listened to me through a stethoscope, holding her fingers to my wrist. A few seconds later, she let go and began jotting on a clipboard.

"Nan?"

"Yes?" She peered at me. Another of her sweet smiles was on the way.

"I'm sorry."

Heat and tremors built in my chest and my skin erupted. I ripped my arm free of tubes and the cuff relaxed. Nan's eyes grew, filling with confusion and horror. My body expanded and I went with it, reaching with a fist. My right connected neatly with her chin and she fell forward, knocked out. I was a little gleeful about that. It was just like on TV.

I did my best to catch her as my wings exploded against the bed. It creaked and gave way. I leaned forward and used my tail to stop myself from landing on the floor with the busted-up bed. The monitors broke into chorus. I dropped Nan on the mattress, looking at the door.

I tucked my wings and stepped toward the hall and stuck my head out. A lighted sign hung from the tiled ceiling, pointing to the right side of the hall.

Somebody screamed. A man dropped some files and a pen with a smack. He screamed again. I stared in irony, fully expecting to see a female making the racket. Beyond his twisted, horrified face the EXIT sign hung illuminated from the ceiling. I shoved past him, speeding up through double-doors.

On the other side of the doors banked by a wall of windows, was a nun. I hadn't seen one since I left Austin. The nuns at the Home for Girls were liars. They were the reason I wasn't adopted with my brother. They were the cause of me losing him. This one was just like the rest. I could practically smell it on her. I'd mistakenly trusted nuns once and ended up trapped with them for nearly seventeen years.

The nun crossed herself, muttering a silent prayer. I approached, surely a demon stepping from Revelations, proof that her Satan and her God were real. She was tiny and very young, with oversized brown eyes that locked on mine. We stared at one another for a second more, my wings beating slowly as I examined her. She closed her eyes, sending a tear down her cheek.

I stepped around her to the right and popped an elbow through the glass, then cleared out a huge portion of one pane before hopping through into darkness.

I jetted into the air to get my bearings, which didn't take long because I'd been taken right back into Kelty.

18

The book was gone. I thought I'd feel lighter at heart. I was, to a point. I didn't want to stay in Scotland any longer.

I had to wonder what was best for Bree, as well. The Logans held something amazing for her, taking her in when she and Crispin grew close. Watching their relationship grow had been one of the coolest events in my life. Bree was happy, despite losing her mortality. Love and guidance surrounded her. Between Crispin and his cousins, Clan Logan were determined to make Bree a Logan, too. I was confident I helped her, as well. Our friendship was deep, and besides, they were all a bunch of guys. There were things Bree and I could talk about together that they'd never be able to sit through or understand. Girl things, and issues with missing people in the States, and missing Austin altogether.

Now I concentrated on what would be best for me. I'd figured going back to the bookstore, what I considered my London home, would be the answer. Iain had taken the news about the old truck I'd totaled in stride. I'd been in a hurry when I told him because I saw him before Bree when I got back to the castle.

I could have used more time to be more convincing. They were good men. I was confident the Logans' would both take care of Bree and facilitate our being able to see one another whenever we wanted. I just needed time to think. I wasn't all that comfortable staying at Logan Castle and being so close to the Grotto, where Kai had nearly killed me. Possibly sometime in the future I'd see the rest of the land and feel differently, but, beautiful as it was, Scotland just wasn't my thing.

I needed the busy work and feeling of accomplishment I got when I'd help run the bookstore last year. I'd spend my spare time making a plan. Finding out what was best for myself.

Little things happened during the day to show me I was right in feeling Bree would be happy staying in Scotland. The way she'd taught Crispin how to text—how to use a smartphone in the first place—was one of them. Her cell phone chimed with the notification she'd set up for his texts. I knew it by sound. It happened all the time. I also knew each text that came in was his because of the never-failing smile that would break out on Bree's face when she got new texts or calls from him.

Things were off currently, though. We were reading and doinking around in the library and Bree kept checking her phone. She held it up again, scrolled a bit, made a face, and dropped it on the overstuffed chair beside her.

"What's up?" I asked, over the top of *I'm Not Sam*. I'd developed a thing for horror stories and Jack Ketchum was my new favorite writer. His writing was incredibly dark, but relatable at the same time. I dug it, knowing well enough we were kindred and twisted spirits, Jack and me.

"I think Crispin messed up his cell again. We had plans to go hiking this morning after he got back from the monoliths."

"Maybe his morning ritual took a little longer than normal," I offered.

"You're probably right." She went back to the magazine she'd been reading through. It was a gardening mag, which was sort of perfect seeing how we had acres of ground with several perfect spots for her to stake out a plot. It was one more thing that solidified my confidence that she'd be happiest staying right where she was.

I'd just gotten back into my story when she huffed and dropped her cell on the chair again.

I sat up and marked my book. "Not everyone is attached to their phone like you are. Try to relax. These guys live differently than we're used to. One of the others might have needed help with something."

"Then he should have texted me about it." She rose and walked toward the window. "Look at this. Perfect morning for a hike."

Bree would always be who she was brought up to be. I loved her deeply, but truth was, she was a little spoiled. Kind as she was, life was about her. She'd come from an affluent family in Austin. When the little things didn't stack up the way she wanted she had the tendency to pout.

"I know this is a dumb question, but did you try calling him?"

"Of course I did. Like, a jillion times." She turned from the window, the sunshine revealing inner workings of her face. It was impressive to see that it really did take so many facial muscles to scowl. "I mean, I waited a while to give him time out there, but it's been nearly forty-five minutes. This is ridiculous." She dropped into her chair.

"That's all? I mean, I think he's probably fine and just got busy."

"Well, it's rude not to let me know."

She had a point there. "Just give him some time. I'm sure he'll get right with you when he's done." I smiled at her, but she wasn't having it. She resumed her pose in the chair and started thumbing through her magazine rather violently.

Iain's voice boomed from downstairs. I couldn't make out what he was yelling about. Bree shot me a look that screamed "I told you so!" and I marked my book and rose. We ran down the stairs and I listened hard, trying to control the urge to sprint. We arrived just in time to see Petra following the rest outside. We ran after them, Petra sprinting to catch up to Iain, and Peter running beside Osgar. The stone and timber circle appeared to be our goal. The stones were pretty far out in the yard.

"What is that?" Bree squinted toward the standing monoliths. We slowed and so did Petra. Dread built inside me like ice. My heart was in my throat to the point of pain. We reached the stones too quickly to be able to process what was happening.

"I have no idea."

Crispin was hunched against one of the stones with his hands and feet bound in knots in front of him. A filthy rag was wrapped around his head and in his mouth, gagging him. Blood streaked down his temple from a gash and goose egg. A dwarfish looking thing held a crude sword against Crispin's throat. Osgar went at it but the thing growled and drew the blade into the skin of Crispin's neck. Crispin grunted against the pain as a fresh geyser of blood splashed down his chest.

Iain put his hands up, stepping slowly toward the dwarf-thing.

"Schop!" it shouted, oversized, brown eyes darting from one of the men to the other. The thing slobbered a lot. The front of its tunic was drenched and stained.

Osgar froze.

"Jesus! Make him stop!" Bree pleaded, out of breath. I grabbed her hand, trying to digest what I was seeing. Somehow familiar, it wasn't a dwarf threatening Crispin. It was a different species, for lack of better word. I knew the name and it hung on the end of my tongue, just out of reach. It was an old memory, one of the goddess's. I surveyed the shaggy head of hair with pointy ears sticking out, hempy looking tunic and oversized, Flintstone feet. It began with a B. I let go of Bree's hand, stepping up next to Iain. The thing looked up at me and actually hissed, then appeared totally frightened, bottom lip quivering. It squinted.

"No, Tezza," it said. "Backing." It stiffened its meaty little grip on the sword, showing how it meant business.

"Brownie." The word finally came forth from old memory. "You shouldn't be here."

"Shorry," it said. Tears built and fell down its dirty cheeks. I was both awed and justified in realizing it recognized me. Brownies were nocturnal, which meant this one might not be able to see well.

"Killing isn't in your nature, beast," Iain said. "Give me the blade." He waved a hand at all of us watching. "There is forgiveness here in exchange for your explanation." He held out a hand and moved forward.

"Schop!" the brownie yelped. He put the blade deep into Crispin's throat. Crispin wheezed and struggled against the ropes at his wrists. All too quickly he stopped, gaze locking with Bree's before his eyelids drifted closed.

"Please let him go," she begged. The brownie didn't acknowledge she'd spoken, still staring at me.

The sight of blood pooling in the grass impacted me. My gaze crept up from the ground, across crimson stained boots and legs. "Why are you doing this?"

The brownie stared nervously, trembling so hard it rocked against Crispin. "Sh-shorry." It began to sob and squeal.

I turned to Iain. "It's being compelled or something. They aren't violent like this."

"Either step back from him or die. Those are your choices." Osgar stood on the opposite side of Iain, arms crossed matter-of-factly. Crispin had lost far too much blood. I wondered what was keeping his head attached as the first thought of consoling Bree entered my mind. Everyone else might not be dealing with it yet, but Crispin wasn't going to survive. I didn't like the way I went straight to emotional numbness.

Being a gargoyle, Crispin could withstand everything he'd gone through and recover fully once nightfall hit. The real problem was that his neck had been hacked badly. If his head came away from his shoulders, he was done. I feared gravity allowed his head to rest against the boulder behind him.

Bree was crying. I had to concentrate on her, even though a part of me was dying, knowing Crispin had likely been killed. Bree wouldn't handle it. She'd been through too much, being recently turned. She hadn't seen her family in too long and for a girl like her, that was huge. She had me, but she'd had Crispin, too. They'd grown close. I remembered from my brief relationship with Kai that it didn't take long to let someone encompass your days, your nights, and your hope for the future. Bree was there with Crispin. If we were looking at the end of him, it was detrimental.

"Please do something." Her voice cracked horribly, and it took a couple tries for her to get all the words out.

"Drop the blade," I commanded. "You don't want to hurt him. I know you don't. Just drop it and run away."

"Genevieve sends words," it grated. "Broken contract. Broken family."

The brownie began to scream as his arm drew back and flew forward again. I turned toward Bree as Osgar and Iain leapt forward. The heavy thump against the turf dictated they were too late. I'm not sure which one broke first, but the sounds of loss and heartbreak took over.

I ran to Bree. Her hands flew to her mouth as her gaze traced the movement of what I knew could only be Crispin's head falling to the grass. It took forever for her to inhale and scream. I wrapped my arms around her as the brownie screamed one last time. I didn't care which of the Logans had ended the thing.

I did all I could to pull Bree away. She tried to get free and go toward Crispin, but I hung onto her somehow and began dragging her out of the circle of stones. She screamed and beat on me, but one foot in front of the last, I managed to keep her from touching any of it. Once we were into the front garden, she didn't fight anymore, but she wailed. I ached, watching her come apart. She shattered. I wanted to trade places with her, hating the pain she felt, but I would have welcomed taking it from her.

"No . . . no." Bree moaned through tears, then broke into a series of screams.

19

The next week was hell, watching my best friend mourn. Bree was a shattered being. Osgar and Iain drank like fish, argued, and then drank some more. Crispin's body was burned on a pyre. Peter skulked around and disappeared for days at a time, only to show up drinking with the Logans. Petra was seldom seen but I was sure she was avoiding me. I couldn't help anyone feel any better, so I did what I always did and tried to fix stuff. It's all I had.

More than anything, I couldn't get the trip to Genevieve's out of my head. I wanted to know who was in the other tank.

Genevieve was bringing Kai back from where I'd sent him, with help from the Tyrens. Asking them who else she was growing in the oversized lab dish was an outside chance, but it was a starting point, so I was back at the Grotto. I also wanted to know how Genevieve managed to kidnap the Tyrens.

If one of the Logans, Peter or Petra was helping her do it, I didn't know how I'd handle that. I prayed Genevieve had found a different way as I hung my towel and waded out into the deep pool in the far corner of the cavern. It was the same place I'd seen my first Tyren over a year ago. Taking a deep breath, I went under and had a look around.

In the past, whenever I needed to find one of the watery beings it seemed to take the better part of a day to get their attention. That wasn't the case this time. One swam straight up to me like a silvery, see through mermaid without fins. The Tyren was a female. At that point I was so relieved at not having to wait forever that it wouldn't have made a difference if they'd sent the family dog. I'd saved one of them from captivity, the least they could do is acknowledge my presence, whether they had answers or not. I waived her forward and waded out after she nodded. Something about the Tyrens still made me feel uneasy. It might have been watching the way they'd made Kai explode by forcing their way into his body through any available opening until he was so overfilled that he simply exploded. I'd had to wipe parts of him off my shoulder and hair. Not a great memory. So yeah, I was wary and extra vigilant when I was close to one.

One of the water being's arms hadn't fully formed. I wasn't alarmed, given the nature of a Tyren. I'd seen a cluster them crawl out of the water in a blob of malformed humanish anatomy before. Of course, she didn't speak, just strode close. She was taller than me, which wasn't a surprise. Most things were, it seemed. The area below her shoulder formed into an arm as she neared. The hand held a long, silvery blade.

"Hey!" I backed off. "You don't need that. What the hell?"

Her eyes flashed. Next thing I knew she ran it straight through my stomach and jerked it out as fast as she could. White hot pain erupted in every part of my body. I was too stunned to cry out for help and my gut was on fire with debilitating pain. The Tyren's expression was stoic as she watched me double over. Before I hit the floor, she jumped behind me and caught my shoulders.

I couldn't inhale. I shook, wondering if I might actually die because it was a magical being that stabbed me. She began dragging me toward the pool. I knew then she was going to drown me before I bled out; it might have been a better way to go. I barely felt the water as we submerged. The Tyren disappeared into the pool. The only thing I could see was a dark swirl of crimson that grew around me. The current caught the seepage. It twisted together, the blood flowing away from me. My chest burned, and pressure built behind my eyes.

Another Tyren shimmered into view, it's skin glistening as it came close. The water churned furiously, and I was tossed like a sock in a washing machine. Rocks passed as the current carried me farther into the stream. Lengths of the creek bed lingered, and some passed. I was able to see a complete 360 of my surroundings. I had no idea how much longer it would take for me to die, but my body would be a part of the Grotto. I'd shattered.

The odd thought that I must have been feeling what Kai went through when the Tyrens took him apart dawned on me, but I didn't have pain anymore. Water was everywhere and everything. Minerals churned around me. I was warm but the sensation of being in touch with my extremities was gone. I laughed. An eye for an eye. My body had broken into the tiniest of pieces. I twisted in the current, mentally reaching for my limbs to see if I could connect or had any control. The sound of water gushing quieted into gentle silence. The surface of the stream reflected above me, the ceiling of the cavern appearing through clouds of bubbles.

Water rushed past me. I allowed myself to swirl and turn, looking around. A twinge of pressure rocked me as a Tyren grasped me somehow. The thought I'd broken apart and become part of the mineral water fizzled out as he yanked me toward the surface.

Instinct took over and I kicked hard, swimming upward. When my face breached I tried to breath in, which was a huge mistake. I coughed uncontrollably, so hard I began to sink again.

Thankfully, the Tyren still had a grip on my arm and he jerked me along until he stood in waist deep water. We trudged toward the rocky bank where I fell down in a heap.

I hacked and vomited water for a long time. Finally, I focused on my savior, in awe. But I got it. I'd just been shown what it would be like to be taken down by Tyrens. The one who'd pulled me out studied me. I didn't like the view from my angle as I looked up. I had to glance past his junk to see his face. I rolled over and started to gather myself. The bikini I'd worn was gone. Perfect. The Tyren walked past, turned, and gestured for me to follow. Being submerged was the only way to hear them when they spoke. He had a message, apparently, to accompany the threat. I walked out to waist deep and crouched. The Tyren was a few feet away, just deep enough so he stood with his feet on the bottom and his head grazing the surface. The female who stabbed me was with him, as well as a couple more I didn't remember ever seeing before.

I stood so my head was out of the water and waited for their heads to emerge above the surface. They popped up quickly, scowling. That seriously got to me. I didn't understand what was happening, so it really pissed me off. I gritted my teeth and scowled back. "I don't know what this crap is about, but I came here to ask for your help." One of the females shook her head and disappeared beneath the surface. "Listen up." I slapped the surface of the water. "There are two things. I've seen Tyrens in captivity and need to know how your kind are being captured. Secondly, Kai is being rebuilt somehow after you guys tore him apart. There's this crazy chick named Genevieve and she is bringing him back, along with someone or something else. Who is it?"

I took a deep breath and went under again hoping to get answers and pretty damned scared.

"We are broken," he said. Sometimes it was tough to understand what a Tyren meant. They could speak English words, but didn't use them properly all the time.

"We owe you nothing. You have broken the system," the male said again. He shook his head. "Now, because you are here, one of your own breaks our family. One: Stop the taking of Tyrens. Two: Join us for always when we next meet." I didn't like the finality in his tone.

They dissolved into invisible water before I had a chance to answer. I guessed that meant the conversation was closed. My lungs screamed for air so I stood up and slogged back to the pebble beach to get my towel . . . which was mysteriously gone.

"Dammit," I grumbled, wrapping my arms around my chest. I really shouldn't have been worried about the lack of a swimsuit, considering most others didn't even bother with suits in the pools.

Petra approached, my towel hanging over one forearm. Her eyes were puffy and wet and so was her nose. She didn't appear hurt and was fully dressed in a plain shirt, jeans, and running shoes.

"Give me my towel please?" I asked, the question hanging in my words. Petra was odd and conniving. She had a look like she'd considered running off with it but changed her mind. She held it out, a new tear streaking her cheek.

"Thanks," I said, so calmly, I was proud of myself. "You okay?" I wrapped up. She didn't respond right away. I considered that maybe she was upset about Crispin.

"What are you going to do?" she asked, in a whimpering voice.

I was lost, and I guess it showed. I opened my mouth, getting ready to tell her I didn't know what the heck she was talking or crying about, but she cut me off.

"I hate the way they talk to you, you know? Tyrens won't talk to just anyone." She shook her head, looking out to the water. "They're mean. Just hear me out. And please don't tell Peter?"

I closed my mouth, listening closely. I didn't respond and she took my silence as an answer. My feet grew cold and started to go numb. I shifted.

"I agreed to help Genevieve catch one Tyren. The rest have been because she threatened to rat me out to the Logans."

"You bitch," I said, astonished.

Petra stopped talking, regarding me. After a moment, she crossed her arms, looking at her feet. "They didn't tell you."

"Mm, nope," I huffed, shaking my head, still in disbelief. That was a lucky thing for her. The more it hit home, the more I wanted to throttle her and then tell her brother. "They didn't say who was doing it, only that it was happening and I had to stop it or they'd dissolve me like salt in that water the next time they could reach me. Do you know how it feels to be blamed for someone else's bad decisions?" I waited a second, and of course Petra didn't respond. "Those things take this kidnapping seriously, Petra. They used words like 'broken family,' and such. They want to kill me," I said, firmly. "Me. You did this." Tyrens were a creature that didn't care if I was half-goddess or half-schnauzer. They'd off me just the same.

"Well, it is your fault. If you'd listened and stayed away from Peter, this wouldn't be happening," she squawked. "You have no business with him. You're dangerous. Wreckless! He tries to tell you to stay safe and out of trouble and you don't listen to him, of fucking course," she yelled. "And then, when you've got your idiot, pigheaded self in deep again, who flies out to your rescue? My brother!"

"I'm not having this argument with you," I said. "You should have kept your nose out of our business. If you'd done that, you couldn't blame me for the kidnap and torture of the Tyrens. And what the hell does that have to do with me and Peter? You've lost your damned mind." I worked hard at not yelling back, which was tough. I could understand if she was mad at both the Tyrens and me for killing Kai. She'd been hung up on him. It was total

Stockholm Syndrome, to her credit, because Kai was an abusive shit and a monster.

She sighed and dropped onto a bench that was a few feet away by the towel hooks, rubbing her eyes. She'd stopped crying. "I found the cell where Kai held the Logans during the moon cycles. Kai sort of let on about the water and I followed him a few times. I saw that he'd just bring whichever brother down here and the Tyrens would hold him in the water until it was time to switch them out. So when you were being all noble and attempting to find Teigan, I knew where he was the entire time."

"He was broken apart in there with the Tyrens," I said. "And you made a deal with Genevieve. She gets to bring back Kai and you get to be a hero by finding Teigan." I didn't wait for her to answer. "But he was in the water." From what I'd seen, merely water wasn't used to bring him back.

"He was. And that's how I got the idea, hoping if I could find a way to bring Teigan back, it was possible you would fixate on him, rather than Peter. My brother would be spared any further"—she waved a hand in my direction without looking at me—"risk on the count of your stupidity." She broke out into tears again. "But she uses Tyrens to do it. Not the water."

I was incensed and creeped out. My temper flared and so did my body temperature. I wiped at the sweat on my face, holding back the urge to rail at Petra. The Tyrens had apparently absorbed Kai and Teigan somehow. They'd been in the water a long time, whereas I was only in there for a matter of minutes. Maybe that was the difference. And the thing with Petra thinking I was obsessed with Peter was ridiculous. Not only did I sicken at the thought of being close to her beloved brother since I'd found out he turned a blind eye to Adam's kidnapping and murder of multiple women, I had a serious issue with being blamed for anyone else's bad choices. I made enough of my own.

One thing that delighted me was the way she assumed the Tyrens had named her as the kidnapper. Maybe it was their limited use of language that held them back. I didn't know, but Petra had confessed, thinking they'd named her. Really, she would have been my first suspect because she was a fink and a sneak and a liar who'd tried to save herself at the last minute by begging me not to tell her twin brother.

I sat beside her on the bench and waited for her to quit with the alligator tears. When she finally looked up, I gave her my best reassuring smile. "You make me sick," I said, with a nod.

I left her there, kicking my own ass as I walked all the way up the steps, across the courtyard, and into my room. The simplicity of Teigan's location, the clue, was right with me all the time. A cell with no walls. Why had I been so thick as not to see when Petra was able to get it? I'd spent so much time worrying and brainstorming, researching and poking around when Teigan's prison was just one mundane clue away. Teigan had been mourned as gone forever by his family, and Petra had known all along right where he was. I owed him my life. With every bit of my being I wanted to thank him.

First, I had to find Osgar and Iain to let them know that Teigan was found. The hard part would be telling them that Genevieve had him and that he wasn't quite done cooking.

20

It's not every day a girl gets the chance to start a war. It was the morning of September 2—my twentieth birthday. I was ancient of soul and young at heart and in body.

Something deep in my ancient soul rejoiced at the thought. From an early age I loved to watch boxing and mixed martial arts on television. Each time I saw conflict coming I was scared, of course, but at the same time a growing part of me looked forward to it. I loved the fight.

The epic battle between gargoyles and Kai's henchmen last year had made my blood boil with lust for the fight. True, I'd had my ass neatly folded up and handed to me, but once I was back in it, hearing the clash of weapons against scaled plates, of blows landing against the body of a foe, I was in heaven.

Using "the goddess" as an excuse for the ancient feelings, knowledge, and cravings I got had to stop. I couldn't count on that part of me being available at all times, but it was *sometimes*. I was her and she was me. Soon, I would go to battle and risk my life, loving every second. It was time to embrace that part of me. I simply craved a war.

After the weirdness in the Grotto with Petra and the Tyrens,

I'd Garged Out and flown around the hillside nearly all night, thinking about who I was and allowing myself to love the new part of me. I couldn't stop it but I'd learn to be my true self with dignity. And besides, I needed all the juice I could get.

Was I using the Logans as a tool for my own revenge? Not completely, since it was their war, too.

They'd lost kin. Crispin was dead because Genevieve had struck back. She had to die and I would use the Logans and every other force I could rally.

I was on the brink of losing Bree, the one person on the planet I considered family. I hated myself as I watched her grieve and she had me worried. It was my fault Bree was changed. She deserved so much more, but on some level I knew it was only a matter of time before I let her down. She cried until she fell asleep and then cried while she slept.

I sat at the table in the great hall, directly across from Osgar. Iain was beside me and Bree on the other side. Peter sat beside Osgar, and Petra was next to him.

"What's this about?" Peter asked, cold as hell.

It was pin-drop silent after I spoke five words: "Petra has something to say." We all looked at her.

Petra's eyes grew huge and she simply stared at me and gasped.

"Go ahead," I mouthed. We waited. Petra's expression rapidly changed from surprise to stubborn pigheadedness. She looked at me, set her jaw, and shook her head sitting back in her chair.

"Okay then," I said, leaning forward. I gave them the gist, being sure to narrate Petra's roll in the events. After the story was out, I sat back in my chair, giving them time to digest. Peter was the first to react, letting out a long breath and rubbing his face with both hands. Bree sat back in her chair and shook her head, looking into her lap. Iain rocked twice with his hands clasped on the wooden table top, then brought both fists down so hard I thought the table might crack. Osgar simply gazed over at Peter. For a confusing millisecond, I was worried Clan Logan would hold Peter responsible for the acts of his sister, due to some odd ancient rule between clans and blood. Then I wondered why it really mattered so much to me.

"Our clan has called you 'friend' for over a hundred years. I do not find you to be responsible for the actions of your sister, before this point in time. Although, from this moment forth, you are her keeper. No further injustice or untruth will be tolerated on her behalf, or yours."

"That's not right!" Petra interjected. "How can you take her word above ours? They've only brought trouble," she yelled, waving her arms at me and Bree. "She is to blame for these happenings, not—"

"Quiet, Petra." Peter regarded his twin sister with a pained, but stern expression.

"Peter, I—" Petra began. She just couldn't shut up, apparently.

"Enough!" Iain bellowed. "I'd trade any two of the four of you lot for one day with just one of my brothers." He shook his head, either at a loss for what to say or fighting of the urge to yell more. He looked up at the ceiling as if asking the universe for guidance.

Ouch. Bare and raw as it was, his statement made complete sense to me. First, he'd lost Teigan, then he'd watched Crispin die. Now there was the news that Teigan was being brought back and was in the hands of a psychopath when we'd been searching for him for the better part of a year. He looked up at Petra, an expression of disgust on his face.

"You knew where Teigan was, but you didn't say anything. Watching us search. Sitting by while we mourned our lost kin."

To her credit, Petra didn't say anything. Her eyes were huge and she watched him, knowing and waiting for the jury to bring the real punishment.

"You are now the property of Clan Logan. Your purpose is to

serve the castle." Iain took a big breath. "You will not leave the grounds. You own nothing. Your last thread of clothing is Logan property. You will repay this clan with your last breath whether it be spent scrubbing toilets or the shit off my boots. Do not attempt to leave."

Bree was fighting back tears. So much emotion in the room made it hard not to react in some fashion. Osgar watched everyone vigilantly.

"My sister will remain under my watch, and under my guard," Peter said, pointedly directing his words at Iain, who nodded back, scowling.

"We will gather our brother." Osgar said, leaning forward with his elbows on the table. "And bring him home."

There it was. In the process, Genevieve would die. I looked over at Bree, who acknowledged Osgar with a nod and trembling lip. She was with me, wanting vengeance for Crispin's death. I needed to diffuse, so I got up.

"I'll be outside if you need me." I didn't know who exactly I was talking to, but I didn't want to just up and leave without letting them know I was there to talk. Bree rose from her chair, too, and we went into the hallway. Iain followed us out but just when I thought he might say something, he turned and stalked toward the front doors.

"I didn't sleep much so I'm going to go chill." Bree said.

"Okay. I think I'm going to go for a walk." I headed toward the doors.

"Happy birthday, Tessa." Bree smiled beautifully at me. "I love you."

"I love you more." I smiled back and watched her until she was gone up the stairs, then went outside to find a place to reflect.

Just a short year ago, Peter and I danced the night away, celebrating my birthday at the bookstore in London. He'd made me feel like the only thing that mattered in his world. I was upset because I'd wanted to read to him, but all the damned books were bespelled. He'd been putting on an act, just luring me in to make it easier to control me. My nineteenth year was a head spin of confusion, disorientation, loss, and isolation. I pulled in a long breath of crisp air. My twentieth year would be a time of holding my own. Of vengeance and taking a stand.

I started that trend off with getting the feel for wielding the shard of Lugh's Light Cian gave me. Out in the open, the light it threw off didn't seem quite as blinding as the first time I'd seen it in the box. I decided it was so bright that time because it had been boxed up for so long. After just an afternoon of practicing strikes with it, the hilt and handle were like a glove around my hand. The jeweled dagger Ezra had given me was a little shorter, but with one in each hand, I was pretty damned lethal. I loved both weapons. One was jeweled with a thicker crossbar and had a gleaming, silver blade. The other held not one gem, but a had blade that was as stunning as it was deadly. The best part of both weapons was that I could lock my claw around the handles when I was Garged Out. I loved the feel of swinging them, slicing through the air. Practicing balance and footwork was a brilliant relief of stress.

I didn't have plans for my birthday and fully expected to let the date go unnoticed. Bree had given me a hug earlier that morning and gone swiftly back to bed. It was likely best to let her sleep her way through some of the grief. I checked on her one last time before I headed out in back of the stables to work out with my twin blades some more. I planned to be fast and deadly the next time Genevieve had the misfortune of seeing my face.

Early afternoon sun dripped down on me. I toyed with catching it and sending reflections in as many different angles glancing off my blades as I could in a moment. My heart raced as I pushed myself to see how fast my amped up speed would go. I wanted to surpass what Bree called a "blur." Hell, I'd love to be so fast, Genevieve and her minions couldn't see me coming until it was far too late, until they were sliced to ribbons.

A twig popped to my right. I stopped practicing and stared as none other than Peter stepped from the trees.

"Hey," he said, tentatively. At least he met my gaze this time.

"Wow. Take time off to do some creepy stalking?" I wiped my chin on my shoulder. I'd worked up quite the sweat.

"I've been searching for you for hours."

"Again, I'm impressed. How did I rate such a substantial chunk of your time?"

"I, um, you must think I've been an ass."

I grinned and said nothing. He was off to an amazing start.

He drew a breath. "It's your birthday."

"And?" I rolled my neck. Everything was tight. I'd been out for a long time without realizing it. A shower sounded marvelous.

"Happy birthday, Tessa," he said. He pulled a handheld from a pocket and hit a button. A familiar, instrumental song began. I recognized it from exactly a year ago. We'd danced to it.

"What are you doing?"

"I just . . . I've wanted to apologize for so long. And tell you I miss you. I miss what we had."

I was stunned for a moment. "Look, Peter, a lot has happened. You've done things . . . I mean, you've been allowing things to keep happening. Like, things I can't condone. I can't be friends— or anything else—with someone who allows women to be preyed on. You're that guy." I shook my head. It sounded harsh, but that was a good thing. He'd stepped on my principles. "I can't have someone like that, like you, in my life."

"That's what you think of me?" He shut down the music.

"Of course it is. I have to go." I turned away, intent on getting that shower.

"Hold on," Peter stepped into my path.

"Don't piss me off. I'm a little amped up and I really don't like you."

"I saw that. Just to clarify, you're speaking of Adam, correct? And you think I allowed him to live for no good reason?"

I didn't answer right away. Peter's eyes were dark as he watched me, waiting. His face was slightly red and his heart rate had picked up from the looks of the throbbing vein in his neck.

"Well, piss off then." He turned on the trail in front of me and started off. A second later, he spun around again. "Don't you ever wonder why you're still alive? Killing a fae creature is certain death." He came closer. Too close. I backed away.

"If you'd succeeded in killing Adam when you snuck off that night, you wouldn't be breathing, and neither would your two nearest kin. So you"—he poked a finger at me—"with your damned stubborn ways, even after refusing to listen to me for your own safety, managed to survive despite your best, yet shoddy efforts at killing him."

"That doesn't explain why you did nothing to stop him, Peter," I shot back. "You thought you were an orphan with a dead sister."

"Were you able to give up hope so quickly when you found out you had a brother?" he yelled. "I wouldn't allow myself to believe Petra was gone. She is all I have. And if I had killed Adam, she really would be gone, because she just happened to show up after a damned century."

"And I'm going to believe you, just like that? Not likely." I stomped around him. His gall amazed me. There was lying and then there was grasping for any words to try to save face. That's where he was. I was done wasting my time with him. "That's the biggest load of shit I've heard since I left Texas."

I surveyed my wings and fangs in my bedroom mirror, balling up my clawed fists. For the first time in two years I wished I could stay in my gargoyle form during the day. Truth be told, in my human form I was soft and weak. I needed my plated scales and the force of my bulky muscle to survive battle. We were going to Petrichor Park, land of odd and unexpected things. Things that would kill and eat me, given a chance. I wished there was a way to get a count on the leftover ranks of Kai's henchmen gargoyles. They had all switched allegiance to Genevieve and we needed to know what we were up against.

"Can we talk?" Cian appeared behind me in the reflection. I stiffened and then relaxed, relieved at finally hearing his voice. Interesting that he could materialize in a girl's bedroom.

"Hey! I've been thinking about you. Did everything work out with the thing that came up?" I smiled. Seeing him was great. I'd been so busy being kidnapped and all that I didn't have much time to miss him. I needed some comfort and he'd showed up at the perfect time.

He caught my claws in his human hands and brought them together between us. "That's what I'm here to talk about it. Do you have some time?"

My smile faded. Something had changed. "Sure. I mean, you've been gone for a long time. I'd wondered if I'd ever see you again." I pulled back. "Which, you know, is sort of a big deal since we're supposed to get married and . . . stuff."

Cian smiled and looked down, shaking his head. "Stuff. Indeed." After a moment, he looked at me. "That is what I'm here about. I don't feel you're ready for that."

"What does that mean?" My little girl voice was back, right when I needed to sound like a capable adult. A woman, not a child, or even a teenager. More than a woman actually. Cian was a god. He deserved and expected a goddess. My tail twitched as I toed a crack in the flooring. I'd just answered my own question.

Cian stepped close. "It's not a bad thing. You just need time." One of his soft hands touched my jagged chin. The next moment I was in my human form, plain old Tessa Conley. Edible, naked, and soft. The girl who wasn't even good enough to adopt as a kid. I was kidding myself to think Cian could be into me. To his credit he didn't look away from my eyes.

"Time for what?" I pulled my chin away, sprouting wings.

"Time to mature. You're very young and . . ." his words drifted away. He sighed.

"And human-ish?"

He didn't respond.

"Maybe it's because I'm a gargoyle?" That, coupled with being centuries younger, had to be it. "Because if that's the case maybe you should use your big, bad god powers to zap me back to looking like a human!" I squawked.

"It's not about what you look like!" His voice boomed, reverberating deeply. "So don't accuse me of something so shallow, so human as that. This is about your continuing denial of your birthright. You've been given guidance and are yet to let yourself become who you were meant to be in the beginning. All this," he gestured at me, "will fade."

"I've been working on that, actually."

He said nothing. I snorted and turned back to the mirror. His behavior was typical. Guys wanted it all and I would always come up short. I'd actually tried and knew I was making progress with letting myself meld with my ancient side. It wasn't easy. "It's not like flipping a switch, you know. It comes in stages. I'm learning."

"I'm sorry if this upsets you."

I didn't respond. Of all the days to reappear, and in dick mode, no less.

"I need to see that you've accepted her, let her come forth from where you keep her trapped. I'll be waiting." He touched me again, and I got a little dizzy when I was snapped into human form again so fast. He kissed me.

I pulled away immediately. Kissing him when he considered me to be merely a cocoon with a tough, unyielding skin wasn't right. He wanted me to be something else.

He turned to go.

"Cian?"

"Yes," he said, looking over a shoulder.

"What if I like who I am now? I mean, or what if there isn't that much of a difference once she's with me all the time?"

"It's simply not possible. I remember her well. She will change you."

"We'll see, I guess."

Cian watched me with unspoken judgement wheeling in his thoughts. I looked away briefly until I heard his footsteps leading away. One thing he didn't understand is that the goddess was sharing *my* existence. My body in my time. I wasn't totally sure it would all go down the way he said.

Cian was gone as suddenly as he'd appeared, but his words rang in my mind. I hadn't been suppressing anything. When the goddess was with me, she was in, one hundred percent. I couldn't do a damned thing about it when she stayed gone, but I could call on amped up speed and fire, for the love of God. That was huge! He had no idea.

The one thing I had tried to look forward to was over, or at least on hold for God only knew how long. Somehow I knew I wasn't the white wedding type, anyhow. I made up my mind to put my life on hold for no one.

And I was no longer the type to take a backseat while somebody else took life's wheel. I would do my damnedest to remain me, despite the inevitable.

21

B ree took her sweet time on the sidewalk, peering up at hanging flower baskets and watching the little creatures fly past, zipping and playing tag above her head. I realized what she must have been feeling. The wonder and amazement of watching something so surreal take place in your space of existence was immensely humbling. She might have been trying to talk herself into thinking they were really big bugs, like the June bugs in Austin. She might have been trying to wrap her head around the fact that they were probably magical flying beings, which was our new reality. Then again, she might have been looking up at them thinking, "I don't give a crap what they are. I'm here to do a job." She flipped a mass of long, brown curls over a shoulder, put a hand to a jutting hip, and held up her phone to shoot an extra smiley selfie beside a gas lamp. After punching a couple of buttons on her device, she adjusted the V-neck top she wore and kept rubbernecking.

Whatever the case, she feigned wonder beautifully. Petrichor Park inspired awe in all of its shady, big-treed glory, but I doubted she was that into it, considering. Each two- or three-story building stood draped with ivy beneath a canopy of trees with multi-colored leaves of differing shapes. There might have been a rule or covenant governing the number of flowers boxes below each window or balcony because there wasn't a single missed opportunity to have an oversized container barfing a rainbow of blossoms across brick or stone walls. The balconies were actually pretty cool. They were made of twisted metal, the same type, on every second story down what I discerned to be the main street in the park. I hunched low, peering through a God-awful amount of foliage to keep an eye on Bree as she made her way along the cobbled sidewalk. She did a damned good job, taking her time. There were moments when I wondered if she'd forgotten what the heck we were there for.

Humans in business attire passed by, all feverish in their daily routine. I didn't get that at first, why the humans were all dressed up. When I'd first found the Park, I had shown up in sweats and had been covered from head to toe in sweat, but no one had batted an eye that day.

"Why are they here?" I whispered to Petra. "The humans, I mean. It looks like they're all on the way to the office." Petra was extremely timid since being found out. Convincing Osgar to let me use her in the plan had taken hours of persuasion. I didn't fully trust her, but I figured if she tried anything, she'd likely be taken out by something after dark.

Petra leaned in close. "That's it. They're at work. There is a trade market here. It is big business and so they wear the part."

"Are they all human?" The words were out before I could stop myself. Of course Petra delighted when I asked a question that had an obvious answer.

She gave me her snooty look for only a second and then wiped the attitude off her face. Over a century of bitchiness was hard to overcome. "Yes. I'm certain each one you see is human. Because why wouldn't they all be just that?" After a moment, she said, "I'm sorry, but you have a habit of saying the most ridiculous things. It would be beyond my nature to let it go."

"I can't begin to tell you the many ways you can piss off right now." I turned a tall shoulder toward her and found Bree again, who had made considerable distance. I shifted, edgy and ready for action. I scanned the rooftops on the buildings across the street. Collectively we'd taken vantage points on several of them. I knew just where to spot Peter, Osgar, and Iain. I wished Petra would have been placed beside Peter. We all knew that's really the only place she'd ever be truly happy. And heaven help us all if he was to spend too much time in the same space as me. She really needed to get over the jealousy. I wanted to say that really badly. I didn't, though, because of all they'd been through to find each other again.

They'd believed one another to be dead. I put myself in her shoes. If I'd somehow found Robbie again after all this time being without him, and now knowing he was dead, if he walked back into my life, yeah, I'd be jealous of everything on the planet that could occupy space near him instead of me.

But I wouldn't be a bitch about it, like Petra.

The only reason we were together on the furthermost rooftop was because of the Logans' belief that fae beings could use olfaction to find a female human instead of a male. Although we were both gargoyles, apparently there was still enough human left in us to throw off a scent—or maybe it was pheromones—and we could be sensed. In this case, they thought that would be a really bad thing. I was on the fence with that. Would it really be a bad thing? My dirks were at my side. I was ready to blow off some steam. Instead of saving that for the moment I found Genevieve, I could use everything else that got in the path as a warm up.

That would blow the plan. I couldn't do that to the others. I was hyped up, angry, and a little ember of warmth glowed in my chest. That meant speed. I loved that part of bonding with the goddess. It was the one way I'd accepted her completely. I could only hope the rest of the road to the inevitable process of melding with her would be so cool and so amazing. I had a feeling fire was going to be even better, but I was still so new with it that I didn't consider it to be part of my arsenal.

Bree weaved in and out of the suits politely, using her sweet, Southern Belle manners, smiling and turning heads. Finally, just outside Jonnie's, someone approached her.

The oversized, baggy jeans, shaggy clusters of brown curls to hide the horns, and gleaming smile I could see from across the street gave away the identity. We had a winner.

Adam stuck out a hand and Bree took it, shaking it gently. She leaned away, looking up to read the sign, just as we'd rehearsed. She'd say she wanted a place to chill for a minute, catch some lunch, and upload all her photos to the Cloud. Adam, of course, obliged with a smile. I was certain he'd been watching her, just out of my view. We'd set it up so everyone had a different angle, so one of us could keep an eye on the street.

"Prick," I said, under my breath. He'd taken the bait. My best friend.

"She'll be fine. She is a gargoyle now, remember?" Petra stood up straight and stretched out her back. I did the same. It seemed like we'd been on the damned roof for hours. It had only been about 26 minutes according to the clock tower adjacent to us.

"She's new."

"She's angry." Petra winked. "And she knows to use it. She impressively smart."

"For an American?" I retorted. I knew that's what she was thinking.

"For a friend of yours."

I sighed. I'd done it again. I'd love to see the day I didn't give her fodder for comebacks.

"Let's go." I pulled my hair into a high ponytail and fastened it tight.

Petra watched me, intently.

"What?" I bent to check my calf scabbards and jerked the legs of my jeans over them. She didn't answer.

I walked toward the side of the building to start the painstakingly slow process of climbing down a trellis. Slow-going was best when we could climb up virtually unseen, into the thick of vines and trees. When I felt I was close enough, I pushed away and landed on the fluffy grass below. Petra did the same after I stepped away to make room for her.

As soon as she landed we both began adding small things to disguise ourselves. We were well beneath the leafy canopy that covered the park so there was no need to cover up. I added too many cheap bangle bracelets and an oversized faux gold necklace with a key pendant. I dug a pair of gaudy, white sunglasses from the depths of my bag and smeared on a thick coat of Roaring Red lipstick. "Okay. You ready?"

"Indeed. I am," she said.

I stared for a second. Petra had thrown on a black mini skirt and sleeveless top and a pair of black boots. The outfit was perfect for the slender, nearly-boy body she had. She flipped her thin, brown hair over and pulled it together, then tied it with a piece of brown twine. Coming upright, she grinned, having put her hair up just like mine. I rolled my eyes. There was really no contest. Petra was beautiful and I paled in comparison. She probably knew it.

"We're hot." She smiled at her own awkwardness and slid a few clacking bracelets onto her arm. Our get-ups would hopefully buy us passage through the park and close to the goat-guy's lair. We turned onto the road and began sauntering around, looking and gawking. I pulled my big purse onto my shoulder. We watched for Adam and Bree for nearly half an hour as the other part of our crew watched from the rooftops. Finally, out they came, taking their time en route to the church. Bree acted slightly giddy, maybe faking a buzz. Adam laughed with her, keeping a hand in contact with her skin, either by holding onto her elbow or gentling her along with pressure against her back. I growled. His hand was far too low on her hips.

"Knock it off," Petra whispered. "She's doing a wonderful job."

"Shut up, Petra. You'd be fine if he was dragging her by one foot, caveman style."

She shrugged. I took a deep breath to rein in mounting anger and started walking. I was already heated up. Little movements happened at staggering speeds. I'd tried to tighten my hair tie a moment ago and the only reason I knew I'd done is it was my scalp started screaming at me. I didn't need Petra's antics to compromise how well I kept my cool. We'd find Genevieve soon enough. In the meantime, we had to pull it all off in human form to get the plan to work.

We crouched behind a seriously shaggy outcropping of ivy that banked a short rock wall, listening. The church was diagonal across a four-way intersection of cobbled lanes. We were close, but we'd have to bust our butts getting inside fast. We'd also have to get the job done quickly so we didn't run out of daylight. We weren't the only things that got scary in the moonlight in Petrichor Park, according to the Logans.

"It's really a church?" said Bree.

"Not so much. I talked my aunt into having it built in replica," Adam said, holding the door. "I love antiques, and that doesn't stop with the small stuff. This building is an exact copy of one close-by in Inverness."

Bree continued to exclaim as she entered but I lost her words in the squeal of the door's hinges as it shut. That was it. She was inside.

And I wasn't.

Petra and I glanced at one another as I counted to ten to slow myself down. She had the look of someone who wondered if I'd explode or hold it together. I closed my eyes and cooled down.

A moment later, we emerged straightening our clothes and walking toward the church like divas invited to a New Year's Eve party. We clicked photos and hammed it up. When we finally made it to the side with the low basement door, we huddled in the stairway leading down and ditched the impractical costume crap. Just for giggles, I tried the door.

It opened right up.

Shit.

I hadn't been expecting that. Luckily, I caught it before it swung wide. Petra leaned back against the stone wall and practically disappeared in a shadow there. She would report to Osgar, per our plan, if things got weird. Low music played inside. I took a step in, being careful to leave the door cracked open.

The familiar smell of old dirt and decaying wood was heavy in the damp air. My eyes adjusted slowly so that's how I proceeded, remembering the details of the night I broke in and thought I'd killed Adam. Piles of clothes lay here and there. I tried not to pay too close of attention to them. A slender, bronzed elbow protruding from one made that impossible.

"Fuck," I whispered.

I skirted the pile of twisted, multi-colored and textured fabric, not believing what came into view. The most beautiful dead girl had been placed on top of a pile of clothes. Care was taken to lay her there, hands folded on her stomach and eyes closed. It could have been guilt driving the act, but I doubted it, considering. There were no marks on her, making her appear as though she was just sleeping. I would have picked up on her breathing or heartbeat at that point, but I knew from the second I saw her she was gone and had been for at least half a day. She had beautiful, olive skin tone and straight, long black hair. Her make-up remained impeccable, right down to the points of her darkened eyebrows and glittering bronzed cheeks. The same glint was on her collarbone and on the top of her arms. Not a stitch of clothing was left on her.

I hated to, but I wondered how she'd died, so perfect like that. It took a second to switch gears, thinking how much I'd like to stick my dirk into the soft flesh beneath Adam's chin, clear to the hilt. This thing where we couldn't simply end him was beginning to push my buttons.

"Tessa, stop," Bree said. "He knows you're here." I jumped at the sound of her voice.

"Are all American's naïve?" Adam sat on a wooden bar stool beside Bree, who was bound to an upright beam with her hands behind her back. "It amazes me you've survived as a nation this long."

Bree didn't appear to be hurt. She wasn't scared, either. "Let's kill him," she mouthed.

Adam's knees bent backward, which made one of his legs appear to be busted in half or dislocated. The other was stretched in front of him. He got up, grinning.

The light wasn't great in the place. I assessed things, mind whirling.

Adam spun around and punched Bree. It happened so fast I was stunned, and seeing her head snap backward and fall forward again seemed to take a full minute. Adam didn't even look at her condition. Bree's head lolled briefly, but she looked up. Her mouth was already puffing up and her bottom lip was split badly at the corner of her mouth. She straightened up and took a deep breath.

"What do you have for me?" Adam pulled a mean-looking knife and held it to Bree's throat. "A trade? You for her? What do the Logans want? Why are they not here with you?" He glanced between me and Bree, ready to cut her if I moved too fast.

I approached, keeping my eyes on his. "Don't do that again."

"Enough posturing. You for her. She'll warn the Logans off or you will die. Tah dah. Happily ever after."

Bree's eyes lit up and her hands dropped to her sides. Petra appeared behind her, holding the thick piece of rope she'd cut away from Bree's arms. Silently, Bree slid away from the point of Adam's blade. Petra swung downward on Adam's wrist hard and fast, popping the blade from his grasp. It all happened in a millisecond.

I couldn't help smiling as I closed in on Adam and to his surprise, rapped him in the mouth.

"You're going to need a new front door." Petra smiled. "Your old one has gone missing, sadly." Adam got really nervous when he saw Petra. It was like he was sure he could take two of us, but three was the magic number to spike fight or flight. Bree wiped blood from her bottom lip and pulled her small dagger from a hidden scabbard on her inner thigh.

"We can't kill him, Bree. I dodged a bullet before. There's that rule with Fate—"

Bree lunged at him. "I don't care." She held the blade to his throat. "Honestly, I don't. I think feeling anything will seriously improve my day. Because you know what? For the last week and two days I have been doing my damnedest to push my feelings away. They all hurt. I heard you have something to do with all that, huh?"

"Whoa," said Petra. She glanced at me with wonder. Bree was acting like a loose cannon and neither of us were convinced it was all acting.

Adam didn't answer. I watched him closely. His expression was different from the time I'd almost killed him. I thought I had. He'd just passed out or something, or maybe he had been faking it so I wouldn't cut him again. That was a funny thing, because that is exactly what Bree did.

She locked eyes with him and simply drug the blade along his face, nearly severing an ear.

For some reason, he didn't scream. He grit his teeth and glanced over at me. Maybe it was association with being sliced up. I had no idea. One thing I knew was that I had to stop Bree from getting carried away.

"Hey, we need to step back and let these guys get to work." I stepped beside her, letting our arms touch to try to reel her in some. She seemed to be spiraling. That was okay. I could totally understand it.

Bree didn't respond. She grabbed Adam's ear with one hand and sliced it free. That time he did yelp. Bree grinned, wiggling the bloodied flesh in front of his face. She tossed it over her shoulder.

"What could this idiot know? I mean, really. Look at him."

"We've done our part. The Logans will do the rest." Petra cut the excess rope behind Adam and yanked on all the bindings, growling and cussing.

"I need a shower." I tilted my head and gestured toward the door. "Let's get out of here."

Bree took a breath, grinning at Adam. "You've got a little something right here." She wiped at her jaw, the same place where a flow of fresh blood dripped along Adam's face. He didn't bat an eye. I snorted, and Petra laughed.

"I don't know why it matters. No one can kill him." Bree surveyed Adam, watching him bleed.

"There's that new thing Osgar brought up," I said.

"Oh. I forgot about that."

"I allowed you to live, bitch. I see now I should have fought you to the death. Either way, in the end, you would be dead right now." Adam's eyes were black with hate. I believed him.

"You're not doing yourself any favors." I smiled. "Now be a good goat-man and tell us where we could potentially go chat up Genevieve."

"Who is that?" He grinned back.

"This can go a couple of ways. Do yourself a favor and just talk to me. We'll be able to find her eventually but if you help, I'll try really hard not to let Bree carve off any other chunks of your protruding anatomy."

Adam smirked.

"We found a way around this dumb curse thing," Bree

chimed. "We can cut you up and dump you in the Thames. We could get crazy, I mean, I'm there."

"Ah, yes you are. Mourning the loss of your pet gargoyle. Stings as bit, I suppose."

Bree leaned in, waving the blade in his face. She scraped it through his scraggly goatee. "It does. I'm willing to share that. Cutting you, watching your face, watching you bleed, it helped. The way I figure it, when I'm through with you, I'll feel great." In a quick movement she sliced off the long part of his chin hair.

Adam cringed and jumped. Bree laughed.

"Crazy bitch." Adam regarded Bree, wide eyed. I hated it, but I understood him. I totally got why he was slightly afraid. Bree looked the part. She had him believing she was half twitchy and willing to hack him up. True enough, we were afraid to kill him, but when it came to torture, he was a believer. He was afraid of all that pain. He understood Bree would break him, nearly to death, and then bring him back just so she could do it all over again.

I glanced at Petra who appeared to be watching Bree the same exact way as me. Bree's eyes danced as she dragged the blade across Adam's collarbone, scoring deep into the flesh. A high-pitched squeal sounded. I preferred to think it was Adam, but in truth I was sure it was the blade chiming through bone. I was nauseated, watching her work on him.

I wanted better things for my best friend. She used to be so soft and kind-hearted. I looked away when she cleaved off a finger, told him to quit whining, and backhanded him. This woman, this weapon, wasn't my friend. She was different than this. She had to be. If not, my God, I'd miss my friend.

Petra glanced my way. I met her gaze briefly before looking at the ceiling. Blood splattered the ground.

Bree turned to Petra quickly. "These guys are like us, right? I mean they'll heal up quickly?"

"They don't shift, if that's what you intend to find out," Petra said. "They do heal fast. Even faster if we drag him outside with the elements in the park."

Bree turned back to her work, using one of Adam's horns to push his head back. His chin hit his chest when she let go. "Maybe he's had it for now."

"Hold on," I said, approaching him. I bent close, listening. Adam's heart rattled in his chest like a rabbit's. "He's acting." I backed away. "He did the same thing to me when I thought I'd killed him. Our little goat-boy likes to play possum."

Bree grinned and kneed him in the groin. Adam grunted and wheezed.

"Aw damn," I looked down, remembering the size and scope of what Bree had just brutalized.

"What the hell does that mean?" Petra glared.

"Playing possum?" Bree said, grunting as she smacked Adam's head to the other side. "That's when someone's been a real dick and tries to dodge his comeuppance by playing like he's knocked out or whatever." She smacked him in the nose with the fist that held the dagger. Adam's head snapped back and fell forward. Blood gushed from his nose and ran down his chest. He didn't move, chin down.

"Oops." Bree backed off. "Now he's out. Shoot." She looked back, apologetically.

"Let's drag him outside." I grabbed at his shirt, choking up my grip. "Once he's out there for a while, he'll be good for round two."

Adam actually sighed, lifting his head. "Perhaps we got off on the wrong foot," he said, looking right at me.

"Please understand"—I got really close, right up in his face —"you and I stand exactly where we need to be."

He released a mouthful of blood, trying to let it go slightly to the side, but it all ran through a split in his lip and sluiced down his neck.

"Aw, that's a shame, now," Petra said.

"Fuck you, garg bitch."

"Hey now. That's offensive." Bree brought the blade up again, signaling she was ready to ring the bell and let the next round begin.

"You two," Adam said, gesturing between me and Bree with a tilt of his head, "I get it. You're new. You didn't ask for it. She, though," he said, glaring at Petra, "she chose to be a gargoyle. She wanted it. Chased it down matter of fact, did you not?"

Bree and I both peered at Petra, who looked like she'd just been backed-over by the Truth Trolley.

"You *wanted* . . . this?" I couldn't imagine what position I would have to be in to actually ask to be transformed into a shapeshifter, into a living monster.

"It's not like that, at all."

"What's it like then?" Bree asked, quietly.

"Curiosity, correct? Or was it chasing down love?" Adam grinned, showing bloody teeth.

"One more word, and your tongue is the next thing to hit the floor, faun," Petra growled.

"Is that true?" Bree said, persisting.

"Mind your business." Petra gave Bree a warning look.

"Watch yourself, Petra. Don't think for one second you won't feel it if you threaten her."

"Seriously, I want to know what the hell he's talking about." Bree approached Petra. "Why in the world would you want to be a gargoyle? Don't you feel like a monster? Miss yourself, or anything? What did you gain?

"Kai."

"What?" Bree studied Petra, who, oddly enough, didn't argue. "You're a first-rate idiot."

"Piss off." Petra shoved one of Bree's shoulders. Without missing a beat, Bree sliced at Petra with the blade. Petra dodged easily, smiling. She threw an easy hook that landed against Bree's face.

Adam grinned, his mission accomplished, as Bree and Petra unleashed on each other. I was a little torn between wanting Petra to get her ass kicked and hoping Bree got to release some angst. Seconds in, though, I could tell Petra's experience would win out and it would be Bree who caught the rough end. Sure enough, Petra swung downward and knocked her straight to the floor. Bree rolled over, looking at the rough-cut ceiling. She didn't try to get up.

"That's enough," I said, warning Petra off. She glared but backed away. That was a smart decision, considering the outcome the last time she pushed my buttons. Bree clamored to her feet, resting with her hands on her knees.

Petra huffed. "Let's collect this rubbish and get out of here."

"Check his ropes," I said.

"I was referring to her." Petra nodded toward Bree.

"Screw you." Bree stood upright, breathing hard.

"Little Yank got her bell rung." Adam grinned at Bree.

"I hope you took some notes, you prick. The Logans are waiting for you."

"Gargoyles hardly inspire fear in Petrichor Park," he retorted.

Adam's cockiness wore thin. I leaned close, searching his face, and tried to keep my cool. It didn't work. The closer I got, the more sweat broke out on his face. Steam, or maybe it was white smoke, rose in swirls above his head. He began to tremble.

"That's exactly why we're leaving. You have things in your perverted, horned, rattletrap of a head. I need to pick it clean."

The stench of burning hair seared my nose. I backed away as Adam's mop of curls began to smolder. Fear gleamed in his eyes for the first time. I triumphed, realizing I finally had a weapon to use against him.

"You don't like fire, do you?" I smiled sweetly. "That's a real shame for you. Because I love it these days. Did you know I can make things practically explode into flame? I can also do things like this." I latched onto his wrist hard, imagining the look of my hand print branded into his skin. Joy of joys, it worked. Adam clamped his jaw on a squeal that he couldn't hold back as his skin sizzled in my grip. He let loose with a rather lady-like scream and I let go.

"Central Square. Second floor. She's always there at sunset," Adam said, through grit teeth.

"Nicely done," Petra said.

"Like I need your approval." I shook my head at her.

"Why didn't you just do that to begin with, Tessa?" Bree sounded slightly exasperated.

"Because you needed therapy."

"And an adjustment of attitude," Petra added.

I couldn't wait to get Petra alone. The realization that she'd been so into Kai at one point in her life that she gave up her mortality was something I found impossibly intriguing and psychotic at the same time.

"It's getting late," Bree said.

"Where are they?" My impatience was plain. The plan was the Logans and Peter would give me and Petra no more than half hour to get things under control and then they'd come and help transport Adam. I didn't want to touch him. Petra had warned them of the door being open quite a while ago.

"You know," Petra said, "it's times like these that make putting up with your arrogance completely worthwhile."

"What the hell are you talking about?" I was going to snap.

"Before you get too flustered, I want you to know that I didn't have to come back here and help cut her loose." She shook her head. "I could have stayed outside."

"Gee, thanks." Bree said. "Really, I think the reason you're here is because no one trusts you to stay at the castle alone without doing something shitty."

"Indeed, you're not welcome," Petra said, shaking her head.

"What about the plan? What about him?" I jabbed a finger at Adam, who wore a rotten, crooked smirk.

"That's the thing with you, Tessa. This," Petra waved a hand at Adam, "begging a fight in Petrichor Park of all places, with beings we can't even kill, this is all you. It's your fight. And that's why they've gone."

I'd started to sweat earlier and was having a hell of a time keeping my temper down. Heat built. Try as I would, there was no helping it. I'd be thermal inside of five minutes. So much for family and new friends and all . . .

"You knew all along." I turned on Petra. "You trounced around this place with me, knowing full well it was a bust. We put my friend in jeopardy for nothing."

"I did not know. I was told when I went back to let them know the bloody door was open." She didn't blink or even look away. I believed her. Sort of. "One other reason I'm here is to tell you to call all of this off. Everyone knew you'd get her out of here," she said, gesturing toward Bree. "Now we can drag this lump outside and simply go back home."

"And what? Wait for the next attack from Genevieve? Hang out, waiting for the henchmen to gather forces and come take your home away? Or maybe all these beings here in this place come at us. That's what we should do when we get back to Scotland—we could all sit around watching each other's backs."

"You sound paranoid."

"You're being naïve if you think nothing's going to happen," I said, shaking my head at her. "I give it a week before everything from gargoyles to goat-men show up at the Logan's looking for a piece of each of us to take back to Genevieve."

"She's right, Petra. And that bitch killed Crispin."

"Things will go back to the way they were if you stop stirring them up," Petra yelled.

"When you get back there, tell all of them they can go to hell."

"You can't seriously be considering staying here after dark. You have her to think about," Petra gestured toward Bree.

"I'm not a liability anymore, Petra. I can fight. And I don't want to go back there and sit around missing Cris. I'm staying with Tessa. Besides," she gestured at Adam, "we've still got this prick, and he told us where Genevieve hangs out."

"You can't kill the things that live here, and its likely Genevieve has many in her guard." I wasn't sure she was right about that. If Genevieve was around, so were the henchmen. I'd killed a few of those badasses. The same rules didn't apply to them.

Petra looked from me to Bree and back. "You're daft. It must be an American thing, or maybe it's because you've never had a family that you're absolutely willing to get your friend killed."

At that same moment, Adam couldn't help himself any longer apparently, because he broke out into a laughing fit.

The dam that had been holding the heat back burst wide. In an instant I had Petra against a wall, pinned above my head. All I wanted to do was put her through the bricks.

"Tessa!" Bree yelled.

Adam continued to giggle and guffaw.

I dropped Petra. "Leave," I said, staring at her until she nodded back. I didn't care if she was my battle buddy for the moment, I was going to kill her if she stayed.

She walked to the door and took a last look over her shoulder before she left. "He's playing with you. Making you look the fool when there's nothing you can do. It might be next year, or even next week, but he will find a way to freedom and more killing."

Petra had a good point, but I was tired of hearing her voice. "On second thought, I'll tell them to go to hell myself. I'll even provide directions."

Adam was downright obnoxious with his bent-at-the-waist antics. He saw me watching him. Then he just grinned.

"I just want to set the record straight." I walked straight up to Adam. "You're very wrong. You've been misled."

"How so?" he tee-heed back.

"You represent the worst of any society. You're a sexual

predator who preys on the opposite sex of a different race because you feel entitled to have them. You sneer at humans and gargoyles like we're low lifes, when it's you that's the lowest bottom-feeder and scum."

Adams hair smoldered away again. He panicked, looking like he might start begging for his life. I couldn't help heating him up a little, and I didn't really want to stop. A switch popped inside me and the hot place in my chest unleashed. Flame licked at the inside of my skin, one of the most divine feelings I've ever experienced. I exhaled a radiating breath at him and smiled.

"So, that's where we're at. With me realizing what must be done, and with you still hiding behind the idea that I won't kill you. You've been misled." I concentrated on all the hair I'd seen on his body, his arms and legs, back and chest, all of it was tinder.

"And you're absolutely wrong. I know the rule of Fate and her threes. But I have no family to consider here and I have a hunch I won't die as part of that."

The smell hit hard just before he burst into flame. I wanted to step closer to him when it ignited, to steal the warmth.

"As for Fate, she's had it in for me since the beginning."

In a matter of seconds Adam was on his knees, screaming. His hands were still bound, but that didn't really matter, I would have torched him one way or another. I caught movement from the corner of my eye when Bree moved toward the door, which brought me back to the moment and out of my lust for flame.

I didn't trust that Adam was dead. Touching him was gag worthy and out of the question. I reached for both dirks and used one on each side of his smoldering neck to slice his head free in a quick, satisfying motion, and managed to move before any blood could get on my Chuck Taylors.

Petra waited at the door looking oddly satisfied. We followed her up the stairs. Once we were across the street I took stock of what was left of daylight. In a matter of moments, the sun would set.

"Tessa!" Peter and Iain ran across the lane toward us. "Hey, what took so long?"

"No frickin' way," I grumbled, looking at Petra.

"You're here," said Bree. She looked between them and then across the street to where Osgar waited. "She told us you left."

Peter looked warily at his sister.

"Tessa broke Fate's rule. She killed the faun."

Of course, Petra tried to rat me out to take the spotlight off herself. I knew about Fate's rule, which stated that anyone who killed a fae being would forfeit the lives of two family members. I didn't get too worked up over that seeing how I had exactly no family members for Fate to harvest.

"You are a first-rate bitch," Bree said. Petra looked to Peter, feigning worry.

"Have you lost your mind?" Peter asked, shocked. I just shook my head, looking away and refusing to answer. They all babbled, and I listened intently to see how far Petra would try to toss me under the bus. I had no regrets. Maybe it was a good thing Petra lied again. I didn't even care that she had. I'd swept the feeling away when I suspected her, because I truly wanted to kill Adam. It was justice, even if it was my fiery brand of judgement and punishment.

"She planned it," Bree said. "She was in there pushing Tessa's buttons, saying how Adam would get loose and pick up where he left off. Then she said you'd all left us and Tessa sort of lost it."

"'Sort of'?" Iain said, watching a few stray tendrils of smoke rise from the basement of the church.

"He's the only thing burning in there," I said, reassuring them that the place wouldn't go up in flames. "And yes, I killed him. And I'd do it again. Besides," I looked straight at Peter. "I don't think Fate can do much in my case." I looked at Petra and then back to him. "Your sister lied to us. She thought she played me. I'm through with this shit."

Bree started back up the lane and I fell into step with her. A familiar iron gate spanned between two buildings, the space above encased in brick. I heard it grating as it opened in my memory of being kidnapped the night of the gala. I got my bearings fast to remember where it was when the time came to come back and get Teigan and kill Kai. Again. While Genevieve watched. Then it would be her turn.

I'd had enough of the Psycho Garg Twins and wanted distance. Actually, from all of them. Peter and his problem of a sister were only part of my it. The Logans. Scotland, too. If Fate was coming for me, she could chase my ass to London. I had the information I wanted and knew where to find Genevieve. I was out.

22

Bree and I flew off on our own. It was a long flight and of course it was raining.

"What do you think about getting our stuff and going back to the bookstore? The thing's like a fortress. I don't want to stay out here anymore." I hoped she'd be good with the idea. Bree puffed along, new with flight and especially with such a long distance. It wasn't easy to go for long periods of time and the rain didn't help. We'd stop in a while so she could rest.

"I don't either, now that Crispin's gone. If he'd been there earlier, I wouldn't have believed Petra when she lied about them leaving us. Cris wouldn't have stood for it. He would have waited right outside, like they were supposed to."

Rain has a way of hiding emotion. I'd used it before and my best friend did now, although I sensed her heartbreak. Bree cried silently for a short time. We flew along, reflecting. I hated when I lost control in her presence. I'd done it up, again. I was pretty happy I hadn't hurt Petra. Adam needed to be dealt with and everyone else in the damned UK seemed pretty frickin' dead-set on not doing anything to stop him. Well, he'd been stopped for good and I was still breathing.

"How are you doing?" Bree asked.

"Oh, you know, just kicking my own ass a little."

"About Petra?"

"Yeah." Bree and I were on the same wave length. She would have killed Adam too, if we hadn't stopped her.

"How about you?"

"I think I have multiple personality disorder." She burst out laughing and the tears started up again.

I nodded and laughed with her. She'd surprised me in a big way. Hopefully, the little torture-fest was therapeutic and she'd gotten it out of her system.

"We need to come up with a plan. We'll need to make a move within a few days, but it will be good to get back and regroup. We'll have some time to recover, get some sleep, and all."

"Good. After making this flight twice, we're going to need all that."

"Yep. You doing okay?" She nodded. My wings burned from exertion, but I didn't want to land for a break if she didn't. Instead, I darted upward with Bree right with me, and we searched for a good wind to glide on for a while. Drizzle coated my scales and soon, our surroundings were silent. A few clouds glowed above after taking out the moon.

Bree shook her head fast, casting off water. Her hair hung in a thick fall of waves on either side of her neck.

"So, I'm wet, cold, tired, and my heart hurts. I don't know about you, but I'm thinking life in Austin sure was a fucking cake walk."

I couldn't help laughing, really loud. "That was me last year. Things were sucking pretty bad and all I could think of is how the crazy nuns really weren't that bad."

"Right? Who knew this is what Fate had in store for us?" She shook her head, smiling.

My grin faded. Fate had something altogether different waiting for me. I'd defied her. Totally waved off one of her defined rules. As soon as she hunted me down—and God only knows what that would look like—I had a seriously bad day coming. I cast the foreboding aside and hoped it was an exaggerated line of lore or something.

"YOU TWO LEAVING IS A SHIT IDEA," Osgar retorted.

I relaxed my arms where they were crossed like bars over my chest. It wouldn't do me any good to be all bunched up. Bree and I were going to speak our minds, Southern Belle-style, get our belongings, and then get the hell out of Scotland.

"Is that supposed to help here, Osgar? All relationships benefit from a degree of separation." I didn't know if that was true, but I wanted some. I shoved a set of keys, which belonged to who knows which of Kai's dusty old cars in the carriage house, into a pocket on my backpack. Kai's collection shouldn't go to waste, the way I figured it. I was about to drive the balls off of whichever started up out there.

Osgar glugged an uncommonly huge amount of amber liquid from a rocks glass. "And here you are, leaving despite my worry."

"We should make a plan. Genevieve and her goons are going to come looking and shit's going to get real around here. We should track her down and finish this."

Osgar shook his head, taking a seat at his desk. "Do you ever stop to think the world might go back to the way it was, pre-Tessa? There was an order here, a system. True, Adam needed to be taken down. And true again, you are the perfect creature to do so. You have to understand, all these things, Petrichor Park, even Genevieve, have coexisted."

"She showed up with henchmen at your gala!" Exasperation owned me. I didn't know if I was missing something or what. "That's not harmony."

"A minor skirmish. Hardly enough to call a war."

Another thick glug of booze slid down. Osgar didn't even wince. I did it for him.

"Enough of those and you've got yourself a war."

Bree set a designer bag full of her belongings down beside mine.

"Aw, so, it's true then?" Iain said, from the doorway. "Stay. This can be worked out."

"I don't want to be here. After what happened yesterday, and Crispin—" Bree shook her head. "It's really hard to want to stay. The wards are up at the bookstore. I need to clear my head. It's nothing personal."

"The wards are up here, too." Peter walked in past Iain, glancing from me to Bree, and back. "What's going on?"

"We're leaving." I didn't spend too much time looking at him. I owed Peter an apology for judging him, for thinking he chose to look the other way instead of taking out Adam. He'd been protecting his sister from Fate's rule. I would have done the same for Robbie. Maybe someday pride would allow me to tell him so. I couldn't afford to get all emotional when we were set to leave. "I'm not arguing with you. All I have to say is that I can't handle being around you and your sister right now with her actions over the last few days. Things can't stand the way she's left them. Tyrens are being bled out. Kai is on his way back." I stopped there, before I mentioned Teigan. Emotions were high enough. I shouldered my bag and turned to leave.

"There are different perspectives at work here, Tessa. Please try to understand other points of view and reasoning." Osgar's gaze held respect.

"I need some time to wrap my head around all this." I still wanted to go back to London and I was certain Bree still did, as well.

"Stop," Peter said. He stepped in front of me. "Fate won't let this stand. You killed a fae being. She won't be denied that price."

"So did Osgar or Iain," Bree said. "Did any of you stop to think about that? Who killed that brownie?"

Everyone got quiet. Osgar held up his glass in a mock toast, then emptied it. "No one. I let it live to save my kin." In my opinion that was best. The creature wasn't acting on its own.

I turned to Peter. "This isn't a discussion you get to have. And besides, it's not just Fate everyone should be worried about. Adam is dead. The things that live over there are going to realize that and they might come looking for some vengeance." I averted my gaze and followed Bree out the door.

WE MADE it to the Edinburgh Airport and ditched the ho-hum of a plain little car in a covered parking lot with the parking tag resting on the dash. Flying would be a lot different on a plane, rather than using our wings, but the trip only cost seventy-five bucks each and we'd simply grab the Tube at Heathrow to get to Cecil Court. The flight was on schedule to land by 1:15 PM. I repeatedly pushed away thoughts of what would happen if the flight was a few hours late for some reason.

It's a short flight. I repeated that to myself several times. I also had to reassure myself again and again that the arsenal we'd packed, which masqueraded as two checked bags, wouldn't be mishandled by the airline.

We had over an hour and a half to kill, so we chose a small restaurant and ordered some food while we waited. Bree perched on a stool along a wooden bar while I scooted our bags underneath our feet and took a place beside her. A grungy guy sat to her left but he didn't seem to smell bad, just wore the second-hand look with long, auburn bed-head hair pulled back in a tail. He turned a half full glass of what looked like beer in his finger-tips, ignoring us. We continued on with the normalcy of ordering and doing our best to keep low until our flight boarded. Bree took out a bracelet that had a broken link and started working it over. I watched people. Just like the US, some in the UK were freaks about the way they dress.

One pale lady paced a long row of windows overlooking the concourse, in a pair of heels that made my feet scream from across the room. The heels narrowed to a vicious point and they seemed far too tight to fit a pair of feet to equal the proportions of her average height. She owned them though, step after step in her path while punching away furiously at a smartphone with delicate fingers polished in pearl white. She looked the part of a lady who had one of the high-stress power-jobs at a firm some-where, all business in a perfectly fitted skirt and matching jacket with a thick messenger bag strapped in the same gleaming white material the shoes were made of. Wash-and-go corn silk soft hair hung past her shoulders, gently swishing away each time she spun in her path. The lady never once looked my way, perfect porcelain face and gaze directed either before her or focused on her phone. The din of travelers passing between us was far too much for me to hear what she said. I could barely make out the tone of her voice.

A fresh glass of room temperature tea was set down for each of us. Bree still had her bracelet out, trying to fix it. I grabbed my glass and took a long drink.

The guy on the other side of Bree pulled his beer close and tipped his chin up. A long fat tendril of flesh emerged from the fold above his Adam's apple, reaching down into the glass. I nudged Bree, who ignored me, oblivious to the alien phallus falling out of this guy's throat, draining his drink like a straw. Little slurps echoed in his glass when it was empty.

What the hell am I witnessing?

"Bree," I whispered, turning my gaze to a spot on the bar directly in front of me. She ignored me, tossing her hair out of the way so she could keep working on the stupid jewelry.

Phallus-man turned on his stool as he pulled a knife,

wrapped a sinewy hand around Bree's wrist, and cut her down in a series of fluid motions that happened equally as fast as I could move using super speed. He grabbed a handful of hair at my scalp and dragged the blade through my neck, sending me into a fit of denial that lasted only long enough for everything to go dark.

I jerked in my seat, nearly knocking my tea over. The glass rocked once but I managed to grab it and slam it down before it spilled. My entire body shook. I pulled my hands away before someone saw them tremble.

Bree looked up from her bracelet. "You okay?"

I nodded. Grungy Guy leaned forward, gazing at me over his glass. The thick penis straw was gone and his eyes were bright and questioning.

"I'm okay. Weird daydream or something," I said.

"You sure? You're a little pale." Bree scanned my face. I nodded and took a drink of tea, refocusing.

They both went back to staring at drinks and prying at jewelry. I looked for the lady in white, but she'd moved on. Probably finished her pre-flight business and boarded first class to her next power meeting.

My breath was ragged and sweat dripped between my shoulder blades into the waistband of my jeans. I sucked in lungs full of air, gently quieting my nerves, pushing bloody images from my mind. I must have started to nod off and had a nightmare in the space of ten seconds, if that. Maybe I was starting to lose it and my state of hypervigilance had induced a vision that was a speedy worst case scenario and fast forward ending to our plight in the UK.

"Got it," Bree said. She held up her wrist and fastened the bracelet above her left hand. "It's been broken for a flippin' month. It wouldn't be a big deal, but Daddy gave it to me last summer."

"So, it's special." I smiled.

"Sorry, Tessa." She sighed.

"Don't be sorry. I love your dad. And you shouldn't avoid talking about your family just because I'm around. They're great people and they spoil me whenever they can."

The robust bartender shuffled up to us and deposited our meal choices on the bar. I'd lost my appetite and the aroma of overcooked meat turned my stomach.

"Besides, my lack of a family is what's keeping me alive for the time being." I took another drink of tea, fiddling with a greasy fry.

"Is that the way it shakes out when Fate's rule is broken?" Bree stabbed her fork into a big leafy bite of salad that had bright red dressing dripping off it. I looked away.

"It's all I got. I don't know how else to explain why I'm still living. What about the Logans, though? They'll all screwed if that's real."

"If it's really a thing," she said, crunching. "I mean, it could be horse shit."

I nodded. "Whatever the case, I'm happy to be breathing."

"Aren't you hungry?" Bree asked, digging through her salad to spear a tomato.

"Not really. I think I'm more tired than anything. I hope I can get a nap on the plane." What I really wanted to do was rush her along and away from the man next to us. I kept seeing a baby fist emerge from beneath his face every time I looked at him. That vibe was going to stick. I looked at her watch, noticeably. It was getting close to time to head over to our gate, thank God.

"Can I get a box please?" Bree waved down the guy behind the bar, who brought over two boxes and a plastic bag. I helped her shovel food into clam shells.

Lately I'd begun forgetting that Bree was the older of us two. I used to look at her like my big sister. Things had totally flipped. One person looked at her cross-eyed and I was ready to split some lips. Watching her being slaughtered in my mind's eye did the trick. I couldn't wait until we were safely behind the warded walls of the bookstore so I could rest knowing we could simply sleep.

And that would be about a week away. There would be no real security anywhere until Genevieve was taken down, and that meant dealing with every rogue gargoyle and henchman I knew of. Which didn't even touch what Kai was capable of.

There had to be a huge, golden reason they'd all joined up with her. Maybe she was paying them off. I understood she was pretty frail and quite, well, killable. She also wasn't the type to get her hands dirty. She'd send her lackeys to do the ugly, risky stuff, like ambushing the Logans. That was a big job. The Logans wouldn't go down easily. She'd send a considerable number of her puppets, the ones who might hear from Clan Logan that Bree and I had gone back to the bookstore. It was the best smoke-screen I could cook up. Appearances meant a lot. Bree and I would do a different kind of flying very soon. When the drones were sent to work, we'd take out their queen.

"WIDEN YOUR STANCE," Michael barked. He was all trussed up in what he called "fighting gear," which still looked all kingly and regal. Wielding a thick cut piece of wood, he worked with Bree, teaching her how to use Crispin's short sword. It was an exercise in patience for them both.

"Again. And this time, don't forget to use your footwork and cover." They were off again, with Michael showing her the actual art of swordsmanship. Bree picked it up quickly. I was a little jealous of the sword. I'd had a year to learn how to be lethal with my dagger and had since started using one in each hand, which worked pretty well, in my opinion. Coupled with amped up speed, I was a decent weapon.

Bree was getting good. Keeping the SCA king's cell number had been a smart move. Michael and two of his "knights" had shown up within a couple hours and were now camped with us at the bookstore, coaching Bree, and griping about the traffic in London.

The back alley, where just months ago Kai had dragged Bree away, which had led to me pummeling Petra for the first time, was now our training arena. I slept in my old bed upstairs and settled Bree into another. Peter's room smelled just like him, all manly and musky, like spice and guilt. I fought off the urge to open up the door each time I passed by in the hall and caught his scent. It was probably locked up, anyway.

Michael and company didn't mind the way our skin went transparent in the sun. They didn't bat an eye. They'd seen us— well me, anyway—Garged Out, so seeing us all skinless might seem tame by comparison.

"All right then, you ready?" The older of the grey bearded knights approached me, holding a mean-looking crossbow.

"Yes. Tommy, right?"

"Good memory," he grinned. "You'll find this to be fairly easy. The hardest part is pulling back the string to load a bolt. After you master that, you'll be hooked."

"Awesome."

Tommy handed over the crossbow, which at first was completely awkward. It was bigger than I expected and seemed to want to fall forward out of my grip. I toyed with the weight and balance, then shouldered the thing so I could aim. That part felt natural.

"We're going to get some water and then I'll be over," called Bree. She and Michael stepped inside the back room. I hoped she'd bring me a water bottle.

Tommy trotted to the end of the alley and propped up a wobbly stand with a paper target strapped to it. Before he made it back to me, Bree was back and ready for crossbow training. We wouldn't be able to cock the things while in human form so they showed us how to use a rope to cock the bows and add a bolt.

Cocking the thing was a drag. Aiming and shooting was cake and a lot of fun. We kept practicing to get faster.

The third guy was very quiet. He was the one who would run out to put up a new target or get us new bolts. Once we sat for a break, he finally said something.

"So, I have some bad news about the bolts. Soaking them in the water you have in there will change the weight, which will change the way they travel. To be accurate, you'll need to keep the shot short, if you can.

"What does that mean?" Bree asked.

"Damn." Michael looked worried. "It means you need to get close to your target."

"Shit." The plan was that Bree would do most of the shooting which would allow her to keep her distance. Once she hit something, I'd kick in with the amped up speed and rush whatever she hit and finish it. The genius part of the plan was to be that we could stay far off, hit a henchman gargoyle with a bolt that had been soaked in mineral water from the Grotto springs, and then I'd rush the gargoyle while it was in human form and finish it. The new wrinkle in our plan would mean Bree would have to get closer, too.

"How short are we talking?"

"I'm not able to put an exact number to the distance. Look at it like this," the man said, putting his hands in his pockets. "The farther away you get from what you're trying to hit, the greater the possibility that you'll miss the shot. Best get as close as you can without putting yourself in too much danger, then taking aim. If you miss, the target will hear the bolt hit in the distance. Then you'll have to start tracking all over again."

Tommy piped up. "The other alternative would be to hit the target with a kill shot with the first bolt. Then you'll be done with it."

"You weren't around for the fight," Michael said. "Those things won't go down with one shot."

"Unless the bolt is soaked with our special water," I said. I wasn't one hundred percent sure it would work so easily, and was even less sure of the results. The theory wasn't tested. The way I figured, one armor-piercing shot would instantly change the gargoyle into human form. I would hopefully have a couple seconds to rush the thing and end it before it Garged Out again. All they had to do was yank out the bolt. All I had to do was tap my amped up speed and end them before they had a chance.

"Okay, I need to put this all into perspective. Now we have weapons. We have a plan. As far as the timeline, Genevieve will probably be sending her gargoyles in any time now. Once she's thinned the herd for us and left some back at her place, we need to make our move."

Bree sunk a bolt into the torso of one dummy and one in the neck of the next target within about half a minute. Michael whistled, grinning.

"Damn," said Tommy. He turned to me. "Well, girl, looks like it'll be on you to jump and finish."

I nodded. "No pressure or anything." I wasn't convinced. It took too long to load another bolt. We needed more shooters. Certainly, Genevieve's crew would outnumber us. Surprise would be on our side. Once that was blown, we'd best unleash and let it all fly or we were screwed. And that was only if they weren't expecting us to fight using the water.

I was certain at some point there had been another attempt at using the mineral water for the purpose of taking down gargoyles. The likely reason it wasn't widely known among our kind was simply Kai and his ability to control everything around him. Maybe I was wrong about that. I'd never witnessed Kai use it. When he wanted me back in human form he changed me right then and there on a whim. He hadn't needed mineral water. That being the case, all he had to do was sit on the secret. Then he was still the guy with all the mojo. Typical Kai.

"Michael, I believe she's ready." Tommy held out his hands

and Bree placed the crossbow in his grip. Michael pulled a large, black case from their gear and popped it open. Inside was another crossbow that was broken down into several pieces. The stalk was engraved wood and all the other parts were gleaming silver, engraved with the same scrolling design. What held my attention most was the large, round barrel that Michael snapped into place once the bow was together. He came to his feet and handed the weapon to Bree. "Try this."

"Wow," I said. "That thing's gorgeous."

"Isn't she?" Tommy agreed. "I call her Kate. Sexiest damn weapon these hands have ever touched."

"Kate?" Bree asked, eyebrows arched. "I've got to know."

"As in Beckinsale," Michael supplied, shaking his head and smiling.

"Aye," Tommy said, wistfully. "And she's fast and mean. You two will be a good team," he told Bree.

She examined the gleaming crossbow, walking back to our makeshift range with Michael.

"This thing shoots more than just one at a time?" I asked.

"Not quite," Tommy said. "It will shoot one bolt at a time, but it is a rapid-fire weapon, with no need to reload after each shot like the one you learned on."

"Why did you make us use that one then, when you had this?" I looked at Michael's pile of gear, noting there were two more identical cases.

"Always learn to ride bareback before the saddle, lass." Tommy grinned. "Now each of those bolts will be a shot in your mind. Each bolt is an opportunity to succeed and survive. If we'd a shown you this first, the value of each bolt would be greatly diminished."

Two bolts slugged into a dummy, knocking it clean off the bracket. We all jumped a little spinning around. A moment later, another slammed into the next target. I expected to see Bree and

Michael shooting again, instead Peter and Petra stood beside Michael. "Your odds have just doubled," he said. "I made a call."

I was so relieved I could have cried. I locked eyes with Peter who, for once, didn't give me a cocky "I told you so" type of glance in return. He nodded at me.

I looked at Michael. "Thank you."

"Of course."

"The Logans will be here tonight," Peter said. "They aren't fond of the idea of traveling such distances in a car."

"Let's break for now then. That's enough practice until tonight." Michael opened up weapon bags and cases and we helped put them away and clean up the fluff from dummies and shredded paper targets.

_____

23

Bree was busy chatting up Tommy, who did his best to convince her she was the best shot he'd seen in decades. I caught her attention with a nod toward the bookstore then walked past everyone and took the stairs two at a time, running to my room. Once inside, I began shucking my personal weapons and tossing them into my reading chair. I laid back on the bed and closed my eyes.

Peter was a distraction. I had guilt that needed to be dealt with since he was now at the bookstore. If only he'd leveled with me and told me why he didn't go after Adam. Instead, he'd let me think the worst rather than allowing me to understand that he'd been protecting Petra. Had he killed Adam, Fate's rule dictated Petra would be taken. I got that. I didn't know what I would have done in the same situation. If my brother was still alive, would I have allowed Adam to live to save his life? Even locking Adam away would have meant bringing a fight to my doorstep. That was a lot to consider. Peter had taken the safe road to save his sister's life and to keep the peace.

I didn't have the whole picture. It wouldn't be only a few occupants of Petrichor Park. That wasn't enough of a risk. I would have locked Adam up and I was certain Peter would have, as well. The stakes were greater, and I just didn't have the whole story.

At any rate, it was all pointless now. I'd done away with Adam. Fate must have been off her game because I was still breathing. I palmed my face, rubbing my forehead with my fingertips. I was a shit for the way I'd treated Peter. If I was going to go have a heart-to-heart with him and apologize, I'd better go do it. The sun was going to set in a couple hours, so I got up and headed down the hall toward his room. It seemed the best place to start looking for him.

Petra opened his bedroom door on my third knock. She leaned against the jamb, eyebrows cocked up, looking down her nose at me. "Can I help you with something?"

"Lose the attitude, Petra. I'm looking for Peter."

"Why?" She asked, staring me down.

"Is he in there or not? And it's none of your business, so keep your big nose out of it."

"You are very wrong about that. And before you get all ready to beat me up, just know, I don't care that you can. It's happened before and I survived. That doesn't mean I will refrain from telling you how I feel." She came out of the door and stood inches from me. "You are not worthy of my brother. He can, and will, do better. He will find someone capable of caring about him, unlike you. Stay away from Peter, Tessa. You deserve no more of his time or his attention. Go back in your room and leave him alone." She turned around and slammed his door.

I walked away feeling pretty shaken up. What if Petra was right about everything she said? Still, an apology needed to happen. I didn't think Peter had been in the room. I went downstairs to look for him.

Petra's word stung. Not only because I was guilty as hell of being bitchy, but because deep down, I sort of felt like I wasn't good enough. The feeling had been there, back in the beginning when I first met Peter. I was so infatuated with him that I would have done anything for him just a year before. That feeling had grown into something heartfelt. Then I'd gotten the wrong impression and let that ruin the way I felt about him, breaking my own heart in a way. And there I was feeling that way again, like I wasn't good enough for him. I felt like a mutt at a pedigree dog show; an orphan that couldn't even get adopted. No one had ever wanted me. No one but Bree. I couldn't let that stop me from doing the right thing and telling him I was sorry, if he'd hear me out.

I searched for a long time, checking each alcove in the bookstore, the alley, the kitchen, and the study. I checked with Michael, who hadn't seen him since he left target practice. After one last look around the store, I went back upstairs. Peter must have taken off into London. Just as I put my hand on the door handle the idea occurred to me that there was one more place I hadn't checked: The rooftop where Peter had taught me to fly.

At the end of the hallway there was a narrow door and an old set of stairs leading up. As I pushed through the exterior door, I saw him standing at the edge of the roof in the same place we'd jumped off together. Quietly, I shut the door and walked over to stand beside him. The sun hung slightly above even horizon. Peter was bathed with brilliant gold and silver. I didn't look past his transparent skin. He was simply a beautiful man. I gazed out at the building across the alley, the same one we'd smashed into during my first flight lesson. We'd cracked the wall up and Peter had gotten in terrible trouble and had paid to fix it himself.

"Hey," I said, sounding lame.

Peter didn't answer or acknowledge I was standing beside him.

I took a deep breath. "I'm really glad you're here."

He snorted and shook his head. "What do you want, Tessa?"

"To talk, I guess."

"To talk. Really?" He glanced down at me.

"I want to apologize for being such a mean bitch lately. I was judgmental and that wasn't right."

"You don't say."

"I'm trying here, Peter."

He looked away again. "Well, thank you. I'm afraid it's a too late. But I appreciate the gesture."

"The gesture? I really am sorry." Not surprising. He was so arrogant, he couldn't even accept a sincere apology.

"You just feel guilty." He spun and headed toward the door. "Don't worry. I'm over it."

"Hey! Don't walk away."

He kept doing just that.

"I mean, you could have explained what was going on. Maybe told me why you didn't do anything to stop him."

He stopped walking and let his chin drop to his chest. When he turned around, I wanted to end the conversation and go to bed. The look in his eyes was half rage and half something else that I didn't get right away.

"Why do you think I owe you any sort of explanation about my decisions? I owe you nothing." He approached, getting really close. "Understand? Not. A. Damned. Thing."

He was right. As much as I wanted my words to make everything better between us, the damage was done. And he didn't have to explain himself. He was correct there, too. "Okay, I get it. Just, please, know that I am really sorry for the way I treated you. I shouldn't have. I am so sorry, Peter."

He searched my face, looking from eye to eye. Without a word, he turned away and left. I didn't want to watch the door close, so I turned back to the sunset and sat down, not knowing what I was waiting for.

My heart hurt. Peter was hurt. I hated myself and would have given anything to step back in time and do things right. The pressure of the days ahead, plus my heartache, added up. A few tears slid down my cheeks. I wiped at them fast. Crying would do absolutely no good at all.

Peter stepped beside me and I started, twisting to look up at him. He sat and pulled me around to face him, one of my feet beside him, pulling the bow from shoelace on my Chuck Taylor and loosening it enough to pull it free. I watched his hands working at my other shoe, stunned, thinking he was doing it because we'd be Garging Out in a short while. I was dead wrong.

We locked eyes and Peter put his hand on my cheek, caressing the skin below my lip with his thumb. I held my breath. Finally, he leaned in and placed a soft, beautiful kiss on my lips. I'd longed for this for months, and it was an answer to my heart's dream, but it was scary as hell at the same time. Almost instantly, heat surged from the pit of my gut outward. I fought it off, determined to be strong and not let it stop me this time. Peter knew what he was getting into.

The last time we'd made out a little bit he'd been scratched, bitten, and teased to a point no man should endure. Maybe it was that another guy would have given in to my wishes when I was under delirium and a head injury. My alter-self had taken the opportunity to "enjoy" being in Peter's bed while I was out of it. I'd missed out on most of it, coming to in a state of confusion and almost sure we'd gone the distance. But Peter wasn't that guy.

When he broke the kiss I got to my knees and pulled his shirt over his head, watching as bronzed sunlight touched skinless muscle and shadow defined the lines of his abdomen. I traced my fingertips across his chest, loving the feel of him.

"Your hands are hot," he said warily. He leaned in, kissing my cheek and whispering. "Doing all right?'

"I'm okay," I said, turning my forehead to rest against his. We smiled together and took the next couple of minutes to remove more clothes. I thought I'd be shy with him, but he took his time and cherished moments by kissing my forehead and the tender skin by my ear. Our hands wandered and so did our lips. I tasted parts of him I'd thought myself far too prudish to touch, let alone put my tongue against. He was amazing and patient and I tried to be just as good to him. I burned inside the whole time, nervous and wanting to get the painful part behind us. He read my mind, easing in and watching my eyes the whole time. My legs began to shake, which was sort of embarrassing, so I wrapped them around him.

"You're like a thermal core," he said, rocking against me softly.

I pulled my hands through his hair, watching as light danced in his silver eyes. "Is that a bad thing? Like weird?" I couldn't help staring at him above me. I'd daydreamed about what it would be like to be intimate with him.

"God, no." He kissed the inside of my wrist when I ran a hand along his cheek. "Please tell me I'm not hurting you."

"It stung a little at first, for only a second. It doesn't hurt." I couldn't say I was as close to being there as he was. I could tell he was holding back.

I had to hold myself back as well. Part of me, that ancient part who knew exactly what she was doing and just what she wanted and how she wanted it was just below the surface. I kept her in the back of my mind but the things that played out there, the visions of doing things with Peter, doing things *to* him, were amazing. His speed picked up and I tightened my legs around his hips, pulling him close so I could feel our hearts beating at the same time. The sounds he made as he finished were something I never wanted to forget. His breath against my neck. The taste of his sweat. I never wanted to remember sex any other way.

Peter turned his lips against my cheek. "Do you feel that?"

I sighed. "Yeah." Skin tingled along the backs of my arms and legs. Bright orange turned to purple as I watched the sun set, casting color on his face. We pulled away from one another, locking eyes as we transformed into gargoyles. I had never known another person on such a deep level. We had an understanding of each other then, knowledge of base parts of one another. It was like I could see his heart through the tough plate of scales surrounding it. I would never think of Peter the same way again. On a primal level, deep beneath my heart, he was there.

And he was mine.

I couldn't help but smile at him. He cocked his head, watching me. As fast as I could, I took off at a run across the rooftop and dove into the air, gaining altitude as quickly as I could. Peter was right with me. The city below was a net of soft lights appearing in bursts as clouds separated. I dropped back and watched Peter soar above me, circling in the moonlight, just as I had months ago. He was majestic and dark up there against the midnight sky with moon light showing through the membranes of his wings. I wanted to be in his arms in human form again. I decided to settle for holding onto one of his claws as we flew. We were so high up that it seemed we were lighter on the air. Peter flipped me over beneath him and pulled my wings closed with his arms. I grabbed onto him for dear life, yelping and laughing. He held me at the right distance so he still had wings. I imagined what it would be like if we touched too much and turned human way up there. We'd fall from the sky like dragons who'd lost their wings.

"Don't panic," he said, biting his lower lip.

"I'm not. I mean, I trust you." I smiled back as we soared, using his wings to glide.

"All right then. Don't let go." He pulled me beneath him, wrapping my thighs around his waist. Had we been human at that point, we could have been intimate again. It was sort of cool just hanging onto him, watching him fly us around. Our chests touched. Soft skin met mine and we locked our human bodies together. We didn't start falling fast right away. We tumbled on the air and he moved so perfectly that way. I kept my arms locked around him as we flipped and I was above him. I bit into his shoulder gently. He flipped us back over and pulled away, his wings catching like a parachute. We were back to plain scales touching where we were joined before. I was burning up, needing more of him wanting to be human and close with him again. Gargoyles couldn't have sex and really, I was fine with that but growing impatient. He must have sensed it because we dropped from the air fast and alighted a little less than gently on the rooftop of the bookstore. Without a word we ran to the door and squeezed through the human sized opening and didn't stop running until we were in my room with the door locked behind us.

Pounding on my door wasn't the ideal way to wake me with a smile. Moonlight peeked through the window blinds. My neck was cricked from sleeping with my head on Peter's shoulder and my chest on his. That made me smile.

Peter sighed. "Who the bloody hell is it?" He yelled toward the door. Footsteps stomped away down the hall. I had a hunch it was Petra. She was likely to have a bad day now. My smile widened. I raised only my head up so I wouldn't trigger the change and ruin the moment.

"So that cat's outta the bag."

"Indeed."

Neither of us moved. Scenes played through my mind and I picked out my favorites of many. The longer we stayed in bed holding each other, the idea nagged and nagged that the night had been a distraction we both needed badly. That didn't mean spending the night with Peter hadn't meant everything to me. The issue was that the next day was when we'd organize and head out to hunt down Genevieve.

Male voices boomed through the hallway, coming in from the rooftop. The Logans had arrived, which was likely why Petra was trying to find Peter.

"I should show them in so they can get some rest," Peter said, with a long sigh. He kissed my forehead and then hefted us both off the mattress. I helped as best I could, keeping close so our chests didn't come apart. Once we both had our feet on the floor, we parted in a heavy gust of leathery wings and scraping scales. I grinned at him, feeling my fangs scratch across my bottom lip.

"I'm going to stay here. But tell them I'll see them in the morning, okay?"

Peter nodded and quietly shut my bedroom door behind him after peering out into the hall to make sure we weren't busted by the other gargoyles.

24

Shooting a rapid-fire crossbow at a stuffed dummy was a damned piece of cake compared to aiming at a live target, even if it was a henchman we shot at, fully Garged Out and pissed as hell. He'd been locked up since Michael and Company snagged him at the ambush, weeks back. I wanted the vile thing to blow apart like a vampire hit with holy water, but the asshole just snarled and baited us with horrible comments about whether he wanted to eat Bree, Petra, or me first, and what he wanted to do to us beforehand. The angrier I got, the farther off-target my shot was. He howled with laughter, his giant head tossing around so his horns reflected what limited moonlight there was shining down on him.

Bree stuck him good with a freshly-soaked mineral water bolt that blew right through his chest plate. I grinned almost as big as she did, grateful she did it, rather than Petra. We three stood there in the back alley, rain dripping off the canopy of our wings, smiling like dopes, waiting for something—anything—to happen to him.

Something was wrong. He didn't change to human form. The

shot hurt like hell from the way he bellowed but the wound, a solid shot nearly dead-center in his chest, wasn't even enough to keep him down if he wasn't chained to a metal parking beam like he was now. The steel post was anchored deeply in the concrete and strategically placed to stop cars from striking the bookstore when they drove through and turned the corner. The setup made for a perfect firing range.

"Shit." Bree lowered the weapon, watching the henchman. "It's not working."

"Hit him again, maybe?" I offered.

She took careful aim as the round magazine on top of the crossbow clicked, ready to fire. Bree sent another bolt into the meaty part of the henchman's shoulder, then another into his thigh on the opposite side. Her motions were fluid, intentional, and killer-fast.

"That was badass." I said, still hoping the target would change to human form.

"Your plan is shit so far," Petra said. "Filling them full of wood won't kill these gargoyles."

"Do you have to be such a bitch?" Bree asked her. "I mean all the time?"

"If not, you'd think me ill," Petra said, and winked at Bree, closing one almond shaped eye. Seeing Petra Garged Out was always a little unsettling. Me and Bree, the Logans, and Peter transformed into humanoid types. Petra was a conundrum. Her torso was long and slender, more serpentine than bulky, like mine. Her scales were gray like mine, but the base of hers had a dark crimson hue. Her appearance wouldn't let me trust her, which was best. She looked like a viper and acted like a snake in the grass most times.

"She's right, even if her delivery sucks. We're a little screwed at the moment." I considered briefly, then bit the bullet. "I need to go see Iain." More apologies were needed. I lived for the day when I didn't destroy the property of others, be it unintentional or not.

Petra piped up, looking at Bree. "What say you and I keep up the attempts to bring this big bastard down?"

"Maybe there's a good place to stick him that will do the trick. But we need to do it in one shot. The water's not working." She handed the crossbow to Petra as I walked into the bookstore.

"Do you have a minute?" I asked Iain, trying not to startle him. He held open his door, with a book in his other hand, quirking a smile. I was reminded of when we touched back to our human forms, buck naked. My cheeks flushed. "I just wanted to apologize again for totaling your truck. I have lots saved up from working so much last year and I'd like to pay you back or help replace it."

"That will do," he said. "No hurry, though, lass."

I smiled, relieved. Paying for part of the replacement would help ease my guilt and it wouldn't put a big dent in my coffer. "Okay." I wavered uncomfortably in the doorway of the guest room Iain was using, wings fluttering a little and tail twitching. "So, did you ever examine what was implanted in my back?"

"Ah, I thought it best to show you. I have it here. Haven't had time to spend looking much into it, although last we talked, you and I were certain it's mineral water." He went back inside the room, dropping the book on the bed as he passed, and produced a small pouch from a larger bag. Inside was the silver canister. He shook it beside his ear. "Doesn't sound much like water, now that you bring it to my attention."

Suddenly, it hit me. "Aw, shit."

Iain arched his brows and laughed, showing all of his fangs and black forked tongue.

"Sorry. Do you know how to open it up?"

"Aye." He shoved a claw inside the pocket of a pair of pants that were tossed over the back of a chair and pulled out a multi-tool. I followed him to the desk where he locked the pliers onto the canister and squeezed it in his massive grip until the metal gave and dented in on one side.

"Looks to be mud," he said, sounding confused.

My heart sank. Of course it wasn't the mineral water from the Grotto. What had been sewn into my back was a quantity I knew to be found after a gruesome system of torture and harvest.

"This changes things," he said

Indeed, it did.

THE NEXT MORNING everyone sat around the breakfast bar in the back room of the Bochord, sipping tea that wasn't hotter than the tempers in the room. Michael had sent the other two gamer humans back home after loading the shot-up henchman into their van. Waiting until daybreak to handle a gargoyle that size was best. Even in human form the old, Ancients were huge beasts.

"Miss Conley?" One of the college students Peter and I had hired to run the store, poked his head inside. "I just wanted you to know we're flipping the sign out here. It promises to be a busy day, judging from all the early traffic."

"Thanks, Bradley. I'll be out to let you know when we're through here."

Bradley nodded diligently and let the door swing shut. The bookstore staff would give us privacy while we talked.

"I suggest we discuss what we do know rather than what we do not. That should aid in keeping control of this tension in the room," Osgar said. "Tessa, please. Explain this material you found."

I nodded, thinking of the best way to deliver a CliffsNotes-type version. "The stuff implanted in my back appears to be the same thing Genevieve is pulling from all the Tyrens she captures. She hooks them up to a system, like a syphon. This thick substance is processed and then pushed through a manifold and a system of tubing, then into two individual like, tubs. The only thing I can guess is the essence in this stuff is powerful enough to put the change into some sort of remission. That's what happened to me. I didn't change, and I couldn't tap any amped up speed, either."

Thankfully, Iain spoke up. "It loses strength after a time. After Tessa removed it, I attempted to duplicate the effects by implanting the same canister beneath the skin at the top of my own spine. I believe after exposure to air and possibly sunlight, the power simply diffuses."

"You say this material is collected in the tubs and that is what Genevieve is using to bring back Kai and Teigan," Osgar said, looking back at me.

"Yes. And I'm not trying to be a shit, but Petra can verify that. She got the information straight from Genevieve." All eyes shot to Petra who simply nodded. I moved on to avoid another scene. "I don't know how much longer it will take until Genevieve is done . . . remaking them, but a human hand—like, fully generated—shot out of one of the metal tubs at me. That's how I knew what was inside them."

"Bottom line, we have to get inside and get to this stuff," Michael said, gesturing to the cracked canister on the bar next to Iain, "and tip the bolts with it if we want to stop gargoyles."

"Getting inside is priority," Peter said. "Teigan needs us and we need him."

I nodded, remembering the first time I saw Teigan in gargoyle form. He stood taller than Peter and was built like a brick shithouse, as we used to say in the States. Massive and dark, he'd been quiet until I pushed his temper. I'd mistaken him for one of Kai's henchmen. I owed him my life and would do anything to repay him. "When we find Teigan, we find Kai." I couldn't help smiling when a little flicker of heat ignited at the thought. There would be a battle involved, just like the last time we took Kai down. We had to get a little tricky last time, but we had more resources now. The thought of seeing him again both made me long for a fight and scared the hell out of me. Kai was torturous and dark, capable of killing without blinking. I guess being alive for centuries sapped humanity after a while. It certainly had with Kai.

"And that's where the book comes in. We have it. We should use it to stop Kai." Petra said. My blood chilled. Everyone nodded, agreeing in slow motion while panic iced my veins. No one knew I'd given it to Cody.

"Do you figure you're up to using it, lass?" Osgar asked. "I ken it's not always easy."

My first instinct was to take the opportunity he laid out for me to lie. I could tell them I couldn't use the book. That it wasn't working for me. Even if I still had it, I didn't know how to use it against Kai. I could skirt the issue and bury that fact that I'd ditched something they considered to be an asset, a weapon we desperately needed. I looked at Peter who gazed back with unspoken confidence that I would say the right thing. Osgar and Iain watched me, calmly waiting for a response. Even Petra looked at me expectantly. Michael looked confused, but hung on my answer. Bree was the only one who looked at me with a degree of wonder. I think she knew I was about to deliver a bombshell. She knew me too well. I took a big breath.

"Genevieve has a plan for that book," I began "which isn't good. I'm not sure why she wants it so badly, but I think she has made significant promises to the henchmen to get them to align with her. Wielding the book coupled with bringing back Kai, makes up for the fact that she is merely human."

"Merely?" Michael interjected.

"Sorry," I said. "I mean she used to be a goddess and was relegated to life as a human because she betrayed Lugh."

Michael looked at me with questions in his eyes.

I went on: "I'm sort of a demigod-gargoyle hybrid. On the

demigod side, my mother was a human and my father is Lugh. All that is in here with me. I was born in Austin, Texas in the United States, where the demigod rescued me after the car crash where my family was killed, except for my brother. I recently found out that Genevieve caused that wreck, along with killing Lugh's mistress, the mother to my goddess side. So, Genevieve has killed both of my mothers trying to get to me out of jealousy. She was Lugh's wife and he like, needed other people. She responded by turning murderous and lost her status as a goddess. Now she's here. I couldn't let her get a hold of that book."

There was a long period of silence. I picked up my mug of tea and sipped, for lack of something else to do. I was sick to my stomach, preparing for the next bit of information I had to share.

"Couldn't? As in you have done something about this?" Iain asked. Of everyone, I knew he'd be the one to get it.

"I sent the book away with Cody. He found a safe buyer for it. Like a collector. He assures me that book is in excellent hands. I didn't know what I was doing with it. It changed Bree with this 'taking a toll' thing the last time I asked it a question. I couldn't trust myself with it." Realizing I was babbling, I shut my mouth, fighting off the urge to put my head in my hands. I had to remember it was the right thing to do.

"Why did you hide this?" Osgar said, after taking a moment to digest what I'd said.

"I didn't mean to hide it. There's been a lot going on. It's only been a few days. There was the wreck and I just . . ." I looked from face to face as they waited for an explanation. "I just didn't."

"Again, looking at what we do know, I have to deduce that Genevieve has the damned thing. She's come across magic enough to bring two entities back from molecular disassembly. She couldn't do that on her own." Iain didn't look at me when he spoke. I read into that.

"There's no way. Cody took the book out of the UK on a flight, minutes after I gave it to him."

"Contrarily, there is a way. That bitch has her hooks in half of England and Ireland, plus some in Scotland," Osgar said.

"I'd wager she has it, Tessa." Peter agreed.

"Since the possibility exists, we have to plan for that. We might be looking at more of a fight from her," said Michael.

"Genevieve wants her status back. She said she wants to go back home where she belongs," I said quietly. I wouldn't allow myself to think I'd made a mistake. We were all better off with that book locked away on another continent. "We have no guarantee she has it. I'm holding out faith that Cody succeeded."

No one had anything to add but we all brooded silently for a moment. Finally, Iain spoke up.

"The security we installed will alert us when she makes a move." He held up a smartphone. "I'll get the call."

"We can still use that part of our plan. We wait until Genevieve sends a number of the henchmen to the castle. Then we go in," said Bree. "They might have us beat with numbers, otherwise."

"I have thirteen fighters," said Michael. "And before you interject some nonsense about my fighters being 'merely' human, I will tell you that these are skilled knights, ready for a fight. They've prepared since our games were interrupted by gargoyles. We have a diversity of weaponry, as you clearly know by now, as well as skills. We are ready for this fight."

"So, we ready ourselves and wait for the sign from Kelty," Peter said.

Iain nodded. "Any ill will, animosity between the ranks here should be diffused at this moment. What is done is final. We stand united in this or we fail. I move thusly."

"As do I," said Osgar.

"Agreed," I said, nodding. Everyone else acknowledged, as well. I was very happy we were in London rather than all the way up in Scotland. Petrichor Park was a little over an hour's run from the Bochord. We would use that to our advantage.

Peter rose from his chair, stretching as the others began talking amongst themselves. He smiled my way and I gave him a half-hearted smile in return. He took a step toward me, his expression going blank and eyes darkening. With one long arm, he reached behind his head and pulled the back of his shirt over his shoulders, discarding it on the floor.

"What are you doing?" I asked, with cold fear building in my chest.

Peter didn't answer. He tipped his face toward the ceiling as his chest heaved and he rocked back on his heels. From beneath his arms on each side, a small bit of flesh protruded, beginning to grow. Within a beat two arms that mimicked his others erupted, fully muscled, attached to his broad chest. I couldn't speak or breath, hit by the same otherworldly feeling that I'd experience at the airport when the homeless guy appeared to cut Bree down. Peter leveled his gaze my way, the beautiful silver color back in his eyes. He smiled, holding up one of his new hands, which beckoned me to him with a "come here" motion of one digit.

I gasped and grabbed the edge of the bar with one hand, knocking my tea mug to the floor in a crash.

"Oops," Bree chirped. I glanced at her as she got up and walked toward the utility closet where the broom was kept.

"Damned gravity," Osgar said, as he ripped free a few paper towels. I watched him soak up the tea at my feet, in shock, then glanced back to Peter.

"Nicely done," he mouthed, with an exaggerated wink. He had two arms and was wearing his shirt. My head spun and my stomach heaved. I came off my seat, ready for some air and needing to put lots of distance between myself and others, no matter how many arms they had. I walked toward the back door and opened it up, gulping cool lungsful of air.

"You okay?" Bree asked.

I sucked in air, nodding. "Do you remember back at the airport on our way here and I lost my appetite? I was feeling sort of sick. Now, too," I said, then took a breather. "I've been seeing some odd things. People changing. Sprouting new limbs. It happened in there." I doubled over and put my hands on my knees.

Bree rubbed my back. "Maybe you need to lie down for a while. It's been a crazy week. Month. Year." She laughed.

I nodded and came upright. "I'm okay. I think I'm going to go check out what's new in the bookstore." Walking around the shop for a while always cheered me up and helped my perspective before.

"Okay. I'm going to go upstairs for a bit. I'll be in my room if you need me."

I turned and wrapped her in a quick hug. "Bree, I don't know what I'd do if you weren't here. I love you."

"I love you, too, Tessa. You should really get some rest. A good nap. Even a powernap." She patted my back and let me go. I stayed on the concrete steps out back for a few more moments to completely gather myself. I was seeing things. Peter had only two arms. The guy at the airport didn't have a huge straw that popped out of his neck. Bree was safe. I needed to get a grip. When I walked back through the breakroom, Peter was the only one there. He'd been waiting.

"You all right?" He got up and came toward me, only two arms and a whole lot of gorgeous. I fell against his chest as he wrapped my up in a hug.

"I'm okay. I think all this stress and stuff is getting to me a little bit. Thanks for being here." I breathed in through the fabric of his shirt. He smelled great, familiar and masculine and safe.

"Okay then." He rocked me a little and kissed the top of my head.

"I'm going to go check out the bookstore. It's been a while."

"Sounds good."

Bradley was straightening shelves by the storefront, where it just happened to be unseasonably sunny. I wanted to go scavenge through the shelves that were bathed in sunlight, feel the radiating warmth, and forget about everything else. Peter and I stopped by the stairs, where he turned to take the first one. I smiled up at him and wrinkled my nose. He snorted a little laugh and started upstairs. Bradley saw us right then and started my way.

"How's it going out here?"

"We had a tidy little rush at opening. It's died down so I'm going to get my stocking done." He smiled. "Another day in book paradise."

"I remember those days well." Back when I was hung up on the mere thought of being a gargoyle. Things were so different now. Sure, I still thought about the change. But there was the whole trying to stay sane while learning to merge my existence with a demigoddess thing, plus ditching the book and not dying in a rollover crash thing. I could have added to the list but mentally shifted gears.

Bradley marched toward the sales counter and cut open a brown carton. I still couldn't help the excitement of seeing what titles and cover designs were in each shipment. He began unpacking the box as the bard's bells chimed, announcing another customer.

Without looking up, I said, "I'll greet this one." I had to wait for customers to come into the store and past the reach of any rogue rays of sunlight. After watching Bradley unload the books for a moment, I turned to look for a possible sale.

I saw a flash of a white dress before the girl turned out of sight, heading toward the back of the store. I followed, intent on tracking her into the depths of the bookstore. I knew my way around through the Bochord and the customer didn't so I wasn't particularly worried. I found her in the back where the books stayed relatively untouched. Old volumes and classics were back there, far from mainstream titles and new releases.

She turned as I pasted on my usual smile, ready to ask what I could help her find and thank her for stopping in. My words died on my tongue as I recognized her from the airport. The white on white outfit should have tipped me off but I was too absorbed with feeling lightheaded and nauseated earlier.

"This is where it all started for you. Right here? Where you saw your first living gargoyle. That wasn't really you, though, was it? Because to be true, you are the first living gargoyle, correct? How's that whole alter ego thing working out?"

Since she apparently knew me, both "me's," I didn't know which name to respond with. "I'm Tessa. Teasa, if you want to go old school."

"Well, which do you prefer? It's you're world. I'm just living in it." She winked.

"Tessa." Saying my same name with emphasis on a different part of it wasn't my favorite aspect of my duality, now that she brought it up. I could choose just one.

"I like that better, too."

"You're an American?" I was floored. And she was sassy, at that. "Who are you?" Being direct was her M.O. and that was very welcome when she broke the ice by reciting by my life stories. Being frank would cut down on the small talk.

"I just flew in from LA," she beamed. "Love all that sunshine over there. And the men," she placed a French manicured hand on her chest and closed her eyes. "My gods. Miles of bronzed muscle and weeks of very satisfying entertainment."

"Glad you enjoyed all of them. How do you know me? Why are you following me? You know, why are you stalking me? All that." My hands were on my hips. I got the feeling she was playing with me, like she thought she was in control or something. It pissed me off. I didn't like being trailed and could care less if she banged the entire state of California.

"Ah, there's that attitude. Love the moxie, Tessa. You amaze us all, by the way. I used to love watching you grow and become what you're meant to be."

"Knock it off and tell me what the hell's going on here!" I snarled. "I don't have time for this shit."

Her pink glossed lips tightened into a line and she stepped right in my face. My hands clenched, ready to defend myself. She was slightly taller than me but of course was wearing outrageously heeled white leather boots. She was slenderer than me and far too worried about her appearance. I could take her.

"Okay then. We can do it this way. Shut the fuck up and listen well, you idiot. You broke my favorite rule. Because of who you are, I haven't ended you like any other shitbag around here." She took a cool breath and backed off. "Lugh is a personal friend. I couldn't kill you and wound him that deeply so consider yourself lucky. And stop sizing me up." She tossed her white-blonde hair over a shoulder. "You don't want any of this."

I tossed my head back and let loose with a loud bark of laughter that came up from the soles of my shoes. She was hilarious. My eyes started to water, and I just let the laughter pour out. It felt sort of great. I wiped at my eyes one at a time, keeping her in view. "Don't stop. I need the levity."

She smiled, almost lovingly. It was bizarre. "See, I really like you. You're bright and funny, and it's good to be suspecting. You live in a crazy few worlds," she said, as if giving me an excuse or feeling a bit sorry. She continued to grin, watching me get a hold of myself. "Let's do this a different way. You've had your ass kicked lately. How about some good news? Maybe a sneak peek?"

"Indeed. Humor me, please." I couldn't wait to hear what was next.

"Take off your clothes."

That set me back a second. but I recovered fast. "Get the hell out of my store."

"What, you think I haven't seen boobies before?" She shook her head, waiting a second while she apparently gave me a moment to change my mind. I shook my head.

"Suit yourself." She shrugged a shoulder and approached me

again. When she was about a foot away, she closed her eyes and simply blew in my face.

Warm air poured across my cheeks. Instead of being grossed out or alarmed, I found it totally comforting. The heat is what made it feel so good. My skin started tingling like I was going to Garg Out though it was the middle of the morning. My shoulders burned in the twin places where my wings sprouted every night. I stepped away from her when, sure as hell, my huge leathery wings busted through my favorite Dropkick Murphys T-shirt. Heat was everywhere, making me want to swim in it. Scales erupted on my skin, but they tightened into a woven top-skin rather than plates of hardened, stony armor. I didn't grow like normal. No bulky muscle expanded, and my hands didn't turn into claws. Heat grew in my chest and radiated outward. In an orange and black flash, my clothes and shoes went up in a quick gust of flame that extinguished as fast as it started. Twin tines of my forked tongue explored fangs that erupted, elongating my canine teeth. My hair grew long enough to touch the tops of my feet, and was streaked with copper and white tones.

I hovered above the floor without realizing I'd come off the hardwood. My body hadn't grown at all so each beat of my wings did substantially more than when I was a gargoyle. I brought a hand up into view and flipped it over, looking at it. When I turned my wrist over fast, a cloud of blue flame formed in my palm. I held it for a moment, a beautiful little fire in my hand. Cold air flowed across my teeth when I smiled. I turned my other palm up and watched, delighted, as another ball of fire ignited in my hand. A quick look down the length of my body revealed that I was naked, but the new scales were much like a body suit. Every curve was visible, but not every detail. I had no nipples or belly button. There was no hair on my forearms, or anywhere else except the massively long mane on my scalp. I let myself down to the floor gently and pulled my wings in.

The girl in white was sitting in a leather reading chair with her perfect legs crossed at the knee. "Well? What do you think?" She beamed at me. "I just want you to know, I'm breaking a few rules doing this. But I wanted to be the one who shows you what's coming. I'm selfish like that. So, I'm cheating."

"It's amazing. I feel great! This is the first time in my life the fever isn't scary."

"It's not a fever," she said, excitedly, coming to her feet. "This is you. You're a fire being, like your father. Being a half-blood keeps you grounded to this plane, but this, beautiful, is what you really are. You can choose to use all this power any way you want. Helping others, saving puppies, revenge, whatever. If I were you, I'd travel. The men, mmhm," she drifted off, savoring the thought.

"Who are you, really?" I asked. She had stunning powers to be able to change me this way. I felt a little shame considering the way I was acting a few moments ago. Hello, game-changer.

"I am Fate." She preened, smoothing her dress and tilting her head, regally. "But you can call me Cosma." She smiled again, and I realized she rarely stopped looking happy. It was addictive. "Preview over." She pasted on an exaggerated half-frown.

I nearly dropped to the floor when my wings vanished. The glorious heat left, leaving me chilled and naked. All the magic was gone, twice as fast as it came on. I wanted to cry for a second but took a breath of cold air and stood up straight. I looked around for anything to wrap up in, but of course, there was nothing. My clothes had been incinerated.

"I told you to remove your clothes. Lesson learned." Cosma sat down again, getting comfortable. "Bradley, bring us one of the new throws from the gifts and baubles section, darling," she said, barely audible to me, let alone loud enough to be heard all the way back at the register. He'd never hear her.

Footsteps approached, and I ran behind a bookcase. Bradley appeared, grinning like an idiot, and handed a ribbon-bound cozy blanket to Cosma. "Thanks, dear," she told him. Bradley didn't look my way. Cosma threw the new throw at me and I caught it gratefully.

"Now, to the business of your recent killing of a fae being. I've had it in for you for a while, sugar."

I wrapped up in the throw like it was a towel, tucking the ends in tight. "You have two names?"

"No. Really, would you like people to call you 'Clerk'? Hi Clerk! How you been girl?" Cosma extended a hand, as if to shake upon meeting with a friend.

I gave her a dull look. "I get it."

"So technically, you're supposed to be dead by now, with your two closest living relatives proceeding you. Thoughts on how to handle this?" She asked, kicking a boot over her knee. "Because you done fucked up."

"Since you brought it up, Adam was a piece of shit. I don't care if he was one of your beloved pets to protect. He was a blight on society."

"Whose?" She shot back. Her smile faded into a stern look.

"What do you mean? He killed people after using them for entertainment."

"Has anyone explained to you, there has been a balance between societies here for eons?"

"Yes. It pisses me off that I'm expected to turn a cheek. I don't work that way."

Cosma sat back in her seat, considering. After a moment, she put both feet on the floor and stood up. "I'm not going to kill you."

I didn't say anything, waiting for the rest of her verdict. Really, I didn't know if she was able to kill me. I was technically a goddess. Or at least a half of one. And she'd gone on about how much she loved Lugh. I'd keep that hunch for later.

"So, I'll take it out in trade. A life for a life."

"You mean I have to kill someone? That's ridiculous."

"Don't get all judgy. You'd be saving me some time. And since you're trying to be all noble, it will interest you that this individual has enabled worse than death for others and needs taken down."

"Who made that decision?" The question fell out of my face before I had time to consider too much.

"Hello, Fate here," Cosma said, waving her pointer fingers in a circular motion around her face. She grinned.

My dimples tugged a little. If things were different, if we were both just a couple girls meeting in the States some place, I'd like her.

"So, we have a deal. You take care of this pesky matter for me and I'll report back to Daddy that you're still breathing. Sound good?"

"I didn't agree to anything." I crossed my arms.

"Okay, it's hardball then. You do this for me, or I'll take a life I feel represents equal payment for what you've done. And mind you, you're no judge. It isn't up to you to go all vigilante and kill other beings down here. So, here's the deal. You bring me this Petra's head, or I'll take your BFF's."

I didn't respond. That was a lot to take in. Apparently, Petra had quite the rap sheet with Fate. Peter's sister. I couldn't kill Peter's sister. "Her head?"

"I'm an old force here, and a patron of the classics. And a bit of a drama queen, if I don't say so," Cosma said, then laughed, a little too genuinely for my comfort. "Do it or I'll treat this matter as if Bree did it. So first, I'll kill her mommy, then her daddy. Then I'll kill her. The thing I love about my job? I can get creative. Movies have been made about my techniques."

Cosma spoke as if taking a life was just her job. She never broke a smile. Just another day at the office. I was speechless.

"I need an answer. Fast. I've got a red eye to Milan. I need to know if I have to take care of business here before I go, or if you're going to get smart and help a sister out." She dug in an expensive looking handbag and brought out a smartphone in a pearl white case. She poked at it for a second and smiled, flipping it around to show me a nude guy who was smiling at his phone's camera. "This is waiting for my plane to land. Let's not give him a reason to stop smiling like that." Without waiting for an answer, she started typing again. "Well?"

"Okay. I'll do it," I heard myself say. Did I really have what it took for cold-blooded killing? When someone was looking at me all murderously I could do what I had to. I couldn't kill Petra. I'd just lied. Again. But what else could I do? Cosma was a magical woman. She'd just had me Garg Out, during daylight, into something that was much more than my normal gargoyle. She'd shown me my true self. I was grateful and disgusted with her all at once.

"Great!" Cosma chirped, and began typing away. It was comical to think that Fate, herself, was addicted to a smartphone. Certainly she could have communicated a different way. She could have any guy, but was a fan of dating sites. Again, speechless me.

"I have a plane to catch and you need to go shopping," she said, continuing to poke around on her phone. "I so love that we can check in online these days. Just like that. I'm heading to Milan, baby." She beamed at me then dropped the phone back in her bag. "Does three days work for you?"

I nodded, not willing to make another lie verbally, like that would make it better somehow.

"I'll catch you after the weekend, then. Walk me out?"

"'Fraid not." It was my turn to gesture at myself the way she did. "I'm going to skulk my way to the staircase. I'm sure you'll be fine." I smiled at her.

"Of course. Have a great weekend, okay? We'll catch up when I get back. Heathrow can be a bitch, though, so don't worry if I'm not here at the crack of dawn." She looked at me one more time before leaving the little alcove where she'd changed my life. Not that she cornered the market there. "Ah, you're upset. Don't be.

Once you get started and realize your position you'll get it that these little things don't matter. Suck it up, buttercup. You'll learn to walk it off just like the rest of us and never look back."

I found myself nodding again.

What if she was right?

25

Thankfully, I was able to walk my skulky self upstairs and to my room without encountering anyone else. The store was quiet. Maybe Cosma had intervened so I wasn't accosted by customers. I turned the door handle just as Petra appeared in the hall. Her eyebrows rose with genuine surprise at seeing me wrapped in a blanket. I looked away fast. Seeing her was horrible, considering the deal I made. I was supposed to just off her and move on. Piece of cake. No big. Another day in the life.

"Unbelievable," she said, as she passed.

"You have no idea. And today's not a great day to piss me off." I pushed my door open and slammed it before she gave me another reason to throttle her. I grabbed a new set of clothes, wondering how much weight it took to pull a human's head away from her shoulders. An ear was supposed to take only forty-six pounds, give or take. I needed to go for a run, so I grabbed a hoodie, checked to see if the hall was clear, and headed downstairs to wander the streets and let my mind cook down everything I had to chew on. I didn't like being told what to do. Worse,

I didn't like ultimatums. Biggest doozy of them all was I found myself wondering how best to kill someone and keep it a secret. I was plotting a murder.

To be fair to myself and go out on a limb and a giant leap of faith on Cosma's word. Petra was, like Adam, a blight. Was she a blight on society as I knew it? She'd aided in killing and torture and kidnapping. My running shoes pounded the ground faster and harder the more I thought about it and ran, tucked away from sunlight inside my hood or in the shadows of buildings.

Tyrens could be called members of society as I knew it. They were the victims of Petra's indiscretion. There had to be more I hadn't heard about. There could have been even worse things. Were the things I knew enough to make me feel justified? Maybe I needed to go back and look in those tanks one more time. The Tyrens were emaciated. Flaking apart. Being sucked dry of their life force, and that was torturous. By the time I rounded back onto Charring Cross Road, I was convinced and needed help feeling better about the decision I needed to make. Thinking about the ways Petra was a shit and a betraying bottom feeder made it pretty damned easy. The more I thought, the faster I ran and the madder I became. I was so into my thoughts that I stepped off a curb and was nicked by a brown bus that was flying toward the alley beside the Bochord. I whirled in the crosswalk, bouncing a little but I didn't fall down. My knee grew numb and so did my hand. I ran the other direction as fast as I could, needing to distance myself with anyone who might have gotten a good look at the skin on my hand as the van swiped me. I circled the block once more and then ran toward Cecil Court and into the alley. The same vehicle was parked in our alley.

Bracing myself for an altercation, I ran into the break room. Peter was there, and so were Petra and Bree.

"Look who decided to show up," Petra said.

"Shut the hell up." I directed every syllable straight at her. A moment of amazing silence ensued where no one spoke. Finally, I looked at Bree.

"Looks like it's happening," she said.

"Who was in that van?" I asked.

"All of Michael's knights, or whatever he wants to call them," Peter replied. "They're out front. We flipped the sign early. Iain got a signal from the front gates. Where have you been?"

I glanced over at Peter. He'd said that last part with a little exasperation. "I went for a run. Trying to clear my head."

"It's been two hours."

"I know when I left, Peter." Seeing Petra smiling gave me a reason to suspect something was up. After just a moment, I got it. "You knew when you saw me," I told her.

"You must mean when you were standing in the hallway naked but for a cover you filched from the store."

"Thanks for the heads-up." I winked at her. Yep, small price to pay for saving three lives. Even the math agreed with my decision. Three lives saved for the cost of one dickbag of an English bitch. Done.

"When do we leave?"

"We could have left before, but now we only have a half day of sun left. Henchmen were spotted at the Logans' about an hour and a half ago. They're still there, I'd wager. Osgar has sent in neighboring forces to monitor for the slightest sign of smoke or destruction. They're already engaged at the castle. Iain has a count."

"Their best chance is to get as many taken down during the day as possible." I had no idea if we were talking about humans engaging the henchmen or more simple gargoyles. When the fight broke out last year it seemed there were many battling right beside us. We could only hope. Humans, even Highlanders, didn't stand as good a chance against henchmen after dark. Certainly, they would take cover as soon as the sun set.

"Everyone should try to get some rest. We should plan to

arrive outside Petrichor Park before dawn. I don't want to risk missing our target." Peter looked at me, likely expecting me to object. I didn't. Petra nodded, all business. She was out to impress her brother, acting all hypervigilant. I hoped she was ready to roll and brought her A game. She rushed at him for a hug and then trotted off toward the stairs.

"See you in the morning, then," I said.

"You two rest well."

"We'll try," said Bree. "I just want to get this over with. It's like an extermination. After tomorrow, the world will be a better place." She started off and I fell in step behind her. We walked in silence until we were at her door. I gave her a hug.

"I love you, Bree. I know you don't want to hear it, but I want you to know I'm sorry for everything. I'm going to make it right somehow."

"I know," she whispered. "Don't be sorry, Tessa. I love you, too." She squeezed me tighter for a second, then opened her door and stepped inside. She smiled at me while she pulled the door closed and I backed toward my own room. I'd no sooner slid my lock close than a gentle knock sounded. It would be Peter, of course. I wasn't in the mood for a lecture, but I wanted to talk to him privately before we left.

"Thanks for knocking instead of huffing and puffing."

"Very funny," he said, stepping through the door when I opened it for him.

"I was actually thinking of getting a shower since I didn't have time after my run. I'm glad you came by, though. I just want to make sure we're on the same page as to how things are going to go tomorrow." I plopped on the bed and he took my wingback chair beside the bed.

"I've spoken briefly with Iain. The castle is crawling with Gen's men."

"Henchmen?" I asked.

"A few, and some not. Some other things," he said, and

smiled. I watched him speak. The way his eyes lit up coupled with his art of smiling with his dimples between words made my stomach do little flips as I listened.

"So, this might actually work."

"Indeed. Osgar agrees. It's good we didn't run to the castle when they were sighted there.

"What about the damage they'll do?"

"The Logan's say it's a small price to pay for gaining the division of her forces. And besides, if they're at all bright, they'll soon realize the place is vacant and will not stay. That will minimize the damage they inflict on the grounds."

I nodded. That was a good point. "They'll alert her somehow."

"That's a chance we take. It will not get them back to her in time."

"We'll be in and out by then."

Peter nodded, watching me. "There something I want to tell you."

My breath caught. "Peter, I—"

"Take it easy, Tessa. I'm not about to propose marriage." He winked.

"I didn't think you were," I said, exhaling. Anything he was about to say was going to be profound.

"I've been talking a lot with my sister. She really is sorry for her behavior before. She feels you wouldn't listen if she tried to apologize."

"So you're here to do it for her." I stood up and so did he. "I really need to get a shower and try to rest up some." I turned toward my door to let him out. He caught my elbow and pulled me around to face him, placing his lips softly on mine. I went a little soft in his arms. My God, he was magic.

He broke the kiss, placing his forehead against mine. "This is why I'm here. For myself and no one else. Promise me you'll be careful, Tessa."

"I will. And I want you to be careful, too."

"Deal," he whispered. Neither of us made a move to break away. Finally, I looked up at him, ready to reiterate how badly I wanted a shower.

"I know. It's time to go," he said.

I grabbed my shower bag from the armoire, stopping with my hand on a folded towel, looking at him. He grinned as I pulled down two towels and tossed one at his chest.

OF COURSE, it was raining like hell at two in the morning when we loaded up our backpacks with clothes to change into when the sun rose. The human section of our force took off driving in their van before we left flying. They'd hooked up an enclosed trailer, in case we brought anything or anyone valuable out with us after we were done. They were decked out with armor, shields, swords, and a few random handguns. Bree and I, as well as Petra, each had an automatic crossbow. It was a lot to fly with, but it was a short distance to go.

I was wound tight. Really, more like a nervous train wreck waiting to leave the depot. Over the last half hour my mind decided to play through every possible bad scenario. My claws kept catching on every bit of cloth or material I tried to touch. I dropped everything in a huff. My bag clattered to the floor. I winced realizing I was hearing my daggers smack the tile.

"Aw. Diddums get flustered?" Petra said, smirking from across the room.

I glared at her. "I'm going to break your damned neck if you don't shut the f—"

"Petra," Petra growled. He stared at her for a second while she continued to smile at me. "You know what? I'm through with this. The next time you open your mouth I'm going to let it happen.

You'll get what you ask for and deserve each bit of it." He grabbed his bag and stomped off.

"Nicely done," Bree said. She zipped her pack and set it aside. "Why do you have to be such a hag all the time? We're all working for the same thing here." Everyone stopped moving and looked at Petra, waiting for an answer. Petra glance at Iain and Osgar, then at me.

"I think it's time for you to stop," Bree said. She grabbed her pack and followed the Scots toward the back door. I was left racing to get my crap packed up before Petra. I didn't want to be left in the same room alone with her. If I started throttling her, I wasn't sure I could stop. I wasn't sure how I was going to fulfill my debt to Cosma, but it wouldn't do to take her out in the back room of the bookstore with my friends waiting for me.

Petra grabbed her bag and stomped out, banging one of her wings on the door way. I breathed in my relief and finished up, then went to join the others, relieved that everyone else was finally coming around to the fact that Petra was the problem.

The next chunk of time blew past like a tornado. It was frantic and unsettling. We took off from the bookstore rooftop and flew like hell. I stuck really close to Bree, looking for any comfort I could get. I was unsure of everything and feeling inadequate. Bree, on the other hand, appeared to be so focused she could deflect bullets. No one spoke. We just beat our wings, the six of us flying in a cluster of death heading straight for Genevieve.

I'd briefed everyone on what I knew about the building she called home. Though I'd been blinded with a black cloth bag over my head on the way out, I knew there was a long tunnel down and a lengthy elevator ride down. From the street, two stories were visible, the top floor hung with balconies and wrought iron banisters and hand rails. Genevieve's great room, kitchen and living spaces were at what I knew to be the bottom floor. Finesse was required. We couldn't go in with our guns blazing, so to speak. Teigan was inside somewhere, and so was a possible herd of Tyrens that could still be alive. That was the "rescue" part of the raid. The other part was extermination. First Genevieve, then Kai—if he was fully cooked by then.

The van and trailer had to wait back on a street that was still recognized as part of London on a typical map. There were few cars or trucks in Petrichor Park. Most people walked. Even seeing a car was odd, and those I knew of belonged to Genevieve and were housed off the lane, below her building. I totally got that. The beings there didn't dig cars.

And then there was the solo mission I had while we performed the other stuff. I had two days and counting to meet Cosma's demands. I didn't know how I was going to pull it off, but being in a place where Petra could potentially be killed did much to open up my options and make it look like an accident or like Genevieve did it. We were all gunning for her anyway. I might as well give the others one more reason to cut her down.

It worked out in my mind, but I was still nervous and scared that I'd screw it all up or get someone hurt. The people I loved were headed into a volatile situation. Any one of us could be wounded or killed. The advantages of breaking in as humans were to infiltrate the place quietly and to be sure other gargoyles were also in human form. Going this soon after Genevieve's forces were spotted far up in Scotland had to happen. If we waited another twelve hours, they'd have time to make it back, just as the sun set and we all Garged Out. The numbers weren't in our favor if that happened. In this case, daytime was our advantage.

Just thinking about conflict chewed at my stomach. My temperature was up, and amped up speed chomped at the bit like a race horse. Even in my undersized, human form, I would be pretty damned fast in action. I silently thanked the universe for letting me access at least that much of my ancient powers. Being able to start a fire, if necessary, would be a totally badass blessing.

There was also the whole Tyren-syphoning situation. The

trailer would come in handy for a lot more than just transporting any living Tyrens back to the castle. If I was right, we'd be taking the whole set up back with us, less the empty tanks. Tyrens could survive out of water long enough to get them to the van, where one of the Logans' stock tanks waited, holding just enough water to submerge a few of them for the trip back to the Grotto.

Half of me wanted to turn around and go back to the bookstore and the other half wanted to get shit over with. Time seemed to be clicking past slowly as we flew. Finally, the dark canopy of trees came into view against the lavender sky. Osgar wrapped his wings in tight, dropping toward the park and we all followed him down between two of the tallest buildings in Petrichor Park. We opened our wings, parachuting to a silent landing in an alley that reminded me of the one where I'd met Tal and his friend.

That was the day I'd screwed up royally and drank cider, jacking around in Jonnie's until the sun set. And that's how I met Adam. Who was dead. And then I'd met Cosma, who wanted Petra dead. I closed my eyes and shook my head to clear it. What a cluster.

We all faded into the shadows at the back of the alley, folding our wings and crouching behind a big trash container or leaning in blackened corners. The sky grew lighter. I slid my backpack to the cobbled pavers and quietly opened the zipper to remove the set of clothes I would need in a few seconds. Bree and Iain were behind the trash container with me. Petra was with Osgar and Peter. I supposed she was okay doing naked in front of her brother. Maybe it was different with twins. The thought gave me an icky "bad-touch" feeling. A white line of sunshine burst onto the top of the building to one side. I didn't gawk and I trusted no one else would either. I jerked on a pair of leggings and tied both dirk scabbards to my calves, fastened my bra and pulled a long-sleeved shirt over my head in about thirty seconds, then yanked my hair into a lopsided but functional pony tail. I stomped into my Chucks and whipped the laces into bows, then slid my backpack beneath the wheeled trash bin. The folded crossbow was easy to sling over my head so it lay across my back, leaving my hands free. The sounds of zippers sliding and clothes being thrown on faded and we all met against one of the walls leading to the sidewalk without a syllable muttered between us. Iain and Osgar each had scabbards strapped to their backs. They were decked out with other weapons that were out of sight. That was something that I found cool about Peter. He could fill his hands with a weapon, seemingly out of thin air, just like the Scots. Petra held her assembled crossbow at the ready and I wondered if Bree and I should follow suit. We had a short bit of running to do so I decided to wait. I took my place at the at the mouth of the alley, preparing to lead the way into Genevieve's lair.

Genevieve's building wasn't far. Maybe two doors down. The backs of the buildings formed a central square with even more overflowing flower boxes and bushes, with strategically placed gas lights. We had to cross in front almost a block of buildings before we came to the sliding gate leading to the long tunnel below the lane.

Petrichor Park wasn't a large place. One block wide by around five blocks long. Just big enough to house some crazy shit but small enough to get lost between two labeled streets on a map of London. It was like a lost strip of cobbled lane running about a quarter mile, hidden between two streets. All over grown with trees and ivy, secluded, quiet, and preserved from the insanity of London's business district inside an unseen bubble of magic. I didn't understand all the rules. Neither did the Logans or Peter. Humans came and went during the day. No one stayed in Petrichor Park past sundown, on purpose.

Unless you were in cahoots with Genevieve.

I glanced down the sleepy lane. Dew hung thickly on all the ivy and flowers, making moss plump in green-blue tufts on the trunks of trees and in the corners of stone steps and buildings. Nothing moved.

I stepped onto the sidewalk and started a brisk walk toward the iron gate. At some point, our intrusion would trigger an alarm. We might hear it and we might not. The trick would be to expect an ambush any second.

We made it to the gate fast and Iain planted a foot beside the wrought iron. I stepped on his bent knee, took one of his hands, and boosted myself over after one quick step onto his shoulder. Landing quietly wasn't something I was great at in human form. My shoes slapped the ground, the noise echoing from stone to stone. The sound spurred us on. In a matter of seconds, Petra landed, then Bree. One by one, we all cleared the gate, with Iain scaling over on his own.

I took a moment to draw out my dirks. Bree popped her crossbow together as we ran into a truck-sized cutout in the side of the building and into the tunnel leading to the depths beneath the visible part of Petrichor Park. Our pace quickened, and we were at the elevator within a few minutes. A metal staircase was off to one side.

Peter's gaze locked on mine, concern in his eyes. We were all-in. Once we descended into the rooms below, there wasn't a way to call for a Mulligan. There was no use putting it off. I took a big breath and started down. Osgar, Petra, and Bree were closest to me with the rest following behind. I locked eyes with Bree. She didn't look at all frightened. A look of resolve and a quick nod, then we were on our way down.

I did my best to remain focused on what was coming up as our feet clanged on the metal staircase. Moments later, we all made it to the lower level.

"Wait here. I'll have us a look." Osgar waited for a nod from each of us and then carefully slunk out into the hall.

Petra leaned beside me, whispering. "You've nearly gotten

these men killed many times and you're the only one who knows your way here. Do not think that irony is lost on me."

"Shut the hell up, Petra," I hissed. "The only reason you're with us is because it will be easier to rescue you here than all the way back at the castle." Petra's words hit a sore spot. I decided Osgar had been out scouting long enough. One more word from Petra and I'd end her where we stood. I walked out, leading the way. I was nervous as hell. I was a risk to the others when I wasn't careful. She was right about that. There was nothing in sight that could give us trouble, just the long foyer leading in.

"Something's got to be off here," I leaned close to Iain and whispered, since he was closest. "This will not be easy. There's no way she hasn't set up a safety net for herself here some place."

"Aye. Watching," he said softly, with a confident nod.

My hackles were up. I listened to all indicators my body sent out. I picked my way across the foyer and into the sitting room where I'd seen Cody. The place hadn't changed at all. Not a brocade pillow was out of place. To our left was the door leading into the long corridor that turned into a sterile environment, like an exam room in a mental ward. We crossed a few doors that I didn't remember seeing last time, but I was pretty freaked out about the Tyrens and coffins where things were growing in goop. The door I wanted was the next one on the right. I turned the handle gently and peered inside.

The tall pillar of tanks was dark. We filed inside. Peter watched carefully when I reached to switch on one of the lights above the first tank we came to.

"Damn." Iain peered deep into the cloudy water. The occupant, an emaciated male Tyren, hung lifeless and grey in the murky fluid. Long strips of what looked like shed skin floated around him. I looked away and backed in the direction of the coffins by the wall. Petra watched me suspiciously and gravitated my way while the men worked their way around the cluster of aquariums flipping on the lights and looking for life. Bree hung back, watching with a sickened look on her face. A few feet from me, a large bubble popped on the surface inside the nearest tub. The clear outline of a muscular male was visible, having come that much farther in the process. The subtle noise caught Petra's attention. She eyed me like I'd made the noise. I turned to the vat, sure to stay a safe distance— an arm's length to be precise—and gazed into the growing ripples that stirred up silty material from the outline of the man inside.

"Stay back some," I whispered, knowing full well she'd take that as an invitation to blow me off. She shot me a rotten, patron- izing look and pressed forward with her crossbow pointed into the vat. That was all it took.

I glanced around quickly and noted how the others were busy checking the Tyrens for any sign of life, which sadly was not there. Bree was examining the monstrous syphon manifold, tapping tubes and looking for answers. Petra stepped past me, short of knocking me out of her way so she could make a big discovery as to who was in the tank beside us. I rebounded and hit her with my shoulder. All I had to do was let it happen.

And I did.

A meaty claw of a hand shot right to her side and tore into her like a treble hook. Her crossbow clanked off the side of the tank, falling to the floor. She grasped at the slick forearm trying to free herself but was jerked into the plastic sneeze guard thing so hard it shattered and snapped, slicing into her face and neck. The event seemed to take an extraordinary amount of time. I processed what I'd done, what I'd allowed to happen, as the man sat up out of the goop, the whites of his brown eyes flashing at me, confirming what I'd hoped. It wasn't Teigan who throttled a flailing Petra to what I hoped was her untimely death. It was Kai. The love of Petra's life. And he appeared fully formed with all working limbs.

I made a grab for one of Petra's boots as her body was yanked into the tub with him. Everything was so slick with a mixture of blood and brown slime that splashed everywhere that my hands slid off. That part happened incredibly fast and unpredictably. I slipped and slammed to the floor in the muck, crashing into the base of the vat. Petra's garbled screaming was cut short. I worked at getting to my feet as fast as I could, which was like a toddler spinning out on an ice rink. The machine shrieked to life, sounding a high-pitched alarm.

Peter flew at the tank with Osgar right behind him. Iain stomped on the hand I'd planted as I attempted to right myself. I couldn't really see the chaos, but I knew what it looked like. No one could get a clear shot at Kai without hitting Petra.

It all happened perfectly. Every one of them would be under the impression that I'd tried to save Petra when she got too close to the tub. I managed to keep one slippery shoe beneath me and assembled myself with the melee happening behind me.

Metal snapped, and I turned in time to see bolts ripping free of the floor as the vat toppled sideways and smacked against the other tub, where Teigan was. Bree hooked both hands around my elbow and drug me out of the mix. Iain worked to pull himself free from beneath the overturned vat. Osgar went down close to Peter's feet. Everyone was yelling, but through the din I heard Peter's voice.

"Don't, please," he said. Kai was wild-eyed, backed against the wall with both hands around Petra's throat. She hung limp against him. Bronzed skin gleamed where the goo had been smudged away. Thick bloody streaks ran down his nude body, dripping onto the floor. He came off the wall, wavering slightly, which could have been from Petra's dead weight. I got the impression he wasn't quite at full strength, or wasn't balancing himself well yet, but he made it past where Bree and I stood and closed the distance toward the door where we'd come in. Iain managed to free himself and scramble to his feet. Peter made a grab for Petra's arm, which turned out to be dangling by a bit of skin. It came off in his grip. He released it fast and it fell to the floor. No one made any threatening movements out of fear that Kai would end Petra for good, but Peter was already unleashed and slammed a fist into Kai's side. Kai barely even grunted. Peter hit him again, trying to stop him from getting any closer to the door. Kai growled and tightened his grip around Petra's neck, which produced a sickeningly loud pop right before he tore her head free from her neck. Peter yelled again as Kai shoved Petra's body toward him, knocking Peter to the floor beneath what was left of his twin. Petra's head landed with a softened thump after glancing off Peter's back.

Kai grasped the handle and jerked the door open, but before he stepped into the hall he looked right at me, familiar, deep brown eyes locking on mine briefly. A crossbow bolt zipped past me and thumped deep into his right shoulder. Bree was beside me, sights leveled for another shot. Kai ripped the bolt loose and let it fall to the floor with a grunt through gritted teeth.

His gaze returned to me. "I see you," he rasped.

I had no idea what he meant by that. He turned and strode through the door with a handful of bolts sinking into the flesh of his back. Bree kept firing until the door drifted closed. Peter wailed, the only sound heard above the machine's alarm.

"Oh my God," Bree said. I traced her line of sight to the second vat where another man was sliding over the side of the tub's wall. He landed on a shoulder, the rest of his slimy body hitting the floor in an ungraceful, greasy heap.

"Teigan," Osgar called, running to his brother with Iain following to help Teigan free himself.

I was at a loss for what to do. The Logan's quietly helped their own. I wanted to help Peter, but something stopped me, as if he could somehow know I was responsible for Petra's death. I quickly shook that off and went to him. There was no way he could have any idea. I pulled at Petra's beheaded corpse, gently working to extricate Peter. Bree helped me drag her remains a distance away. Peter sat up, head bowed forward. I carefully stepped around Petra's severed head, which was still behind him, and grabbed one of his hands to pull him to his feet, keeping him facing away. He grabbed onto me, pulling me close, his sobs silent but wracking both of us.

That's when the guilt hit.

26

W e gathered ourselves slowly. I managed to hit enough buttons on the computer monitor to make it shut up. My ears rang. Osgar dragged Petra's remains to the other side of the downed vat to get them out of sight. Peter had stopped crying but remained pale and quiet, and I was certain he was in shock. I didn't know how someone like Peter, who'd experienced centuries of life with veins of grief running through it, would react to watching his only family, his twin, being pulled apart just inches from him. I would do everything I could to help him. Maybe that would help dispel the guilt building at the back of every thought I had about him.

Teigan was awkward on his feet and awkwardly naked. He was a huge guy, easily half a foot taller than Iain, who I guessed was a strong six foot three. There wasn't a single hair on his head. That was likely the case with Kai, too, but I was too busy being terrified to care much about his looks. We managed to wipe goo off our faces and hands, but we were all coated with a thick layer of the stuff. It overpowered my senses, smelling like really rich dirt, the kind the nuns used to cultivate in their gardens back at the Home for Girls in Austin.

Peter was quiet. I contemplated how we could possibly move forward with our plan after Petra's death and Teigan not being able to walk well. Certainly, that was an elephant in the room. Recovering Teigan was one of our goals so we couldn't consider the mission a complete loss. I didn't want to think about it much, but I was good with Fate at that point so Bree was safe. I'd see Cosma soon enough, in just a couple days. She probably already knew I'd fulfilled my part of the deal. Truth was, I'd walked into the ordeal looking for a way to come out clean after I made sure Petra didn't survive the trip. There were no witnesses among us, but I considered Fate to be all-knowing. Somehow, she knew.

Hair stood up on my arms so tight it prickled my skin. I looked around to see if anyone else had the same thing happen, but the others were still wiping off and talking to Teigan. My stomach heaved, and I clamped down on a strong gag. A chill came from the hallway like an exterior door left open in an ice storm. I stepped closer, peering out. Nothing seemed out of place or odd, but I did see a bathroom across the hall with the door standing open. Running water would be a big blessing for all of us. I hoped to find some towels or something to help cover Teigan.

I approached Osgar, who was surrounded by everyone else with Peter on one side and Teigan on the other. "There's a bathroom across the hall and to the right. I'm going to check it out and scope out the hallway and I'll be right back."

"I'll come with you, lass," Iain said. He stepped up beside me.

I nodded and so did Osgar. "Be right back," I said, looking at Bree.

"'Kay," Bree said, with a quick nod.

Iain and I neared the door and I turned to him and whispered. "Look, I can do this in a split second if I use my amped up speed. I can run there"—I pointed to the bathroom doorway, then to the opposite end of hall—"then I can head up there to see if we can get out okay. I really think our best bet would be to get back to the bookstore and let Teigan get his bearings before we move forward." I gestured and stepped into the hall and out of view of the others.

Iain nodded, fully knowing I was right. I could do all those things and be back at his side in under ten seconds. Maybe even half that once I got moving good. "Be quick," he said. "I'll be right here. Call out if you need me."

I bounced on the balls of my feet a couple times. I'd look up the hall first to have a look and then swing into the bathroom next. With a huge deep breath, I started off and reached a sprint fast. The end of the hall and the doorway out came up quickly. I was about to turn the corner and check the hall when I smashed face first into a cold, wet wall. Even though the surface gave a little, my face went numb and my nose filled with blood. I turned my face away.

Reality set in that second but everything else seemed to move in slow motion. "Iain! Run! Get out!" I was suddenly into the invisible wall with my arms and hips. Back at the doorway, Iain swung his head into the room with the others and then took a step back into the hall. I squinted to keep it out of my eyes but I had to leave them open a crack so I could see. My surroundings were coated in a yellow hue. Every motion slowed. Sounds were liquefied. My stomach rolled and churned. With everything I had, I threw it in reverse and pushed backward. I was stuck. My mouth filled with vomit.

I'd run into a ward at full speed.

Garbled sounds grew louder. Shapes moved in front of me. Some were upright and appeared human, but others were dark and low to the ground. I struggled to process what they could be. Dogs? Some climbed along the walls or crept with elongated limbs. The sounds became grunts and shrieks as they grew closer. I hit reverse again, but it was no good. I'd hit the ward so fast my momentum pushed me forward. My lungs screamed. Amped up speed used a lot of oxygen and I had none. I fought against the urge to inhale. Blood ran down the back of my throat. I tried so hard to twist around but I could barely move my arms. The opposite wall of the ward grew closer, but I wasn't going to make it out. My vision narrowed to a shrinking tunnel though I could see a little clearer since I neared the other side. Kai was over there, that was plain. And Genevieve, wearing a red pant suit. That I expected. Most unnerving were the other things. They were thin boned and sinewy with dark eyes and hungry faces. I'd never seen such madness. The hallway on the other side of the ward that trapped me was filled with monsters. I was blinking out. I needed air. Certainly, Iain was on his way to help, to pull me out. My heartbeat spiked to that of a rabbit's and heat burst inside my chest. Involuntary muscle memory took over and I gasped in a chest full of cold gel. Everything burned against darkness that overtook my existence. My last thought was the hope that Kai and Genevieve wouldn't let me die inside the ward. I prayed to the universe to let me wake up.

MY LEG TWITCHED and pain launched both ways, through to my foot and up into my hip. I ignored it. Moving made it hurt so I just wouldn't move and that would be good. The muscles twitched again and this time it was more than pain. A burning sensation spread in my thigh. My breath caught on a surge of vomit. At the last second, I turned my head and let the gush of puke fly out. My head pounded in rhythm to the shaky beating of my heart. I pulled in a breath and worked to get my eyes open. Something sticky held my eyelashes and lids together. A sliver of white light seared my retina. Everything smelled and tasted like bleach, puke, and blood. A subtle beeping broke the silence, accompanied by the sounds of something being arranged on a table by my side. Breathing. Tapping of computer keys. A sigh.

"Good morning, sleepy head." A bespectacled man peered

down at me, holding up one eyelid and then the other so he could shine a really bright damned light into my eyes. My stomach lurched, grotesquely loud. He backed off. I blinked hard, trying to remember where I'd seen him before.

He held up a hand, which was missing an index finger, and wiggled it at me. "Remember me?" he said, grinning.

Ah, well fu—

"Ah, that's recognition if I ever, old girl."

I tried to swallow with a gritty, parched, and sore throat.

The doctor tilted his head to a handset that was clipped to the collar of his shirt and spoke into a mic. "She's awake." He turned and went to a machine that I could only see a little part of. Everything was strapped down.

I took stock of the place. It wasn't the same room I'd been in before. This room was darker and smaller. The walls gleamed with the reflections of lights from monitors and an overhead light off to the side where the doctor worked. I wasn't on my back this time, either. I was strapped to what I imagined was the wall. My legs were separated, but not spread by any means, but my arms were held tightly, straight out at the sides. I couldn't even turn my hands over by rolling a wrist. Straps were everywhere, at my waist and chest, and high on each thigh like a harness around my pelvis. There was something thick holding my neck. I could move my head slightly and my clothes were in place but still coated in brown goo from the vats. I'd been saved from dying inside the ward. That was something. I was dizzy but worked at blinking and breathing to shake the waning grogginess. I had to use everything I could to get loose. I locked my eyes on the doctor's back and did my best to imagine the fabric of his shirt growing hotter and hotter. A wisp of grey grew between his shoulder blades.

He spun, eyes wide with fear.

"Stop, drop, and roll much?"

He screamed into the mic, dipping his head to his shoulder. "Dammit, I said she's awake!"

"Hey. Hey!" I yelled, trying to get his attention as he tore the smoldering shirt off without bothering to unbutton. "The next step is a nice, toasty fire, but if you want, we can make a deal. I don't need your shirt."

The doctor stared at me with fear in his eyes.

"That's right. You're flammable."

He opened his mouth and then closed it again, looking at the door.

"I promise you, my man, I'll light you up far before you reach that door. Come over here and get me down."

He didn't move, just glanced warily between me and the door.

"Three." I watched him, intent and fully ready to go to camp fire mode. For the first time, I had no doubt I could light him up, maybe even any others that came into the room.

The doctor had a full head of cropped, silver hair. I studied the texture, imagining the ends smoking and growing hotter. "Two."

He smelled his hair cooking before he felt the heat but it all happened pretty fast. With a yelp, he patted at his head to extinguish the potential fire on his scalp.

"One." The vision of him bursting into flame bounced through my head. Everything was orange and red. He was out of chances. The door burst open and Kai entered. My concentration blown, real color returned to my surroundings as I realized just how screwed I was. The shaky, easily scared doctor was one thing. Kai could end me without blinking. Suddenly all the pain I'd felt just moments before returned. I pulled in a trembling breath, wondering if I might start crying.

The doctor breathed a big sigh and bent for his shirt. "I'll need a moment," he said, looking at Kai, who simply nodded as the doctor blustered past him and out the door.

"You found some clothes," I said, not wanting to let him think I was freaked out.

"Ah, that wit. I love that about you." He approached, taking stock of all the straps and the wall or board I was strung up on. "Remember just some months ago when I tried to win you, to convince you to come away with me?"

I didn't respond. I remembered his attempts at controlling me quite well. I hated him, and hate was an emotion that didn't come easily for me.

"You're soon to wish you'd taken me up on that." He smoothed a wayward piece of my hair back from my forehead and out of my face. "We're at different times now, which call for a stronger approach, you see. We have to separate you two." He smoothed his knuckles along my jaw bone, brown eyes glinting with everything but compassion, no matter what his words or actions told me. Many things swam in his expression. Curiosity. Familiarity. Hostility. Arrogance. I jerked my face away from his touch. Everyone who knew my situation knew that was pretty freaking impossible. I was bonded tightly with my alter ego.

Heels clicked, coming up behind Kai. "Let's get started, then," Genevieve's tight brogue tumbled into the room with a shallow echo. Kai turned away.

"What is that smell? Her?" She looked at me with a good dose of disgust.

"Burnt hair." Kai said, smiling.

Genevieve peered up at his bald head. "It's not yours. Where the hell—"

"Here," the doctor said, rushing into the room. His hair was wet and slicked back and he'd put his shirt back on. He appeared fresh and under control, pulling an electronic tablet from the table to my right. He swiped and tapped for a second.

"The ward had minimal effects and none that lasted past about five hours. She is at the same strength as before we captured her." The doctor looked between Genevieve and Kai. "If I may, miss, I have to bring up the fact that I mentioned before we should go straight to the more invasive methods as I was attacked

—brutalized really—by this monster and had warned both Kai and yourself of the potential—"

"Enough." Kai growled. "You may not. It was on my suggestion, not hers. Understand? I set this up. I have the most experience with the creature she's become."

The slight doctor began nodding furiously as soon as Kai cut him off. "Of course. Please excuse me."

"I'll consider it. One more syllable out of line from you and I'll let our guest set you alight and use your burning bones to warm my feet."

"Understood." The doctor pulled in a steeling breath. "Selection two is prepared and can be launched upon your command." He went back to his tablet, swiping and reading.

Genevieve smiled in my direction. I ignored her and watched Kai. "What are you going to do?" He couldn't possibly want to just break a finger or something subtle like last time. I had the biggest sense of dread I'd ever known. "Kai, please don't do whatever you're thinking here. You know I'm stuck together with her for life. It's not a physical thing."

"Shhh," he said, walking toward me. We were close to eye to eye, with me held off the floor. He put a hand around the back of my neck and placed a kiss on my forehead.

I didn't stop pleading. "I mean, just please, please don't let this idiot hurt me. Look at him. He's a mess and he's angry and he's going to screw this up." I locked eyes with him, desperately trying to reach him, to go back on all the things I'd done to him and now somehow appeal to any remaining humanity he had left to stop the process.

"You want your life back, right? You want to go back to Austin. To lie about in the sun and teach British Literature at an American university." He didn't blink while he recited my plans, pre-gargoyle. Quite a memory. He wasn't serious, though. He was playing with me. I'd groveled, and he was mocking me in response.

I pulled my head away from his grip gently, looking away. He was setting up to kill me. At least the human me. Maybe the goddess would be set free to go back to the realm of Celtic deities and see her father. She could keep saving wayward children and be herself again.

I'd begun to tremble and the fact that I wasn't crying surprised me. Kai walked away, watching what the doctor was doing on his tablet. Genevieve was perched on a tall chair with her legs crossed, kicking one foot, watching the men. My right arm grew cold and an instant later a burning sensation grew, like ice had fused to my shoulder. I turned my head as far as I could but only saw series of tubing extending from me to a machine to my right. One tube was full of clear fluid but the lower one had a flow of blood pushing through it. I was set for dialysis but my veins were being filled with something else.

Heat spread through my shoulder blades, growing excruciating. I grit my teeth and glared at the doctor, who was watching the machine intently. I readied myself to cook him where he stood and cleared my mind the best I could to light him up. Heat grew in my chest, stirring my hope. The wall I was strapped to shuddered and banged, rattling my senses. Pain continued to grow and spread. I lost sight of the doctor briefly but found him again when he wheeled the machine away to a work station across the room. My straps tightened and seared into my skin. The pain grew stronger. I screamed, trying to burn through the straps and free myself. They held tight as the wall slid backward and glass came down around the contraption I was strapped to. Air kicked up around me as one final sheet of thick glass came down in front and sealed me in. All I heard was the machine hissing. Concentrating hard, I sent heat out to the glass walls, intent on making them even more liquid than glass normally was. They should have melted into puddles, but they stayed strong. I poured more heat out at every surface of my surrounding. The clear material held tight and didn't even crack. Steam built on the surface and the air inside with me grew foggy. An alarm sounded outside my glass box then stopped abruptly when the hissing quit.

A *pop* sounded by my feet and flames erupted. My knee-jerk reaction was fear, but I remembered myself. My Chuck Taylor's burst into flame and so did my jeans and clothing. The heat seared into my skin, but the time I'd totaled Iain's truck in a fiery wreck reminded me that I wouldn't be harmed by fire. All it really did is piss me off. Then I began to cough. Smoke and steam came from my nose. I hacked and more smoke, accompanied my blue and green flames flew out of my mouth. My eyes burned but I could still see everything. Fire crackled and snapped inside me, churning through my limbs with the beat of my heart. My body lurched against the wall board as I boiled inside. Flames continued to spray at me from all sides, in deadly shades of orange and red. The fluid inside me gradually burned out, which made me ache inside, dry and lacking oxygen. I let my head fall forward, thinking about how I would free myself when they stopped trying to cook me. They must have thought immersing my human flesh in a box of flame would somehow draw the goddess away from me. Apparently, it didn't work that way because I held tightly to her, and the best part was, she locked down inside me, inside of us, telling me she wasn't going anywhere. The biggest problem I had was the wait. Fire pounded and surged around me and all I could do was listen to it wail. I'd seen a garden cottage burn once back at the Home for Girls in Austin. I'd never forget the sound that little house made as it screamed its death throes, nor would I forget the fascination, the urge to get closer to the heat. Of course the nuns had shooed me back and then the Austin Fire Department had been there with their loud sirens and too much water. Too much of everything. Just like now. Too much fire that lasted too long for no good reason.

I tried my bindings, hoping something would have burned

through. If the incineration was hot enough to ruin a newer pair of Chucks, I figure it was worth a try. I had a little room to wiggle but couldn't pull my arms down or move my feet. The harness thing that held my middle was gone but that part did me no good. If they ever turned off the broilers, I would be completely bare for all three of them to see. Of all I had to worry about, that wasn't a big thing. There was something about being strung up and vulnerable that way that prickled some anxiety. I didn't really care if Genevieve saw me that way. She was nothing more than an uppity human bitch now that Lugh had reduced her. That spun a few more thoughts through my mind. I rolled my neck and shoulders, trying to loosen them up. If she was just a human now, merely mortal and very killable, would Kai try to protect her? She'd brought him back to life, but would that bring enough allegiance for him to step in if I was about to end her? Did he need her for a future plan of some kind or was she now expendable since he was obviously back to himself, minus all the hair? I had to try to get rid of her, no matter what Kai might do. I would get out, pry myself off the board and find a way to succeed at purging my world of her. And then I'd concentrate on Kai.

Fire didn't work to make the goddess give up on me. I wondered if I could fake it. Act human and frail or something. It wasn't likely. Kai had sensed her in me all along. The bigger worry was, what did they have to try next? I was admittedly a newbie to melded personalities like mine. Really, I was a step down from a demigod. Teasa was a demigod, the offspring of Lugh and one of his mortal concubines. I was fused to her, soul to soul, and our existences and thought processes had begun to meld. Sometimes her thoughts were mine and probably the other way, as well. That type of thing wasn't something you could undo with paint thinner and a match. Did they expect the goddess to be flying around in the tank and me to be a hanging, charred bunch of bones? Kai had to know better. I could see Genevieve thinking it might work, but would Kai really expect it?

A really long tone sounded above the moaning of the burners. I rolled my neck again. It had to have been around an hour I'd been in the flames. Another loud *pop* sounded and the fires extinguished. Soot hung on everything so I couldn't see out, but my skin was clean and pink as the day I was born. Or so I imagined it was.

Things creaked and snapped into places. I hoped it was over. Maybe I'd Garg Out and be able to bust my way free come nightfall. What if nightfall had already come and gone and I wasn't going to change again, like last time? Certainly, they wouldn't risk letting me transform. I let my head loll. Time passed and I drifted in and out, waking to fresh bouts of pain and surges of anger that led me to rage and fight my bindings. Nothing worked. I slept. A new type of hissing sound erupted some time later. The tubes that had launched fire at me for God knows how long started spraying cold air. I wasn't susceptible to cold when I was human, much less after the change. It didn't worry me. The cold started to burn, which changed my mind. Now they were trying to freeze me with some type of gas. Probably nitrogen. Pain started in my hands and feet. The sensation blew past numb in a millisecond and went straight to making me scream. I did. I was broken. They'd heard me beg and scream before. I just let it out. I couldn't move my head. Everything went white. The hissing sound drifted off. Somehow, I remembered feeling the bindings snap and wondered if that was planned or if they suspected it might happen. It didn't matter much. The last binding gave and I dropped to the floor like an ice sculpture that refused to shatter. I felt nothing and saw nothing. I assumed I was face down but couldn't remember what position my head was in when I passed out from the pain. Still, I knew they hadn't succeeded. A small spark remained under layers of ice, a tiny pilot light of hope. I would be okay.

My trouble was that I was emotionally finished. In between the times I drifted off, I thought about missing having a family growing up. About barely missing getting to know my brother before he was killed in Iraq. I wondered about Bree and whether I'd be able to see her again and if she would remain angry at me till the end of time if I was truly able to escape Kai. Worst of all, I wondered about myself. I was a living, breathing, missed opportunity to make a mark on the world.

I wanted to make a difference. Being a gargoyle I should have realized earlier that I could save people. I was completely able to take down bad guys. I could have watched over children. Maybe I was getting that from my alter ego. It didn't matter where it came from, it was the right thing to do. My heart broke. I was a waste. If only I'd made a different choice, to save people over vengeance and just trying to take down one person I considered to be a mark. Had I been thawed, I would have cried. I couldn't even do that. I begged for sleep and concentrated on staying out for as long as I could. I vowed to myself, if I made it out, I would go where I was needed and I would make a difference. I would help those who were preyed upon. I would stop those villains. If. It was all about if. If got out.

I'd start with Kai. Then I'd look for the next blight.

I slept.

The front panel decompressed somehow and slid upward at a slow crawl. The first face I saw was Genevieve, who raged, "Get a damned blanket over her. Now!"

I laughed. The sound that came out wasn't pretty. I was exhausted and let my head roll to the side. Before I knew it, I was passed out.

27

"She doesn't need air. She won't freeze. You're not dealing with your own brand of physics. This is a waste of time, you idiot." Kai stopped yelling briefly. "Even she knew you'd fail." I cracked an eye open to see him rail at the doctor. I was strapped upright again with new bindings and a blanket tied around me like a towel after a shower. Kai continued his latest rant. "We agreed to skip that selection and move on."

"It was an honest mistake," Genevieve chimed in. "I assumed we were starting at the beginning. So we burned her. We froze her a little. On we go." She paced around to stand next to Kai, placing a hand on his forearm. He jerked away.

"You wasted my time." He stalked over to the doctor and ripped the tablet away. I didn't think Kai was very techy and I was right. "This," he jabbed a finger at the screen. "This is next."

"I'll prepare the metals." The doctor stepped out of my line of sight, but I could hear him working next to me.

Genevieve, of all people, looked a little stressed. She'd changed clothes. When I noticed that, I checked out Kai. Both he and the doctor were in different outfits. I'd been out of commission for at least a day.

That set me off. I hoped everyone got out okay. That would have to do. I had no way of finding out for sure. Genevieve wasn't looking so swell at all. She and Kai weren't speaking. Something had happened.

"Trouble in paradise?" I asked, to no one in particular. Kai watched the doctor's hands as two metal tubes were taped off at my thigh. I'd been out when they'd installed them. It looked like bigger IV stuff.

Kai squinted at me. "It seems my book has made it to the US. You wouldn't happen to know anything about this occurrence, would you?"

"Not a damned thing." I didn't even blink. Smiling inwardly in the face of impending torture was a new trick for me. I pulled it off. Genevieve had let all that happen. Of course, it was with my help, but she looked like shit and it had to be because Kai knew she'd screwed up.

"This man, Cody Allen, does his name ring any bells?"

"You're really asking me to think straight right now? Screw off." I looked intently at the doctor as he taped down the second rig of tubing. Either he was really good at installing needles or my pain threshold had been reset to screaming-ass high.

"Ah. There she is." Kai leaned in, really close so I had to look up at him. He looked from eye to eye. "This is the one that will separate you two. Then I'll never have to listen to your smart mouth again. It's nearly over. Then no more Tessa." He backed away, giving me a view of what the doctor was preparing. The dialysis machine had been revamped with lots of metal gears and the side of it was attached to a large kiln.

"Are you aware of an alloy named electrum?" he asked, without bothering to look at me.

I knew what it was. Electrum was a metal the Celts fashioned jewelry out of that was fit for royalty. Kai wore a torc around his neck that was pure electrum. I didn't answer, just watched silver hot liquid metal begin to slide into the shunt. The tubing lit up, turning a muted copper color that got closer and closer to my thigh as the machine pushed molten metal toward my open veins.

"Electrum is the perfect conductor of magic. Most amateurs still try to use lead. I've prepared this mixture just for you, love."

My leg stung for a second and then felt like it was melting. It didn't, of course, but in just under a minute everything in my field of vision turned to differing shades of grey. My heart surged but kept beating. I had expected more pain.

"Cut it off," Kai said. The doctor bent over the machine, working at switches. "Someone's got a choice to make." He smiled my way. Once the doctor was done with the machine, he removed the tubing using thick, Kevlar gloves.

"Now, freeze her again."

Screams broke out in my head. I panicked, trying the straps at my wrists, doing my best to get free. If the goddess was that horrified, I was absolutely done for. Just like before, the clear partitions slid into place. Cold air rushed me from all directions. The screams turned to wails and sobs. White ice took over and soon it beat at my core where my heart slowed. The smallest flame continued to burn in my chest. I was comforted by that but sobs still resounded in my mind. It took no time at all for me to pass out. I actually welcomed it but this time I didn't get the oblivion I hoped for.

I woke up in the dark, strapped to a wall. Teasa approached, gown frothing over the ground and hair flowing behind her, nearly dragging the ground. There were fresh tears on her cheeks. She was so familiar to me. I knew every line of her face. Although we were similar in appearance, subtle differences existed.

"Why are you crying?" I asked. After all, she wasn't the one strapped to a damned wall will veins full of metal. Even if I was free, I wouldn't be able to move from the weight of the stuff.

"Kai is forcing my hand." She smiled gently, moving to release first my right arm and then my left. I continued to question her as she worked at the rest of the straps.

"How? I mean, we're bound for life now, right? Are you sure he can really do that?" She offered a hand and I took it, stepping away from the bindings. The wall faded out of our reality.

"I am the reason the electrum is still in a liquid state. But I cannot remain. If I do, the odds are against survival for either of us. I am so sorry, my darling." She started to cry again, her broken heart plain on her face.

I let that sink in. She had to leave to survive. If she left, I would die with electrum setting up in all of my veins and blood vessels. If she stayed, there was a slender chance that we would survive together but the odds of that were almost zero. Either way, I would die. But if she left me now, she could live on. Probably go back to where she belonged.

"Look, you don't have to stay. At least that way you can live. Looks like I'm just screwed anyway." She listened to me with new tears streaming. "I know you miss your dad." I smiled. "I'll probably just keep sleeping. I mean, the worst is over. I just won't wake up." I tried to play it tough but my legs started to tremble, so I sat down and pulled the blanket around my legs and feet. Teasa sat down with me.

"The reason I picked you wasn't just for me. I was running from Genevieve. I needed you. When I looked inside you, even when you were but a wee child, I saw your heart. Overlarge and pure. Beautiful. That is why I am here."

She looked off into the darkness for a time. I did too, letting my imagination wander. I was afraid to die. I'd taken other lives. Maybe Fate could pull some strings on the other side. Maybe I would simply "know nothing else" as the nuns taught, waving their Bibles and lecturing me to be a good Christian. Either outcome scared me. Maybe I'd see my family. That sent me over the edge. I put my face in my hands and started to cry.

A warm arm wrapped around my shoulders. "I canna let this happen," she sighed.

I didn't look up. I was beat. Exhausted and overcome.

"Listen closely, Tessa, and remember I love you." She nudged me. "These are the reasons for my father's ire." She laughed softly. "I will not leave you. We will defy the odds. You are good in the place of monsters. Be patient with yourself. Guilt has no place in a hero's heart."

"I'm okay," I said, wiping my nose on the blanket. "What do you mean?" I wiped tears out of my eyes so I could see.

"When we wake up, do not be frightened. The electrum must be expelled from my presence. Kai, he remembers well. Electrum is prized by mortals from history for reasons that go far beyond value for trade. Many wore it for protection from the Celtic deities, not all are benevolent. A sure way to protect a babe from an angry god was to bind her tiny wrist with a cuff fashioned of electrum. Once older, mortal royalty adorned themselves for protection and to show status."

"Like Kai." I said.

"Kai. Yes." She looked away for a moment. "'Tis true we were lovers. But I canna be with someone with a dark heart such as his."

"You don't owe me an explanation. I completely get it. And he wears electrum because he doesn't trust you?"

"There was a threat made by Lugh," she grinned and looked down again. "My father put a price on Kai's head long ago. Just after the creation of the Book of Divisions. Most don't remember, but I certainly do. And Kai does well to remember, also. There you go. Electrum. It repels our kind. And time runs short."

"You're staying to fight with me?" My heart jumped. Hope can cause butterflies.

"Aye. To leave you now is to go against my character. I am—

forgive me," she smiled and continued, "we are the protector of the innocents. I will not leave you to die." She nudged me again.

I nodded.

"We will be victorious in this, Tessa. I am forever affected by the electrum. Although, in the days after, I will be at your side completely."

I took a big breath to get a grip. "That's good. Because I hate to half-ass things."

She nodded. "When the times comes, we will go thermal, by mortal measurements. Do not fear. We are bound. We will break apart and we will come together again."

"Thermal." I said.

Teasa nodded.

"Okay then."

28

Fire ignited deep in my chest. I couldn't move, cocooned in frost and ice. Stirring as much as possible, I fed the fire, drawing warmth into my existence. Thawing hurt like a mother. I bit back a moan as nerves awoke. I opened my eyes and leveled my gaze on Kai.

His eyes shot wide for a brief moment, taking me in.

"You bitch," he mouthed.

I nodded as well as I could. But I was able to pull together a pretty big smile.

"Turn it back on!" he yelled. The doctor scrambled around behind him while Kai watched me thawing out. The fire inside me had grown into a source of radiating heat. I rolled my neck once and shook my head to clear the ringing in my ears and the slight grogginess. Kai peered through the barrier at me, looking arrogant and confident that he would be able to freeze me again.

So not the case.

I flipped up a palm and blasted a hole through the container, a fist-sized fireball blazing straight at him. Kai dodged it, but poor Dr. Nine Fingers took the brunt, getting smashed into the wall behind him. A neat hole smoldered at the hollow of his collarbone and he slid to the floor in a heap. Genevieve screamed and then unleashed with a tirade of profanity and threats. She ran toward the door, but I decided it wouldn't be a good idea to let her out. I hit the door with a smaller bit of fire. She ran to Kai.

"Stop her!"

Cute. My Gods, I loathed the woman. Kai, too, for that matter. And the dead doctor. Might as well add two more to the count of lives I'd taken. At least these three would be sacrificed so the world could be a better place. Heat built faster and more intensely than I could ever remember. A twinge of fear rattled me for a second, but I remembered myself. I'd come back together.

A curious look came across Kai's face, part disbelief and part realization that he was completely screwed if he didn't put a move on. Genevieve stepped up beside him, watching as I built strength. Each breath I took in was converted to energy.

"What is she doing?"

"Stay here for a moment," Kai murmured. He turned toward the door and simply walked out. Genevieve stepped closer to me, intent on keeping an eye on me.

I smiled at her. "Light's out, Gen." She screamed. A lot. I closed my eyes against the white light and sent fire in all directions, fracturing myself into the air like powder in a gale.

THE SCENT of lavender was one of the oldest memories I had. My human mom used it to clean our clothes in a wooden tub by the brook. The aroma was a strong one if you were close to a few plants or a large lavender bush. I opened my eyes a sliver and pulled my head up off a shoulder. Everything ached. I took a deep breath and sat up straight when memories poured into my mind. I was slumped against a planter full of blossoming lavender on the lane outside of Genevieve's compound.

I pulled myself to standing and realized I wasn't wearing any clothes. A breeze became a blustering gust of wind, blowing to the left of me. An odd sound accompanied the wind and it lasted for about a second and simply died, like a pulse of energy that broke loose from somewhere and was on its way out. I turned in a circle looking for some place to get something to put on, the breeze kicked up again and the same sound, like a bit of whale song without the ocean, surged past me again. Every nerve in my body was on edge.

The door to Jonnie's had blown open so I ran toward it, hoping no one would see me run in and steal the first towel or tablecloth I came across. Petrichor Park was hidden beneath a thick canopy of trees. I could only hope the sun would be setting sometime soon. The breeze dropped. I ran to the door and leapt at the nearest booth, sitting my bare butt on cold vinyl and leaning forward against the table to cover my breasts.

The place was eerily vacant. The scent of old fry grease hung around but there was no one in the kitchen either. I got up, walking around a little, my bare feet sticking to spots of spilled beer and soda. Just inside the kitchen door was a rack of white aprons. I grabbed two of them and tied one on forward and one on backward, tying them tightly into a makeshift halter dress. The wind gusted again and the whale-type noise was just as loud and resonating as it was in the lane. I waited a moment for the wind to drop and went back outside. No winged faery things bussed around the pots of flowers. Petrichor Park was deserted. I started in the direction of the bookstore. I needed to see my friends and make sure they were okay.

About every fifteen seconds more winds and whale song would erupt. By the time I was at the end of the Park, a constant pull of air swept up from the cobbled street into the area just ahead of me. I cleared the last of the tree cover and was about to step out into a real London street when a blast of wind and the mournful song kicked up, the loudest I'd heard it get. Leaves and dirt drifted inside the breeze, over my head and through what looked like a ripple in pond-water. The sound built and when it hit a crescendo the ripples drifted downward like a set of curtains parting. Sound, wind, leaves, and debris blew through the gap. The wind dropped and the ripple closed up, except for the place above my head where it looked like water. I stared for a while, mesmerized. Fifteen seconds flew by. The sound started up again. This time when the ripple touched down a squatty, green and brown footstool-type of creature with a row of beady little eyes on its back grunted past me and right through the curtain.

"What the hell . . . ?" I looked back into Petrichor Park where the deserted lane was dark beneath the trees. All the things that used to be there when I arrived were out running about in London. Had I blown a hole through some barrier or veil that held the creatures inside the Park? Maybe Kai had done it when he made his escape. Although, he likely didn't need something like a cut in an invisible wall to go anywhere.

I didn't wait for another breeze to kick up. I'd never needed any mojo to come in or leave so I simply kept walking. The sun was due to set soon. I scoped out safe places to walk while I waited for twilight to find me.

Blessedly, my skin began to tingle so I ducked into shadows between a building and a row of parked cars so I could change in private. The sun dipped, and I closed my eyes, waiting for my body to shift and expand, for bulging muscle to pop out on my thighs and biceps. Wings sprouted from my back a little faster than normal. Scales erupted, weaved together, and then flattened out into soft skin, rather than a plate of thick scales covering my body. My tail appeared, wrapping neatly around my slender right leg. Things were much different. My tongue was forked but after feeling my face, it wasn't chiseled into a stony, doglike image. My face felt like my face. My hair had grown and hung around my hips and calves in a long, copper and grey fall.

Cosma stepped up beside me where I was hidden in the shadows against the building. "Hey." She smiled.

I stopped fidgeting and crossed my arms over my chest. My breasts were there but my nipple weren't visible. "How was your trip?" I asked.

"Amazing," she answered, and dug in her bag. "I have got to show you these photos."

"Oh, yeah. I'm okay," I said. "I'm glad to hear you had a good time."

"Thanks. So, you came through. And it looks like you've gone through some personal growth." She laughed.

"I guess I got tired of meeting myself coming and going." I smiled, feeling my fangs grate into my bottom lip.

She nodded, pulling a strand of sun bleached hair behind an ear.

"Listen, I need to get back. My friends have got to be worried sick and I don't even know if they're all okay."

"Spoiler alert," Cosma said, grinning. "They're all fine."

"Oh, thank goodness." I tipped my head back and closed my eyes, thanking the universe. "Okay. I'm going home."

"See ya around!"

I didn't look back. It felt pretty awesome to launch into the air and dance with the breeze in the moonlight. I flew as fast as I could to the Bochord.

WHEN I ALIT on the rooftop I nearly landed on top of Peter, who'd seen me a second before and practically caught me in his claws. I wrapped myself around him as fast as I could and warm skin replaced our scales. I shoved my face into his chest and just stayed there for a moment while he kissed the top of my head.

"I knew you were alive. I told them all. I didn't give up on you," he said, against my scalp. "You've changed."

"I am so sorry," I said, holding my breath so I didn't start crying. "And yes. This is me, Garged Out now."

He nodded, taking me in. "You certainly have no reason to apologize, Tessa. We were able to get Teigan to the van, and one of the Tyren's was still alive. You saved some lives, sacrificing yourself that way. Iain told us all about it."

I took a moment to gather myself so I didn't blather on about things I could never tell him. "I didn't know the ward was there. But I'm glad I held everything off long enough for you guys to get out." I peeled my face off of his warm chest and looked up at him. "I need to go see Bree. How is she?"

Peter didn't answer right away. My heart jumped. "Peter? Bree? Is something wrong?"

"She's okay," he said, finally. "She's been in a very dark place since we got back. Coming out without you took a toll on her."

I backed away so we would Garg Out again. I stepped back again so I could look into his face without craning my neck. It was so easy to forget how tall he was in his gargoyle form. My tail twitched and snaked around my feet. "Okay. I'm going down to find her." Peter nodded, and we headed downstairs into the living quarters of the bookstore.

I knocked on Bree's door and Peter kept walking. He nodded toward the hall to let me know he would give us privacy.

Bree pulled her door open, looked a little confused by my new gargoyle form, then recognized me, immediately put her claws over her snout, bursting into tears. She stepped back and I followed her inside where we sat down on the floor beside her bed and cried together. The "sister" feeling was back, and I was so thankful. I didn't need any family as long as I had Bree. We pulled pillows and sheets from the bed onto the carpet with us and crashed out on the floor.

EPILOGUE

Healing takes time and no one does it at the same rate as anyone else. Seeing the brutal murder of a loved one has to be the worst event to recover from. I could only think of one thing that would be worse, and that would be finding out the person you're sleeping with was responsible for that death. I vowed to keep my mouth shut about it. I'd lured Petra to her death. I was responsible for Peter's grief. Case closed.

I did a fairly good job being supportive of his process. He wasn't weepy or angry, but he did drift off sometimes, and other times he would tell me he needed a moment and then go to his room for a while. He knew where to find me when he wanted my company, but he withdrew. He came looking for me less and less. My guilt kicked up and I let the distance grow. I had to wonder if I was best for Peter. I had to consider everything I'd brought his way and the pain I'd caused him in the last year. Sure, he'd done some damage and was sort of domineering in the beginning, but I'd done much worse. Distance was what he deserved.

Teigan's recovery was a long, slow time coming. He appeared physically back to normal and he spoke fine. But he woke up at night in fits, sure he was being dissolved in the water at the

Grotto. He was back at the castle with Osgar and Iain, who sent updates to the Bochord. I wondered if he had hair or if he remembered me, at all. Someday I'd probably be able to see Clan Logan again. But it wouldn't be soon.

I shared with them the tear in the bubble around Petrichor Park. If anyone could dig up a way to fix it, they could. At any rate, I didn't know who else to tell. The whale noise had since stopped. The place remained deserted as far as I knew. I couldn't worry about that with everything else going on.

I had all kinds of reasons to go back to the States, the largest being the fact that Kai was off on a trip to find the Book of Division. My fear was two-fold. He would tear apart my country whether he found the book or not, likely hunting down Cody in the process. If he did find the book, it wasn't just the US that would be affected. Kai was a blight that had to be stopped as fast as possible. Bree, being the smarty pants she is, went back to Genevieve's lab and then claimed she'd devised a way to keep us in human form for a night. She wanted to go home to see her family. I wanted her to be happy. We had some time to work out the details.

My journey continued. I was a walking, talking learning curve. My powers fluctuated. Amped up speed was a kiddy trick compared to a couple of launches I'd pulled off. All the electrum had been blasted away during my "thermal event" in Petrichor Park. I never wanted to come into contact with that again. It was like my Kryptonite. After that, I made a promise to myself that was the last time I was going to die.

I knew I should have used what I'd be cursed with as a way to help others. I'd been spared. It was time to hold up my end of the bargain. I owed that much to no one other than me. So, I thought about ways to achieve that, and each time my journey began with first stopping Kai. He'd likely taken a force of henchmen with him. After that, I didn't know.

One thing I did know is that monsters roamed when no one

suspected or was looking. Their existence wasn't known until it was too late; until a class room was shot up or a bomb detonated during a marathon in a crowded city. Just saving one life would make it worth the while, but I'd do my damnedest to save them all.

My journey continued.

ABOUT THE AUTHOR

Amity Green is an award-winning essayist and author of urban fantasy novels and horror stories. She has enjoyed professions as a truck driver, bartender, and raft guide. Her debut novel, Scales, was released in 2013. A Colorado native, Amity resides in Manitou Springs with her pug mix, Dempsey, and cats, Milk Dud and Shadow, where she produces works of supernatural alternative history, horror, and urban fantasy and renovates her historic Victorian home. When not writing, she hikes, gardens, and tries to quit wasting time on social media.

Join Amity's Readers Group at www.amitygreen.ink.

ALSO BY AMITY GREEN

SCALES: Book I of the Fate and Fire Series

THE WITCHER CHIME: A Haunting